DARK HIGHLAND FIRE

KENDRA LEIGH CASTLE

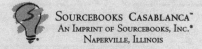

SOURCEBOOKS CASABLANCA™
AN IMPRINT OF SOURCEBOOKS, INC.®
NAPERVILLE, ILLINOIS

Sourcebooks and the colophon are registered trademarks of Sourcebooks,
Inc.

Published by Sourcebooks Casablanca, an imprint of Sourcebooks, Inc.
P.O. Box 4410, Naperville, Illinois 60567-4410
(630) 961-3900
FAX: (630) 961-2168
www.sourcebooks.com

Library of Congress Cataloging-in-Publication Data

Castle, Kendra Leigh.
  Dark highland fire / Kendra Leigh Castle.
    p. cm.
  ISBN-13: 978-1-4022-1159-1
  ISBN-10: 1-4022-1159-7
  1. Werewolves—Fiction. 2. Supernatural—Fiction. I. Title.
PS3603.A878D37 2008
  813'.6—dc22

                                    2008013687

          Printed and bound in the United States of America
              QW 10 9 8 7 6 5 4 3 2 1

Dedicated to Mom and Dad—
for believing

Chapter 1

ROWAN CLOSED HER EYES AND BREATHED DEEPLY.

I am in the Great Tent of the Dyadd Morgaine, she thought, concentrating until she could almost believe it was so. In her mind's eye, she stood under a ceiling of gently billowing crimson silk, the lush carpet beneath her bare feet the grass of the forest. The faint calls of night creatures just awakening drifted to her on a breath of sultry evening air, already rich with the scent of spice. Tonight the Dyadd would feast, and well.

But first, as they always had, they would dance.

Rowan stood poised, still and silent as a statue alongside her sisters, her mother, waiting for the music to begin. The villagers who had gathered to pay them homage held a collective breath, the desire of the men who would offer of themselves already prickling her skin with anticipation. The drums began to beat. *She was ready …*

"Hey babe, wake up. You're next."

"Shit," she muttered, using one of her favorite human curse words as a curvy brunette wearing nothing but a G-string brushed past her, jerking her instantly back to reality.

Memories of spiced summer air and forest drums vanished instantly, leaving her with nothing but stale cigarette smoke and the opening notes of Rob Zombie's "Living Dead Girl."

It was just another Saturday night in Reno. And like it or not, she was on.

Rowan stalked out onto the strobe-lit stage, mile-high stilettos clicking in time with the thudding beat of the music. Wild howls and catcalls erupted from the packed floor of the club at her entrance, the individual faces of the usual motley crew of patrons obscured somewhat by the haze of white pouring from the smoke machine. The fistfuls of green already waving in the air, however, were readily apparent. And that, she reminded herself, was all that truly mattered these days.

Survival.

Even if it involved red satin hot pants and corsets.

She prowled her way to one of the golden poles that flanked the stage and wrapped one long, shapely leg around it. Rowan coiled sinuously around it, arching so that the long red mane of her hair nearly brushed the floor. She spun, slid, gyrated to the music, expertly whipping the crowd into a boiling frenzy of lust. They hung on her every smoldering glance, shuddered each time she bared her fangs in a seductive snarl. Simple men, powerless before wicked beauty, nearly coming to blows in the crush to give her their money.

Rowan accepted it all with a boredom that was increasingly edged with despair.

It wasn't the work, really. Her kind had always reveled in the unusual beauty of their physical forms, wielding that power like a sword when need be. If these human men really wanted to throw precious money at her for doing nothing more than dancing around without any clothes on, drooling over a body that would bring them a universe of pain should they ever attempt to touch it … well, that was their stupidity, to her way of thinking. She felt no shame, though she was often annoyed. But the monotony of it, night after night in this dingy place, all the while not knowing if she would ever be able to return home or whether there was anything to return to, ate at her very soul. She worried that in time the fundamental decay would begin to show. But for now she could only wait, work. And worry.

In the meantime it was just unfortunate that she'd grown to hate this damned song so much. Rowan watched a big bald-headed man with numerous tattoos attempt to pound a scrawny youth into the ground to get nearer the stage and wished desperately that Zin, the manager, would let her switch to something she could lose herself in. As it was, the fights were the only things that kept her from falling asleep in mid-wiggle. But according to him, her Stripping Vampire routine had put his sleazy little dive on the map, and she was going to keep doing it until either the men tired of it or her legs fell off.

Since neither thing had happened yet, she was stuck being The Pretty Kitty's own Living Dead Girl. But that didn't mean she had to like it.

Just as Zin didn't like her conditions for continued employment, Rowan thought with a smirk as she worked the crowd. No lap dances. No private shows. In fact, no *anything* she didn't specifically feel like doing. She showed up, she did her thing, she went home, end of story. Lucky for her that was all it took to bring in more money than all the other dancers combined.

Lucky for him he had a blood-drinking demigoddess desperate enough to continue to do the job. Much to Rowan's chagrin, in this realm neither her considerable talent nor her legendary beauty was any match for having gone to the place humans called "college." And what would have been her preferred methods of getting what she needed had been flatly condemned by her brother as *way too conspicuous,* seeing as they tended to involve flaming infernos of destruction.

But she could dance. And she could remove her clothes.

And whether or not it had been the best decision, here she had been for the nine months since she and Bastian had fled the smoking ruins of the camp of their people, breaking through to this strange realm on a terrifying burst of magic she still didn't understand. Rowan could comprehend the blinding flash that had thrown them from their own realm of Coracin into Earth no better than she could the horrible fate that had befallen their people. All she knew was that it was undeserved. And that whatever fault there was lay with her.

The Dyadd Morgaine were Drakkyn sorceresses who took little for their own and wielded their power wisely, holding court beneath the endless canopy of their forests and accepting the offerings of those who revered them. They had done nothing but what the Goddess had asked of them, to look after the Orinn villagers who had no magic of their own to protect themselves, often from one another. Now her mother, sisters, aunts were gone, borne away on leathery wings of death or fled in terror to who-knew-where. All because they would belong to no man.

But in truth, because *she* had refused to belong to a hateful *one*.

Lucien Andrakkar. May the Goddess curse you wherever you walk.

Rowan shed her hot pants in a series of fluid movements, then spun across the stage in her matching G-string, trying to escape the sudden swell of revulsion and anger within her. She'd gotten good at blocking it out, the black rage at the Drakkyn shifter who, with his blind lust, had stolen everything from her. Still, it seeped through from time to time, threatening her hard-won control over her emotions.

Her life on what these humans called Earth had been a carefully cultivated façade of apathy. Fortunately, that seemed to suit the so-called *vampires* who had taken her and Bastian in just fine. The pain, the crushing grief from that night had been buried deep in a place she could not touch. If she did, Rowan feared that the one her mother had called *Little Flame* would consume herself and everything around her in the blaze of her own fury. Instead, she played along, dancing for the pleasure of the weak, turning a blind eye to the perverse appetites of the Earthly vampires, and praying to the Goddess Morgaine that she and Bastian would soon be returned to their own world.

Returned … and granted vengeance.

Unsettled, distracted, she allowed yet another sweaty admirer near enough to slip a twenty under the thin strap riding her hipbone. He let his chubby fingers linger overlong against the smooth skin of her thigh, giving a tentative stroke to what wasn't his to touch. Rowan whipped her head around in a flash of temper and hissed, baring razor-sharp incisors.

He loved it.

She meant it.

The offending fingers were removed, but by now Rowan recognized that the slight tremor in the man's hands had nothing to do with fear and everything to do with unmitigated lust. He would touch her again in a heartbeat given the chance. She knew it, and her mood shot straight to potentially violent. It was that more than anything, the utter lack of respect accorded her by the males of this realm, that had her once-famous temper on an increasingly short leash these days. Well, she grudgingly admitted, that and the fact that she was so blood-starved at this point that she probably couldn't blow a leaf across a street, much less defeat the army of winged reptiles who certainly awaited her return in her own realm. But either way, every night it got harder to let the little things go.

Just as it got harder not to simply give up and put the fangs everyone here assumed were fake to good use. Rowan took a great deal of pride in her discipline. But she was so *hungry*.

Again, she wished for the freedom dancing had once brought her. Back when she had moved to the wild music of pipes and drums beneath different stars, a different moon. When blood had been something given in homage, taken and offered with love and honor.

Not coerced or stolen, ripped from the necks of the deluded, frightened, or simply unwilling. She had not been able to take what was not freely given, though she had tried. But instead of the warm flow of life, all she'd been able to taste was sick, nauseating fear. Her refusal to drink for many months now infuriated Bastian, and though it was not his place to question her, she could understand. She saw it every time she looked in a mirror, her loss of strength from this slow starvation. Yet though she had lost almost everything, she still had both principle and pride.

She only hoped they would not end up being *all* she had left.

Rowan shook her head to clear it, hating herself for letting the same old things interfere while she was performing. She would be blank, uncaring. She would do what must be done until there was another option.

I will control my temper. I will not bite. I will not cause any of the nice people to burst into flames. I WILL control my temper ...

Just then she caught a flash of something, a familiar face materializing in the haze beyond the stage as it pushed through the crowd. She continued to move to the beat as she tried to get a better look, craning her neck as her long fingers began to work at the scarlet ribbon that held her corset together. The face vanished, then reappeared. Electric blue eyes caught her own, and held while the mouth frantically repeated the same words over and over again.

Rowan paused, letting the ribbon fall. *Bastian?* What was her brother doing here? He made a point of avoiding the club at all times, since the one time he'd taken her to work had nearly caused a riot among the other dancers. Rowan hated to admit it, but her brother was almost as pretty as she was. He might be odd in that he was the only male ever known to have been born into her tribe, but his looks held the same startling perfection as all Dyadd. Bastian's looks were ice to her fire. Just as his temperament was the still, deep pool to her raging tempest. Though none of her tribe would ever admit to being dependent on a man, Rowan knew that without Bastian's unwavering calm and reason to cling to, she would have been utterly lost these last months. He was all she had.

And the only thing that could have brought him here tonight had Rowan's stomach clenching with sick dread. She watched the words he formed once more, just to be certain.

Outside. Run. NOW.

Rowan gave a faint nod, feeling glued in place for precious seconds as Bastian struggled against the sea of people to get to her. When the crowd only shoved him back, he repeated himself even more emphatically, then shot a sharp glance at the front entrance. Her eyes went there as well, and the senses she'd had to suppress just to exist here unfurled like the petals of some dark flower. Suddenly she could feel the power gathering somewhere just beyond, out there in the night. She swallowed, hard, with a throat that had become as dry as sand. And despite the raucous noise in the club, the jeers now directed at her as the music continued, her ears picked up a sound that kicked her heart into such a quick beat it might have flown out of her chest.

Thunder. A storm. Oh, by the Goddess, no.

She snapped into action then, moving at a speed not remotely human. Rowan snatched up her discarded shorts and raced from the stage so quickly that for most, a blink found her vanished. It was bound to cause talk. It would possibly get her fired. And none of that mattered now, she thought as she burst through the back door of the club. After all these months of relative safety, she and Bastian had been found. The dragons had come for her once again.

But this time she had no idea where to run.

The darkness in the dingy alley was alive with a malevolent energy that raised each separate hair on her body. It crackled in each breath she drew, coiling into a leaden ball at the very core of her as she raced down the narrow passage. She veered sharply left where the sagging old buildings gapped, barely slowing as she emerged onto the cracked and heaving sidewalk of Virginia Street. And then she stopped so quickly that her ungainly and hated shoes tangled in each other, sending her sprawling into the street. The empty, dead-silent street.

There was nothing but the ragged sound of her own breathing in the oppressive heaviness that had descended over what should have been a bustling Saturday night on a busy, if seedy, strip. Instead, the street was utterly deserted. Windshields of parked and empty cars winked dully, reflecting streetlights that began to wink out as she watched in mounting horror.

One by precious one.

Rowan got slowly to her feet, eyes darting from place to place as she hunted for any sign of life, of possible salvation. But there were only empty windows, the low moan of a rising wind, and the sinister rumble of rapidly approaching thunder. The streetlights continued to expire, three blocks away. Then two. Creeping, ever closer, like the thunder.

A crumpled burger wrapper blew past her feet, tumbling off into the alley, while other bits of discarded trash danced away down the road and sidewalks with no traffic to impede their progress. Rowan kept her head high as she turned toward the encroaching darkness. Even now, isolated as though she were the last person remaining on Earth, she could not lower her head and accept such a fate. Still, she cursed herself silently for allowing her powers to wane to where they had. Blood Magic was the blessing and the curse of the sorceresses of the Dyadd. In refusing to drink human blood, she had neglected her gifts for far too long. And in so doing, Rowan realized with a heavy heart, she had sealed her fate.

She looked around one final time, but Bastian was nowhere to be seen, somehow locked out of this strange and lifeless moment her enemy had so cleverly trapped her in. Rowan inhaled deeply, scenting air that carried the coppery tang of blood. Even together the Dyadd had been no match for the great winged beasts that served the House of Andrakkar, most powerful of all the Drakkyn. But she was all that was left. And so she would make her stand as best she could.

Alone.

She looked down at the scrap of material crumpled in one fist, and after a moment of thought, slid the skimpy satin bottoms on. The hungry eyes that sought her would see no more than she could manage. It was a small act of defiance, but there was comfort in it. There was no part of her that would belong to him, nothing he wanted that would not remain hidden.

The darkening streetlights continued their march. One block. Three lights. One.

Blackness.

Rowan squared her shoulders in the middle of a street that had faded to shadow and addressed the source.

"I am Rowan *an* Morgaine, a Daughter of the Goddess and future *Dyana* of my people! Show yourself, or feel the wrath of a sorceress of the blood!" She shouted into the darkness, showing no weakness and standing firm even as the thunder rolled loud and threatening overhead.

The wind picked up, toying with her hair with its invisible fingers and swirling like warm breath over her exposed skin. When the thunder sounded again, it was a grating chuckle. Beneath it there was the seductive whisper of a voice that haunted her every nightmare.

"Have you not missed me, my beautiful witch?"

Rowan curled her lips into a disgusted snarl, ignoring the greedy way the breeze pawed at her. "How could I miss what was never interesting enough to notice in the first place?"

"Oh, come, now," the thunder rumbled, sounding amused. *"We both know you've lost, Little Flame. And I have every intention of tasting the fire you've so long denied me. The game is done. You're mine."*

"I'm not your Little Flame," she spat, hating to hear a nickname so beloved spoken by one so foul. "And all you'll ever feel of me is my teeth and nails. All you'll taste is the scorched flesh of your own tongue if it should get too near me. I'll die before I let a foul dragon touch me, this I swear."

"Your defiance of me is pointless, Rowan an Morgaine. But I'll enjoy breaking you of it."

Rowan glared into the abyss around her, her nails biting into her palms. The invisible hands of the wind grew rougher, more possessive as they roamed brazenly over her body, caressing a buttock through the thin material, cruising over her breasts. They raked through her hair viciously, tugging and pulling, willing her to drop her head back and bare her throat.

To submit.

She gritted her teeth and stayed still. "You will never break me."

"We will see."

The blow plucked her from the pavement and flung her back down as though she were nothing more than a rag doll, slamming her to the earth with a force that would have broken the bones of any but a Drakkyn. The breath rushed from her in a forceful hiss, her knees and elbows stinging from the small wounds the contact had opened. Rowan gathered herself, closing her eyes beneath the veil of hair that hung over her face. She couldn't believe that it had come to this at last, that there was no more hope. To become a woman of the Andrakkar, a slave in all but name, was a fate worse than death. There had to be something she could do.

If only Bastian could find a way into this madness … she knew in her heart that it was he who had somehow transported them to Earth initially. He had a deep magic that none of the other Dyadd had, though he refused to acknowledge it. But they'd all sensed it. If only Elara, their mother, had told them who had fathered him, perhaps it would have been more easily understood. But the *Dyana* loved many men, and bore many children, without ties or explanations. It was their way. So Bastian's existence remained a mystery in all ways, and would, it now seemed, for all time. If only she could make him hear her, maybe he could get to her. But she was so weak.

"How did you find me?" she gasped out, thinking to buy precious time. Lucien, like her, was next in line to lead, and dragons were famously vain. Rowan hoped he would jump at the chance to display his cunning to her.

She was not disappointed.

"The Dyadd Morgaine may hide in the forests, sweet, but the dragons have many cunning allies. With access to such power, did you actually think I would give up over such a small thing as a change in realm? And the barrier between worlds is thin here in these mountains. Do you not feel it? I found a way to come for you. I will always find a way. Because you are mine."

The truth of it twisted like a knife in her gut. They never should have stayed here, she and Bastian. Not in the very place they had managed to break through, in the shadow of mountains that were ominous reflections of those the dragons themselves inhabited. Should never have decided that dependence upon the questionable kindness of creatures who could kill without remorse, who couldn't even walk the day for fear of the sun, was acceptable. Was enough.

Was safe.

But in their need and confusion, they had. There was no changing it now. And oh, how her part in that grave mistake cut deep.

"Why?" she finally asked softly, barely caring whether he could hear her or not. "You knew the Dyadd do not bind themselves in marriage. Your kind has never shown any interest in ours before. We never even leave the forests. Why me?"

For long minutes there was nothing but the howl of the wind and the low, almost pensive voice of the thunder. Rowan finally looked up and was startled to see the figure of a man standing only feet from her. Tall and broad shouldered, his form was possessed of a lean and muscular grace even at rest, and his skin, fair like hers, was luminescent with power in the darkness. He was dressed simply, in the way of his people, in a severe black cassock that barely moved in the high wind. Ebony hair was kept ruthlessly short, setting off sharply hand-some features and burning violet eyes that pierced her to her core.

"Lucien," she murmured, feeling herself shrink back but unable to help it. *Please, my Goddess ... whatever may come, give me the strength not to beg.*

She waited for him to approach, to grab her by the hair and do what he would. But to her surprise, he stayed where he was, looking at her with an inscrutable expression. Finally he spoke, and the words chilled her to the bone.

"It is you because when I look at you, I can actually feel. For the first time in my wretched existence, I am

something other than dead and cold. But only when you are near. And so, though you will not be bound, I will bind you to me. Though you would hide, I will hunt you to the ends of a thousand worlds. I will do anything to make you mine."

Terror and rage ripped through her as she looked at the one who had destroyed all she'd held dear. "You and your people burned our camp, killed my family! You desecrated the bond that exists between all Drakkyn! And for what? Because I make you *feel*?"

He looked at her somberly. *"I had no control over that. Your defiance enraged my father, whose solutions, I admit, would not be my own. But if his actions have brought you to me at last, I cannot regret what was done. If I am to be all you have, so be it. You will love me, Rowan. I will accept nothing less."*

Words tried to come, but she choked on them. How dare he? *How dare he?* It didn't matter whether he had ordered the attack or not. Condoning it made him just as guilty as his father, that fiend Mordred. A traitorous tear slipped down her cheek as she struggled back to her feet, all that she felt threatening to break her apart. She took a shaky step forward, then another, repulsed by the hope she saw in those glowing violet eyes. She stopped, just out of arm's reach, and spat at his feet.

"You may gain my body, you sick son of a bitch. But I swear on the blood of the Goddess herself, no matter what torment you devise, I will *never* love you! I hate you, do you understand me? *I hate you, and will hate you with every breath I have until my dying day!*" She screamed the last at him, willing him to understand what he had done. If he took her now, he would be getting nothing more than an empty shell. For the first time in her life, she cursed the lineage that had given her such terrible beauty. Beauty that could inspire such love as to destroy everything in its path.

No wonder the Dyadd did not wed. It seemed that for her kind, love was destined to be nothing more than poison.

Lucien's eye twitched, the only indication her barb had hit its mark. His voice, when he spoke, was soft and deadly. *"But you will belong to me. And perhaps that will be enough."*

Rowan knew then that the game was up. No matter what she said, what she did, he would have her. She would disappear into the Black Mountains of the dragons and serve this monster until she died. Her future flashed before her, the emptiness and despair of it, and it was suddenly too much. Despite her determination to stand bravely before her fate, she spun blindly away from Lucien and began to run, his cold laughter following her.

"Do you wish me to chase you, little witch? Very well, then ..."

She heard the quick clip of his boots against the pavement as she raced, cursing the spike-heeled instruments of torture that bound her feet. Her speed was far greater than any human's, but still she knew he was gaining on her. Toying with her, really. She hadn't the strength to challenge him. Desperate, she summoned what she had within her and turned to cast it behind her, balls of flame rocketing from her fingertips. Again he laughed, this time seeming genuinely amused.

"Is that really all you have left, my love? How sad ... it's always better when you can fight ..."

There was a sudden loud *bang* as something behind her exploded, followed by Lucien's enraged roar. Hope swelled just as her ankle twisted sharply, and she began to fall forward, offering up a prayer that somehow, some way, fate had seen fit to spare her one last time.

Strong arms caught her just before she hit the ground, and she was lifted and spun at dizzying speed to be crushed against a familiar chest.

"Bastian," she sobbed, even as her vision began to go dark.

"Hang on," he breathed against her hair.

She had one final impression before her consciousness left her—that of an enormous black dragon, wings spread, shrieking at the sky as she rapidly left it behind. Then there was only that sweet, mysterious burst of magic she had encountered but once before.

And cocooned in the safety of her brother's arms, Rowan knew no more.

Chapter 2

GABRIEL MACINNES SAT QUIETLY ON THE LARGE, TIME-worn boulder, nursing a beer and staring at a sky brilliant with stars. A warm night breeze ruffled his hair, carrying with it the scents of pine, of rich earth, and fathomless water. The scents of home, he thought, taking another pull on the beer bottle. Though he'd gone off to make a place of his own in Tobermory several years ago, no place had ever held the same allure for him as these sixty square miles of wilderness, the Pack's since time immemorial.

Iargail would always be his heart.

A pity, then, that he'd never been quite able to figure out his place there. Gabriel sighed, allowing himself to wallow a little. He figured it didn't hurt as long as he acknowledged that wallowing was exactly what he was doing. The sounds of laughter and conversation carried to him from the back of the house, along with the occasional soft drift of music from the stereo someone had dragged outside. He knew he should be there, entertaining his cousins, playing the charming host to the few stragglers who hadn't yet left from last week's Pack gathering. He normally thrived on that sort of thing.

But this year had been different, and for the first time in a long while, Gabriel purposely set himself outside the warm circle of light that the stately manor house cast. He was tired. Tired, and so disinterested in the things that usually amused him (women, his pub, and women, in about that order) that he'd actually begun to worry about himself. It unsettled him. Worrying had always been Gideon's area, and that had suited him just fine.

Until he'd almost lost everyone he actually gave a damn about.

A sudden merry burst of laughter from the terrace had Gabriel turning his head, briefly considering making his way back. Then another soft breath from the woods beyond turned his head to contemplate the deep and welcoming darkness of the Highlands. His home. The place he wished he knew how to protect.

The whole family had been on tenterhooks since December, no surprise considering what had happened with Malachi and the Stone. Gabriel frowned and took another swig, his anger beginning to rise at the memory of the way his cousin had betrayed them all. How he'd tried to hand over everything the Pack had ever built, ever stood for, to the Drakkyn. To Mordred Andrakkar, horns and scales and all.

Andrakkar. Drakkyn. The words were strange, almost poisonous. And yet it seemed that his people were bound somehow to the men with the cold violet eyes who had used the sacred Stone of Destiny to enter this world from their own. But try as they might, none of them, not even Malcolm, had managed to figure out much beyond just that. Nothing beyond what Mordred had told them himself, right before Gideon had ripped half his bloody throat out and sent him back to wherever the hell he'd come from.

Now that, Gabriel thought with a small smile, was a much better memory.

"I'll drink to that," he said aloud, raising the bottle of Harp only to discover it empty. "Hell," he grumbled, glaring at it as though doing so would provide him a magic refill. You'd think there might have been some extra benefit in being related to a bunch of nasty, super-powerful creatures from another dimension. As it was, he couldn't even manage to get drunk by himself without bollixing it up. Later maybe he'd Change into his Wolf form and go be sick on the daisies. That would truly make his night complete.

Gabriel was heading into a comfortable solitary sulk when a familiar voice pulled him back to the present.

"It's an odd night when I feel like I have to ask you if you'd like some company." His brother, Gideon, settled on the rock beside him and handed him one of the beers he carried.

His answer was a sidelong glance. "And still I don't hear you asking."

Gideon grinned, the action brightening his normally serious countenance like the sun after a storm. "Night didn't seem that odd."

Gabriel snorted, but decided to accept both the brother and his offering. It would do him good if just a little bit of Gideon's newfound bliss rubbed off on him. Of course, he didn't happen to have a beautiful blonde wife who was madly in love with him to help with that process as Gideon had. Marriage, Gabriel decided, agreed with his brother. And Carly Silver, now Carly MacInnes, agreed with everyone who met her. Thrown together by evil and a northern New York snowstorm, he thought with a shake of his head. Love was to be found in the most unexpected of places.

It was one of the main reasons why he stayed as far away from those kinds of places as he could manage.

"All right," Gideon sighed after listening to nothing but breathing for a few minutes. "I hate to ask, but I might as well. What in God's name are you so busy brooding about out here?"

"I'm not brooding. I'm … philosophizing." Gabriel kept a straight face for all of three seconds before both of them dissolved into laughter. At thirty-one, he was old enough to be amused at the fact that he was not a man known for his depth. Hell, he'd carefully cultivated that reputation. And it felt good to have a moment alone with Gideon spent laughing instead of worrying.

"And after the minute or so that took, I'll assume you've just been sleeping out here," chuckled Gideon, clinking his bottle against Gabriel's before taking a long drink.

"You're lucky I'm not in the mood for a fight." Gabriel never lost his grin, though the nudge he gave his brother was hard enough to push him halfway off the side of the boulder.

After the requisite scuffle, the two of them sat in companionable silence for a while, drinking and staring into the night. Gideon appeared to be waiting. Before long, as he no doubt expected, it was Gabriel who broke the silence.

"I just don't understand why they don't *do* something!" he finally growled, letting some of his frustration seep into his voice. "It's been nearly eight months. We've alerted the Pack, we've upped the guard." He turned to his brother, knowing his eyes were blazing. "They're toying with us, and there's nothing we can do but sit here! There has to be more. I can't accept that there isn't more we can do." *More* I *can do,* he silently added.

Gideon's voice was quiet, thoughtful, eyes giving off a faint glow of their own. "What would you have us do, Gabe? Everyone is on watch, everyone takes this as dead serious. But the only ones who know for sure how concerned we need to be, and how this all actually works, are back on the other side of wherever the Stone leads. And they won't be coming through it again. We're making damn sure of that."

Gabriel clenched his teeth and said nothing. He'd been there, in the chamber of the *Lia Fáil.* He'd seen his father's blood used to open a door into some other godforsaken realm, seen a man begin to change into something he'd only read about in fairy tales. He'd been berated for being the descendant of creatures he could scarcely imagine, threatened with attack until he and his Pack were wiped from the face of the Earth. *This is not the only door,* the Andrakkar had warned them. And Gabriel had assumed it would be only days, weeks at most, until they met again.

Instead, eight months of silence. And all he could do was sit around waiting for the other shoe to drop. It was intolerable.

"The Drakkyn didn't seem the type to simply lick their wounds and go home," he said flatly. "You'll forgive me if I've found it a bit hard to concentrate on much but impending annihilation."

"I thought Wolf at the Door was *mostly* about impending annihilation," Gideon replied, referring to his brother's scrubby yet successful pub with a faint smile. When Gabriel just glared, he cocked his head at him, looking closely. "It's called humor, Gabe. Otherwise known as your second language. Christ, you really are knotted up, aren't you? Look," he tried again, rubbing a hand through his wavy mass of hair the way he always did when he was out of sorts. "It's entirely possible that they can't come through again at all, period. They certainly can't do it right here. And it may be tens, hell, hundreds of our years before anything happens, even if they *can* get through somewhere. We just *don't know.* And as miserable a thing as that is, it's something you're going to have to accept."

Gabriel glowered and shook his head, a definitive *no.* "I'm not at acceptance yet. But I'll give you miserable." He shifted slightly, sliding down enough to brace his weight on one long leg, the other propped against hard stone. He knew Gideon was looking at him, trying to puzzle him out. He'd been looking at him that way with increasing frequency since the encounter in the chamber, as though he sensed there was a storm brewing beneath Gabriel's always-cheerful surface. But even that surface was full of ripples now, Gabriel knew. How to calm them was the part that he hadn't even come close to figuring out.

"Listen, Gid," Gabriel began, on the verge of simply spilling it all and seeing whether his big brother might be able to make some sense out of what didn't make a bit of sense to him. It had, after all, always been one of Gideon's particular talents. Whatever else he might have said, however, died in his throat as a strange noise rose into the night. Low at first, but rapidly increasing in both volume and urgency, it was a sound that vibrated in every fiber of Gabriel's body. At first it was almost a song.

Within seconds it was a scream.

"What the hell," he heard Gideon murmur beside him as they sat frozen, ears ringing as the shrieking escalated further. Then the ground began to tremble beneath their feet, making the branches sway on the trees, and Gabriel knew.

"It's the Stone," he whispered, his voice strangled. He'd only ever heard the relic's legendary song once, full of heart-wrenching beauty as it opened a door to another world beneath a full winter's moon. This, though … this was the sound of someone's heart being ripped from their body, of soul-searing pain. Gabriel shot a quick look at the sky, but he already knew what was wrong. The Stone of Destiny only sang beneath the full moon, unheard and secure in the underground chamber where it had rested for centuries. But the moon was on the wane tonight. And something was forcing the precious *Lia Fáil* to waken anyway.

The brothers shared a grim look before racing off across the grounds, heading for the ruins of the old chapel. The MacInnes werewolves had only been charged to guard the relic, not use it. If they'd ever had the knowledge or power to do so, it had been lost to the ages long ago. But the Drakkyn had proven without a doubt that they had not forgotten. And from the little the MacInneses had seen, the dark beings who existed on the other side of the Stone had more than enough power to cause something like this.

Gabriel steeled himself for the inevitable, perhaps final, fight. He'd wanted this, he reminded himself as he saw Duncan up ahead at the ruin, speaking the words that opened the hidden door sunken into the ground. Figures he recognized as Malcolm and Carly were right behind, and he heard Gideon swear at the sight of his wife descending into the chamber.

He couldn't blame him. But Carly was one of them now. She had a right to stand alongside the rest and fight.

They reached the crumbling foundation together, Gideon taking the lead when they started down the narrow and winding stone steps that had been revealed and disappearing quickly under the earth. The noise was head-splitting now. Gabriel clapped his hands over his ears, though it was no defense against a sound that seemed to vibrate in every cell of his body. The ground was shaking violently, causing dust to rain from the ceiling and onto their heads as one by one they emerged into the low circular chamber that housed the Stone.

The torches that lined the wall were aflame, casting wildly dancing shadows on the wall while the room rocked like a ship in rough seas. The Stone of Destiny itself sat on a pedestal in the middle of the chamber, a large, rectangular block that glowed like dark fire, carved with strange etchings that burned gold. The screaming seemed to emanate from the very core of it, making the light pulse as it poured out. All at once, the torch flames turned blue and blazed higher. Gabriel looked to his father, so different from the last time they'd all been in this room. Then he had been slumped before the Stone, covered in blood.

Now Duncan stood with his massive chest thrown out, fists clenched, appearing decades younger than his sixty years. He was Pack Alpha, Guardian of the Stone … and he was visibly ready to be just that. Gabriel caught his father's eye and gave a slight nod. *Ready,* he thought, *because here they come.*

The same blue light tore from the top of the Stone in a violent rush as the room rocked harder, and a deafening *crack* bent the air. Gabriel felt his claws lengthening, his muscles bunching as his body sought the form it could best protect itself in. The last time they had fought the Drakkyn, he had felt almost supercharged in his Wolf form, fighting with a power he had never felt before and hadn't since. Gideon had admitted afterward that he'd felt the same. Gabriel prayed that strength would see fit to return to aid them now, whatever it had been.

From the looks of things, they would need all they could get.

The Stone gave one final deafening roar, and Gabriel felt a trickle of blood begin to leak from his nose. Still, he held his ground, caught between Wolf and man and ready to do his part for whatever the situation required. Two figures shot from the light, one ripping out of the glowing doorway at a run as it carried the other. Their features were indistinguishable as they emerged, surrounded in a nimbus of shimmering fire. Then, as quickly as it had begun, the terrible sound stopped, though it continued to echo away into the night. The blazing spear of blue collapsed into what looked like thousands of tiny fireflies before vanishing completely.

The sudden silence was jarring.

An imposing Nordic god with ice-blue eyes and short, spiky pale blond hair regarded them warily. In his arms he held a woman either unconscious or dead, her long fall of hair like a wave of blood.

For a long moment no one spoke. No one moved. Then, in a soft rasp, the man addressed them. His accent was mostly American, but with a flavor that was unidentifiably exotic, Gabriel noted. And while his words weren't specifically threatening, they did little to shake the feeling of dread that had settled over the chamber.

"Shifters," he said softly, and not without a hint of surprise. "Am I still on Earth?"

"Bloody well right you're still on Earth," snapped Duncan, teeth bared. "In fact, you're also on my land. Which is to say that if you even think about changing into some horrid beastie or spitting fire at us, one of us will be happy to tear you limb from limb and set your head on a pike out front. We've dealt with your lot before." Gabriel's mouth twitched despite his pounding heart. Whatever happened, he had to give the old man points for style. Duncan curled his lips into a sneer.

"Next question?"

To Gabriel's shock, the man grinned with delight. "By the Goddess ... *arukhin* shifters! I had never thought to see your kind, not in this lifetime at any rate." He laughed with obvious relief, and Gabriel suddenly saw the strain written all over his deceptively cool features. It was quickly becoming apparent that this was not going to be the battle they'd thought, and fear and anger were rapidly being replaced by complete confusion. Gideon caught his eye and raised his eyebrows. Gabriel shrugged lightly and gave a barely perceptible shake of his head. No matter how happy this man appeared to be to see them, it was not yet prudent to stand down.

"I don't know what the hell an *arukhin* is," Duncan said flatly. "But the last creature that called us that went back through the Stone with a hole in his neck. You'll go the same way if you don't explain yourself."

Gabriel saw the puzzlement in the man's eyes as they swept across their stony faces. Duncan was right, however. Mordred Andrakkar, the dark being who had come through with the intention of making himself a new little kingdom on Earth, had referred to the MacInneses with the same strange word. The difference was in how it was said. This man had seemed pleased. Mordred had spat it at them and implied that an *arukhin* was an incredibly vile thing to be. It was a mark in their current company's favor, if a small one.

"Forgive me. I didn't realize … a stone, you said?" He paused, finally seeming to notice his surroundings. His strange eyes seemed to miss nothing as they darted from face to face, floor to ceiling. Then they widened as they lit on the Stone of Destiny itself. He exhaled softly, reverently, before raising his gaze to Duncan's.

"You are keepers of a *Na'an Taleth*, a gateway stone," he murmured. "I had no idea there were any on your Earth. No wonder I was drawn here."

"Enough of this nonsense. What do you want with us?" Duncan's voice was little more than a growl, his eyes ablaze with the instinct to fight, to defend his territory.

The man's eyes finally narrowed at the hostility in Duncan's tone, but he kept his own voice even when he replied. "I am Bastian *an* Morgaine. This is my sister, Rowan. I've come to ask for your help, noble *arukhin.* To beg, if need be. The ties between our kinds were strong once. I hope you will honor that, though I can see you have lost the memory of it."

Malcolm, Duncan's second in command and trusted adviser, had stood thoughtful and silent until now. At this, however, he spoke up. "You're Drakkyn, aren't you?"

Bastian frowned, as though not understanding. "Of course. We are of the Dyadd Morgaine, the Tribe of the Goddess." He saw their lack of comprehension, and his frown deepened. "You don't know of the Dyadd, or the *arukhin,* and yet you know of the Drakkyn. How can that be, if I may ask?"

"Are you associated, then, with the one called Mordred Andrakkar, or his son?" Malcolm asked. At the mention of that name, something dangerous flashed in Bastian's eyes and he drew his sister closer to his chest. For the first time, Gabriel noticed that there was something odd about Bastian's teeth.

"Are *you*?" was his flat reply as he regarded them all with renewed wariness. And suddenly Gabriel began to understand: Drakkyn must come in more than one variety. Considering the only sort he'd met so far had been evil and semi-reptilian, that could only be a good thing. His father seemed to agree. Duncan sighed wearily and stepped forward, putting out his hand. After considering it for a moment, Bastian accepted it and shook.

"It seems we have a common enemy, Bastian *an* Morgaine. But I'm not sure what we can do to help you. We barely know what to do to help ourselves at this point." Briefly, Duncan explained the encounter with the Andrakkar in December, the shock of discovering themselves to be descended from something called Drakkyn, the disdain and threats of annihilation from Mordred. And of course, and with great pride, the way Gideon had taken a chunk out of Mordred and driven him off. When he finished, worry had settled again into Bastian's expression.

"I'm afraid I don't even have time to explain. Rowan can tell you more when she awakens. But if the Andrakkar have become interested in this world, that makes my leaving all the more urgent." He looked at their faces again, seeming to search deeper than just the visible. It was discomfiting, Gabriel thought, to have those eyes settle on you even for a second. They passed over his face once and then returned. To stay.

"You," Bastian said. "What is your name?"

Gabriel stared back unflinchingly. He suddenly felt just the way he always had every time a teacher had sent him to stand in the corner, which was quite a few.

"Gabriel. MacInnes."

Bastian was silent for interminable seconds as he continued to stare, making the hackles on the back of Gabriel's neck rise in reaction. He couldn't shake the sensation that this man, or creature—whatever he was— was looking not *at* him but *into* him … searching. For what, he couldn't know, but he had a sudden wild hope that it wouldn't be there. That he would be found lacking, and therefore excused.

Bastian's sudden brisk nod crumbled that wish into dust.

"I give my sister into your keeping until I return, Gabriel MacInnes." Bastian approached as Gabriel's eyes widened. *Give? Sister?* He took a step back despite himself. He'd signed on to protect his family, the Stone. But it looked as though Bastian was about to hand him a living, breathing woman he'd never seen before. Gabriel searched frantically for something to say that would stop Bastain in his tracks. In his horror an image flashed through his mind, that of the unfortunate goldfish he'd once attempted to keep in his apartment that had managed to die of some bizarre form of aquatic leprosy. And he'd actually *tried* with that one! But a woman ... a *Drakkyn* woman, no less.

"Wait just a damn minute!" Gabriel growled, putting his hands up in front of him. "I'm no babysitter. And where the hell do you think you're going in such a hurry?"

Bastian advanced on him, undeterred. Gabriel shot a glance at the others, who didn't appear to be in any hurry to help him. In fact, if he wasn't mistaken, Gideon looked suspiciously relieved. Gabriel frowned at him. Just because the man had Carly to take care of shouldn't exempt him after all. And what of Duncan, or even Malcolm? They were ostensibly running the show here.

Reflexively, Gabriel's traitorous arms lifted to catch the woman who was being unceremoniously shoved at him.

"I have my own score to settle with the Andrakkar. As does she," Bastian said, inclining his head to his prone sister. "But she's too weak right now. You'll need to make sure she feeds, though she'll fight you on that." He sighed, his gaze upon her both affectionate and irritated. "The Goddess knows I've had my hands full trying."

"Uh, sorry, but what exactly do you mean by *feed*?" Gabriel asked, suddenly understanding what was bothering him about Bastian's teeth. The incisors were long and deadly sharp. Just like a …

"In Nevada, where we were, Lucien Andrakkar entered this world. I intend to find out how. Then," Bastian said, his voice a dangerous rasp, "I'm going to make sure it never happens again."

"We'll come with you," Duncan said, his jaw set, his expression grim. "I'll do whatever I can to blow those bastards out of the damned universe."

Bastian gave a slight bow, but he was already backing away from them. Gabriel felt the weight in his arms and was overcome with the desire to hurl it right back at Bastian. He couldn't be responsible for her. What could Bastian possibly have seen in him that would indicate this was a good idea? He had a *life,* for Christ's sake!

"I thank you, more than I can say. But the most important thing now is keeping Rowan safe. She is precious to the Dyadd, our future leader … whosoever may be left of us, at any rate. Something she and I will find out together once I return." His gaze, bright and determined, flicked back to Gabriel. "I warn you, Lucien is nothing short of obsessed. He is still searching for her. He can't be allowed to have her. No matter what."

Gabriel opened his mouth to protest, but incredibly, he heard Duncan's voice answering for him.

"Gabe'll keep her safe. Just you be sure and shut whatever back door he's found into our world."

Gabriel turned his head to look incredulously at his father, who pointedly ignored him.

Feeling like a man who had just been tied to a sinking ship, he tried to think of something, *anything* he could say to pass this off to someone else. All he could come up with, though, was one outraged question.

"Why *me*?" he roared.

"Because you're the only one who might be even more stubborn than she is," answered Bastian. There was a quick smile, a disturbing flash of teeth, before his look turned somber. "Just be sure she feeds. She's been starving herself, and her power is all but gone. She'll need all she has for what is to come."

"If you think," Gabriel began, his temper heating to a full boil, "that I'm just going to let her …"

"Luck to you, brother *arukhin*. You'll need it. May the blessings of the Goddess Morgaine rain down upon you all. I will return."

There was a blinding flash of light, a deafening *crack* like a massive tree splitting in two. And when his eyes could focus again, Gabriel saw that the woman Bastian had called "precious" remained in his arms, silent and still frustratingly real. Looking up, he saw that all eyes were fixed on him. All, that was, but Bastian's.

For as suddenly as he'd appeared, Bastian *an* Morgaine had gone.

Chapter 3

AT FIRST SHE WAS ADRIFT IN NOTHING BUT SOOTHING, SILENT darkness. Wrapped in warm arms, unaware of other eyes on her, Rowan let herself enjoy the novelty of feeling protected, safe. Willfully blind, floating beneath the surface of consciousness, she knew nothing but that for once she was at rest without the company of her terrible dreams.

Then, gradually, there were voices.

Unfortunately, they were irritating.

"… that I'd take care of her, but what if she takes care of me? She's a Drakkyn, for Christ's sake …"

"… just lucky for her she isn't a goldfish …"

" … all well and good for you, but did you get a look at his bloody teeth?"

"For the love of God, Gabriel, stop being such a whiny jackass."

Rowan frowned at the unfamiliar rumbles of several male voices, none of which sounded happy despite carrying an accent that was both strange and beautiful to her ears. They echoed at first as though coming from far away, a meaningless conversation carried over distant hills. But as Rowan came somewhat unwillingly back to herself, she became aware that one of the voices vibrated against her ear each time it sounded.

She also slowly became aware that the unpleasant subject under discussion was none other than herself.

"What am I supposed to do with her? I've got to get back to Tobermory in the next few days or Jerry'll have my head. I've been gone a week already! It isn't as though I can just drop everything and move back to *Iargail,* you know that."

"You gave your word, lad."

"You mean *you* gave my word."

"You heard what the man said. Those Andrakkar bastards are after them, too. How can you refuse when he's off to push them back again? I only wish he hadn't disappeared so quickly on us. We've as much right to go and fight as he does, whoever the hell he is."

A beleaguered sigh, to Rowan's rapidly increasing irritation, came from whoever belonged to the arms she'd just been so obliviously enjoying. She was being held, her body still curled into the gentle embrace that was so at odds with the words being spoken. *I am not enjoying this,* she told herself. And truly, what with the insulting manner in which she was being discussed, she wasn't. Mentally, anyway. But her tired limbs firmly refused to peel themselves away from the delicious heat. A lovely smell, clean and altogether male, filled her nostrils and threatened to muddy her already fuzzy thinking. Then the voice again, low and slightly rough with that thick and rolling accent, thrummed against her ear.

"No, you're right. I know you're right, all of you. It's just … honestly, what is a simple werewolf going to do with some … some bloodsucking Drakkyn? Ideas? Anyone?"

That's it, she thought, opening her eyes to glare directly up at whoever had his damned hands all over her person while referring to her with the distasteful title of *bloodsucker.* If she'd had just few less principles, she would have simply chomped down on an arm to see how he liked *that.* As it was, words would have to do.

"Putting me down would be a nice start, thanks." Her voice, Rowan was pleased to find, was a little hoarse from her confrontation with Lucien but strong enough to be heard.

It was also strong enough to find her immediately on her rear end on a cold stone floor.

"Oh, hell, sorry! Are you all right? You just startled me ..."

Gritting her teeth against the feel of her smarting backside, Rowan looked up to find herself surrounded by four men and one sympathetic-looking woman. Even from this low vantage point, Rowan could tell that either the woman was tiny or the men were huge. Or possibly both, which didn't sit well considering her brother was nowhere in sight. From the little she'd heard, it sounded as though Bastian might have gone running off to do something stupid. That was bad enough without leaving her with a bunch of pushy, overbearing *werewolves.* She had heard of these Wolf shifters, though she knew little of them.

As of right now, she knew all she wanted to.

"Nice one, Gabe," said one of them, shaggily handsome and with a serious countenance, an effect that was enhanced by the long and deadly scar across one eye. He was shaking his head at someone behind her while two older men—one stocky and imposing, the other slim and clever-looking—eyed her as though she were some new and potentially dangerous species of animal. Rowan narrowed her eyes at them. Truly, they had no idea.

Those familiar arms tried to scoop her up into them again. "Here, let me help you."

Rowan yelped angrily, swatting at the hands, then struggling out of them as quickly as she'd found herself in them. That earned her rear end another sharp jolt, but this time it was, in her opinion, worth it. She was not accustomed to being manhandled. Ogled, yes, but not manhandled. And if she'd had her wits fully about her, Rowan swore she would have managed to singe her erstwhile protector's overzealous fingers. As it was, all she could do was scoot away from him and try to gain her footing before she found herself tossed over someone's shoulder in the name of assistance.

"Just … could you just … hey, look buddy, *hands off*, okay?" She finally shouted this last at him, pleased when it shocked him just enough to immobilize him. Quickly, Rowan got her feet under her. Though her legs were shaky, they held her well enough, despite the fact that she was still wearing those ridiculous, toe-numbing shoes.

Which meant she was also still wearing the equally ridiculous corset-and-hot-pants stripper ensemble, Rowan realized with an unpleasant jolt. What a wonderful way to begin to command some respect from whoever these people were. Well, just let them say anything about it, she decided, settling her hands on her hips with a deliberately arrogant toss of her head. She might not stoop to biting, but her mouth was well proven as a weapon vicious enough in its own right, fangs aside.

"Now," she began, "would someone like to explain just exactly what is going on here?" She swept her eyes over the lot of them before turning her attention to the one who'd been so vocal about his objection to her presence. Since he'd been holding her, she could only assume he was the one in charge. After all, her brother would have made sure she was left in the most capable hands. Not, she thought irritably, that she needed to be left in *anyone's* hands, but the two of them would take that up the next time she saw him. He'd just better hope that there was nothing flammable anywhere near him when that happened.

The gift of Fire was not one she had always cherished, but it did have its uses.

The silence that greeted her question had her temper at full boil before she even looked at him. Then she got her first eyeful of Mr. Tall, Dark, and Irritating, and temper mixed with an unexpected punch of a different kind of heat that left her momentarily speechless.

Speechless, but steaming.

He was as obnoxiously tall as she'd feared, Rowan noticed just before her brain function fried completely. She had never been considered short, but this man absolutely towered over her. *Wonderful ... he's probably just as high-handed as Bastian if he's used to hulking over everyone to get his way, and ... oh. OH. Uh-oh ...*

It was the eyes that did it. Large and expressive, framed by thick, dark lashes, those eyes watched her with the silent intensity of the most powerful creatures of the forest. Their color, a luminous golden green, had the hue of the sunlight as it filtered down through the endless canopy of trees that she had once lived beneath. *Hunter's eyes,* she thought dazedly, tearing her own away from that unblinking gaze to see if the rest of this so-called werewolf could possibly measure up to that kind of singular beauty.

Unfortunately, the rest, if at all possible, was even better.

He was bold-featured and dark, with a mouth that looked custom-made for all sorts of delicious mischief, and a physical presence that, coupled with his height, made it seem as though he occupied twice the space he actually did. His stance was deceptively casual, but she could sense the power coiled just beneath the surface, ready to strike if she did. What would it be like to spar with such a creature? she wondered. Would he toy with her before moving in for the kill, leaving her breathless with the need for him to pounce?

Would she let him?

Rowan hissed out a frustrated breath, commanding herself to concentrate on the matter at hand. She may have been raised among women, but she was certainly no stranger to men. Attraction, even so unexpectedly intense, was nothing to her but an unwanted distraction. She could deal with it, just brush it off and move forward. And by all that was sacred, she would keep it to herself. Blind, unrequited lust had destroyed everything she'd had. She shuddered to think how much more damage might be done should she ever reciprocate, for however brief a time.

You will love me, Lucien whispered in her memory, and her skin went cold. Once, she had been blissfully ignorant of the destructive power of the beauty of her kind.

Never again. If she were ever so lucky as to assume her place as *Dyana,* she would leave the wild affairs and intrigues, the inevitably brief attachments, and by default, she thought with a pang of regret, the children, to whoever of her sisters remained. She would drink from men because she had no choice. But her body, and her heart, would forever remain her own.

She lifted her gaze back to meet his, intending to show nothing but disdain and defiance. Her reaction to him was troubling, yes, but thankfully that had no bearing on his to her. And she would make sure he saw nothing but cold, proud, utterly indifferent beauty. He would feel nothing, she told herself. And her feeling would then fade quickly away.

Except the heat that blazed back at her when her eyes locked with his told another story entirely, kindling an answering slow burn at her very core.

Damn you, Bastian, Rowan thought. *Of all the places on Earth ... why here?*

Gabriel watched in helpless fascination as one emotion after another crossed the most stunningly beautiful face he'd ever had the fortune to see.

Whether that fortune was good or the worst in all of MacInnes history remained to be decided, but in the meantime he was content to just stand there and be utterly annihilated by beauty.

He'd seen (not to mention bedded) plenty of women in his life. It was a point of pride with him that he was a bit of a connoisseur of the opposite sex, though Gideon had never done much but shake his head and laugh over

Gabriel's tales of his many conquests. All had been lovely in their own particular ways, some had been widely considered to be rare beauties. None, however, held so much as a candle to Rowan *an* Morgaine.

The eyes that reflected everything from amazement to anger, from fear to what looked suspiciously like animal lust (please, God), were tip-tilted and jewel-bright, an exquisite shade of purest emerald green that seemed lit from within. Her face was a perfect oval, her features delicate yet regal, while her skin was the closest thing to alabaster he'd ever seen. And as for her body … he had barely restrained himself from shouting his thanks to the heavens that female Drakkyn apparently dressed like some Goth teenager's wet dream. A tiny waist, miles of leg, and curves enough to keep his hands busy for several eternities were all showcased perfectly by her revealing ensemble. And all that outrageously red hair was the icing on the cake.

Gabriel felt the memories of all the women he'd ever had in his life vanish in the face of pure female perfection. His heart stumbled along in his chest as he stared, unable to tear his eyes away. His breathing felt constricted, and he was suddenly grateful for the baggy cargo shorts and loose Hawaiian shirt he was wearing. They went a long way toward camouflaging the rest of his body's reaction to her.

It astounded him that he'd just been holding this exquisite creature in his arms and complaining about being saddled with her. Why hadn't he bothered to actually *look* at her before opening his big, stupid mouth? And now, having gotten off on the wrong foot, this

Rowan was doubtless convinced he was a complete and utter ass. Which might not be far from the truth sometimes, he reflected, but it wasn't something he generally cared to display right up front. Leave it to him to put a foot in it but good.

"Well?" she asked, tapping one long, red fingernail against her hip and glaring at him. All traces of that flash of lust, he noted with disappointment, had been replaced by pure, unadulterated pique. It also appeared to be directed entirely at him.

Gabriel opened his mouth to answer, and then realized he had absolutely no clue what she was talking about. He thought quickly, trying to come up with something at least semi-astute to say.

"Um," was what came out. He frowned, and then tried again. "Er."

One red brow arched so high it looked as though it might reach her hairline. "Are you," she asked slowly, "impaired in some way I should know about?"

His frown deepened as he wondered whether such radiant beauty could be hiding a somewhat less stunning temperament and tongue. "No," he heard himself grumble, and was gratified that he had at least managed a one-syllable word that made sense.

Rowan looked unconvinced. "Well. Whatever." She turned away from him to look at the rest of their small party, which Gabriel found insulting, though the feeling was softened somewhat by the view.

"Where is my brother, and where am I? And who are all of you?" She glanced back at him dismissively. "Except for you. You don't have to answer. Wouldn't want to tax you."

Carly, Gabriel saw, bit down so hard on her lip, it was almost certainly going to bleed. She also refused to look back at him while he was glaring at her, and her shoulders shook suspiciously. Gideon looked at the ceiling. Malcolm coughed.

Duncan, damn him, simply answered her politely. Not too terrible, except for the unmistakable look of sympathy he also gave her. Gabriel balled his hands into fists and silently counted to ten. It was that or bash someone's head into the *Lia Fáil,* and since with his luck that would bring about the apocalypse, he thought it better to stay silent until he could control himself.

"You're on *Iargail* Estate in the Western Highlands of Scotland, lass. Your brother, er, seems to have dropped you off here. My son Gabriel, there, gave his word he'd look after you, though, so you're in good hands. I swear it on the honor of my Pack."

Rowan frowned. "*Your* Pack?" she asked, sounding perplexed. She rounded on Gabriel then, her expression oddly accusatory. "You mean you're not the leader here?"

Gabriel shook his head slowly, wondering what the hell that had to do with anything and why the woman was so displeased by it. "No. My father, there, Duncan, is Pack Alpha. Next in line is my brother, Gideon," he continued, even as he watched Rowan's eyes darken with what looked like fury, "then myself."

"Do you mean to tell me," she growled, "that Bastian didn't even have the decency to dump me on the most powerful of you? That he thought some ... some random, semi-coherent shifter was sufficient to help hold off a wizard who fights as a *winged serpent*?" Her voice was strained, coming in harsh pants as her anger rose. It would have been maddeningly erotic, Gabriel thought, if he didn't want to throttle her pretty neck right about now.

Gabriel distinctly heard Gideon mutter something like "ouch" before the red haze of his own temper finally kicked all the way in. He took one menacing step toward her, then another, until he and Rowan were toe to toe. He glared down at her. She glowered up. Gabriel inhaled once, and then decided that might be a bad idea.

She smelled good.

Damn her.

"That's about enough out of you," Gabriel snarled. "In fact, I think I've heard about enough out of the entire Drakkyn race in general. If we're so bloody damn inferior to you, O Great One, then why do you and your ilk keep turning up on our doorstep wanting things? And how did we manage to toss Mordred Andrakkar back into whatever miserable place you've come from with a gaping hole in his neck?" That gave her a start, he saw, but he was on too much of a roll to let her get a word in.

"I didn't …"

"And furthermore," he continued, "I might not be next in line for Alpha, but I'm as much of that blood as either my father or my brother, so you can shove those condescending comments right up your …"

"Look, no one mentioned …"

"And *finally,* while honor might be a foreign concept to your particular breed of lesser life form, I gave my word to your brother that I would look after you until he came back from kicking one of those 'winged serpents' out of Earth, *again.* And that," he informed her, enjoying the trepidation that flickered across Rowan's face, "I will do, whether I have to bind you, gag you, or tie you to a tree." His voice deepened, softened, as he leaned down until his nose was almost touching hers.

"Are we quite clear, your highness?"

Rowan opened her mouth to speak, shut it, and then opened it again. And no matter what else she said, Gabriel knew she'd seen his determination, and that it had unsettled her. Good, he thought with dark pleasure. He'd always been a stubborn bastard. He'd take great pleasure in teaching her just *how* stubborn. He didn't want to look after Rowan *an* Morgaine. But he'd be damned if he wouldn't do it just to spite her.

Finally, she said, "I'm going back to Reno."

Gabriel sighed loudly. "Woman, did you hear nothing I just said to you? If not, let me recap: *over my dead body.*"

She bared her fangs at him, an action that Gabriel found both irritating and arousing (which, come to think of it, was also irritating). He'd never liked vampires, and even though he knew Rowan was technically something different, it didn't stop his distaste at the sight of those teeth. The bloodsuckers were a lazy, selfish, self-indulgent lot, and his people and theirs tended to steer very clear of one another. The largest clans of them, one of which it sounded like Rowan and Bastian had fallen in with, were all the way over in America. It was far, though Gabriel would never call it far enough. The bottom of the ocean or possibly outer space might be, but he really wasn't sure.

He'd been in a bar fight once with one of the members of a low-class little pocket of them that insisted upon existing right here in Scotland. That had been interesting. And more than enough.

"Do I look like I need taking care of?" she hissed. Gabriel used the question as another opportunity to peruse Rowan's interesting outfit. Well, what was under the outfit, really, but she didn't need to know that. No, he damn well didn't want to look after her, but just plain wanting her … he'd have to be dead to avoid that.

Though he had a nasty feeling Rowan might do him in if she hung around long enough.

"You look," he finally replied, "like you need a body-guard or three. Who told you how humans dress, anyway? A gang of gothic strippers?"

Her hands clenched into fists at her sides. "For your information, genius, I *am* a stripper."

Gabriel's eyes widened as his imagination kicked into high gear. A stripper. Well. That was one he hadn't seen coming. He pictured Rowan undulating against some pole, minus the corset, and was suddenly, irrationally jealous of all the grubby, leering men who'd gotten to see what he could only imagine.

"So what?" Rowan snapped with a stiff jerk of her head. "It's not as though I had so many options in your world. Besides, Bastian didn't like my other idea."

He couldn't resist. "Which was?"

Her slow, sexy smile was thoroughly predatory. "World domination."

Gabriel felt his laugh bubble up and decided just to let it come. It left him in a long, lusty roll that brought that intriguing heat to Rowan's gaze again, if only fleetingly. He wondered what it would take to keep it there.

He also wondered if he needed his head examined.

Still, at this point it was either laugh or run screaming. This was going to be impossible. Rowan might look like sex incarnate, but her appearance was camouflage for a stubborn and sarcastic nature that, coupled with those teeth and whatever powers she usually had, might even rival his own. He would do well to remember that she was at least as dangerous as he was. Possibly more.

Probably more.

And to get her to accept this arrangement, he might very well *have* to tie her to a tree. Her next words proved him right.

"Look, I appreciate the concern. Really," she said with a glance at everyone, speaking in a tone that indicated she didn't appreciate this one iota. "But if anyone should be back in Reno fighting off Lucien Andrakkar, it's me. Besides, Bastian may not have mentioned this, but he has no authority to order me to stay anywhere. The opposite is true, in fact. So if you'll just direct me to the nearest airport or boat or something, I'll be out of your hair." She tried for a smile. It looked pained.

Gideon spoke softly, and the backup did Gabriel's heart good. "I'm afraid not. We're a little remote here, you see."

She frowned at him. "What do you mean, *remote*?"

"Not to mention," he continued as though he hadn't heard her, "that unless there are pockets sewn into that costume that I'm unaware of, you have no money to travel. I'm assuming that the way your brother left isn't the way you intended to go."

"No, I can't … I … but …," Rowan stammered angrily, and two bright spots of color appeared high on her pale cheeks. Finally, she chose to fix her ire on

Duncan. "You can't just *keep* me here!" she screeched in a voice that could have awakened the dead. "I'm *Dyana* of the Tribe of Morgaine, for the love of the Goddess! You, you're nothing but a bunch of big, furry… *nuisances*! I demand to be let go!"

Duncan simply raised his eyebrows. "You demand to be locked out of the house all night and sleep on the damp ground?"

The flush spread to her cheeks in their entirety. It appeared Rowan was finally figuring out that she was stuck, Gabriel thought with a disturbing amount of pleasure. It wasn't just her looks that intrigued him, he realized. Rowan was proud, and arrogant, and had more spirit in her pinky finger than most women probably had in their entire bodies.

He wanted her, badly. The strength of that need shook him when he tried to gauge it, and had him trying futilely to put it in perspective, turn it down, shut it off. *Just another woman,* he repeated to himself as he raked his eyes over strong shoulders, taut buttocks, hands planted defiantly on deliciously curved hips. *She's no different than any other.*

Except she *was* different. And Gabriel realized if he spent anymore time with her, he might, just might, be in very big trouble. Gabriel had to fight off a sudden strong urge to run howling into the forest and hide until Rowan, and all the trouble she'd doubtlessly brought with her, were long gone.

Duncan looked past Rowan, who was beginning to both look and sound like she might just spontaneously combust, and quirked a small smile at Gabriel. There was a wicked twinkle in his eyes, and Gabriel wasn't sure which Duncan was enjoying more—causing a Drakkyn, any Drakkyn, such distress, or the prospect of Gabriel being saddled with that same Drakkyn for days on end. It was probably a toss-up.

Gabriel glowered.

"Ah, well, it's getting a little late for abuse this evening, I think," Duncan said mildly. "We can all get some rest and pick up again in the morning, though, and won't that be a joy? Gabe will show you to one of the bedrooms, of course." Duncan gave a small bow then as Gabriel watched incredulously, turned on his heel, and walked out the door. Following suit, Malcolm bade the rest of them good night. Gabriel turned his head to his brother, narrowing his eyes threateningly. He and Carly wouldn't actually leave him alone with this spitting hellion, would they?

Damn it, yes they would.

Gideon flashed him a quick grin and caught up Carly's hand in his own. Carly, at least, had the decency to look apologetic as she followed her husband toward the stairs.

"See you both in the morning," Gideon called back cheerfully.

"Rowan, if you need anything, please don't hesitate to ask," Carly said, turning her head as Gideon dragged her away at increasing speed.

"Hesitate until at least morning," Gideon amended. "Good night, all." And with that, they were gone.

Gabriel and Rowan were alone.

"Well. Shall we?" he asked after an uncomfortable moment's hesitation.

Rowan looked back, her eyes flashing in the dim light. "Nothing good can come of keeping me here," she said in a soft voice that managed to be both lilting and ominous.

Gabriel simply sighed and rubbed a hand across the back of his neck. "Don't I just know it," he replied, and started toward the doorway. He heard her pause, then begin to follow. What choice did either of them have, really? But her words, both warning and threatening, echoed in his ears as he started toward the surface, and refused to let him be.

Chapter 4

"DO YOU ALWAYS DO THAT?"

Gabriel started, the soft and smoky voice beside him jerking him back to the present. After a silent walk back across the grounds to the *Iargail* house, with Rowan trudging along beside him with a ferocious look that quite eloquently said, *Don't even think about talking to me,* he'd been free to let his mind wander in peace. And so it had—up long and shapely legs, under a particular clinging corset to skim a slim waist and bountiful curves, and over one long, ivory neck. He'd thought, since she was paying him no attention anyway, that he was being discreet enough.

Apparently not.

He would have been if he'd been able to quit gulping down the Rowan-scented air that surrounded him, he thought darkly, stopping just at the top of the stairs and turning to look into a face that was indisputably irritated. He opened his mouth to fend off what was sure to be a complaint about his ogling, er, *admiring* of her exalted person. Instead, he got another whiff of his own personal werewolf heaven.

It was so unfair, he thought, dangling somewhere between annoyance and bliss.

It was also utterly glorious. And in the end, bliss won out.

Helpless to resist, he drank in the smoky musk of a blustery autumn afternoon, exhaling on a sigh after he'd filled his nose with the crisp bite of October air and the warm aroma of fallen leaves. As impossible as it seemed, Rowan smelled just like his very favorite sort of day, the kind he dreamed about when he needed to escape for a bit. He'd done it ever since he was a child; one minute there was only stress, and the next, he was racing through trees turned to Highland fire.

There was nothing childish about his reaction to that scent, though. He would have been mortified about the decidedly boyish burst of butterflies in his stomach had he been thinking of anything but having this glorious creature beneath him tonight. All night. Every night.

Jesus.

"Do I always do what?" he finally managed in a voice that sounded like he'd recently taken up gargling with razor blades. If only she'd tell him he was driving her mad with lust, or that she found werewolves completely irresistible …

"Sigh," she said instead, tilting her chin down to give him a beleaguered look that might have been charming had it not so plainly meant she thought he was an idiot. "Loudly. Heavily. And at least ten times since we got in the house. Is it a medical condition, or are you just naturally annoying?"

When the words sank in, he wasn't sure whether to laugh or be offended. It seemed to be the way with this particular Drakkyn, which meant he was well on his way to a headache of epic proportions if he spent much longer with her. Gabriel jerked his chin up, crossed his arms over his chest, and glowered. It was a look that had intimidated many a would-be brawler at his

place of business. Unfortunately, Rowan looked decidedly underwhelmed.

"And are you always such a charming conversation-
alist, or is it just me?" he shot back, keeping his voice
deliberately even. He didn't think it wise, when he knew
so little of her, to let Rowan know he felt like throttling
her every time she opened her mouth.

"It's you," she replied, not quite suppressing what
appeared to be an amused quirk of her lips. "I know
when I'm being a bitch."

The honesty, strangely charming, caught him off
guard. "Ah," he murmured, "that's ... astute of you."

"About as astute as telling you I don't plan to reform
right now," she said, not looking concerned in the least.
"So just quit sighing. It's giving me a headache, and all
I want to do is sleep."

She might as well have ended with *I have spoken*,
Gabriel thought as he watched her flounce off without
him. He found himself in no hurry to catch up, taking
the opportunity to enjoy the way her hips swayed when
she walked, as though she were moving to music only
she could hear. He could imagine her dancing, the
sinuous motion of those long limbs and perfect curves
to some sensuous, bass-heavy song.

Gabriel shook his head, wishing the motion would
clear it, and made himself follow despite every ounce of
his better judgment. It was bizarre, his reaction to this
acid-tongued creature. He preferred his women on the
"doting and delectable" side, of course. But if a man's
tastes ran more to the wild and wicked—and thank God
his didn't—Rowan would be desire personified. She

would also, he had no doubt, be more than happy to abuse the besotted into eternity.

Could be interesting, some traitorous part of his mind piped up.

The rest, obviously brighter than his libido, simply retorted, *For Christ's sake, you idiot, get some sleep.*

"You're doing it again."

Gabriel gritted his teeth and jogged to her side, taking her around the corner and stopping in front of a door in the east wing, the part of the house generally reserved for family. "This'll be your room, for the time being," he informed her as he pushed the door open, flipping the light switch just inside. She stepped in warily, and Gabriel felt a surprising tug of sympathy for her in that moment, left alone in a strange place with nothing but the clothes on her back. Well, what little there was of them. He had a strange urge to follow her, to try to put her at ease. After all, he reminded himself, it sounded like she'd been through a lot. No matter how tough she played, he'd bet she would become vulnerable once the door shut on her.

Then her sarcastic voice reached his ears from within.

"Oh. Pink. My favorite."

Okay, so, maybe not so vulnerable.

Gabriel barely suppressed a chuckle, remembering now that this particular room was a bit frilly. Lots of eyelet lace and rose accents. Guests often came to *Iargail* for its charm as a Victorian country manor, and much of the decorating had been done with that time period, the time when the original castle ruins had been incorporated into a stately yet charming brick home, in mind. But with her bold looks and fiery temperament, it was one of the last time periods he'd associate with Rowan. She was more warrior queen than retiring lady, more likely to be toting a spear than a doily. And the woman was the absolute antithesis of pastels and pink.

It seemed, he thought as the smirk lingered, that Rowan was inclined to agree.

He knew he should just leave her be to get settled in for the night, but found himself stepping in behind her anyway. She had stopped in the center of the large but modestly appointed room, looking over the heavy, old four-poster bed, nightstand, low mirrored dresser, and armoire like a queen surveying her domain. Apparently she found everything but the wall color adequate enough, as she turned to look at him with an imperious air, hands on hips.

"Thanks. I can take it from here."

Though he was obviously being dismissed, and *here* was the last place he really ought to be until he formulated some sort of rational plan of action, Gabriel still hesitated. In the soft lamplight, the woman who'd introduced herself as Rowan *an* Morgaine looked even more tired than she had when she'd so abruptly arrived. Though the dark smudges beneath those jewel-bright eyes and the hollowness of her cheeks did nothing to mar her beauty, it was obvious that she hadn't been getting the care she needed. And her brother's words slithered through his mind with an unpleasant hiss: *Just be sure she feeds. She's been starving herself, and her power is all but gone.*

Gabriel heaved another exasperated sigh and rubbed a hand across the back of his neck, prompting Rowan to glare daggers at him before unceremoniously turning her back on him to turn down the bed. It was, he knew, an invitation to leave. Now. And also to shut the hell up with the sighing, which she was bound to point out if he slipped again.

He started to do just that, but caught himself at the last minute and settled for glaring at the back of Rowan's head instead. Pity her brother hadn't been more specific about just *when* she'd die of starvation, since then he might have had the luxury of dragging the task out for a while. But then maybe it was better to just get it over with and move on from there. Perhaps she'd thank him, he thought, though there was a better chance of Gideon dancing the can-can in drag at the pub. But in her purportedly weakened state, at least she probably wouldn't be able to kill him. That was something.

Christ, his standards were getting low.

"Right," he said, more to himself than to Rowan. She turned back to him, looking suddenly wary. "Except first I, ah, promised your brother I would do something." His reward for this admission was feeling like a prize idiot when Rowan simply looked at him blandly. Perhaps she hadn't understood him. Then again, perhaps pigs would someday learn to fly.

"For you," he added meaningfully.

"Uh-huh."

Gabriel tried his best not to glare at the woman, who he was sure was being deliberately obtuse. She knew she was a bloodsucker. He knew she was a bloodsucker. It wasn't as though he was skirting the issue. Well, not exactly. He took another step closer, and Rowan narrowed her eyes into slits. All of that outrageous hair seemed to pulse with a life of its own in the glow of the antique wall sconces that framed the bed, and Gabriel had a sudden intense urge to simply twist it around his fist and use it to hold her still while he took a long, hard taste of that luscious mouth and sharp tongue.

He'd taken two more steps toward her before he even realized what he was doing, and by then Rowan was beginning to look like she was seriously considering ripping into him with those long, manicured fingernails. Gabriel gave a short, angry growl. Hell with this. He hated vampires as much as the next werewolf. Blood-sucking Drakkyn were close enough. And the best way to cure himself of this ludicrous fixation he seemed to be working on was by doing exactly as he'd been asked.

By getting up close and personal with her particular pair of sharp, pointy teeth.

That should dampen his ardor well into the next millennium.

"Look, let's just get this over with, all right?" Gabriel snapped. "Only be quick about it. And try not to leave a mark or anything." He'd never been big on hickeys. Bite marks, in his opinion, fell into that general category. Especially when he wasn't getting a damned thing out of the experience, Gabriel thought irritably. Still, if nothing else, he was a man of his word. He closed the small remaining distance between himself and Rowan, leaned down so that his neck would be easy to access, and closed his eyes, anticipating the pinch of her teeth. He waited as a few seconds passed … then a few more. But it wasn't teeth he finally felt, just the warm tickle of breath against his skin. Her tone, however, was arctic.

"What *exactly* do you think you're doing?"

Gabriel pulled back just enough to frown at her. "Letting you bite me."

She frowned back at him. "I don't want to bite you, thanks."

"Your brother …"

"Worries too much, and is lately obnoxious about it. Look," she said, pushing her hair back in an agitated gesture and huffing out a breath, "I don't care what Bastian told you, or made you promise, or made you sign in pig's blood. I'm not hungry; I'm just tired, which requires you to leave rather than presenting yourself as dinner. But, you know, thanks. Really." She waited a beat, eyebrows raised expectantly. "Good night, Gabriel."

Damn her, but that spicy, intoxicating scent she carried with her was beginning to affect him again, clouding his brain just when he needed his wits about him. Because if the hostility in her expression was any indication, he was going to have to *make* her do what he didn't really want her to in the first place. Though it was futile, he wished desperately he'd gone home days ago and was curled up in his own bed with some luscious, willing blonde who didn't make his head feel like it was going to explode.

"I gave my word," Gabriel began, in a tone he might use with a young, tantrum-prone child.

She glowered. "Not to me, you didn't."

"I intend to keep it," he continued as he began to lose his patience. "I don't like it any better than you do, by the way, but there's nothing for it. I know you're starving. I may not be able to fix your personality problem, but I *can* fix that. So I'm going to indulge your nasty little habit so that your brother can come back to something other than your corpse. Now bite me, damn it. You're not the only one who wants to go to bed."

She looked outraged, crossing her arms over her chest and glaring murderously at him. "My 'nasty little habit' is what keeps me alive, you insufferable jackass. And if that's how you feel, you can absolutely forget me *ever* doing you the honor of drinking from you."

Gabriel snorted. "If that's considered an honor, I've found yet another reason to never cross into your world. But be that as it may, I'm afraid we're both going to have to make do."

Her expression turned mulish. "No."

"Yes."

"No."

"Oh, for the love of ... this is ridiculous!" Gabriel snapped with an impatient wave of his hands. And finally, for whatever reason (his visible stress being the most likely), Rowan smiled. It had a wicked edge to it that left him feeling slightly weak in the knees.

"I haven't even gotten started," she informed him. She spoke with the self-satisfied air of one who had won many a bloody war of words. Unfortunately for her, though, he had no intention of continuing to spar with her verbally. Sometimes fighting dirty was the only option.

With no warning, he advanced on her. Gabriel was darkly satisfied when this time she backed up, stopping only when she hit the edge of the bed. "You're going to bite me so we can both get some sleep," he informed her, letting her know with his tone that he would brook no refusals. A low, sinister noise reached his ears in reply.

"Are you … are you *growling* at me, woman?" He stared at her curiously, this being an utterly new one on him. He'd had women throw things at him, curse at him, and threaten to send him to the devil himself, but not a one had ever growled at him. Not since he was just a young pup, at any rate, and the few female cousins he'd played with had hardly qualified as women at the time. Gabriel cocked his head, considering. It was actually sort of erotic.

And he really needed to get this over with before he lost what was left of his mind.

Rowan glared at him, her jade green eyes so hot he wouldn't have been surprised if they'd started shooting off sparks. "I'm telling you to get the hell out of my room before I make you. I'm. Not. Interested. Now for the love of the Goddess, *go away.* The last thing I need is some mangy shifter dogging my heels and trying to fill in for my brother, who, I might add, has no right to order me around anyway. You and your kind, Gabriel MacInnes, have less. I'm only here until I can get back home, I only care about defeating the Andrakkar in the most violent way I can think of, and what I really need is sleep. Are we now clear?"

Her chest rose and fell rapidly in her anger, and a light flush had suffused skin that was the color of cool alabaster. Her nostrils flared faintly, and the lush lips she was using to hurl invectives at him were pursed tightly. As he supposed she'd intended, Rowan now had Gabriel's undivided attention. He doubted, however, that its nuances would please her. The thought made him smile, what he knew was a big, Wolfish grin. Battling her was proving to be a twisted pleasure, but his instincts told him she was in no shape to refuse him. It was time to go in for the kill.

"All that may be true, but you're our guest. We're not going to let such an exalted guest starve to death. You need blood. I happen to have some. And as I've already mentioned, I gave your brother my word. I'm not going back on it."

Her eyes widened and her gaze darted past him, around the room, looking for escape. Gabriel closed in on her, knowing there was none. She must truly be weak, he knew, if she hadn't any magic to throw in a last-ditch effort to stop him. Part of him hated to force her. The other part was entirely focused on the scent of delicious, desirable prey, ready to be taken down.

"I … I don't want your blood. I haven't been able to drink human blood," she stammered, her unease finally showing through. "It makes me sick."

"Ah, but you forget. I'm not human," he replied, stopping only when he was so close that their bodies were almost touching. "And I insist."

She was cornered.

Rowan stood seething as Gabriel MacInnes smirked down at her, acting even more overbearing than Bastian had become since the attack. It was a feat she hadn't thought possible, but this shifter was surprising her at every turn, and not, she decided with clenched jaw, in a good way. If only she had an ounce of power left in her. But as the room tilted slightly again, challenging her balance enough to make her worry that her captor had seen her wobble, Rowan knew without a doubt that it was gone.

Blood magic. The Dyadd's gift, and their curse. Before the Andrakkar had come for them, she'd had it in abundance. Rowan wistfully remembered calling down a rain of stars, joining with her sisters to create a pillar of white fire to celebrate the Fertility Rite. In those days, her only true complaint had been that her own particular gifts seemed tailored more for destruction than helping the villagers who so depended on them, despite her mother's assurances that her abilities were greater than she knew. But that time was long past, and from the way Gabriel was now dealing with her, she was sure he knew it.

If only she could be certain she wouldn't react to his blood the same way she had to the "gift" the vampires had given her.

The man, as she remembered, had been what the vampires had laughingly called *thralled,* his mind clouded and convinced that he wanted to be bitten. And yet, when she had reluctantly begun to drink, the life force that ran through his blood had screamed through her own body in horror until she'd had to run from the room. She'd been violently ill for hours, Rowan remembered with a shudder. And the taunting laughter of creatures that were her distant kin echoed in her memory still.

Only a monster could drink fear. She, Rowan *an* Morgaine, was many things, but monster was not one of them. But for the Dyadd's sake, and for Bastian's, she knew she would have to try.

She was no use to anyone otherwise, least of all herself.

"Fine," she finally snapped, suppressing another growl. The last thing she needed right now was for him to smile again. She wanted to focus on the unpleasant task at hand and be done with it. Gabriel MacInnes excited her in a

way a man such as he definitely should not, and the closer
he got, the more unsettled she became. Just now he'd
looked like he wanted to devour her. And for a moment,
just a *very quick* weak moment, she'd wanted to let him.
It was nothing, Rowan told herself firmly.

And yet her mouth went instantly dry as she watched
the pulse in the hollow of his throat beat quickly and
steadily. Rowan swallowed, and it felt like a rock had
lodged in the desert of her throat. She could smell him
now, the living essence of him, blood and earth and
wilderness, man and animal joined. It was raw, and male,
and brutally arousing to Rowan's deprived senses.

And now, though she could hardly bear to let herself,
she began to truly *want*.

"Well? Do you think you could get it over with?" He
had his eyes shut tight, so Rowan let herself truly smile.
He so obviously found this distasteful, and yet he was
going to let what he considered his natural enemy sink
her teeth into his neck, all for a hastily given promise.
Had he fallen at her feet in her old life, she realized with
a twinge of regret, she would have gladly taken him to
her bed, though she gave into the erotic impulse that
feeding provoked only seldom. She would have let him
run those strong hands over her body, stoking her inner
flame until both of them were consumed in the heat.
There was something about him that pulled at her; that
she could admit now with no one able to read it in her
expression. But the heat in his eyes when he looked at her,
the raw desire to possess so clearly written there. That sort
of need was something she didn't understand, and didn't
want. It was too close. Too close to the things Elara, her
mother, had always warned would cause her pain.

Too close to Lucien.

"Just be still," Rowan said quickly, recognizing the sensual rasp in her voice and hating that she couldn't contain that evidence of her reaction to his closeness. She cleared her throat, but it didn't help. "Relax, and don't be afraid. It …" She swallowed hard against the stomach-roiling memory of the thralled human. "It makes it much more difficult."

That instruction met with an amused grunt. Gabriel opened one eye to look at her. "I've heard three-year-old werewolves with scarier growls than you. I wouldn't worry."

She glowered at him, indignant. "I'm scarier than you think I am."

His only response was an unconvincing *Mmm,* and Rowan knew her time for stalling was up. She said a quick prayer to the Goddess Morgaine that she could tolerate this blood, that one feeding would be enough to restore her. For with this man she didn't think she could afford more than once.

Then she moved in.

She took care to touch him as lightly as possible, but it did nothing to dull the knife edge of Rowan's need. Now that she had decided to feed, that her body *knew* it was about to receive sustenance, it seemed that every one of her senses was filled with nothing but Gabriel. Her supplicant. Her victim.

Hers.

She pushed the odd thought away even as she felt her incisors lengthen and become even sharper. However much attraction there was between them, it was only that, nothing more. Nothing unusual, nothing difficult to suppress. Nothing.

Rowan closed her eyes, sliding her hands up his chest. *Nothing,* she told herself firmly even as she nuzzled against the side of his throat, unable to deny herself the pleasure of filling her senses with him in the moment before they joined. He was so wonderfully *alive.* After so many months of keeping company with those who would rather exude death, Gabriel's nearness filled her with a sudden savage joy. She heard his quick intake of breath, felt his pulse begin to skip along more quickly beneath her hands. And as she bared her teeth, hesitating a breath away from fulfillment, she realized she would have to cling tightly to what control she had left. She should never have waited so long.

Oh, it's been so long.

She bit in, flesh giving way to fang, and her senses burst in a slow, shimmering implosion. Rowan barely felt Gabriel's jerk as her teeth slipped into him, as her mouth was filled with rich, pulsing life. It was like nothing she'd ever tasted, she thought as a low sound of pleasure escaped her throat. Dark wine flavored with the light of the moon. She smelled it, tasted it, *felt* it as she never had anything else, moving her hands to his back and clinging more tightly as sensation rocketed through her. And within her, at her center, the flame that sustained her magic flickered into life once more and began its seductive dance.

Unable to help herself, Rowan rubbed against him like a cat in heat, her nipples tightening into taut buds beneath the thin corset and sending tiny shock waves through her each time they brushed his chest. Her fingers bit harder into his skin, the fabric of his shirt in danger of giving way beneath nails that were sharpening to claws in her excitement. And still that delicious elixir flowed from him, filling her until she could no longer tell where she ended and Gabriel began. The joining was intense, erotic. But just out of reach and yet frustratingly close was the promise of *more*. She had always felt it there, each time she fed. This time, though, was different. It would have terrified her if she hadn't been caught in a hurricane of hunger and lust.

Because this time she sensed that if she reached far enough, she might be able to have not just *more,* but *all.*

She heard a soft noise, Gabriel's broken moan as he slid his hands up to tangle in her hair. Caught in the spell of their joining, Rowan lapped his neck ever more greedily while she suckled. Dimly she heard herself purr in pleasure, felt herself arching against her captive. There was no leveling off with Gabriel, she thought with dazed wonder. Only a stoking of her passion higher and higher, until it threatened to consume them both. It was madness. Her hunger only seemed to grow with every pull of her lips. For the first time in her life, that elusive promise of completion seemed almost close enough to touch.

Rowan drank deeply, wanting, needing to get closer, to be inside his skin with him. She began to move more urgently against him, the heat between them threatening to ignite into an inferno. Even right up against him it wasn't close enough. She rose onto her toes, sliding her hands lower to grip his hips and press him into the liquid heat at the juncture of her thighs. That sudden exquisite pressure had her instantly trembling at the edge of what she knew would be a blinding climax.

Yes, love, there … please, there …

Stop, I have to stop.

The dim warning barely registered, lost as she was. Gabriel was hard, deliciously hard against her, and his harsh breaths as she pulsed against him coiled her tighter, tighter. Desperately, Rowan clung to him, drawing deep, needing more. She was rushing toward some shimmering peak on a river of molten sensation, mouth and hips moving together in the ancient dance of her people. But it had never been like this, never brought her so close to coming apart.

She clawed at his shirt, desperate for contact. The thin material tore easily, shredding apart and baring a broad, muscular chest that radiated the heat she couldn't seem to get close enough to. Rowan surfaced with a gasp, tearing her mouth from Gabriel's neck to crush against lips that were as eager as her own. His kiss was hot, hard, demanding. He dug his hands into her hair and held her there as his tongue swept into her mouth, plundering, rubbing against her own until Rowan could no longer hear her own breathless cries for want of him.

There was a tearing sound as the corset was ripped from her body and thrown to the floor. She barely felt it, reveling in Gabriel's harsh groan when skin finally connected to skin. They fit together as though they had been created solely for each other, her curves molding against the hard planes of his broad chest. The taste of him was still on her lips, in her mouth, making her dizzy with need. And still he ground against her, the tip of his cock pressing insistently against the thin silk of her hot pants. He could be inside her in seconds, she realized. All she had to do was let him. All she had to do was let go …

STOP!

But the only thing that stopped her was the blinding light of her climax, shocking her with its ferocity. She gasped, then gave a hoarse cry as it crashed through her, tossing her head back as she rode wave upon wave of pleasure while strong hands held her tightly. Then his mouth was back on hers, velvet lips open and hot as he tasted his blood on her tongue. Rowan moaned softly as he crushed her to him, melting against the solid heat of him. *Gabriel,* she thought languidly. That one name was now imbued with all the emotion, all the sensation that had shaken her to her core. All the blessed things that for her had no name now joined to form his. *Gabriel.* Rowan was dimly aware of being lifted as he moved to settle her on the bed. Impossible though it seemed, though her thirst had been slaked, her hunger had only intensified. And she wanted, how she wanted more.

But there can be no more. And I can't let this happen.

Slowly she returned to herself, forcing herself into awareness no matter how much her mind and body wanted to stay adrift. And though his essence was still shimmering through her, setting off tiny explosions within her as his blood mingled with her own, Rowan knew she had gone far enough. Too far. But it was time to end this and salvage what she could. To give herself now was to make a promise she could not keep, not to this stranger who stirred her, not to anyone.

Her hands came up to push at him as he began to press her back against the mattress.

"Don't," she said softly. "Don't. You have to go. Please."

"But we're only just getting started, love," he murmured, caressing her gently as he settled himself against her. Rowan felt her stomach clench as she looked into Gabriel's face, getting her first clear look at what she'd done to him. His singular eyes were glazed, but glowed with almost desperate desire. And she had done this to him, with her carelessness. Fear shot through her, like ice in her veins. It seemed laughable that just a short while ago she'd been afraid that *he* might hurt *her.* After all that had happened, it was clear that she herself posed one of the greatest dangers of all. Truly, what more could she find to destroy? Yet if the Goddess was kind, there was still time to rectify this mistake. Rowan pushed again, harder this time, overcome with shame.

"Gabriel," she repeated, her voice quavering slightly in her growing desperation. "If you don't stop, I'm going to have to make you."

No response as he kissed a line down her jaw, sparking the first unwanted flickers of renewed desire even as her gut twisted with guilt. She, who had condemned the vampires for thralling their victims, had turned out to be no better. She'd just used beauty and sex instead of dark magic. It was not the way of the Dyadd. It was not her way. But then nothing about this encounter had been.

She had lost control. It was unconscionable. And it was dangerous. Perhaps, she thought, seething with anger at her own foolishness, she would have been better matched to Lucien after all. It seemed they both had a tendency to destroy things with their emotions.

She looked back at Gabriel, who had only been trying to help, and knew he would pay the price. But better now than later. She didn't understand her insane, over-whelming reaction to him, and didn't particularly want to. But one thing was crystal clear.

This could never happen again.

"I'm sorry," she said with true regret, "but this is for the best."

He spoke again, and though his words were rough with desire and difficult to make out, they made her blood run cold.

"Don't go," he sighed against her neck. "Need you … my only …"

Her reaction was reflexive, and instantaneous. She coiled her renewed power into a ball and pushed outward, *hard.* One second Gabriel was on top of her, the next he had flown through the air and slammed against the wall in the hallway. The force with which he hit caused the furniture to shudder, and Rowan leaped from the bed, rushing to the doorway, hoping with all her might she hadn't hurt him.

Apparently, however, the man was built like a rock. Gabriel sat crumpled against the wall, rubbing the back of his head and looking as though he didn't quite know where he was. At the sight of her, though, his thoughts seemed to clear with unfortunate speed. Rowan fought back a cringe as his eyes, only minutes before fogged with desire, blazed back at her with violent anger.

"What," he asked, his voice deadly soft, "the bloody hell was *that*?"

"A warning," she said, her own voice just as soft. This was for the best, she told herself. Nothing good could come of this … this stupid infatuation with some other-world shifter. It had been her own damn fault for waiting so long to feed, or she never would have had such an intense reaction to him. She shoved aside the insistent feeling that there was more to it, not wanting any of it. Soon she would be rid of this place, and rid of *him*. And he, she thought with a pang, of her. It looked like that couldn't happen soon enough, for either of them.

"Stay away from me, Gabriel. For your own good, and mine. And never touch me again."

"No problem," he snarled, leaping to his feet in a movement so fluid and graceful that it surprised her, seeing it in someone so big and imposing. "And by the way, your highness, *you're welcome.*"

He stalked off down the hallway and was around the corner in an instant. Rowan sagged against the door frame, feeling as though she'd had the wind knocked out of her even though she knew her body to be restored, awakened with new life. She listened as he thundered down the stairs, as he slammed out into the night. *This is for the best,* she told herself again. She was *Dyana* of the Tribe of Morgaine now. She belonged to all and none, and there was no future in a dalliance with Gabriel MacInnes. He would recover soon enough, she was sure, from his desire. But she could not forget the words he'd murmured to her.

"My only."

Rowan closed her eyes against it, and then shut her door to get ready for bed. She needed the rest for all that lay ahead.

But as a distant howl pierced the night and filled her with unwanted longing, in her heart she knew. There would be no sleep for her tonight.

Chapter 5

"IT IS HOPELESS," JAGRIN SAID. "I CANNOT GIVE HER TO YOU."

Lucien Andrakkar glared at the pale, slim, red-eyed figure who stared silently back at him from across the small table. After all he had done to take the flame-haired witch as his own, to now have Jagrin tell him that it was for naught was a knife in his cold and blackened heart. It was a measure of how he loved her that he could suffer so for her, when no other woman had produced so much as a twinge of feeling in him in so many years.

No. It could not be. He could see the greedy glitter in the *daemon*'s eyes. There was something yet to be had here … if he was willing to pay the price.

Twin ribbons of smoke curled lazily out of Lucien's nostrils, a mark of his displeasure with the man whom he had summoned from the borderlands of the Blighted Kingdom. He wanted to shift, to rip and tear the meager flesh from the bones of his reticent companion. But Jagrin was highly placed in the *daemon* king's house, and the slight was one he could not afford.

Especially since Mordred had not sanctioned this meeting. The dragon king had obsessions of his own to tend to, none of which involved matters of the heart. Claws and teeth, however, were another matter altogether.

"Come now, Jagrin," he said softly, relaxing in the cold stone chair as though he had never been more at peace. "The dragon and *daemon* have been allies since the time the great Drak fled to the higher realms. You can't deny it's been a beneficial relationship, especially for your kind," he said. He knew full well about the caverns full of fat and glittering gems that rested beneath the endless desert, had been on the patrols that circled the Blighted Kingdom during the day when the *daemon* were at their weakest. Annoyances … and yet they were a small price to pay for access to the dark magic the wretched creatures possessed.

Jagrin's lip curled slightly, his lips a gaping wound against the white of skin that would burst into flames at the first hint of sunlight. "Be that as it may, my lord Lucien, I speak the truth. Moving between realms is no easy feat. It would take months to prepare another traveling draught, and even then there are no guarantees." He paused, lifting one corner of his thin red mouth in a half smile. "You saw that yourself, after all."

Lucien kept his expression impassive, though beneath the table his nails sliced thin red crescents into his palms. He hardly needed to be reminded of how he had failed to capture Rowan just several nights past. He relived it a thousand times a day in his mind, obsessing over the tiniest details: the way her strange clothing had molded to her exquisite flesh, the defiance in her eyes when he had professed his devotion, the scent of her, rich and sultry on the warm night air. The perfection of her people was legendary, but for him, upon finally seeing the hidden tribe of unsurpassed beauty that was the Dyadd Morgaine, there had been only one. And for once in his life, his father had wholeheartedly agreed with his choice, going so far as to order the camp raided, the witch stolen, on his son's behalf.

If only Jonas had done as he'd been ordered, then he had no doubt Rowan would already have been his. If only Mordred's prized warrior had captured her at the beginning of the raid, there would not have been the carnage that had so turned her against him. Instead, the bloodlust each of them fought to control in battle had consumed Jonas whole, and many of the Dyadd had been destroyed as the others followed his lead.

He had not been there. He had waited in the tower, ready, so ready, to claim his bride. That the act itself would involve more a need to possess than true lust on his part, at least at first, didn't disturb him; he had been dead inside for so long that he felt such need must take time to cultivate. But he felt pulled to Rowan as though the ties that bound them were visible. The need to be near her was nothing short of painful. So he had waited that long night, anticipating what it might be like to hunger that way, waiting to be stirred as he had never been. Certain that her touch would at last make him whole.

As it turned out, he waited still. But glimmering at the center of the darkest magic was hope, if only he had the courage to grasp it. And so he had summoned Jagrin once more, praying to the strongest gods that he might be granted one more chance. Without Rowan he had so little left to lose.

"The *daemon* know dark magic better than any," Lucien said smoothly, seeing that the flattery had hit its mark when his companion smiled. "I fault myself for the failure, of course. To see her so immediately, to have everything happen so quickly … I was utterly taken aback by your handiwork, Jagrin. I only ask this of you because I know that you, above all but the king himself, have the ability."

"True, true," Jagrin preened, steepling long fingers beneath his chin. He looked pensive, but also deeply pleased. That gave Lucien hope. Still, even if the ploy had worked, there would be a price. With the *daemon* there was always a price, ally or no.

"Well, perhaps there is something more," he finally allowed, speaking slowly, thoughtfully. "Though I warn you, it will be difficult." *And come at great expense,* Lucien thought, not missing the malicious glitter in Jagrin's red gaze. Still, he found himself hard-pressed to care. If he succeeded, he won the ultimate prize. If he should lose, well, he was used to torment. Maybe suffering it at the hands of the *daemon* would be a pleasant switch from a lifetime spent as the only son and heir of Mordred Andrakkar. It wouldn't matter anyway. He had cared for nothing before he had found her. If he should lose her, the numbness would simply consume him.

Rowan had awakened some mysterious part of him that he had never known a dragon to have. He cursed himself for having ever denied that he could love her, for this ceaseless longing could be nothing else. It had taken root so rapidly, and then grown, the one thing that finally awakened his interest in assuming the rule of the dragons. But only with his queen at his side. It seemed he did have a heart after all. And if Rowan chose to shatter it … well, Lucien thought grimly, the *daemon* were welcome to what was left.

"What can be done, then?" Lucien asked.

Jagrin simply looked at him for a moment, his expression inscrutable. "That would, of course, depend," he finally said, his voice a near whisper, "on what you are willing to give for such a service."

Lucien closed his eyes, thinking of the priceless scepter—a family heirloom—that he had parted with for the ill-fated traveling draught. There was more, of course; the riches of the House of Andrakkar alone, not to mention the dragons in general, were beyond most beings' imagining. To barter with such treasures would be considered nothing short of treason, he knew, if he were caught. But he had already doomed himself with the scepter, he supposed. There was no point in becoming principled about it now.

"There are many other riches," he began, only to have Jagrin cut him off with an impatient wave of his hand.

"No, no. The scepter is lovely, but useless to me as anything but a bauble. Fine payment for a traveling draught, of course. But the thing I may or may not share with you has been a secret among my people for over a thousand years. We kill those who reveal it," Jagrin said with a considering tilt of his head, "but I might if you agree to my price. The Andrakkar are not, after all, the only ones who desire things from the Earthly realm. And the *daemon* have known about it for far longer than you."

Lucien tried to hide his shock and remain impassive, but it was difficult. The *daemon* know about Earth? How, he wondered? And what could Jagrin possibly want from such a place? He knew he had no choice, in any case, but to say yes.

"If it is in my power to give it to you, it will be done," Lucien said, getting in response a ripple of ugly laughter.

"Oh, it *will* be, my lord Andrakkar. I refuse to come away empty-handed for such a service. But a thing so secret, so sacred, demands a high price. And so I will help you if you will bring to me what I truly desire: a slave."

Lucien shook his head, somewhat relieved. He didn't give a damn about humans. If Jagrin truly wanted one, it should be easy enough to get. "A slave is nothing to me. I will return with whatever human I run across."

"But I don't want a human," Jagrin smirked. "I want one of the *arukhin* your people are hunting."

Lucien inhaled sharply, shock warring with pure fury at the *daemon*'s audacity, his insolence. How he had come to know such things was a grave concern, of course. But having his father's mad quest dangled in front of him like some diseased carcass was almost more than he could bear. Almost.

If only this wasn't his last hope, Lucien thought, the misery that had dogged him all his life rising up in a sudden wave, threatening to consume him. To pull him under, once and for all.

Though sometimes he wondered if that might not be a sort of blessing, too.

Jagrin took this in, seeming to savor it, before continuing. "Yes, yes, my lord Andrakkar. We *daemon* have known about the lost forest shifters almost from the time they escaped. You forget … the dragon kings have not always been kind to my people. The Tunnels have swallowed many to assuage a serpent's anger. Why should you think that with our abilities we wouldn't be able to connect in some way to the realms that touch ours most closely? Your father has been clever with his charmed stones," Jagrin sneered, "but we are far more clever, our powers greater. And we have been watching our descendants on Earth since long before your house was strong enough to even dream of stealing the throne."

Lucien could only stare, his eyes burning with rage, thinking of the slave stones that dangled from the collars of the banished. They allowed his father to keep track of his victims, to communicate if he so desired ... just in case one might prove useful.

It was how Mordred's madness had begun, Lucien thought disgustedly. Now he thought of nothing but finding a way back to Earth, ignoring the continuous infighting of the various dragon houses, and dreaming of nothing but conquest and *arukhin* blood. And though those houses were now weakened enough from years of breeding with the weakest of the non-magic Orinn, there would, Lucien knew, eventually be a challenge.

He was the last of the Andrakkar. And if he did not mate and produce an acceptable dragon heir soon, he might one day soon be awakened as his own black blood was being spilled to make way for new rule. It wouldn't matter, except for the flame-haired witch who haunted his dreams. He had to have her. She would love him, even if he had to have her spellbound by the *daemon*.

And then he would have all.

"So," Lucien rasped, his normally deep and silken voice roughened by barely restrained violence, "you know ..."

"Everything," Jagrin chuckled, relaxing in the stone chair. "The traitors your father managed to recruit, the embarrassment that was your little skirmish with the Pack leaders. Mordred's foolish vision of a realm ruled by dragons." He shook his head, mocking. "Earth is a much larger realm than our own, you know. Full of endless delights and wondrous destruction. Trying to control it would be madness," he said, eyes flashing. "But partaking of its riches ... its flesh ... its pain ... now *that* might be a worthwhile pursuit."

"Do the *daemon* have a way of going there at will?" Lucien asked, hardly daring to believe it might be that easy. And it wasn't, he saw as Jagrin waved one long, pale hand dismissively.

"Sadly, no. We have no gateway stone, and as you know, there are no Drakkyn left who can control the Tunnels. It's said that it takes strong emotion, for one thing." He smirked. "Something that, fortunately, my people are not afflicted with. The traveling draughts work for such a short time that it's hardly worth it, as you saw. No," he said again, with a sigh that was almost wistful. "We have no interest in drifting about a world so large, where there is no respect for magic. And humans, though occasionally entertaining, are really only good for food. Our own Orinn make far better playthings."

"But you said you have descendants there," Lucien pressed, leaning forward across the table. It was so imperative that he know exactly what he was dealing with, what channels he would have to go through to get to his prize.

"Indeed," Jagrin replied. "Thanks to the last king of the House of Ragnath, who was most displeased to find his Dyadd lover consorting with a *daemon* on the side. Into the Tunnels they both went, naturally, as the Ragnath had roughly as much compassion as brains. And so were born the vampires of Earth, nightwalkers, blood drinkers. Wonderfully twisted, for the most part. And they do like to keep close to their roots, sharing tales of their little pleasures. As we do with them, of course."

"How? How is that possible?" Lucien bit out, his black claws lengthening as he gripped the table. It seemed impossible that the strange, weakling *daemon* should have had such knowledge for so long and kept it to themselves, that they had populated bits of the Earthly realm with their own seed when the dragons had only just learned such a place existed. But Jagrin's obvious pleasure in finally sharing the secret told him it was indeed so. And the dragons had badly underestimated those they grudgingly protected.

"It matters not. Not to you, at any rate," Jagrin said mildly. And Lucien could see that he had gotten all he was going to, unless he could get his claws on the *daemon* and try to extract the information in the way his kind was most talented at. All things considered, that seemed like a particularly bad idea. He would have to work with the scraps he had been thrown, and hope they were enough.

"But you will help me get to Rowan, provided I bring you one of the *arukhin*?"

"Yes. One will do. We saw what happened when the House of Andrakkar got greedy with them. Lost them all, and really, the gods were bound to notice you'd broken the laws about Drakkyn races and enslaving one another. Hotheaded, as always," he murmured, though he looked thoughtfully at Lucien. "Though you, I think, are a bit more like us. Cold. Ruthless, but cold. My king feels, and I agree, that your leadership would be far preferable to any of the other available alternatives. So I am to help you."

"Cadmus knows about our meetings?" Lucien asked, surprised. He hadn't expected that the *daemon* king would bother to get involved with the Andrakkar heir's mating concerns. But then that backing would be useful, he supposed, when Mordred finally became insane enough that he would have to be removed. It was high time the dragons reclaimed their glory. But they needed an iron leader to do it. The *daemon* could watch these vampires all they liked, Lucien thought. But as far as he was concerned, the Drak's circle at the foot of the mountains could remain nothing but lifeless stone, and the *arukhin* could stay on Earth forever. All he wanted, all he needed was Rowan.

"I'll speak to my king," said Jagrin, standing. "And see what can be done. The witch and her brother were staying with a nest of vampires for some time, though we only recently realized that their guests had been Drakkyn. And that they hadn't simply been more casualties of your father's temper, of course." He paused, considering. "The brother, is he of any interest to you?"

Lucien shook his head, a sharp, jerky movement. All this time, she had been right under his nose. All this time ... but now he was close, he told himself. "No. A male Dyim, some obscene twist of nature. Useless."

It wasn't true, of course. But the look on Jagrin's face told him that there were some things that he, Lucien, still had to himself. Bargaining chips, he told himself. And Bastian was the largest one he had. It was the only reason why the surprisingly powerful Dyim was still alive.

"Good," Jagrin smiled, showing a mouthful of dagger-sharp teeth. "The vampires will wish to be rewarded for their help, of course, and he'll do nicely if he hasn't run off. And you will bring us the *arukhin* warrior. Quite a useful pet he'll make, I think. So many secrets to learn. And such fun to train."

"You will have a forest-shifter. I swear it," Lucien said softly.

Jagrin's red gaze was piercing. With a quick motion, he produced a tiny, glittering gold bottle from beneath his long cloak and held it toward Lucien.

"And if you fail," Jagrin hissed, his voice like sand across the bare stone floor, "you forfeit yourself to us, to do with as we please. Our slave in the *arukhin*'s stead. Swear it now, and on your blood, Andrakkar. And you will have your chance to claim your woman, and your throne."

It was as he'd feared. The price, should he fail to meet his end of the bargain, was as high as it could possibly be; it would cost him nothing less than himself. Lucien stared at the bottle, a simple, stoppered thing of beautiful craftsmanship. So small it nestled into the palm of Jagrin's hand. So large it seemed to encompass his entire universe. The key, either to his future as king or to some eternal prison. But it was a key he needed. And at this point there was no turning back.

Slowly, deliberately, Lucien drew back the sleeve of his cassock, exposing the skin of his wrist. As he lengthened one nail into an ebony claw and sliced open the skin, Jagrin removed the stopper and held it out to catch the black blood that welled to the surface.

"My promise," Lucien whispered, and it echoed around him while his blood flowed.

"Your blood," Jagrin responded with a solemn nod, completing the ritual. When the wound began to heal itself, and the flow ebbed, the *daemon* placed the stopper back in the bottle, sealing the pact.

And though Lucien tried to think only of how it would feel to finally hold the beautiful sorceress who he felt he had been waiting for all his life, the air seemed to weigh on him, threatening to crush him beneath the weight of what he had just done. He no longer felt like a man in helpless, undeniable love.

He felt doomed.

Chapter 6

GABRIEL AWOKE SURLY, RUMPLED, AND FACE-DOWN IN A thick carpet of grass.

Needs mowing, was his first thought. Then, as his mind crawled sluggishly into awareness, he had another.

Bloody hell.

He was an absolute mess. His legs ached. His head was pounding hard enough to split open. There was a persistent twinge in his side, and his mouth felt like it had recently been shellacked with something foul. Gabriel felt like he was just waking up at the end of a three-day bender, though he'd had nothing to drink.

And this was no less than he deserved for making such an absolute ass of himself, he thought, as the memories of his "heroics" where a certain malnourished redhead was concerned resurfaced with perfect clarity. His intentions had been good, he recalled, or as good as his intentions ever got, which was close enough.

As it turned out, the only part he'd gotten right was when he'd run out of the house like the hounds of hell were at his heels. Kept running, in fact, until he was senseless with exhaustion and his abused body had simply refused to go any farther. As a Wolf, he'd raced for miles over the Hunting Grounds, silent and swift as the Highland winds through the trees.

As a man, he'd apparently decided to curl up and have a nap in someone's yard. At least he seemed to have put his shorts back on. That had to count for something. Still, he wished he'd managed to run all the way back to Tobermory. A little perspective was badly needed, some time to clear out his head and decide what exactly he needed to do about one infuriating, hypersexual, maddeningly reticent Drakkyn. Maybe he'd been mistaken, Gabriel tried to convince himself. Maybe he didn't want her as badly as he'd thought.

Then he remembered the feel of her curves pressed against him, the way she'd trembled as she came just from the contact with him, and the surprising vulnerability in her eyes when she'd told him to stay away. Gabriel groaned, squeezing his eyes shut. As tired and muddled as he was, one thing was crystal clear: he still wanted Rowan *an* Morgaine. He was still mad as hell at her for hurling him out of her room just when things were getting interesting, but at the same time, his blood was up, his hunting instinct alive as it never had been. Rowan was full of secrets, passionate, and obstinately inaccessible.

He'd be damned if she was going to get away from him so easily, no matter who or what she was. Gabriel grimaced a little as he shifted, trying to assuage the nagging pain in his side. He'd never had to chase a woman before. He had a bad feeling that chasing Rowan might damn near do him in, either from whatever violent form of magic she was sure to possess or sheer frustration. Still, he was going to have his hands on her again, and soon. Just how to do that, however, was going to require a bit more strategy. Maybe he'd talk to his recently love-struck brother about it. First, though, he needed a bit more rest. If he slept for just a short while longer, Gabriel reasoned, maybe he could get a handle on his options—murder, escape, insanity …

He sighed, staying spread-eagled and nuzzling deeper into the fragrant green, and let himself drift back toward sleep. The twinge in his side, however, suddenly grew biting. It also began to feel decidedly more like the toe of some insensitive individual's shoe. Gabriel gave a soft growl. It wasn't hard to guess who that might be.

"That's right, Sleeping Beauty. Rise and shine. My wife is getting tired of coming out here to make sure you're still breathing. I tried to tell her that if stupidity hasn't killed you yet, it isn't going to. But she won't listen."

Gabriel opened one eye to focus blearily on his brother. Gideon, he noted, looked to be taking an inordinate amount of pleasure in continuing to kick at him. He licked his lips, wincing at the taste, and tried to speak. When that produced nothing but a strangled croak, he cleared his throat and tried again. It was only slightly more productive.

"Gah. Fuff. Bastard. Stoppit." He slapped irritably at Gideon's leg, which produced no effect except for a snort of derisive laughter from somewhere above him.

"Not a chance, little brother. It's almost noon, and frankly, you make an ugly lawn ornament."

Gabriel stopped slapping and instead extended his middle finger. Gideon laughed in earnest then, just before Gabriel felt his brother grab him beneath the arms and haul him to his feet. He finally opened both eyes, blinking owlishly in the sunlight and swaying unsteadily. Just ahead of him, Gideon and Carly's stone cottage rose from a well-groomed lawn of verdant green. From one of the second-story windows, framed by white shutters that were flung wide to the warm July day, Carly waved cheerily at him. He couldn't help but think she looked a bit more amused than was necessary over his current unkempt, half-awake state.

"Morning, sunshine!" she called, then ducked back inside once he'd managed a halfhearted raise of his hand. Her soft laughter echoed to where he was standing. Gabriel frowned. Obviously, living with Gideon was rubbing off on her, and badly.

He turned his attention back to Gideon, annoyingly clean and well rested, who was looking at him appraisingly with his arms crossed over his chest. Gabriel simply gave him a beleaguered look, hoping against hope that his brother would simply let him stagger away in peace. He wanted to talk to him, yes. But after a shower. And some food. And possibly twenty-four more hours of sleep.

A pipe dream, as usual.

"What in God's name did you get up to last night? You look like something's been gnawing on you."

"Piss off." His throat felt like he'd been swallowing gravel, and Gideon's commentary on his appearance this morning was the last thing he wanted to hear. Besides, though it may have been intended mockingly, his brother was awfully close to the truth.

"With pleasure, your ripeness." He gave a mocking half bow before waving his hand in front of his nose. "I doubted you were interested in what our new houseguest had to say for herself this morning anyway." Gideon turned with a knowing smirk and started back toward his house, not stopping when he called back, "Figured as much, really. And she seemed happier without you there anyway."

Gabriel paused, digesting this bit of unpleasant observation, then staggered after his brother. "Just what is that supposed to mean?"

Gideon didn't look at him, but he did slow a little to let his brother catch up. "Just that I've never seen someone look so happy to hear that someone else was passed out on the lawn and unresponsive."

Gabriel frowned mightily. Between her destructive little fits of temper and her sharp tongue, he was beginning to suspect that the woman had a mean streak about a mile wide. Why that interested him so was an infuriating mystery. It was going to be a pleasure to teach her that he wasn't to be gotten rid of so easily.

Gideon was looking at him strangely. "Are you smiling, or about to bite me? Because if it's the latter, I have to tell you, you're in no shape. I might actually feel bad about kicking your ass."

"Then it's a good thing that would never happen."

"Try me."

"Maybe later. I'd hate to make you feel even worse about having someone in my condition beat you to a pulp."

They grinned at each other then, and Gabriel was pleased to feel his stiff muscles loosening up a little. He made a point of keeping himself in shape, but he'd obviously outdone himself this time.

"You might as well come in and have some lunch," Gabriel said. "Carly made enough food for an army last night. There are leftovers galore."

Gabriel followed his brother in, knowing Carly had only made that much because Gideon had asked her to, being that she didn't much care to cook so she didn't do it that often. He wasn't quite sure he wanted to get into everything right now, but his growling stomach refused to let him walk away from the promise of Carly's food. She'd learned the art of Italian cooking at her mother's knee, and learned it well. Sadly for all concerned, actually catching Carly cooking was a rare occurrence. Gideon's wife claimed to miss takeout when she was here, but since that wasn't an option in a place as remote as Lochaline, the rest of the MacInneses were more than happy to reap the benefits of her deprivation when she got bored enough to fuss in the kitchen.

They walked through the warm, open space of the great room Gideon had redone himself and headed for the kitchen. Gabriel envied him the space, and the patience that had allowed him to renovate what had once been the factor's house on the estate. Once boxy and outdated, the interior of the house was now open and inviting. A cozy cave for his brother, Gabriel thought, noting the little touches that had sprung up since he'd married Carly. Bright flowers in a red vase here, a scattering of photos in artfully mismatched frames. And of course, her beloved romance novels lying on nearly every available surface.

In the time since he'd met her, Gabriel had decided Carly only ran her own romantic bookshop to feed her addiction. Gideon was supportive, as long as he never had to go there. The two of them had invested in a run-down old place on Lake Ontario that had once been a captain's mansion sometime in the 1800s, Gabriel knew, and Gideon spent most of his time working to remodel it with a loosely organized group of skilled friends. If he knew his brother, they'd sell it for a handsome profit before long and then start all over again.

Of course, it was all just temporary. Eventually, Duncan would decide to hand over the reins to his elder son, making him Pack Alpha and Guardian of the Stone. Gideon and Carly would move back permanently, which he was selfishly and unashamedly glad for, and Duncan would finally get to enjoy being an eccentric and irritating old codger. And *he* ...

Well, that was the problem, wasn't it? Gabriel opened the fridge and grabbed the plastic container full of some sort of pasta heaven while Gideon settled himself at the breakfast bar. He could see the future for everyone else, clear as day. But he'd never really known (or cared, truth be told) what he'd be doing. Probably still living in a shabby apartment above Wolf at the Door, he'd figured, bedding beautiful women, imposing on everyone at *Iargail* from time to time, and doing as he pleased.

Which did no one any good, he now realized. Least of all him.

Gabriel plopped a heap of pasta in a bowl and slammed it in the microwave, scowling.

Gideon relaxed at the counter, studying him as one might a particularly fascinating new species of insect. Gabriel knew he was waiting for him to spill his guts, as he always had, so he took malicious pleasure in remaining silent. The microwave ran, then beeped. Gabriel kept his mouth shut, removing his bowl and rummaging in one of the drawers for a fork.

He tried not to look smug when Gideon began to tap his fingers on the counter.

Carly wandered in just as Gabriel was settling himself at the square wooden table tucked into the nook on the opposite side of the kitchen from his brother. She stopped short when she saw the odd seating arrangement.

"Hey, guys," she ventured, then raised a critical eyebrow when there was no response. She looked slowly from one brother to the other, noting the impatiently tapping fingers of her husband and the mulish look on her brother-in-law's face.

"Can I get you something, babe?" she asked Gideon, who gave a grunt that could have been taken as either affirmative or negative. Carly pursed her lips, dissatisfied, and turned to Gabriel.

"How's the food, scrounge?" When that earned her nothing but a nearly identical grunt, she frowned and settled her hands on her hips. A beautiful, petite blonde with big blue eyes and a mass of loose waves that were currently in the process of escaping from the elastic she'd pulled it back with, Carly had a hard time passing for intimidating. Her looks, however, were deceiving. Having grown up with two loud and obnoxious older brothers, it took a lot more to rattle her than the two massive men now filling up her kitchen with the unmistakable air of masculine bullshit.

Unfazed, she simply crossed her arms over her chest and fixed her husband with a glare that Gideon had often sworn could burn holes in things if she looked at them long enough. "I'm waiting," she announced.

Gabriel continued to eat peacefully. Carly was a favorite of his, but he wasn't worried about upsetting her. After all, part of Gideon's job as her husband was to catch hell for anything and everything first. He figured he could be long gone before she ever got around to giving him his turn. Gideon must have been thinking the same, because he heaved an exasperated sigh as he shoved his hand through dark, tousled, chin-length hair.

"He's being an ass," he snapped, and Gabriel barely suppressed his smirk when the outraged finger was pointed at him. There were few people who could get the stoic Gideon MacInnes to revert to childish behavior. He was inordinately proud to be one of them.

"He does God-knows-what all night with some strange Drakkyn woman, then spends half the day passed out on my lawn, and *then* decides to eat leftover pasta instead of blabbing about it like he normally would! And I see you smiling over there, Gabe—don't think I don't. You're lucky I don't come over there and take it off your face for you."

"But then how will I share my innermost thoughts with you?" Gabriel managed between bites of food. It was so delicious, he truly was torn between tormenting his brother and just shoveling in as much as he could before Gideon started chasing him around the kitchen. "What is this anyway?" he asked, turning his attention to Carly. "It's brilliant."

Despite herself, Carly grinned. "Penne a la Puttanesca. And I'm glad you like it, even though you're wearing like half of it on your oh-so-bare-and-manly chest. I didn't know you were suddenly into trailer-park chic, by the way."

Gabriel glanced down at his shirtless torso, which was, as Carly had said, decorated with a few splashes of sauce. His shrug was casual, though the memory of where his once-favorite and now-shredded Hawaiian shirt had lain crumpled the last time he'd seen it ignited a slow and seething burn inside him. Not to mention how it had been removed from him in the first place.

It was suddenly a struggle to focus on the conversation at hand.

"It is," Gabriel smirked, hoping it didn't look as forced as it felt. "Quite manly. Thanks for noticing, love."

"Knock it off, you," grumbled Gideon, "before I punch you in some other amazingly manly place. And she's not your love."

"Oh goody, just what I wanted in the house today. More useless testosterone." Carly rolled her eyes, then walked to her husband to wrap her arms around his neck and plant a noisy kiss on his cheek. "And of course I'm not his love," she continued, voice matter-of-fact. "Rowan is. Duh."

She continued to nuzzle Gideon's cheek, unconcerned, as Gabriel began to choke on his pasta.

"Now why didn't I think of that?" Gideon wondered dryly, though his hands slid around Carly's waist to draw her close to him. "Gabe and the Red Plague. It would almost be fitting, but even I'm not that cruel. I'm glad you are, though." He smiled lazily. "Evil's sexy on you."

"It's not nice to call her that," Carly admonished him, and then giggled when he tickled her sides, ruining her attempt at sternness. "And I'm not kidding. Your brother has one hell of a hickey on his neck, which I kind of doubt he got from the sheep." She then paused to look back at Gabriel, who was now pounding away on his own chest. "Um, I sure hope he didn't anyway."

Gabriel tried to formulate an appropriately snide response to this, but he couldn't seem to clear his airway enough to do more than continue coughing. That was what he got for inhaling an entire mouthful of Penne a la Whatever, he guessed. And for failing to recognize from the start what his sister-in-law had apparently noticed in the five minutes she'd been in the room.

Rowan.

His love.

His bloody damn mate.

Oh, God in heaven, no.

Except that Carly's simple, matter-of-fact statement had slapped him in the face like nothing but the truth could. He'd had all the pieces of the puzzle. They'd finally just been arranged in a way that made sense. A sick sort of sense, granted, but sense nonetheless.

Gabriel could think of nothing more masochistic, more twisted, more mind-bogglingly self-destructive than falling for the mouthy Drakkyn who had spurned him last night. And yet the facts spoke for themselves. As much as he'd ever wanted any woman, he'd never slept in anyone's yard for want of one.

Gabriel wracked his brain for a better, more palatable explanation. Anything but the one thing he'd been running from for so long. But there was nothing for it.

Rowan *an* Morgaine was his one true mate, the only woman who could satisfy him, the woman he would long for as long as he continued to draw breath. For a were-wolf, love came but once, and like a ton of bricks from above. It was also, like everything else concerning his kind, rife with complications.

Since there were so few of them, and since so few humans were strong enough to survive the bite that his kind were compelled to give their mates, it was fairly common for a MacInnes Wolf to remain single. Even if they experienced that singular bond, with humans it was often safer to just let them be and go on alone. It was, Gabriel reflected, even what his brother had decided to do with Carly. Of course, he hadn't counted on Carly being bitten by the Drakkyn scum that was his would-be assassin.

Nor had Gideon realized that the near-Herculean strength of Carly's love for him would see her through her first Change and allow the two of them to be together. Some things, Gabriel supposed, were just meant to be.

And some things were obvious karmic payback for a past littered with carelessly broken hearts. Gabriel shoved the mostly eaten bowl of pasta aside and put his head down, resting his forehead on his arms. His appetite, much like his higher-order thinking, had evaporated into thin air.

"Bloody hell," he groaned.

"Don't pretend she's right, Gabe," Gideon warned him, a note that sounded a lot like panic in his tone. "That's not even funny. And I …" There was a sharp intake of breath as Gideon got a look at the purplish bruise Carly had mentioned, complete with two unmistakable tooth marks in the center.

Gabriel raised his head to look blearily at his brother. Gideon stared at him as though he wasn't sure who he was looking at any longer.

"Please tell me you just let her have a bit of a drink. Out of the kindness of your heart, right, Gabe? And nothing else happened. You didn't feel a damned thing. You just walked away and ... and ..."

"And passed out in your yard from the exertion of being so disgustingly kind," Gabriel inserted flatly. "Yeah. You must be psychic. You know what a giver I am, after all."

Gideon looked horrified. "Tell me you're joking."

Gabriel thought a moment, and then shook his head. "I'm afraid not."

Carly glared between the two of them, looking thoroughly disgusted. "What is *wrong* with you two?" she cried. "It's a *mate,* not terminal cancer! Rowan is obviously a very strong woman, not to mention completely gorgeous! What about that is so bad?"

"She's a Drakkyn, remember?" Gideon replied, earning a look from Carly that indicated he was seconds from having his beloved pasta dumped over his head.

"*And*?" she snapped. "She's not an Andrakkar, and I'd bet she'll do a lot better with a werewolf bite than any human could."

"That's true," Gabriel muttered. "She'll kill *me* instead."

"Oh for the love of ..." Carly threw up her hands in complete exasperation and stalked from the room, heading up the back stairs. "I give up. I would rather yell at the boxers Gideon is always tossing on the floor right beside the hamper. Those have a better chance of listening."

"I don't know what you want me to do about it," Gabriel snapped as Carly stomped off, feeling both angry and slightly desperate. It wasn't just that Rowan was a dangerous bloodsucking sorceress of some kind, either (though that was definitely part of the whole nasty equation). After hiding from it for years, he'd finally found his mate. He'd always assumed that if and when it happened, the lucky woman would be both thrilled and grateful to have the prize that was Gabriel MacInnes.

It was a nasty jolt to realize that he had precious little to recommend himself as quite that caliber of a catch. And it was probably too much to wish for that Rowan had come from people who thought of clutter and aimlessness as virtues. His only hope was that she'd grown up in some sort of primordial mud hole with scrawny, weakling men.

Gabriel closed his eyes in defeat. He was doomed.

"She doesn't even *like* me, Carly!"

Carly didn't pause as her shapely legs disappeared from view. "I don't blame her. Now quit being such a wussie and do something about it before she's no longer stuck with you."

Gabriel watched his sister-in-law go, and then he slouched over to the breakfast bar to settle himself beside his brother. Gideon, it gave him some small amount of pleasure to note, looked nearly as unhappy as he himself felt. It was true, after all—misery loved company.

"Your wife is a hard woman."

Gideon snorted. "You have no idea. I'm going to catch hell for the bit about the hamper after you leave. Again." He sighed, looking up at the ceiling as though contemplating his fate. Then he turned his attention back to his brother, the worry clear in his golden gaze.

"I suppose I don't have to ask if you're sure. God knows you've been through enough women to know."

Gabriel shook his head, a part of him still playing last night's encounter over and over in his mind. She'd taken his blood, but it felt as though Rowan had left a bit of herself behind to rush through his veins. If only he had any idea what he was supposed to do next.

"Don't look at me," Gideon sighed as though he knew what Gabriel was thinking. "I fell for a human, remember? And I was the one being hunted. Never thought I'd say this, but I think Carly and I had it easier."

"You're telling me."

The two of them sat in unhappy, contemplative silence for a long time. Gideon toyed with a cold cup of coffee that sat on the counter in front of him, while Gabriel simply brooded. He really didn't think he'd been overstating the problem. Rowan might have gotten lost in some sort of blood lust–induced haze with him, but any woman who would pick him up with nothing but the power of her mind and throw him bodily out of her room was *not* interested in his company. And women always liked him, he thought with a spark of insult. He was charming, damn it! But then it was possible, he allowed, that he might not have been as charming as he'd intended with her. Something about her quick, sharp little tongue had rained a bit on his usual good humor.

Hell, who was he kidding? Rowan's temperament mixed with his caused more of a torrential downpour. A tornado. An apocalyptic thunderstorm. Something.

"Bollocks," he growled. It didn't pain him to admit that he had a healthy need for control, and the fact that he had exactly none over his reaction to Rowan the Stripping Drakkyn was apt to drive him mad within days. Especially if she resorted to violence every time she saw him from now on. Her instructions, after all, had been rather clear.

Stay away from me.

Well, he was just going to have to find a way around it. The MacInnes stubbornness, legendary in its own right, was going to come in handy. He was going to have to use every weapon in his arsenal to win her. Gabriel glared at his clenched fists. He hoped like hell that Rowan was worth winning. Because there was no way he was going to be one of those Wolves who let his mate go for their own good, and he was certainly not going to spend the rest of his life wishing he were having sex with someone he couldn't bloody well have. He liked sex. A lot. And he'd already surmised that sex with Rowan was going to blow anything he'd ever experienced to microscopic pieces.

He was already having to rethink his distaste for the feeding habits of the vampirically inclined. Being bitten himself had been … interesting. Might even be worth trying again.

"You've got that look on your face," Gideon sighed, scattering his thoughts. Gabriel looked up at him, one eyebrow raised.

"Look?"

"Yeah. The one that says you're going to pursue this no matter how inadvisable, dangerous, or flat-out stupid it might be." He smirked then. "You know. The MacInnes look."

Gabriel chuckled. "The Pack has never been known for running from a challenge, Gid. I can't help what my instincts are telling me, any more than you could last winter. I don't know a thing about her. Well, nothing I much like, in any case," he qualified, shaking his head. "I just know I have to have her."

"That may be easier said than done."

"Because she's a Drakkyn?"

Gideon laughed, but there was little humor in it. "I think that's the least of your worries. We had a short conversation this morning—she and Dad and Carly and I—over a rather abbreviated breakfast. She's still, ah, unhappy about our refusal to see her back to the States."

"Shocking, considering her obviously even temper," Gabriel muttered.

"Exactly. So we only got the bare bones of the issue at hand before your Rowan excused herself. But it sounds like most of her family was killed by the Andrakkar and their friends, who, as our luck would have it, *all* command the ability to shift into fire-breathing dragons. And they're still hunting her."

"You mean *them.* Don't forget the accommodating Bastian." The root of all of his current trouble.

Gideon gave him a sidelong glance. "Not really. It sounds like he's utterly secondary. Bastian is only trying to protect her. Because their tribe was slaughtered over Rowan's refusal to marry Lucien, Mordred's son."

Gabriel exhaled, long and low. "God. That's terrible." He thought of her, proud and beautiful, shrugging off offers for help as though she needed no one. And he wondered what deeper feelings she was fighting so hard to conceal—loss, he imagined, and anger and fear at her brother's abandonment. And then there was the guilt. From the little he'd seen of the Andrakkar, he could understand why Rowan would not want to chain herself to one of them. But he knew how he would feel if one of his decisions compelled the destruction of his loved ones.

He would probably never forgive himself.

And whether it was an instinctual reaction because of his bond to her or simply a natural human response, Gabriel was suddenly consumed with the need to be with her, to help her. To protect her in any way he could.

He stood quickly, the decision made in an instant. If she would accept nothing else from him, then he would start with friendship (no matter how much it pained him, Gabriel thought with a cringe). She'd been given into his care because he was the only one who could match her for sheer, asinine intractability. He planned to exert some of that right now.

Anyway, he consoled himself, it wasn't as though people were going to be lined up to spend time with such a moody, prickly creature. The woman was going to need *someone* to talk to. He hoped.

"Is she still at the house?" he asked. Gideon eyed him speculatively.

"She said something about going for a walk. Alone."

Gabriel smiled. "I imagine that part was emphasized."

"You imagine correctly." He paused. "She looked a great deal healthier today, I have to say." His eyes dropped to Gabriel's neck, curiosity evident in his gaze. "I know you promised you'd feed her, but I didn't necessarily think you'd do it yourself. Or quite so immediately, for that matter."

Gabriel shot his brother a withering look. "What, you thought maybe I'd lure in some unfortunate sheep? She was *starving*."

"Not to mention scantily clad."

"An added bonus. Did you happen to see which way she went?"

Gideon sighed. "Utterly one-track today. No. But I'm sure you'll sniff her out. I will say, she doesn't *smell* like a vampire, even if she does appear to act like one … at least in the nutrition department. And she looked a lot less like one in that old T-shirt you gave her to wear." He smirked. "Smooth, by the way. Though it inspired my wife to take pity and donate a few things that might fit." He shook his head. "I can't think why everyone always likes her better than me."

"T-shirt." There had been clothing removed, Gabriel remembered, but none given that he could recall. And he recalled a great deal about last night, though he wasn't yet convinced that was a good thing.

Gideon lifted one inquisitive brow. "Yeah. A fairly nasty old specimen from your college days, which covered a lot more than her getup from last night did. I assumed you'd given it to her as a sly way of getting your scent all over her. I take it she pilfered it instead?"

Gabriel thought about Rowan slinking into his room, the room that of course contained the bed he longed to get her into, and pawing through his things with those long, slender fingers. What was she thinking of as she'd gone through his clothes? he wondered. *How* did she think of him? She'd breathed in his scent all night, Gabriel realized. Willingly. Maybe he had more than a ghost of a chance with her after all.

And if he ever got that shirt back, he was never washing it again.

Gideon groaned. "Your eyes are glazing. I'm sorry I mentioned she'd been intimate with your clothes. Tell me, honestly, was I this mind-numbingly boring about my wife?"

"You have no idea." Gabriel shoved the stool back beneath the counter and headed for the front door, completely focused on the tasks at hand. He was going to get back into Rowan *an* Morgaine's good graces if it killed him. He was going to do whatever it took to keep that foul Andrakkar away from her. And he was going to stick to her like glue until she accepted him as her mate, either out of undeniable love or extreme battle fatigue.

The first order of business, however, was simply finding her and getting her to speak to him. It might, he worried, be easier said than done.

"I just hope she hasn't teleported out of here or whatever the hell her brother did in the meantime," he muttered.

"If she could have, I think she would have by now. And I doubt she'd look quite as unhappy as she did this morning." Gideon followed him to the front door, grabbing his arm before Gabriel could step through it. It was all Gabriel could do not to snap at the offending hand.

"What? I'm busy, damn it!"

Gideon looked at him blandly, but he didn't move his hand. "You might want to consider being busy after showering and putting on a shirt. You look like you just crawled out of a cave. After eating pasta, I might add." He poked a finger at the dried spots of Carly's pasta sauce dotting Gabriel's collarbone.

"Later," Gabriel replied, pushing past him and stalking out into the sunshine with purpose. "I have every intention of selling myself, but it's going to have to be as is. Besides, with my luck she'll be hiding up some tree or invisible and it'll take me hours to find her."

Gideon watched his brother go. "Only if she knows what's good for her," he called after him, the only response being an irritable little backward wave. He leaned against the door frame, thinking, until he felt Carly slip beneath his arm and snuggle into his side. Gideon smiled despite himself, toying with her hair as she sighed contentedly. He'd found his heart, against enormous odds, he reminded himself. No matter his misgivings about the situation with Rowan, which were greater than he'd let Gabriel know, he needed to remember that. There was no reason his brother shouldn't be allowed the same happiness. Even if the mate he'd found was decidedly … unconventional. He'd worried about Gabriel for years, knew his younger brother had never really felt he had a purpose or a place. This could be just what he needed.

Then again, it could be an unmitigated disaster. Only time would tell. But he would be there to back him up, either way.

Chapter 7

ROWAN SWUNG HER LONG LEGS AS SHE PERCHED ON ONE OF the gnarled branches of an ancient oak tree, trying to simply enjoy being surrounded by nature for the first time in almost a year. A soft breeze ruffled her hair, which tumbled unbound down her back. The temperature was perfect, warm but nowhere near hot, and she was thankful that the pretty blonde who'd been crazy enough to attach herself to this family of werewolves had brought her some shorts and T-shirts. The men might be hulking, barely civilized cretins, Rowan reflected, but Carly seemed almost normal. A little lacking in the height department, she thought, casting a critical eye over the vast amount of leg left uncovered by the shorts, but normal.

Of course, she was married to a MacInnes. *Something* must be wrong with her, the poor thing. Atrocious taste in men, at the very least. Rowan sighed and took a bite of the apple she'd swiped from the bowl on the kitchen table as she'd snuck out. She chewed contemplatively, continuing to swing her legs and savoring the ripe sweetness of the fruit on her tongue. She might need blood, but oh, how she still loved food. And the American vampires hadn't been much on grocery shopping, much less fresh fruit. This, at least, was a welcome change from buffets, frozen dinners, and takeout.

Real food was good, but what was better was that she was feeling like her old self again, Rowan decided with a languorous stretch. No more dizziness, no more hunger pains that human food could do nothing to assuage. If only she weren't beholden to the delicious, desirable, disastrously sexy Gabriel MacInnes for the return of her strength.

If only, she thought with a pained frown, she wasn't already hungry for more of him. And not just his blood. That she could have handled.

That wouldn't have had her up a tree with a pilfered apple.

The shirt had been a mistake, Rowan knew. But she couldn't help thinking (hoping?) that Gabriel might come back, and confronting the man she'd so nearly let ravish her after knowing him for less than an hour would have required more armor than her tiny little costume could have provided. So she'd slunk into his room, an easy guess when she'd followed her nose and his scent, and borrowed a little something.

Rowan had then spent a restless night surrounded by the aromas of forest and male and, above all, Gabriel. For once the nightmares had stayed away. But she wasn't sure her feverish dreams of her Wolf-eyed would-be protector counted as an improvement. At least he'd gone when she'd told him to. Because she hadn't really wanted him to go.

It wouldn't be long before he figured that out. Which was exactly why she couldn't stay here.

He'd nearly gotten in, she thought with a shudder. The fact that Gabriel had barreled most of the way through her carefully constructed defenses with so little effort horrified her. Something about him, the warm, solid strength of him, sent shock waves through her system that had already put irreparable cracks in the walls she'd erected around her emotions. She couldn't fathom why, after all the men she'd encountered in her life, this one alone struck that hidden and all-important chord in her. But really, the why of it mattered substantially less than how, exactly, she was going to manage to avoid him. She wasn't so stupid as to think her rejection would have put Gabriel off his idea of "protecting" her, despite the way he'd run off into the night. He seemed to think it was a matter of honor, keeping his word to her brother.

Yet another issue she was going to take up with Bastian when she got her hands on him. *If* she got her hands on him. And she'd promised herself she wasn't going to torment herself over this one more time, hadn't she?

Rowan sighed and tried to clear her troubled thoughts, closing her eyes and listening to the myriad songs of the birds coupled with the soft rustle of leaves in the gently moving air. *Inhale. Exhale.* Slowly, she felt the tension leaving her as peace trickled through her veins to soothe her. She was in the forest. She was alone. This was her place.

It wasn't something Rowan had any intention of admitting, but there was something about these so-called Highlands that resonated deeply within her. Endless green rolled away into the distance while the waters of Loch Aline flowed deep and dreamless, whispering ancient secrets. This was a place she likely would have sought out had she known it existed.

Of course, as she was being kept here against her will, the shine of *Iargail* was diminished somewhat.

Rowan took another bite and stared up through the leaves into the brilliant blue sky, lost in thought.

"I'm not sure whether to be offended or flattered that you've climbed a tree to be rid of me."

The voice, the deep, all-too-familiar burr of it, nearly startled her off the branch. Rowan clung to the branch for dear life, dropping her half-finished apple in the process. She'd be damned if Gabriel MacInnes knocked her on her ass more than once. It was as though she'd summoned him with nothing but a thought, Rowan fumed, wishing she could make him go with the same ease, and knowing he'd make it difficult. Inwardly, she cursed the acceleration of her heart, the flush that rose unbidden to her cheeks at the mere knowledge of his presence.

Outwardly, she dealt with him the only way she knew how.

"I would have climbed one farther away if I'd known you were going to seek me out to complain about it."

She looked down through the branches and saw him peering up at her. The sight of him, rumpled, disheveled, and (oh the Goddess help her) bare-chested had her digging her nails into the wood beneath her. The audacity of him, to come to her in such a state ... to come to her at *all* when she'd expressly discouraged it ...

"No complaints," he offered with a smile that would have melted a lesser woman's heart (and in truth made hers feel frustratingly gooey). "But I would like to talk."

"I'd rather not." And really, if this was how it was to be with him, she would rather he took a long vacation in another country. But she had a nasty suspicion it would take a great deal more than that to rid herself of this bizarre affliction. Not to mention ridding herself of him.

Gabriel gave a beleaguered sigh, as though he'd expected exactly that response, and leaned against the trunk of a neighboring tree with one arm. The muscles across his broad chest flexed with the movement. Rowan bit her lip hard enough to draw blood. It had been so long since she'd been compelled to hunt for prey that she'd forgotten the instinct was there. She knew her pupils dilated even as her breathing slowed, every breath filling her nostrils with the scent of Gabriel's life essence. She focused completely on him, the rest of the forest falling away into darkness, and the part of her ancestry that was clever and wild threatened to override every other thing. Rowan struggled to stay put, her rational mind only barely holding the advantage over the part that wanted to pounce and bite. Among other things.

Gabriel, blessedly oblivious to her reaction to him, frowned up into the branches. He cocked his head, trying, she knew, for a better look at her, so she made an effort to keep her face obscured. She was grateful he couldn't see what he was doing to her. Last night had been bad enough. This could be decidedly worse.

"Damn it, Rowan, I know you'd just as soon live up in that bloody tree as look at me, all right? I'm not that dense. I've got it. But since we're going to be having some sort of relationship for the immediate future, I think we'd better come to an understanding. And unless you want to give passing notes a go, you and I are stuck with speech."

"I'm not interested in having a relationship." Her voice at this point was a feral purr. Rowan hated it, but she had little control over it. Wretched instinct again, and she didn't even want to speculate why Gabriel's presence, more than any other, seemed to bring out the beast in her. She could almost see Gabriel's ears prick up at the sultry undertone. His eyes narrowed, and he seemed to be scenting the air for some clue about what he'd heard in her voice.

"Relationship in the most professional sense," he finally clarified, still looking intrigued. "I am, after all, supposed to be your acting bodyguard for the time being." He craned his neck further, and for an electric instant their eyes connected. Rowan quickly tore her gaze away, feeling foolishly lightheaded. Gabriel's voice deepened with concern. It was the absolute last thing she wanted this man to feel for her.

"Look, are you all right up there? You sound a bit … odd."

"Well, you look like you've been sleeping outdoors, which I was going to be too polite to mention," she growled. "And you have no idea how little I need a bodyguard."

You *might, though,* she silently added, unable to help licking her lips at the sight of his rock-hard abs.

"Oh, that's lovely. You know full well that you're the reason I slept outdoors. During which time, I understand, you raided my T-shirt drawer. Not," he bit out, "that it has any bearing on this conversation." Gabriel's voice had grown heated, that wonderful accent of his thickening until all of his words seemed to roll together into one. He'd come to find her with some sort of an agenda in mind, Rowan thought. A "let's be friends," shiny, happy kind of agenda.

It was more fun than it should have been to shred it to pieces, but she couldn't seem to help herself.

"We're not having a conversation," she replied. "I told you to leave already. Technically, you're talking to yourself."

His handsome features telegraphed a moment of surprise, which quickly transformed into barely leashed fury. "Bullshit," he snapped. "And if you don't get down here, I'm bloody well coming up."

Rowan didn't respond, drawing her feet up to rest on the branch as she leaned against the sturdy trunk. Her movements were slow and deliberate, the product of the intense effort she had to exert to move at all. For some reason, the only command her body really wanted to obey was to throw herself on her erstwhile savior down below. And that was absolutely, positively not going to happen.

"Rowan?" he asked, waiting a few seconds for a response. When she continued to ignore him, mainly out of a twisted sort of curiosity to see what he would do next, she saw his large, rough hands clench into fists. "*Rowan,*" he said again, not a question but a warning.

He moved so quickly she didn't even have time to be impressed. One second he was glaring upward at her. The next he had leaped up and landed, crouched and still glaring, on her own personal branch. His jump had been so surprisingly light and graceful that the limb barely moved with the added weight. Her eyes widened. Gabriel grinned, and it was both triumphant and not very nice. Predatory, even.

Her traitorous stomach burst into a hurricane of butterflies.

"You," she stammered, "you … you can't just …"

"Damn right I can," he said, cutting her off neatly. "These trees belong to *my* Pack. You, therefore, are trespassing. You're also being a royal pain in the ass, which seems to be more or less a constant in your case. My tree, my rules. Now shut up so we can have our talk."

Rowan bared her teeth at him, which produced no discernible reaction but a faint smirk. As though he thought she was just being, well, *predictable.* How utterly offensive. The Dyadd were never predictable. Perhaps he needed to be taught that particular lesson.

"Apparently you've never heard of squatter's rights," she growled, pleased to be able to use one of the bizarre little terms she'd picked up during her time in the desert. The look on Gabriel's face as she shifted position to grip the part of the branch that lay between them was priceless. That was probably because of the flames that burst through her hands and burned almost instantly through the wood. Rowan felt a surge of triumph as Gabriel began to fall away.

That was, until he snatched her from her place in a blur of movement and crushed her against him to fall the short distance to the ground, rolling when they hit to protect her. Then rolling so she was pinned beneath him.

Oh my, she thought, eyes widening in shock as the full-length connection between their bodies burned through her. It felt terrible, she tried to tell herself. Just … awful.

In the most intensely amazing way possible.

Rowan gave an outraged scream and began to thrash. A little over the top, she knew, but otherwise it was going to be mere seconds before she started rubbing against him and purring. Apart from being a bad idea, that kind of behavior after last night's debacle might damage her pride permanently, so she threw herself into it. Gabriel, however, was having none of it. And she had to admit, with grudging admiration, that she was nowhere near his match for sheer brute strength. He made short work of gripping her wrists and pinning her arms above her head, then immobilizing her kicking legs neatly between his own.

His eyes flashed so hot that they looked like they might begin to shoot sparks, indicating she was moments away from being skinned alive. But how much worse could that be? She was already burning up from the inside out.

"Let go of me, damn you! You're … you're …" Rowan searched frantically for the words that might make him go away, but as she'd feared, her brain was already going fuzzy with lust. In desperation, she reached for the first thing that popped into her head. "You're invading my personal space!"

And it was true. He was, though she'd never found the expression anything but ridiculous. The whole "personal space" thing had been a major issue with the employees at the Pretty Kitty, but she'd been the best at maintaining hers. Fangs and claws would do that for you on Earth, she'd discovered. But Gabriel would be inherently immune to those sorts of tactics. The man obviously had no conception of breathing room.

Rowan wished futilely that she weren't enjoying the invasion quite so much.

There was a flash of perfect white teeth as Gabriel's mouth curved upward into a surprised grin. It lit up his entire face, and the angry heat in his expression faded, to be replaced by cautious curiosity. He was so close to her, Rowan realized, his soft, playful mouth inches from her own. If she raised her head just a little, she could feel it on her own again. The traitorous *something* that wanted to take Gabriel for her own whispered and cajoled through her veins, making her ache. Making her want what she should not have almost to the point of screaming.

Gabriel sensed the change in her. Rowan could tell by the way his eyelids dropped lazily to half-mast, the way he angled himself over her, a position of gentle dominance. There was a haziness in his gaze that she was certain matched what he saw in her own. When he spoke, his voice was low and scraped pleasurably across her nerve endings.

"Your personal … where did you learn English anyway? American cable television?"

"I …" Breathe, she instructed herself. And for the love of all that is blessed, do *not* moan. "I could speak English because it was the first language I heard when I arrived. I'm not sure how such a thing is possible," she confessed, compelled to keep talking in the hopes that it would stop the inevitable. "But I think it's because our worlds are so close together. Because they," she paused to wet her lips with her tongue, unwittingly drawing Gabriel's eyes to her mouth, "touch."

"Hmm," was his only response, a soft growl that left no doubt as to his intentions. Rowan swallowed hard. She wanted this. She didn't want this. Oh, the Goddess help her, maybe she should just keep talking.

"I actually think," she continued breathlessly, "that they might be twinned. Two halves of the same whole. It would explain … quite a bit …"

"Fascinating," Gabriel murmured, and somehow Rowan doubted he was talking about anything to do with worlds. He was a breath away from her, only seconds from a searing kiss should she wish it. And she did, with an intensity that left her quivering. But reason, unwanted though it was, finally penetrated the sexual haze that enveloped them. The connection had to be broken. It was the only thing to be done.

"Let me up, Gabriel," she said softly. She hoped he would do as she asked, though it shouldn't have mattered to her if she had to push him as she had last night. More force might even have been preferable, possibly swaying him once and for all into letting her be. But though there was a flash of regret in his eyes—so quick Rowan nearly missed it—he eased himself off of her to sit on the ground beside her. She waited to see whether he would show any anger, even frustration that might turn to something darker. Something that would make it easier to push him away, to rip into him enough that he would gladly leave her alone. But Gabriel's strong features gave away nothing but warmth, faint concern, and that simmering undercurrent of attraction that seemed to connect them despite the space between them.

It shouldn't have pleased her that he gave her no excuse to hurt him. But it did.

She had never been easy with men such as this, who wore their power and confidence like a comfortable cloak. Or in Lucien's case, brandished it like a weapon. But where that type of man had always seemed to her to consist of nothing but hard edges, she sensed a playful sweetness lurking just beneath the surface of Gabriel MacInnes. It made her want to know more about him, made her want to give a little instead of only taking.

These were feelings that should not be. But they were undeniable.

She raised herself to sit beside him, close but not touching, feeling the shift between them as fully as if the ground beneath them had moved. Being angry at Gabriel, even with the insane lust all mixed up in it, had been easier. Now, the anger having vanished like so much smoke, how was she to deal with him? There was more here than she had suspected or wanted. Rowan felt it shimmering in the air of the forest, a teasing promise that gave no hint whether it would be for good or ill should she remain to explore it.

Rowan sighed, regretting, just a little, that her path was set. She could not remain to know what fate had hidden for her here should she stay.

But that did not stop her traitorous heart from wishing, just a little, that she could.

Gabriel sprawled on the ground, watching her while he struggled with his frustration. He'd seen Rowan begin to open up, and just now she'd closed herself off completely again. It was as though a veil came down over her eyes and her face that shielded her innermost thoughts from him. He badly wanted to rip it away and see what she was so determined to hide. All he knew for certain was that Rowan's reaction to him was no less intense than his to her. Her long, lithe body had actually seemed to vibrate beneath him, Gabriel thought, shifting uncomfortably as his body responded to the memory. It had taken—was *still* taking—all of his willpower to behave himself.

He was actually rather proud of that. Behaving himself wasn't generally his strong suit.

He had no illusions about the situation. Though she wanted him, the woman seemed determined to torment him by holding herself back. He had no idea why, and wanted desperately to remove that roadblock she was hiding behind. But he had every expectation that once she collected herself, Rowan would either make a run for it or hurl some choice bit of invective at him to make him go away. Gabriel decided with grim determination that if she thought she could get rid of him so easily, she was in for a rude awakening.

Of course, so was he if she decided to shoot flames from her fingertips again. It had been one of the shocks of his life to see her burn away that branch with so little effort. He wondered what other neat little talents Rowan was possessed of, then decided he probably didn't want to know. If she could, say, make things explode or fly, it was bound to scatter his focus. Not to mention make him jumpy.

So, not knowing what to say, he simply watched and waited, enjoying the way her hair seemed almost to pulse, vibrantly red, against the cool green of the forest. Eventually, as he knew it would be, his patience was rewarded. Gabriel had decided to let her set the tone. He was ready for everything from contentiousness to outright violence. It was a surprise to discover Rowan was in the mood for neither.

"So," Rowan finally began, flicking her eyes over him, then away. It betrayed an uncertainty he hadn't been expecting, and a dim flicker of hope sprang to life within him. It was true, she'd looked at him with unusual softness before asking him to let her up. And she also hadn't taken what would have been a prime opportunity to hurl him against a tree.

Hell. He was too big a boy to be grasping at straws here, Gabriel told himself as he waited for the inevitable insult. Getting Rowan not to despise him was going to be an uphill battle all the way, and he'd do well to remember it. She surprised him, however, by staying cordial.

Well, mostly.

"What did you have for lunch?"

It was a strange question, he thought, but one he was happy to answer if it kept her talking to him more like an equal than a subhuman.

"I stopped in at Gid and Carly's. She makes excellent pasta, which I took advantage of. Why?" Was she hungry? he wondered. Did she eat regular food when she wasn't sipping from someone's neck? He should have asked Gideon, Gabriel realized, if he'd seen her eat anything this morning. Feeding her, in a more normal sense this time, would be an excellent opportunity to stay by her side for a bit longer.

"You're wearing it. I was just curious." Her smile was placid, but Gabriel couldn't miss the wicked twinkle in her eyes before she turned her head to study a leaf that lay on the ground.

"Er. Oh." Gabriel pursed his lips and racked his brain for another possible avenue for talk, all the while wishing he'd done as Gideon suggested and at least grabbed a shirt.

He watched her for a bit, trying to pretend she didn't know he was staring at her. She looked refreshed, he noted, her fair skin luminescent in the half-light of the forest. She wore a simple tank top and shorts that exposed what seemed like acres of shapely leg. On loan, Gabriel surmised, from Carly. He smiled. His sister-in-law was a soft touch with everything from stray animals to stray semi-vampiric sorceresses,.

"I hope you're feeling better today," he finally said, unable to think of much else.

She continued to study the leaf. "Of course I am." She paused, seeming to struggle with herself for a moment, before continuing. "Thank you, by the way."

Gabriel cocked his head to study her. A thank-you wasn't at all the sort of thing he'd ever thought to hear out of her. Intrigued, he pressed her a bit more.

"You're welcome. I, ah, wasn't sure how you felt about it. Considering." *Considering you tossed me out on my ass after driving me half insane with lust,* he silently added. Rowan gave him a sidelong glance.

"I was starved and had no magic left. How else would I feel? And if you're talking about after …" She trailed off, her tone indicating that if he was, it was extremely bad form.

Fortunately for him, being considered rude was low on his list of current worries.

"Damned right I'm talking about after!" Gabriel growled, frustration bubbling quickly to the surface. He'd planned on keeping this lighter, but maybe it was best she knew what she was doing to him. Just looking at Rowan, sitting calmly with her wild red hair tumbling around her shoulders while he could barely keep a handle on his need for her, made him want to roar. To force a reaction from her, *something* to bring the woman he'd encountered last night back to the surface.

"I was weak, and hungry," she said, her husky voice clipped. "Feeding is a very intimate experience for my kind. I lost control. I'm … I'm sorry," she grated out with obvious difficulty, "if you got the wrong idea. I'm not interested in you."

Gabriel waited, but that was apparently intended to be Rowan's final word on the subject. It irked him, more than he knew how to adequately express, that she thought she could dismiss him so easily. "Like hell you're not interested," he finally snapped. That got her attention squarely back on him, and those bright green eyes weren't quite so cool.

"Like hell I *am*. I appreciate the service you did for me, but it isn't going to happen again. I am sorry for the way it ended last night, but that part hasn't changed."

Gabriel glowered at her, feeling his temper begin to bubble and churn beneath the surface. He normally had a long fuse, but Rowan was possessed of the singular ability to burn up the length of it with a simple word. It was going to make for an interesting future together if he could keep himself from strangling her in the process. The *service* he'd done for her? Was she kidding?

"I'll assume the part that hasn't changed was the one where you mentioned you'd like me to stay away from you?" Gabriel asked.

"You'd be a lot better off if you did," Rowan replied, and just for an instant there was a haunted look about her he didn't care for at all. He'd assumed she must be carrying some guilt. Seeing it, seeing evidence that she carried a burden he was already certain she didn't deserve, was another thing altogether. It was all he could do not to pull her into his arms. The fact that she would reject it if he'd tried only incensed him further.

"You've got an awfully strange way of showing your disinterest," he said, voice flat.

"It isn't going to happen again," Rowan repeated firmly, now with the faint edge of irritation. "Understand. *I don't want you.*"

Gabriel gritted his teeth at the stubborn set of her chin, the regal way she held herself while she attempted to dismiss him.

"I've been with enough women to know when one does or does not want me. You do."

Rowan's crimson brows drew together at this bit of information. Gabriel figured she was going to take issue with his contradiction. He was wrong.

"How many women?"

The question startled him, but he wasn't in the mood to be coy. "*Many* many."

"Yet another reason I don't want you," she snapped, beginning to flush with anger. "I have no interest in being one of a meaningless *many*."

Gabriel grinned, unable to help himself. No matter how easily Rowan managed to push his buttons, it seemed he had the same ability where she was concerned. And this was much preferable to the calm, disinterested façade she'd been trying to project.

"Who says they were all meaningless? And why are you even interested, considering how unimportant I am to you?"

Rowan sprang to her feet, teeth bared in a fit of temper. Gabriel stayed where he was, curious to see whether she was going to destroy something and hoping that if she did, it wouldn't be him. This was all too interesting to go up in a ball of flames in the middle of it. Because if he didn't know better, he'd say Rowan *an* Morgaine was jealous.

It might be a negative emotion, but it was a hell of a lot more promising than simple disgust. Jealousy he might be able to work with.

Rowan, on the other hand, didn't seem to be quite so at ease with it.

"This is pointless, Gabriel," she snarled. "Even if I wanted to be with you … which I *don't* … there is zero possibility of it happening. All I care about is finding a way to defeat those vile Andrakkar, finding what's left of my people, if any, and leading the Dyadd as best I can. There is no room in that scenario for a werewolf of Earth. The Daughters of the Goddess belong to no man, Gabriel MacInnes. I would ask that you respect that for the short time I'm here."

"What the hell is that supposed to mean?"

Rowan stood glaring down at him, her bearing stiff. "I mean that my kind haven't bound themselves to any one man since an entire tribe of Drakkyn shifters fled our forests a thousand years ago. None of my sisters, or my brother, have the same father. And like my mother, when I return as *Dyana,* I will be owned by no man. I'm used to being desired, Gabriel," she bit out, "but if I refused even the most powerful Drakkyn of my world, what possible reason could I have for considering you?"

She'd intended to cut him, and she had. More than she could have known. He had already considered that he had little to offer a woman like this. She was powerful, heart-stoppingly beautiful, and the future leader of her people. He was the aimless second son of a secluded family of werewolves, his only power that of charming his way out of sticky situations, usually involving women. The urge to let her be, to just concede defeat, was strong. Even though it meant he could never give his heart to another.

But his need for her, even as he bled from her sharp and careless tongue, was stronger, as was his pride. And despite the oceans of self-doubt he had always silently struggled with, that pride, once stirred, obscured everything else.

He had been raised a MacInnes Wolf, and he was damned proud of that. Aimless he might well have been. But it was a far cry from worthless. Everything had changed the night the Andrakkar had appeared, but perhaps it was he most of all who had changed. Gabriel knew he'd never been lacking in talent or drive. He wasn't Duncan's son for nothing. But as the second son, what he had lacked was purpose. That was, he realized, until one had been pushed into his arms by a determined Drakkyn. Bastian had been adamant that Rowan stay with him, Gabriel remembered, in what was the first time in memory that he alone had been singled out as the only Wolf for the job. And Bastian had called them all that strange word Mordred had also used, albeit with reverence instead of disdain …

A thought occurred to him out of the blue, crazy on one level but making perfect sense on another. He stood up quickly, facing Rowan, who looked furious and also a little frightened. *Of what?* he wondered.

"What were they called?" he demanded, possessed of a sudden burning need to know the answer. Feeling as though his everything, his life, his future, depended on it.

She stared back as though he'd lost his mind.

"What …"

"The Drakkyn who disappeared? What were they called?"

"I … *arukhin,*" Rowan stammered, and it was obvious she didn't understand what it had to do with anything. "They were guardians of the forest as my own people are, the Dyadd's only equals in power and strength."

"And your people, this Dyadd, only bound yourselves to these *arukhin*?" he pressed.

"With few exceptions. We were the only ones who could handle one another," she replied, shaking her head. "Marriage to an Orinn, who have no true magic, has never led to anything but misery for both. Other Drakkyn races are only ever rarely seen in the *Carith Noor,* and the Dyadd never leave there." She shook her head, the light reflecting in her eyes and making them glow. "I don't see what this has to do with anything. It was, like I said, a thousand years ago."

Relief surged through him along with fierce hope, a balm to the wounds Rowan's refusal of him had inflicted. Bastian had known what they were, as had Mordred. Why Rowan didn't, he couldn't say, but she was about to find out. The pleasure he felt about being the one to set her straight was only slightly malicious.

"The *arukhin* shifters weren't lost," he said quietly. "And I'm afraid I'm not quite as unsuitable for you as you think."

She stared at him, disbelief etched plainly across her face. Before he could think, before he even understood what he was doing, Gabriel grabbed her hand and pressed it against his chest, directly over his heart. Rowan's long fingers splayed over his skin, and in her shock she didn't struggle right away, only gasped at the electric charge of her skin against his.

Gabriel willed his inner beast to come to him, holding it at bay just beneath the surface. And without knowing just how, what was in him called to what was in her, fierce and magic things that were made far from humankind. Images raced through his mind, sensory fragments—a howl rending a summer's night, the feel of paws on softest grass. And there were other things that he had never known, like the feel of his teeth sinking into a supplicant's neck, the first sweet burst of pleasure as blood flowed like nectar upon his tongue. The beautiful broken moan as he took from one who demanded to be taken.

His heartbeat slowed, pulsing through Rowan's hand and into her own breast, coaxing her own heartbeat into a matching and sensuous dance. In moments, the two hearts beat like one, that connection thrumming through both of their bodies as they faced each other in the hazy and scattered light.

"Two halves," Gabriel murmured as he watched her eyes grow blurred, "one whole. Your heart knows mine, Rowan *an* Morgaine. Even after a thousand years."

Rowan lingered, swaying faintly with the rhythm as though entranced. Then, without a warning, she ripped her hand from his grasp with a strangled cry, staring at her hand in horror as though he'd burned it. When her gaze connected with his, all Gabriel saw was stark terror, so raw that he wanted to drop to his knees and beg forgiveness for having put it there.

"My heart," she forced out in a near-hiss, "is my own."

She clutched her hand to her chest, casting one more burning look at him before turning to race away through the trees back toward the house, picking up speed until she vanished, just a blur, in the distance.

Gabriel stood, silent and alone, staring after her long after she'd vanished. Finally he let out a soft, sad sigh and ran a hand back through his hair to shove it out of his eyes.

"I wish I could say the same," he said. But what he had just done, he could never undo.

And after a time, he started home.

Chapter 8

THE GOLDEN SILK WALLS OF THE CAVERNOUS TENT *billowed gently in the night breeze as she walked, feet bare upon sumptuous rugs. All around her was silence as she moved, every eye upon her. The revelers had paused in the midst of the nightly celebration, the Orinn from the nearby village dressed in their muted browns and greens mixed in with the women of her tribe, who stood out like bright jewels in bursts of color. The music, which had been a wild and sensuous beat, had ceased as abruptly as the nightly celebration at the sudden appearance of the two black-clad interlopers. The foreign Drakkyn. The Andrakkar.*

Waiting, with their burning violet eyes, for her. And an answer.

People parted to make a path for her as she approached the dais from which the Dyana *presided over the festivities. Elara, curled like a beautiful and aging lioness upon the pillows of the raised platform, watched her come, her expression inscrutable. Rowan felt her heart pounding in her chest as it never had, not even the first time she had tasted both blood and that first electric surge of her own power. Though she had never seen these two, she knew who they were. Their names had been whispered with fear and a sort of terrified reverence as befitted those from the Black Mountains, the lair of the dragons. Their territory might be far away, but the reach of their claws was wide. Only fools would fail to accord them the respect that demanded.*

The tales of those who had not were, after all, both legendary and drenched in blood.

Rowan kept her head high, determined to meet Mordred and his son and heir, Lucien, as equals, though she knew they would not regard her as such. While there was no particular hierarchy among the Drakkyn, the dragons were most feared, and so considered themselves above all others. It had caused problems from time to time.

She feared this would be one of them.

At last she reached them, extending her arms out at her sides and dropping into a graceful curtsy as the tiny silver bells she wore at her wrists and ankles jingled softly in the oppressive silence. She felt their eyes on her, the cold burn of them, and had to force herself to rise up and meet them with her own. Violet fire bored into her from the twin gazes, making her skin crawl. Rowan struggled with the urge to scream.

"She is lovely, is she not, Lucien?" It was the older of the two who spoke, silver-haired but with a sharply handsome face that was practically unlined. Still, Rowan had no illusions that his beauty was anything more than skin-deep. There was a coldness that radiated from him, so strong that it raised the flesh into tiny bumps along her bare arms.

"Indeed." The voice was barely a whisper, a sound that did nothing to soothe her frayed nerves. If anything, Lucien was more frightening than his father. There was a dangerous kind of heat in his gaze, along with a sense of immense power and barely restrained violence. He too

was darkly handsome, she thought, recognizing it without letting herself be touched by it. His light skin and ebony hair were a striking contrast, setting off features that were almost hawkish. His tall and elegant frame gave an air of sensual grace, though it no doubt hid a terrible strength. He was, after all, Mordred's son. And "terrible" was a word often applied to him.

No, he might be beautiful to look at. But no woman who valued her life would ever see him as anything but what he, like most dragons, must be: a harbinger of a long, slow death.

And yet something about him, something Rowan couldn't quite place her finger on, was familiar, as though they had met long ago. As though some traitorous part of her recognized him, and instead of recoiling in fear and loathing, wished to know him better. It made no sense. And it unsettled her so deeply that she buried the feeling as best she could. She wanted no part of this dragon, or any other. And she knew for certain that what-ever that odd connection was, she would never have any desire to lay with Lucien Andrakkar.

That much, at least, was a relief. She might occasion-ally be foolish, but she had never been self-destructive.

"I thank you for your kind words," she managed, schooling her expression into one of regal indifference. It was disconcerting, this sick unease roiling within her. She had always been supremely confident, fearing nothing. And yet in the presence of these men, she wanted desper-ately to be allowed to go back to hide among her sisters. A flash of bright blue caught her eye off in the far corner, and Rowan caught the barest glimpse of Bastian's troubled

expression before forcing her attention back to the matter at hand. As difficult as it was to believe, there could be little doubt as to what these men wanted.

Her.

This, despite the fact that the Dyadd, descended from the Goddess Morgaine herself, had not bound themselves to men since the arukhin, *their beloved warrior shifters, had disappeared so long ago. Since the Andrakkar had enslaved them, only to see them escape into the unknown darkness beyond this world.*

The Dyadd's choice had always been respected by the other Drakkyn. But it should come as no surprise that Mordred, of all dragons, should have decided to cast that aside. His house had overseen the enslavement of the arukhin, *against all of the natural laws. And now, after all of this time, he had turned his eye to the forest once again.*

Rowan shivered slightly. There were reasons there were so few women among the dragons. She did not want to find out whether she would have the strength to survive such an existence. They were not known for their kindness toward what they regarded as the weaker sex.

"She will do nicely, Elara," Mordred said, not bothering to acknowledge that Rowan had even spoken. "I believe my son has chosen well. You did say she would have succeeded you one day, yes?"

Elara's eyes flashed as golden as the long waves that coiled around her shoulders. "Rowan will one day become Dyana, yes. Of all my daughters, she is most suited. And I have not given her to you, Mordred. Nor will I. For reasons known to us both."

Mordred brushed this aside with a graceful wave of his hand, as though Elara's objections were a mere trifle. "Those reasons are exactly why I have come. Her power makes her ideally suited. In all of our travels, no other has come closer to being worthy. No, your daughter will bear the strongest rulers the Andrakkar have yet seen. My house will be reborn. And in return for her compliance, the forests of the Noor will remain untouched."

Though his voice was light, there was a thinly veiled menace in his words. Rowan's mouth went dry as she looked between the two rulers, Elara's expression both haughty and defiant, Mordred's faintly threatening. She didn't understand their exchange ... what "reasons"? Though her gift did not always please her, she had never considered it a detriment. But puzzling it out would have to wait. Her thoughts were scattered as Lucien continued to stare at her. She felt his eyes as they touched upon her body, on the high full breasts so proudly displayed by her low-cut bodice, on the hints of leg teasingly shown by the shimmering strips of material that comprised her long skirt. Rowan had never shied away from attention, but now it was all she could do to remain still, to look elsewhere so Lucien could not see the disgust in her eyes that she knew would be there.

"The Noor has no reason to fear attack, Mordred," Elara said pointedly. "The Drakkyn are at peace."

"Mmm," he said softly, toying with some invisible thread on the long, black cassock he wore. "And yet you are in an enviable position here. So many resources ... so much this land has to offer should anyone decide to take a closer look."

Fear slipped down her spine like ice water. Had the ruler of the dragons just threatened attack should she refuse his son? Was she truly worth so much? Rowan took a deep breath. Impossible. They must want more than that. She was hardly worth such a display. All Dyadd were beautiful. She wasn't unusual in any way at all. And as for her power, Elara insisted that great things would come from her in time. She herself, however, was by no means convinced. No, the Andrakkar couldn't possibly resort to such things over a mere woman when everyone knew the ill regard they had for her gender.

Except Lucien continued to stare at her like a man possessed, lust mixed with some indefinable emotion in his gaze that she didn't want to understand. No woman could ever give enough to take that away, Rowan thought. Though she might kill herself trying ... if he didn't kill her first.

"I'm sorry," Rowan said, determined to be heard, "but as it's my fate you're discussing, I think it should be my decision." All eyes shot directly to her, unnerving her, but she pressed on. It must be said. And it must come from her. She was a woman now by virtue of her twenty-six years. It had been many years since she'd hidden behind her mother's skirts. And there was no reason for Elara to bear the brunt of the blame for the refusal Rowan knew she had to give.

"Then give us your answer," Mordred said silkily, "and let us hope that you have more sense than your exalted mother."

There were soft gasps in the crowd at such an open insult. Elara was viewed by the various people of the

Carith Noor *as little different than a goddess who walked amongst them. Her benevolence was legendary, true enough, but so was her wrath.*

Elara, however, simply arched a golden brow and smirked. "Why Mordred, I had no idea you were still nursing a grudge after all this time, when our encounter was so brief." Her laugh was taunting. "Very brief, from what I can recall. How flattering. And how typical. But you will not have your way in this. It would be an abomination, and well you know it."

Rowan fought back a cringe. She didn't want to think of Mordred Andrakkar laying so much as a finger on her mother, but it appeared that at sometime in the distant past he had. It was not a history that she cared to repeat. Nor, it seemed, did her mother desire it for her, if her use of the word "abomination" was any indication.

"You know the Dyadd do not marry, Lord Andrakkar," she said, sensing from Elara's look that it was acceptable for her to speak.

"I know the Dyadd choose *not* to marry," Mordred replied with a malicious glint in his eyes. "There is quite a difference between the two."

"Not for me," she said firmly, catching Elara's approving nod with a flood of relief. Immediately she felt lighter, straightening to throw her shoulders back. Her mother understood and approved. All would be well. "Not for us. Leading my people is the most important thing. I can't give that up. Please understand." After a moment's thought, she grudgingly added, "I thank you again for the compliment of your attention."

Mordred's lips peeled back in a snarl, and all sugges-tion of handsomeness vanished in an instant. Now there was just a veneer stretched too thin over an angry serpent.

"You ungrateful little ..."

"I will give you all you could ever desire," Lucien interrupted, and his father fell silent in surprise. Lucien's voice was still soft, but deep and rich as well. Seductive if she would let it be. Perhaps it would have been had she not known him for what he was.

"You will want for nothing," he continued, the faint glow of his eyes almost hypnotic. *"Only belong to me, and all I have to offer, all the world, is yours."*

"And will I have your love?" Rowan asked, chin tipped up defiantly. She knew what the answer would be even before his expression became guarded, before Mordred gave a mocking snort of derision.

"A dragon cannot love," Lucien replied softly. But instead of the reproach she'd expected, there was a hint of melancholy in his tone that puzzled her.

"And the Dyadd do not marry," she countered. *"But since you ask that I do so anyway, why can't I ask whether you would at least love me in return? It's hardly an impossible price."*

"This is pointless," snapped Mordred, and Rowan knew it was. She had only wanted to hear the words, to have the crowd hear the words, to seal her refusal. But the burning look Lucien gave her held fathoms more emotion than she had expected. She looked away quickly, shaken, feeling as though the violent longing she had glimpsed had torn a hole right through her. Though she would never admit it to another soul, it frightened her.

They frightened her.

She wanted to send them away and be done with it.

Mordred was out of what little patience he had. "My son has offered you everything but the moon in the sky. It is more than I would gift a wench like you with, but the choice, fortunately for you, is his. So consider carefully. What is your answer, witch?"

"Your son has given me his," Rowan said coolly, wanting nothing more than their departure so she could regain her balance. "And so you have mine. I will not marry. And I would never marry for anything less than love." Naïve, perhaps. But the words were true. She had grown up a nomad, the traveling court of the Dyadd Morgaine her home wherever it might be, often different parts of the Noor's vast network of forests every few days. She had learned to love beautiful things, but not to value them above nature, family, the things that could not be purchased. She felt that she wanted for nothing.

Almost nothing.

And so she would dream of the arukhin warrior who would return from the blackness to give her his heart, as the tales all said they would. She would belong to no other. But especially not an Andrakkar.

"There now, you have your answer, though I can't see how you would have expected any other," Elara was saying to an obviously furious Mordred. She was, to her credit, trying to contain her smile a little, though not having much success at it. Rowan relaxed. Her mother approved of this choice. She would send them away, use her strength to make sure they never bothered them again …

In the blink of an eye, the great tent was gone, dissolved into a night full of screams and blood-colored flames that seemed to have set the night sky itself on fire. Rowan stood, horrified, in the doorway of her tent as she watched Elara battling a massive red dragon that she knew could be none other than Mordred himself. Green venom dripped from his fangs as he hissed and circled, long neck curved back as he readied for the death strike. Elara fought valiantly, power flowing from her fingertips, attempting to mortally wound the beast. A haze of sparks floated around them as they grappled, neither truly getting the upper hand. Until a drop of that vile green liquid fell in just the right way to touch Elara's fair skin, burning a hole in the flesh just as quickly as the poison it contained was surely burning through her system.

Rowan opened her mouth, knew she was screaming though she couldn't hear it over the cacophony surrounding her. She had to go to her, she thought wildly as the dragon gave a triumphant roar and closed in for its feast. There must be something she could do, some way to stop this madness …

A hand closed over her wrist, jerking her back into the darkness of her tent even as a scream she recognized as her sister Lari's rose tortuously into the night from somewhere close by. And everywhere, louder than all, was the terrible sound of great, leathery wings moving through the air.

She had cried the first time, Rowan remembered as she was pulled backward into darkness. Many times, as she had relived this night countless times since it had happened. Now, however, there were no tears left. Elara was dead; Lari too, no doubt. And Bastian had found her once more, ready to take her from this world into another with some strange magic only he possessed. To save themselves while everyone else burned.

"Hold on to me, love. I can save you."

Rowan turned slowly at the voice that was not her brother's, though it was as familiar to her as her own. And instead of bright blue, eyes of gold and green blazed forth at her from the blackness. This wasn't right, she thought, confused as the dream began to break up around her in a fury of light and sound. None of this was right. It was Bastian who had come to save her. Bastian who had taken her away.

"I can save you if you let me," Gabriel said, pulling her to him in a night that had gone suddenly silent and still. And she wanted, how she wanted, to let him embrace her, to believe he could protect her. To feel his strong arms around her forevermore.

"Will you love me?" she heard herself asking.

His voice echoed faintly back to her as the hot winds returned to tear her from him, dragging her up, up toward consciousness and away from the torment of dreams.

" … if you let me."

Rowan gasped as she awoke, struggling against sheets that seemed to have wound themselves around her while she slept. A thin sheen of sweat covered her body, which was bathed in the faint glow of moonlight filtering in through the window beside the bed.

The dream again, same as it had been every night since her escape. Except the end.

Never, in all the nights she had been forced to relive the consequences of the decision she had made, had there been any variation. Until now. Until Gabriel.

" ... *if you let me* ..."

The words echoed in her ears as she shoved the covers aside and swung her legs over the edge of the bed. She shot a quick glance at the little clock that ticked away the hours on the nightstand, its face barely illuminated in the dim light.

11:30.

Time to go.

Rowan closed her eyes, listening, expanding her senses until every breath, every whisper in the house was as loud to her as a shout. She had to be absolutely sure that her departure would be unnoticed. Since she was given to understand that the werewolves had senses nearly as developed as her own, the best option had seemed to wait until they were asleep. After a moment she let out a breath she hadn't even been aware she was holding. There was only silence, and the gentle inhalations and exhalations of deep slumber. She moved as silently as a cat around the room as she readied herself. Silly though part of her knew it was, she was by no means certain that she wouldn't find one werewolf in particular guarding her door.

Gabriel. She frowned as she pulled the shorts and tank she'd worn earlier back on, eschewing underthings simply because she had none. She'd done nothing to encourage him, everything to send him as far away from her as possible, and yet the man seemed determined to hover around her. She no longer even had the privacy of her dreams, Rowan thought irritably. She picked up the pair of old flip-flops Carly had dug up for her and then, after some consideration, placed them back on the floor. Bare feet would be quieter.

Not to mention faster.

She had to get the hell out of here, and as soon as possible. Because not only was she dreaming of Gabriel MacInnes, she was hungry again. For his touch. For his blood, though what he had given her should have sustained her for weeks. And that was impossible, inexplicable. Or it would have been had he not told her he was a descendant of the *arukhin* warriors she had dreamed of as a young girl. The fanciful tales she had grown up on had done nothing to prepare her for the flesh-and-blood reality of the big, determined shifter who had made no secret of his desire for her.

Though she could admit to herself, at least, how badly she had begun to want him, there was no way she would sacrifice any more of her people on the altar of her own self-interest. It was so tempting to slip into the room where Gabriel was sleeping just two doors away, to give herself to him and damn the consequences. And, Rowan felt, damn herself in the process. Which was why she had to leave now, while it still seemed a better idea to walk away.

Rowan slipped out into the dark hallway and padded silently past gilt-framed portraits of MacInneses past. Just glancing at them, she knew they were all dark-haired, strapping men with intense eyes. Alphas, as Gabriel had called them. A position Gideon would hold someday, being the elder son. Did it bother Gabriel, she wondered? She hadn't even asked him what he did, how he made his own living. There was doubtless money in the family, from the looks of the estate, but a man like that was too vital to simply sit still and wallow lazily in what good fortune heredity had seen fit to impart. He would need to make his own way.

And wondering about it wasn't going to get her down the stairs, Rowan thought with an exasperated sigh, speeding up as she turned the corner at the end of the hall and quickly descending the narrow steps. Past the kitchen, through the door, and out into the night Rowan flew. When the night air enveloped her she took a deep breath of the wild, sweet fragrance of the wood. She headed in the direction of the chapel ruins, relying on memory to take her to the place where the all-important Stone rested.

She had known the moment she'd laid eyes on the smooth black piece of rock that had brought her and Bastian to the lost *arukhin*; this was to be her way back to her own realm of Coracin. Her brother refused to accept her help keeping the Andrakkar out of Earth, so rather than taking his obstinacy as defeat, she'd simply reassessed and decided the best thing would be to go back, find as many of the scattered Dyadd as she could, and fix the problem at its source.

She had resolved on the night of the fires to kill both Lucien and Mordred Andrakkar. And so she would, falling upon them when they would least expect it. *Where* they would least expect it. In their own home— the Black Mountains. And though it might mean her own death, ridding Coracin of such a scourge would be well worth it.

But first she needed to get to the gateway stone.

It took no effort at all to locate the hidden passage to the chamber, though it was well covered. A human would never find it, Rowan knew. But she could feel the power flowing upward through the ground as strongly as her own heartbeat, and with a quick wave of her hand, slabs of heavy stone slid aside to reveal a passageway lit by torches that would never extinguish.

Her breath came fast and shallow as she descended, as the realization of what she was about to do hit her full force. She was, after so many months of exile, going home. She didn't know how much there was to go back to, but it had to be better than wandering aimlessly in this crowded and alien place where she did not belong. Down and down, her feet barely touching the cold stone floor, Rowan raced. At last she reached the massive wooden door that swung easily inward at her barest touch, revealing a large circular chamber, its walls awash in flickering light from the heavy iron chandelier suspended from the ceiling. And in the middle of the room, the sleeping Stone, black as night but etched with golden letters in a language so ancient even she did not understand.

The hair on her arms and the back of her neck stood up as magic wove through her. Rowan approached slowly now, feeling pulled. As though it sensed her, the golden letters began to glow, and the Stone emitted a soft, musical sigh. She stopped, uncertain, then forced herself to take the last few steps to reach it.

The Stone sighed again, a strange and longing sound. Rowan raised her hands, relying on instinct now rather than any true knowledge of how to go about this. The gateway stones had been crafted by the Drakkyn in the time when the gods and goddesses still walked among their people. So many of the secrets of that time had been lost. But the Stone recognized her blood. And Rowan knew without a doubt that it would do as she commanded.

An odd shiver of foreboding rippled through her in those last seconds before she laid her hands on it, a sudden cooling of the air around her even as the words etched into the Stone grew flame-bright. She could turn back, her slightly panicked voice of reason insisted. She could turn away, wait for Bastian as he had wanted. Stay, and only increase her longing for a man she was always going to have to leave.

Or she could begin to seek the revenge that was her right.

Rowan stiffened, drawing her shoulders back. It was time the Andrakkar remembered the wrath of the Goddess. In her mind there was suddenly a whirl of screams and smoke, and the unmistakable smell of burning. All because of her. She had chosen to defy the dragons.

Now she chose revenge.

Rowan slammed her hands down atop the Stone, which came up slightly higher than her waist, and felt a quick shock at the connection. The Stone, surprisingly warm, awoke at her touch. Power roared through her like a great river. Her skin lit like a candle, glowing bright white against the dark, and Rowan didn't think she could have removed her hands if she'd wanted to.

Not that she did. Because at that first touch, she'd felt just how close she was to home. She'd actually felt the ripple of the cool forest breeze through her hair, smelled the rich scents of wood and earth. It gripped her with a longing she hadn't expected, so strong she barely cared what happened to her, as long as she could breathe the sweet air of the *Carith Noor* once again. She opened her mouth to speak the words that would open the portal.

At the last second they died in her throat. The image of Gabriel's soft green eyes rose in her mind, along with a whisper full of an emotion she both yearned for and feared. She had a sudden wild urge to tear her hands away and race back to the house, to whatever awaited her there.

"Stay with me."

Magic pulsed through her, home close enough to touch, only a simple word away. So why was she suddenly so uncertain? Rowan shook her head, trying to clear it, that strange foreboding pricking at her nerves again. She'd made her choice. *Arukhin* protector or no, Gabriel was not an option, not in any sense. It had been too long since her kind and his had been intertwined. He would doubtless try to bend her to his will, deny her the freedom she required. He was strong, yes. Too strong. She didn't want anyone who was capable of harming her and hers.

She didn't want anyone at all, Rowan told herself firmly.

And if it rang a little false even to her, well, she was certain that would change with time and distance.

Her decision made, she forced out the word she knew she must speak.

"Open."

And as the chamber was plunged into darkness, the light snuffed with a single, sinister breath, Rowan was filled with the sudden terrible knowledge that she had made a horrendous mistake. Very likely, her final mistake.

"I've been waiting for you, my love," murmured a soft, deep voice.

"No," Rowan choked out, feeling an icy lethargy stealing over her. With her last ounce of strength, she threw herself backward, as far away from that familiar voice as she could.

"Please, no."

"You may beg me all you like later," Lucien replied, his tone full of dark anticipation. *"But we have an eternity for that. Now come to me. Come to me ... and come home."*

Lucien Andrakkar stood before the churning darkness of the Tunnels, deep in the bowels of the mountain his kind called home, hardly daring to believe the vision that stood before him was real. He blinked once, then again, but she didn't vanish. His beloved. His intended. His beautiful tormentor.

He'd come here this night, to the place most men avoided unless they'd been dragged, to do nothing more than brood. Days had passed, and he had received only one irritatingly vague missive from that wretched Jagrin. He knew that he might go weeks before the *daemon* would decide to toss him another meager scrap of information. Still, he could do nothing, say nothing that did not remind him of his promise, or his woman. Or his fate should no *arukhin* present itself at an opportune time. So he had come here, knowing himself to be a fool for what he had done, and more foolish still because he would not change it. He had also, for the first time in a long time, said a silent prayer to the great Drak, god above all, master of the serpents. He asked for a way to have everything, for a way to find Rowan on his own. For the strength to unlock the secrets of the Tunnels. Now.

He had not expected to receive an answer.

And yet there she was, standing before the same gateway stone that had once brought him so much trouble. But tonight it had somehow brought him Rowan. His thoughts must have called to her just as she touched the Stone. Perhaps, he thought with a dark thrill, she had been thinking of him as well. He stared through the opening of one of the whirling cylinders at the beauty who looked less than pleased to see him.

This was fate. It had to be. After all, the Tunnels, a nexus at the boundaries of worlds, were not known to bend to the wills and whims of any mortal. Not even the mighty Andrakkar had ever been able to control them.

Lucien smiled serenely, though inside his heart beat so quickly he thought it might burst. His irritation with Jagrin, and *daemon*-kind in general, evaporated as he looked at the missive he'd received just this morning in an entirely new light. It had contained little of interest to him, true. But he now possessed information that his reluctant witch was going to find quite … motivating. He was sure of it. And in seconds she would willingly take his hand to be pulled through the portal that had opened. How could she do anything else? They would be bound. And in finding Rowan purely through his own power, he would no longer be held hostage by the bargain with the *daemon*.

"Come to me," he repeated, reaching out until his fingers brushed the rippling surface of the portal. It was like water, and he knew that he had only to reach through the surface to pull her through. If he could just get her close enough.

"Why can't you just accept my refusal and leave me alone?" she snarled, curled on the floor like an exotic cat ready to lash out with claws and teeth.

"You are my choice," he replied, drinking in the sight of her like a parched man led at last to endless water. Again, as always, there was that strange pull, that sense of familiarity. It was as though this woman possessed some secret part of himself, though that could not be possible. "That hasn't changed, no matter where you run."

She glowed in the darkness, her vitality fully restored since the last time he'd seen her. She must have fed, and recently.

Lucien fought back a surge of violent jealousy. He wanted so badly to feel her teeth on his own skin, to have her open the door to all the sensations his wretched life had so long denied him. And entwined with that jealousy was a slow burning rage that even now, confronted with such beauty, he could not truly want her physically. As though all the years of deadened emotion had robbed him of the ability to bond with a mate in the most fundamental sense. And yet he knew, from the tales of those dragons who had experienced it, that to touch her for any length of time should awaken all his absent desire. Lucien clenched his fists, hoping with all he had that it would be so. And fearing that he would feel nothing at all.

If Rowan *an* Morgaine, whose mere presence made him feel more whole than he had ever known was possible, could not incite him to passion, then he would never be able to truly have a mate. He would always be alone. And cold.

His instinct demanded that he keep Rowan near him. But he wanted more. To forever be denied it, the intangible *something* that hovered ever just beyond his reach, would destroy all that was left of him.

"I'll keep running, Lucien," Rowan hissed, no doubt wishing him destroyed already. "You've taken everything from me. There's nothing you could give me that I want."

"Ah," Lucien murmured, savoring the moment, "but I think there is. The Dyadd Morgaine are … *were* … a rather fiercely loyal lot, yes?" When she simply glared at him, green eyes venomous, he continued. "So I would think that any Dyim would do whatever it took to protect another. For instance, a wayward brother whose return to a certain forest has been a woefully ill-kept secret. Drak knows what might befall him if he attracted the wrong sort of interest, what with his, mmm, *interesting* abilities. Pain. Torture. Or worse …"

He watched her digest it, saw the defiant light in her eyes gradually fade as the implications of what he'd said set in. Saw her mouth the name of the one who had stupidly, unwittingly allowed himself to be the thing that would at last drive Rowan into the arms of her waiting dragon.

Bastian.

The Drak still smiled upon his dark children after all, Lucien thought. In his hour of need he had been saved.

He laughed, though it was barely audible over the whispering rush of different realities brushing constantly against one another. The Tunnels had a deceptively soft sound, one that had been known to cause madness in those who listened too long. Lucien's smile widened, now much closer to a triumphant snarl. If the *daemon* were right, Bastian *an* Morgaine, only son of the Goddess and doting brother to his beloved, was back in this world. If he had to hunt him down with the blackest magic in order to make Rowan accept him, he would do so. She would not refuse him again. And though he thought that what had been done to her people was distasteful at best, he was ready to do whatever must be done.

Rowan was a lone bright spark in the cold darkness that had been his existence. Ironic that the pain he sought to escape might be all that could bring her to him.

But if that was so … then so it would be done.

He knew she was gone the moment he awoke.

Gabriel didn't bother to dress. He'd opened his eyes with fear rippling over his skin, gooseflesh raised over every inch of his body. Not thinking, running on instinct, he'd Changed before his paws had even hit the floor. Limbs lengthened, fur sprouted almost instantaneously as he'd sensed trouble better faced as a Wolf somewhere out in the night. And of course it had to do with Rowan. The woman's middle name was probably "trouble," or whatever the Drakkyn equivalent was. It would almost have been funny, the way she seemed to embody absolute disaster, had he not been gripped with the terrifying certainty that this time she'd put herself in mortal danger.

It was the dream that had wakened him, Gabriel thought as he raced down the hallway, not even bothering to look into the room where she was supposed to be sleeping. Rowan had been standing in the midst of some sort of terrible battle, watching the carnage with eyes that seemed to hold all the sadness of the world. He'd pulled her away into darkness and safety, desperate to remove the defeat he saw so clearly stamped across every beautiful feature. And when she'd finally turned to him, instead of the brash and difficult woman he'd met at *Iargail*, there had been a wounded and fragile creature with the weight of the world upon her shoulders. It might have been nothing but a dream, but he didn't think he would ever forget the hope and fear intermingled in Rowan's gaze when she'd asked him whether he would love her.

In his sleep, he'd been sure he could. Upon waking, all he knew for certain was that he was feeling *something* strong for her. Whether it would wind up being love or just an uncontrollable need to throttle her was still, in his mind, completely up in the air.

But he was never going to find out if the woman managed to destroy herself and/or the world as he knew it. Unfortunately, he had a bad feeling that was exactly what she was up to. And the closer he got to the chamber of the *Lia Fáil*, the more certain he was that Rowan was down there. Worse, that she was not alone.

Gabriel growled low in his throat as he approached the old chapel, seeing the gaping hole in the ground just as it had been that terrible night Malachi had tried to destroy them all. He raced toward it, feeling the warm rush of sensation that he had come to understand was his own awareness of the Stone. In the months since his cousin's betrayal that sensation had become a comfort. But something was wrong. The entrance was dark, the torches extinguished. And from the deep darkness beneath the ground poured waves of icy air that slapped at the skin beneath his fur and stung his eyes.

Gabriel's massive paws made no sound as he descended, the cold seeming to thicken as the steps curved ever downward. His night vision, always exceptionally sharp, threatened to fail him in the oppressive darkness. It was only memory, and the fact that he'd been down only the night before, that kept his feet from faltering. He slowed as he approached the door at the bottom, sensing rather than actually seeing that it was swung wide. It was no real surprise. What he hadn't expected was the absolute pitch blackness that poured from the chamber itself, nor the low, insistent rushing sound that seemed to be coming from inside. It wasn't exactly loud. But something about the noise scraped against his nerves so badly that he wanted to cover his ears and howl.

Gabriel stopped just outside, crouching low to the ground, ears pinned back against his head. His impulse was always to rush in. But if, as he suspected, Rowan's would-be lover had shown up to claim what he believed was his, caution was necessary. The little he'd seen of what the Andrakkar were capable of had taught him that, if nothing else. Still, it was hard to stay motionless when a deep and disembodied voice echoed through the chamber and reached his ears.

"Your tears disappoint me, Rowan. Did you really think I'd just let you go?"

"Don't worry, you bastard. These tears aren't for you. I would never waste them like that."

Her voice, at least, sounded strong. But the thought of Rowan in there, making her stand alone with tears still wet on her cheeks, was more than Gabriel could bear. His muscles tensed, claws digging in for purchase on the weathered stone floor. He squinted into the chamber, but there was nothing, not even a faint hint of where Rowan stood. Gabriel gritted his teeth. He was going to have to go with scent alone. It would have been less nerve-wracking if he were going to get more than one chance. Thankfully, he found he was already so attuned to her that after only a few quick breaths he had no doubt as to where she was.

Or where *he* was, for that matter. Gabriel bared his teeth, razor-sharp, as he caught a faint whiff of smoke and something unsettlingly like incense. Childhood memories of attending the occasional mass flickered dimly in his memory, and in his animal form there was only one impression that kept repeating in his mind, strange but somehow fitting—Lucien Andrakkar smelled like a burning church.

"They're wasted, nonetheless. Come to me, and all will be forgiven." That voice was like dark velvet, sinfully soft but with an undercurrent of evil that raised Gabriel's hackles as almost nothing ever had. Such a voice could have belonged to the devil himself. And perhaps it did. He waited for Rowan's tart retort, knew

this was the moment she would bring things to their breaking point. But the silence simply spun out for long moments, leaving Gabriel beginning to shiver in the frigid air, until at last he heard her reply. It was quiet, thoughtful. And utterly defeated.

It was the last thing Gabriel had ever expected.

"If you'll keep your word, then I will come."

In that instant he knew how she must look. She would be as he had seen her in his dream, a broken goddess, resigned to a future so bleak that to look into her eyes was to see nothing but an endless abyss. He could not let it happen.

Not to his mate.

That dark voice was now laced with delight. *"Reach out ... that's it. Just grasp my hand, and I'll pull you through ..."*

Hot rage seared his soul like nothing ever had, not even the first time he had battled this very Drakkyn scum. That he would even presume to lay a hand on her, to touch what was not his to take, caused a fury to coil tighter and tighter within Gabriel's chest until it became no less than a killing rage. His blood boiled, his heartbeat roared in his ears until the darkness, the cold, the world outside the chamber was all but forgotten.

I am Wolf. And she is mine.

At that simple thought something within him snapped. Gabriel sprang forward with a deafening roar, clearing an incredible distance and pistoning into Rowan, knocking her to the ground. He barely heard her pained gasp as he slammed into her, his only thought to keep her here, keep her safe. One quick snarl to warn her to stay, and Gabriel moved to place himself between her and the Stone. It was, he now knew, the source of that horrible, pulsing blackness. Their precious beacon of light, used for blasphemy.

For once Rowan did as he asked and stayed silent and still. Small consolation, considering what he was now facing. One of the Andrakkar, the serpent-sorcerers who wanted to kill his Pack. This one in particular sounded extremely displeased.

"A thousand years without the arukhin, *and now it's impossible to be rid of them! Is this who you choose to hide behind, then? A lesser shifter of polluted blood and questionable skill, so far removed from our people that he barely knows who he is?"* Lucien stood just beyond the Stone in some other chamber, cassock flapping in an alien breeze, violet eyes burning. He was so furious he was nearly spitting. As Gabriel stood still, a menacing growl his only answer, the ground began to shake ominously.

"I will make you pay, wretched shifter, for this insult. You are not fit to guard your pathetic world, much less a woman such as she. Leave now, or you're about to learn an entirely new definition of pain. This is no business of yours. Rowan is mine."

Gabriel remained where he was, hearing Rowan's rapid and shallow breaths behind him. Her terror was a palpable thing. So, now, was his determination to protect her. He was barely capable of intelligible speech in Wolf form, but with a guttural snarl, he managed to make his position perfectly clear.

"Mine."

There was a moment of disbelieving silence before Lucien replied. In a cold, flat voice, he left no doubt as to what sort of enemy Gabriel had just made.

"Then let this fall on the heads of you and yours, foolish arukhin. *I would have let you be. Now I will not rest until I have seen you utterly destroyed. It is no less than you deserve, in truth … yes,"* he hissed, *"I remember you from that night now. Your fate will be fitting, I think. An eternity of torment. How I will enjoy watching. And know this: no matter what you do, or where you run, she will still belong to me. As for you, traitorous witch, I will come for you, and soon, make no mistake. If you accept me, I may yet turn a blind eye to any remnants of the Dyadd who cross my path. But you've already doomed your companion."*

The rushing noise grew louder as the portal began to collapse, making Lucien sound farther and farther away. The cold began to retreat, and little by little, the glowing letters of the *Lia Fáil* became visible. Rowan remained silent. Lucien did not.

"I know where you hide now, Rowan an *Morgaine. Must I teach you again that you will never have anyone but me? We are two halves of the same whole. I will always find you … find you … find you …"*

Lucien's voice echoed into the distance, followed by a hollow boom and a final blast of hot breath as the portal shut upon itself. At once the torches flared back into life, casting dim light around a silent room that looked no different than it ever had. Gabriel and Rowan stayed frozen for a long while after, eyes averted from each other, entirely focused on the still and silent chunk of rock that stood before them. But Lucien, for all his fury, was gone.

The Stone of Destiny slept once again.

Chapter 9

ROWAN STARED AT THE HUGE BLACK WOLF THAT HAD JUST saved her life. It was the most magnificent creature she'd ever seen, a combination of long-limbed grace and tightly coiled power. Its jet-black fur shone in the fire-light as it waited, still watching the Stone for some sign that Lucien was returning. For her part, Rowan wished he would. Maybe then she could do what she should have done to begin with and thrown herself through the portal. It was far from a perfect solution, but Gabriel's blood had given her the strength she needed. She could have tried to deal with her ardent suitor on some sort of familiar territory. But that was never going to happen now. Because she had hesitated, because she'd been afraid, Lucien had just gained the advantage.

Bastian was back in Coracin. And unless she found a way to throw herself on the mercy of the Andrakkar heir, Bastian was going to die. Why her brave, seemingly invincible brother had decided that he could triumph against an army of serpents was a question she couldn't begin to answer.

Figuring out how to save him was going to take all that she had. Not to mention that she was now going to have to do something to protect her self-appointed protector. Lucien's words, a twisted echo of what Gabriel had said to her earlier, played over and over in her mind: "We are two halves of the same whole." She was a whole

unto herself … why couldn't these ridiculous men understand and accept that? Frustration and an unbearable
sense of helplessness swirled within her. They would all
be killed, throwing their lives away when the answer was
so ridiculously, horribly simple: let her go. Let her go,
and the madness would end.

The only issue was how to get around one very large,
very unaccommodating Wolf. She decided to make a run
for it, going over him if necessary.

Unfortunately, he was ready for her. The moment she
took a step forward, Gabriel sprang directly into her path.
He lowered his head and growled, a definite warning.
Rowan hissed at him. He might as well have shaken a
finger at her, and she was in no mood.

"Move, Gabriel," she snarled. "Lucien was right about
that, at least. This is no business of yours."

The obstinate werewolf stayed put, growling once
again. Rowan looked at him for a moment, then held out
her hand, palm up. A swirling mass of flame material-
ized there, glowing brighter with each passing second.
Gabriel stared at it, transfixed by the ball of rotating reds
and oranges floating above her hand. Rowan watched
him, waiting for him to become completely absorbed.

When he was, she threw it at him.

Gabriel let out a sharp, startled bark and sprang side-
ways. The ball passed close enough to his ear that there
was a smell of singed fur, but that was all. Rowan pursed
her lips and exhaled sharply. Gabriel looked almost
comically incredulous, an interesting expression on a
canine, but Rowan was more angry than amused.

"I'm going home. Move," she commanded him. The
expression on the Wolf's face immediately became what

could only be called intractable. And of course he stayed
right where he was, blocking off access to the Stone with
a mountain of muscle and fur. Rowan hissed again, utterly
infuriated. Since stomping her foot and throwing an all-out
temper tantrum seemed a bit beneath her, she conjured an
even larger ball of flame and hurled that at him.

This time he danced easily out of the way, and the orb
exploded in a burst of fire and smoke against the far wall
of the chamber. And again he was right back in her way
in the time it took her to blink. Rowan glared at him and
gave a small, angry scream. While the cold that had
come with Lucien had sapped both her strength and her
will, both had returned in force while sparring with
Gabriel. Her blood was up, along with a heightened incli-
nation to violence. If she could only have felt like this
when Lucien had been there, she was sure she would
have at least been a match for him. As it was, all she
could do now was try to barbecue the world's most irritating werewolf.

And really, as Gabriel was currently serving as the
physical representative for all of the failings of the men
in her life, that would be a very satisfying thing.

"Damn you, Gabriel, get out of my way!" she
snapped, and in her agitation flung a quick-fire volley of
flame at him that sent him bounding around the chamber
to avoid it.

This time, his growl was an unmistakable "No."

That did it. Rowan snarled as she sprang forward,
leaping high into the air with feline grace. She would
just throw herself atop the Stone and hope Lucien was
still waiting for her. And given the evasive maneuvering

Gabriel had undertaken, she truly thought she was going to make it. Until, that was, he slammed into her side just before her feet touched the smooth black surface of the Stone, knocking the wind out of her in a single, pained *whoosh.*

She was too busy trying to breathe again to see the shift, but by the time Rowan hit the ground beneath him, Gabriel had become less of a giant werewolf and decidedly more of a big, handsome, *naked* ...

"Where are your clothes?" she gasped, dismayed to find herself in such an uncomfortably familiar position. What was it with Gabriel and body slams? "Get off of me!"

"Like hell," he snarled. "If you're going to set me on fire, I'm bloody well staying right where I am!"

"I wouldn't set you on fire if you weren't so determined to butt into my affairs!"

"Oh?" he asked, green eyes blazing. "Like surrendering to that worthless, disgusting piece of ..."

"You would think that," Rowan spat back, "since I'm a pitiful, helpless female, that not heading straight for his jugular means surrender! And now he's going to kill you, Mr. *Mine.* Of all the brainless, asinine ..."

"Anything I've done couldn't possibly be as brainless and asinine as taking advantage of people who are trying to help you, or slinking off and trespassing on holy ground so that you can give our enemy exactly what he wants. Yeah, you're right, I *do* think that's pitiful! And don't even think about burning me again, or I'll bite your damned arm off!" Gabriel glared down at her, his hot stare and even hotter tone making her feel more aroused than contrite. She did, at least, think better of trying to hurt him again. She had a feeling he wasn't kidding about biting her.

"If you had just let me go, you would have been saved," she bit out, trying again even though the look on Gabriel's face was anything but receptive. "You would have been fine instead of a big, hairy *target*."

"I don't need saving. You do."

He might have been right, she thought. Rowan was suddenly, overwhelmingly aware of his big, muscular body pressed hard against her own. Each point of contact seemed to sizzle, sending little bursts of electrical current running just beneath her skin in dozens of places. He was breathing hard, from exertion and anger, she knew. But she couldn't stop herself from imagining how it might be if it were from other, far more pleasurable things. Her chest tightened up at the thought, and suddenly her own labored breathing had very little to do with the fact that he was flattening her. She swallowed, then bit her lip as hard as she could to try to clear her head.

The bright burst of pain did absolutely nothing to make her forget he was naked.

It was so wrong, the way he got her so worked up, even when she wanted to hate his guts. It should have been easy, like with the nameless, faceless masses who had come to see her dance. They'd meant nothing … had been entirely beneath her notice. Those men had inspired nothing in her but a vague sense of disgust and, occasionally, pity.

If only there were anything vague about how Gabriel made her feel.

"You're a bastard. You don't understand anything," she hissed at him.

"If you can't say anything nice," he growled, his breath hot against her skin, "then shut the hell up."

Rowan jerked her chin up defiantly. "Make me."

Gabriel bared his teeth at her, and Rowan's belly twisted into knots of lust when she saw his teeth had grown just as deadly as her own. She had never been with another Drakkyn. There were not as many of them as there had once been, and in any case, it was a potent, dangerous combination. She had thought his *arukhin* blood was hopelessly diluted. Now she had to concede that Gabriel MacInnes was perhaps a little less human than she'd thought. Right now he was mostly beast. One who looked about to devour her whole.

It was a wickedly tempting thought.

"Let me go!" she demanded, baring fangs of her own. "Why do you even care? You heard Lucien. Your people are safer without me here! Even if I can't kill him, he'll have me. He would have forgotten about you." She twisted beneath him, only to find herself pinned even more firmly. Rowan grimaced, biting back a shriek until it was just an infuriated little growl.

"Trust me," he replied with a humorless smile, "he wouldn't have forgotten. I'm just adding insult to injury at this point."

Rowan narrowed her eyes at him as an unpleasant thought occurred to her. She hadn't yet discovered what had occurred between these shifters and the dragons, but it seemed it had been bad, whatever it was.

"Is that it? You're so determined to keep me here just

to flaunt me before the Andrakkar?" She began to struggle again in her anger. "This isn't about Bastian and me at all, is it? I see now!"

"I'm beginning to think you can't even see past your damned nose. Don't push me, woman," Gabriel snarled, and she saw that he was furious with her. Furious, and right on the edge of doing something drastic. She wanted to hate him for giving a damn about what happened to her, because for whatever reason, Gabriel did. It certainly wasn't a stretch to stay mad at him. But the part of Gabriel that was Drakkyn pulled at her, refusing to let go. All of the previous night came rushing back to her with perfect clarity, the taste of him, the noises he'd made deep in his throat as they'd moved together. And though she was still so, so angry, the desire raged through her like a tempest, obscuring everything else.

Unable to help herself, she gave him what she knew would be the final push. Slowly, deliberately, Rowan arched up, took his lower lip between her teeth.

And bit.

She saw the heat in his eyes ignite into an inferno in the split second before he crushed his mouth to hers. Rowan gasped as he claimed her in a bruising kiss that left her gasping for air. For *more*. Something deep inside her ignited, so hot it felt as though the thin clothes that were the only barrier between them should have simply melted away. Something seemed to have snapped inside Gabriel as well. He plundered her mouth ruthlessly with his own, nipping, sucking as he moved against her with a passion so intense it was almost violent. Rowan shuddered with raw pleasure, her wrists chafing against his hands where he still held her to the floor. Unable to do anything else, she pressed up into him, letting her body speak for her.

For once she was completely beyond words. All she had were breathless moans. He must know what he was doing to her. But she found there was no way she could stop.

"Stupid, thoughtless little idiot," Gabriel murmured. He traced his tongue over her full bottom lip, teasing her with his delicacy before again crushing his mouth against hers. Rowan moaned deep in her throat as they tasted each other, rubbing her tongue slowly against his in slow, erotic rhythm. Her mind clouded, the way it always seemed to be where he was concerned, struggled to process the words. He'd just insulted her, hadn't he? She should respond, fight back. But, the Goddess save her, he felt so amazingly *good*.

"Nosy, overbearing … *big* idiot," was all she managed to get out. She couldn't be sure, but she might have caught a flash of something that was almost a smile before Gabriel shifted so that his hardness was pressed snug against the very core of her. In an instant she was all liquid, throbbing heat. Rowan arched into him, lifting her hips from the floor to grind against him in tight circles. Gabriel closed his eyes, and his low groan brought her right to the edge of climax. She heard his ragged intake of breath, felt him release her wrists to move those big, rough hands to her backside and squeeze.

"Slow," he said roughly. "God, Rowan, slow down or I'm not going to last."

"Fast," she retorted, just to be obstinate, but he managed to hold her back enough to control the pace. His erection, hard and thick, slid against the thin cotton of her shorts in long, deliberate strokes, creating friction that had her nearly sobbing with pleasure. If she'd still been capable of thought, it might have shamed her. She had never truly lost control.

Until now.

Gabriel buried his head against her throat, nipping at the sensitive skin with newly sharp teeth as he rocked against her. She pressed her breasts against him, wishing desperately to be free of the clothing that separated them. With the thought, the simple garments vanished into thin air, leaving nothing but the delicious connection of skin against skin.

She heard Gabriel's sharp intake of breath as he felt the change, and he rose up to stare down at her. Rowan could only look back, lost in a sexual haze. He was a beautiful man, she thought dazedly. His dark hair hung roguishly in his eyes, which were fathomless in the dim light. Skin like dusted bronze shimmered with a faint sheen of sweat, and his breath came in short, sexy pants. He was hers for the taking, she realized. All hers. As long as she was willing to be taken in return.

Perhaps just this once she could allow it. Something inside of her had been winding tighter and tighter since she had come to Earth, coiling until everything threatened to simply snap and break. She needed a release.

She needed Gabriel.

"If you want me to stop," he said raggedly, "it has to be now. I can't stop again, Rowan. Not when it feels like this."

She could send him away, and he would go. Rowan sensed it, and that he would do that for her touched her unexpectedly. And she suddenly knew, in that instant, that Gabriel would never force himself on her, no matter how much he wanted her. It meant that much more because she sensed the strength in him, which was greater than he was probably even aware of. No matter how difficult it might be, he would walk away with a single word.

It might be better if he did, she knew. Breaking such an intense connection would probably drive him away for good. But even though that would probably be best, that letting this happen would only complicate everything a thousandfold, Rowan found she couldn't let him go. Not now. Not tonight. Tomorrow would bring a world of new problems, she was sure. But she was so weary of having to always think one step ahead of everything, of denying herself and pretending and hiding.

So just for tonight she would be the Rowan she had been in the deep green forests of her home. Tonight she would be who she might have been for Gabriel, in a different time, in another place.

She would deal with tomorrow when it came.

How he had gone from near-destruction to making love, Gabriel had no idea. But with Rowan beneath him, red hair spread around her like a glorious crown and eyes full of desire, he would be the last man on Earth to complain. Still, he had to ask, had to be sure. Because if Rowan told him to stop once he was inside her, it might very well kill him.

He sincerely hoped that wasn't part of her plan.

"Should I stop?" he asked again, aching with the need to be in her, his cock slick with moisture from rubbing against her. Her body was ready for him, he knew. It was the rest of her he wasn't sure about. Rowan was like a living, breathing volcano. Her eruptions were completely unpredictable, and if he was being honest with himself, endlessly fascinating. Even when she was trying very hard to maim him.

Rowan tipped her head to the side, watching him intently with her bright green gaze. What she was thinking about he couldn't begin to guess. But when she reached up, almost tentatively, to slide her long fingers through his hair and bring his mouth back to hers, he wanted to shout with joy. A breath away from her, he heard her whisper.

"My clothes just *burned off*. No more stupid questions. Just kiss me."

Her smile, a rare and beautiful ray of light across features that were too often troubled, provoked one of his own. He had a feeling that "stupid" was going to be one of Rowan's endearments. If it was always accompanied by that smile, it was one he would gladly live with.

"As you wish, your highness," he laughed softly, nuzzling lips that were full and sinfully soft. He teased her a moment, flicking his tongue against the tip of her own when she opened impatiently for him. Then, in one quick movement, he plunged, claiming her mouth with his own and swiveling his hips so that he was inside her with one hard thrust.

God in heaven.

Gabriel stilled, closing his eyes in shock as pleasure like he'd never known rocked him to his very core. Rowan was so wet, so unbelievably tight. She fit him as though they'd been made for each other, a slick, hot sheath only for him. Rowan arched back, exposing her long, pale column of a throat.

"Oh," she sighed, a simple word she managed to imbue with everything she was feeling. He knew, because he felt it, too. All of his muscles tensed as he withdrew slightly, then pushed tentatively forward. Sensation rocketed through him so hard that for a moment he feared he was going to do what he hadn't done since he was a green youth and come immediately. She throbbed around him, pushing back against him insistently, asking without words for more.

Gabriel drew in a shaky breath. This wasn't just another of his endless carousel of women. This was Rowan. And this mattered.

"Gabriel," she pleaded, sliding her hands to his hips to press him into her, nails digging into him with sharp little pricks of pleasure. "Now," she moaned. "Please, now."

"Now," he rasped, giving in to his need. He barely heard Rowan's cry of pleasure as he began to move within her again, thrusting with excruciating slowness as she writhed beneath him. His hands cruised up her long waist to cup her breasts and squeezed lightly, rhythmi-cally as he rocked against her. Rowan arched into his touch as she slid her legs up to lock around his waist, urging him into her deeper, harder. Still he kept the pace slow. He rubbed his thumbs roughly over her nipples, playing with them until they were hard little pearls beneath his fingers.

Rowan gasped her approval, raking her nails up his back to grip his shoulders and licking at his lips until he opened for a searing kiss. He could feel the scrape of her fangs against his lips, and the slight pain mixed in with such intense pleasure was taking him places he'd never dreamed possible. She fit him so exquisitely, every curve and hollow melded perfectly against him. There had never been a woman who had come close to this, never been one who had burned into him until it seemed she was an extension of himself. He traced kisses over her stubborn jaw line, nibbled at her earlobe until she was growling in frustration. Gabriel knew what she wanted. It wasn't hard to see that this was a woman who didn't care to be dominated. And as much as he loved covering her body with his own, setting a pace he knew was driving her mad with desire, he understood.

She'd had control over so little. But if it would give her pleasure, he would let her have it tonight. After all, he reasoned, it wasn't as though he was exactly losing out.

Gabriel rolled them so that his back was now against the stone floor, with Rowan draped across his chest and straddling him. She blinked, startled, as she looked down at him, a question in the glittering depths of her eyes. Her hair fell around them like a curtain, closing the two of them off from the rest of the world. The only sound in that silence was their ragged breathing as Gabriel throbbed deep inside her.

"Ride me, love," he whispered. Rowan hesitated, her expression full of some intense emotion Gabriel couldn't quite understand. Then, with a soft kiss pressed to his lips, Rowan rose above him.

Hadn't she mentioned something about being descended from a goddess? Gabriel wondered. Suddenly he could believe it. Because in the soft glow of the torch-light, with her head tossed back and her alabaster skin shimmering, that was exactly what she looked like. A goddess. His goddess.

Mine.

He felt it then, his heart and mind cleared of everything but Rowan in that moment. She was going to fight him at every turn. She was going to push him away, infuriate him, and probably try to kill him more than once. And he'd be damned if Lucien Andrakkar ever laid so much as a finger on her.

Because she was his mate, well and true. And he was going to love her until there was no breath left in his body. It didn't matter what she was, where she'd come from, or what she thought she had to do. Though he barely knew her, his heart knew hers. It was a fundamental connection he hadn't begun to fathom yet, but it was there. And as it was with all of his kind, once forged, it could never be broken. They could spend forever learning about each other. He would see to that. But for now he loved her simply because she was his.

And was grateful for what he'd been handed.

She could hardly believe it, but there could be no mistake.

Gabriel meant to let her have the control, to take him as she would. It was a gift she hadn't expected from him, understanding as she did his fundamental need to assert his dominance. She gave a small smile. It was a need she understood well.

And yet he would give it up for her, a woman who had been foisted upon him not twenty-four hours ago. And who, she thought with a twinge of guilt, had not been putting much effort into making his life any easier for it. Yet still he handed over the reins of power as though they were nothing, the warm light in his eyes telling her she meant a great deal to him.

It frightened her, the thought of his feeling something for her. Almost as much as it intrigued her. Almost as much as she wanted to return it.

She had been with men, handsome and brave, strong and virile, sweet and unassuming. It was the Dyadd's way, and there had always been pleasure in the lovemaking. Sometimes she had taken, sometimes she had allowed herself to be taken, but always she had known that none of those men were her equal. There had never been any danger, not to her heart or her body.

This time, she sensed, was different. In ceding to her power with nothing but a soft request, Gabriel had just rocked to the core all of her assumptions about Drakkyn men. Dragons were cold and arrogant. Sorcerers were difficult and faithless. *Daemon* were violent and needlessly cruel. And the *arukhin,* the noble and courageous forest shifters, were gone.

But the man nestled so snugly between her thighs was very much there. And her awareness of him as both lover and equal was dizzying in its implications. She didn't want to think of it now; she only wanted to enjoy this one night without fear or expectation.

So she rode.

Rowan shifted her weight as she rose above him,

gasping with pleasure as she gave the first, testing glide. The thick, rigid heat of him filled her completely, and each small movement sent delicious shocks of awareness singing through her body. Gabriel moved his hands to her hips, urging her forward as he gripped her. Rowan grinned wickedly. He had deliberately tormented her with his slow pace.

It was her pleasure to return the favor.

She slid up and down the length of him with excruciating slowness, taking a moment to enjoy Gabriel's broken moan before tipping her own head back and cruising on pure sensation. Slowly she rocked, savoring it each time she sank down upon every inch of him. Lust coiled in her lower belly, winding ever tighter as she arched into the rhythm of their mating. And as the pressure inside her increased, so did her pace. What had begun as a slow and sensuous assault soon became quick, hard strokes, and at last, tight, frenzied pulses. Rowan gasped his name over and over without realizing she was doing it, senseless and lost in a haze of sexual need.

Gabriel's hands moved over her breasts, her thighs, touching, stroking in all the right places. She loved the way he watched her, hungrily, reverently with his wild eyes. And all the while he was murmuring things to her, telling her how she was making him feel, all the things he wanted to do to her. Wicked, decadent, brutally arousing words. The want was so sharp she was nearly begging for release.

He was riding that knife's edge as well, Rowan saw. She pushed harder, lowering herself against him once

again so that there was as much contact as possible
between their sweat-slicked bodies. Another hot, open-
mouthed kiss, and she knew she was nearly there. Gabriel
panted harshly beneath her, thrusting upward to meet her
every downward stroke. His fangs, long and deadly, were
bared. The sight of them now, so close to her own climax,
sent a shiver of pure animal instinct through her. And she
knew suddenly that however good it was going to be this
way, there was one way to take it even higher.

Hunger rocketed through her, not just for anyone, but
for Gabriel. His essence. His blood. Her fangs lengthened in anticipation. Everything in her was hurtling
toward a single point in space.

"Gabriel," she rasped into his ear, feeling the rapid
pulse of his heart and wanting to take it into herself,
"bite me."

He must have felt it too, some ancient instinct to join
completely, because she only had to tell him once. She
felt his teeth slide into the tender flesh at the base of her
neck just as her own broke his skin. Immediately her
senses were flooded with an intensity of taste, of feel, of
sound. It was like the night before, in a way, but joined
as they were it was exponentially more.

She drank deeply, filling her mouth with Gabriel's
lifeblood. With the power it seemed only Gabriel could
give. And when she heard his muffled groan of release
against her neck, felt him buck upward as he came inside
her, Rowan reached the edge of the cliff.

And let go.

Her orgasm hit her like a bolt of lightning, whipping
her body back like a tree in a storm. She tore her teeth

from his neck and screamed her release, wave after wave of unspeakable pleasure crashing through her. And as she came, her mind was filled with Gabriel, with quickly flickering images from the life he'd had before she'd arrived. He filled her up until she knew him completely, even the parts he barely knew himself. They were entwined in that incredible moment, fused into one. Strange words in her mother tongue echoed in her head as she shook, as the orgasm went on and on.

Ta na'am maire, airan y rannan ...

You are mine, now and forever ...

Gabriel quaked beneath her, gasping her name. Until at last she collapsed, boneless, atop him, and he stilled. It seemed to take ages until the last tremors subsided. Until she found herself slipping numbly into exhausted, beckoning sleep. And as she drifted downward, breathing deeply in the arms of the man she had somehow just bound herself to, a single thought formed in the encroaching blackness before fading away into dreams.

By Morgaine and Drak, and all the gods and fates wound together ... what have I just done?

Chapter 10

By night, he had loved her until she could barely move.

By day, some walking, talking facsimile of Gabriel was acting like she might possibly have given him the Earthly equivalent of the Seventh Plague. Not only that, but she'd awakened to the sound of her meager (not to mention borrowed) belongings being stuffed into a knapsack and Gabriel's voice informing her that the two of them were leaving *Iargail*. Now. Immediately. No questions. That, when all she'd wanted was to stretch her well-used body and possibly find breakfast.

It had been an awkward morning, to say the least.

It only got more so when Carly MacInnes peeked in just as Rowan found the mate to the one ancient flip-flop she was wearing.

"You might as well come in," Rowan grumbled as she slipped it on. "It'll give me an excuse to keep his highness waiting a few more minutes."

Carly, looking bright and lovely with her pale blonde hair pulled back in a bouncy ponytail, slid around the door before shutting and leaning against it. She looked unsettled, and sported a blush that was as red as the sky at sunset. The flush did nothing to mar her natural beauty, but it telegraphed Carly's feelings loud and clear: Carly might have married a werewolf, but she was more than a little afraid of Rowan *an* Morgaine.

Rowan sighed, thinking it might have had something to do with the wonderful mood she'd been in since being dumped at *Iargail*. She'd tried to keep her ire pointed squarely at Gabriel, but she had to concede that some of it might have accidentally spilled over. It was the residual guilt as much as the need for a friendly female face that had Rowan taking pity on the woman. She'd been sweet enough to give her clothes, as well as a wide berth. Rowan appreciated both; some of her sisters had never learned to recognize when to just leave her alone.

Just now, though, she found she could use the company.

"Come on," Rowan said, softening. "I don't bite. Well, okay, I do, but I won't bite *you*."

Carly's blush faded a little as she offered a faint smile. "You look ready to bite *someone,* anyway, so that's comforting. Mind if I sit a minute?" When Rowan shook her head, Carly moved to perch lightly on the edge of the bed, watching Rowan search the room for anything else she might have missed.

"No, no more biting. It's gotten me in enough trouble lately." Rowan dropped to the floor to take one last look under the bed.

"I see."

"I doubt it, but it's a little complicated to get into right now."

"No," Carly replied, and the humor in her voice had Rowan looking up at her. "I really do see." She pointed at Rowan's shoulder, indicating the bite marks that still throbbed distractingly. "Now you and he match, at least."

Rowan stood, tried to think of something to say that might explain it, and finally had to settle for a shrug. "Oh."

"It's okay," Carly said with a faint smile. "It's a problem I've had some experience with before. Though I'm going to go out on a limb here and assume that you acquired yours under more pleasant circumstances."

Rowan frowned. "You were bitten?" It surprised her to hear it. Diluted though the blood must be here, the bite of the *arukhin* of Coracin carried a powerful magic. For pure Drakkyn such as she, the magic in such a bite would only blend with their own, able to seal the mating bond and connect two beings on the deepest level under the right circumstances (which, she thought darkly, seemed to include fits of passion in mystical caverns). But that type of power could easily kill an unsuspecting Orinn. It could be no different for humans. Carly's reply confirmed this.

"It almost killed me, until I accepted the Change. It was the only way Gideon and I could be together." She grinned. "I keep telling him he's lucky I like him, because the fur would be kind of a big dating impediment."

Rowan raised her eyebrows as it dawned on her all at once. "You're a werewolf too?" It made sense, of course. With no power to blend with, the Wolf magic would simply change its host to accommodate it. She found herself impressed, a state she wasn't often in. This small Earth woman must have as much of the warrior in her as any of the Dyadd Morgaine. Still, Carly's revelation was going to severely limit most of the derogatory comments Rowan had wanted to make about Gabriel this morning. Calling him a stupid hairball probably wasn't going to fly.

"Yeah," Carly replied, acting as though her condition wasn't any kind of news. "So, um, are you going to be one too, now?" The hopeful look on her pretty face had a sweetness to it that had Rowan coming to sit beside her on the bed. The rush of comfort she felt at Carly's presence surprised her, but told her she'd found a kindred spirit. And oh, how it made her miss her own sisters.

"I'm not anything but sleepy and annoyed right this second," Rowan said, prompting a sympathetic chuckle from her companion. "Though I predict that the 'sleepy' will go eventually. It's different for my kind."

Carly wrinkled her nose in irritation, "Damn it," she grumbled. "I figured."

Rowan couldn't help but laugh. "Tired of being surrounded by MacInnes males? Shocking."

Carly gave her a baleful look as she tucked a stray curl behind her ear. "You don't even know. I grew up with two brothers, no sisters. Gideon and I spend a lot of time back home in New York, but when I'm here, with the exception of the female cousins at the annual gathering, it's testosterone city all over again. Insults, bathroom humor, random body slams … I start to crawl the wall after about a week without female company. I can talk to Regan, my best friend back home, on the phone, but it's not the same. And she has limited tolerance for whining, sadly."

"What about Harriet?" Rowan asked, referring to the fifty-something MacInnes cousin who ran the kitchen.

Carly's wince said it all. "Uh, I love Harriet, but she's my mother's age, and also thinks that watching marathons of *Upstairs, Downstairs* on DVD qualifies as a wild and crazy night." She rolled her eyes. "If I'm going to watch a movie, I'd rather put up with one of Gideon and Gabe's everything-blows-up-athons."

"Sounds interesting." Just like the warm feeling she got when she thought of Gabriel in his normal state, relaxing and joking with his family. He seemed to be a naturally friendly creature, at least to everyone but her. It was just a shame that getting uptight and snappish did nothing to mar his incredible appeal. She thought fleetingly of his hands twined with hers as they'd made love, dusky gold against ivory, and was dismayed to find that she wanted to be near him again, even as abrupt and difficult as he'd made the morning. Her stomach knotted with both desire and dismay.

"Oh, it is," Carly chuckled, tilting her head as she studied what Rowan knew was a sudden bloom of color in her pale cheeks. "They victory dance, yell encouragement when the good guys get something flammable. Sometimes rope me into carnage-related drinking games. I have tossed a blanket over Gabe's sorry, passed-out carcass several times thanks to *Terminator*. So is being his mate going to be a problem for you?"

Rowan blinked, utterly taken aback by the question.

"Mate?" she asked, and even to her own ears her voice sounded stupid. It was one thing to think it. It was quite another to have someone else mention it.

Carly just groaned. "Oh, Rowan, not you too. You're supposed to be rational and make sense, not make a yucky face." She stood, then leaned down into Rowan's face. Her tone was only half joking. "You need to make sense. You're Gabriel's mate, and *one* of you needs to make sense!"

Rowan began to stammer, knowing she was doing just the opposite. "I … I don't think … you see, there are a lot of factors, and …"

"Yeah, I know. It's complicated. You don't have to tell me." Carly finished for her with a sympathetic little half smile. She moved to the door, turning back just as she laid her hand on the knob. "I know that I don't know you. And I'm absolutely sure you've got enough on your plate without adding Gabe into the mix. But he's a good man. And I think he's been waiting for someone just like you."

Rowan slumped on the bed, tipping her chin down to regard Carly while raising her eyebrows in disbelief. "A blood-drinking ex-stripper with commitment issues?"

Carly laughed as she opened the door. "I was thinking more along the lines of 'force of nature with ample willingness to kick his ass,' but either way. Have a safe trip. And I hope you stick around, for what it's worth. God knows I could use the backup. And the sympathy."

"Thanks," Rowan managed as Carly disappeared back into the hallway with one last sunny grin. She still had no idea what this short, beautiful human was doing married to a big hulking werewolf, but her initial impression of Carly MacInnes had been correct: she liked her. So the brothers MacInnes must have some really impressive traits to recommend them as mates, she supposed.

Rowan sighed as she got to her feet and took one last look around the room. It was time to go. And she now had exponentially more to chew over on the drive to Gabriel's. Which, she was quite sure, was just what Carly had intended. Sneaky little human.

Rowan smiled. The two of them were going to get along just fine.

A little over an hour later, Rowan found herself buckled into Gabriel's rattletrap car, trundling off the ferry at the tiny, oddly named town of Fishnish and heading for Tobermory. How exactly she'd come to be heading away from the one thing that was going to help her get to her brother was a little beyond her at the moment.

Still, one thing was certain. Gabriel might have been more than willing to have mind-blowing, earth-shaking sex with her. But he didn't trust her around the Stone. That he was right not to currently wasn't making any difference. His lack of faith pissed her off. Among other things.

Thankfully, he was too broody to notice. Rowan sighed irritably and shifted in the uncomfortable seat. Or maybe it was just her rear end that was uncomfortable. Making love on hard rock was something she might want to reconsider in the future, she decided. It had undoubtedly been a lousy idea. Not only had she all but crawled inside the one man she knew damn well she ought to stay away from, she'd also tied herself to him in some fundamental way she was still trying to figure out. She knew, from the old stories, that a special bond had existed between the Dyadd and the *arukhin*. She hadn't known it was something you could actually *invoke*. So it went without saying that she had no clue how to *un*-invoke it, which was something she needed to do as soon as possible. Otherwise, she was going to want to jump on him again.

Oh, hell. She already did.

Damn it.

Rowan slid lower in her seat and tried to ignore the stinging, faintly throbbing reminder at the juncture of her neck and shoulder of exactly how too far she'd gone. In the chamber. On the lawn. In her bed.

So much for avoiding Gabriel MacInnes.

Carly had seen it before she herself had wanted to look that closely. In sharing that one mutual bite with him, Rowan had done what for her people was unthinkable. She had forged a bond with a male. There were many ways to bind yourself to another, Drakkyn and Orinn, none meaning more than any other. She didn't pretend to be familiar with even half of them, never having intended to wed. But the effect, in the end, was the same.

She felt Gabriel in every breath she took, in each beat of her heart. She had, without intending to, taken some essential part of who he was and fused it to her own inner self. Once bound, never unbound, such was the Drakkyn way. Only the sorcerers strayed, and even then they were compelled to return, ever and always, to their ill-used mates.

At least Gabriel was not a sorcerer. In fact, in light of the information she'd gleaned at their joining, Rowan knew him to be a fundamentally good man. She had scraps of memories now that she knew were his, quick flashes of a young boy bedeviling his serious brother to make him smile, of a young man trying to stand out from his Pack as more than his impressive heritage. But still, staying with him, *loving* him, was out of the question.

Losing her family and her home had almost destroyed her. If she let herself truly feel for Gabriel, it was one more tool for the Andrakkar to use against her. And for her to belong to Lucien, as far as the dragon was concerned, Gabriel would have to be killed. She had no illusions about that. She said a silent prayer for help to Morgaine, the heart of her people, to whom she had always been taught to go with her troubles.

Ama Dyana, how do I get myself out of this mess?

The answer, as it had always been, was silence.

Rowan slid her hands up to her temples and began to massage them, closing her eyes. She had the beginnings of a foul headache if she didn't clear her mind for just a little while.

Gabriel, sensing this was the time she least wanted his conversation, decided this was the appropriate time to start one.

"Listen, I'm sorry for getting us out of there so quickly. But considering what that asshole said, we're both probably better off at my place for now."

Rowan didn't bother to open her eyes. She wished desperately that she were asleep. Then she could at least pretend that none of this was happening.

"And you actually think we can hide from an obsessed dragon prince."

"That's the idea."

She opened her eyes to pin him with a glare. "In your apartment."

"Well. Yeah. You could say that." He had already sounded tired, and worried. Now she could add "cranky" to the list. It didn't do her frayed nerves much good.

They both fell silent again as Rowan watched the landscape roll by, ocean and beaches on one side, lush green hills on the other. Agitated though she was, it was impossible not to be touched by its raw beauty. Especially in the lovely quiet, where she could gather her thoughts and worries in peace. But after roughly five minutes had passed with only the soothing rumble of the car's engine for company, Gabriel, who she was beginning to understand had no appreciation for the absence of noise, tried again.

"So, ah, last night, after we … you know, after you and I …" He trailed off, seeming uncertain about how to continue. Rowan shot him a sidelong glance, annoyed. She had seen into his mind. She knew full well that Gabriel had had his share of "fun" with a vast number of reasonably attractive and very willing females (though none, in her opinion, of much quality). If he was going to try to skirt around the reality of the far superior act he had experienced last night, well, she was having none of it.

"After we had mind-altering sex, you mean?" she asked placidly, then had to bite back a grin when Gabriel's ears turned distinctly pink. Chivalry, it seemed, was not truly dead here, though it was rather misplaced.

"Yes. That. Thanks." He paused a moment to collect himself, during which time Rowan gazed back out the window at the rolling and endless green of the scenery. It had at least had the decency to be a cloudy day, which suited her mood just fine.

"Anyway, I couldn't sleep, so I went out for a bit."

Rowan frowned at him, not liking that he'd left her and she hadn't noticed. She should have sensed it, should have awakened immediately. She had always noticed the smallest things, never having been a very deep sleeper. Last night, though, she'd slept as though she'd been drugged. Bliss was obviously as dangerous as it was restful.

"Out?"

"Yeah. You know. For a run. It helps clear my head, usually." He gave her a look that told her last night had created a lot of fog for him that needed clearing. It should have made her feel better about her own confusion, and in truth it did, in a way. But she never should have let it happen. He didn't need to feel what he was feeling.

Inwardly she cursed herself, even as the thought of Gabriel's lean, powerful body entwining with the power of the Wolf out in the night sent heat straight to her core. She had been born to become the most powerful of women. Why had the Goddess seen fit to make the yearnings of her heart so poisonous, and so impossible to refuse?

"And did it work?" she asked quietly, already knowing the answer.

"You know it didn't," he returned just as softly. "And that's something we're going to need to talk about. But I know you're just going to fight me on it right now," he continued, cutting her off neatly just as she opened her mouth. "So that can wait. Not long, but it can wait." He paused, as though considering, and Rowan's irritation at having been so easily read dissipated quickly to be replaced by a sinister little chill down her spine. There was something more. Something besides just Lucien's threats that had driven him so quickly from his Pack's home.

When he remained silent, she pressed. "Did you see something? Hear something? What?"

"Not so much saw. More like … smelled."

She raised an eyebrow, puzzled. "Smelled?"

Gabriel took his eyes from the road to give her a pointed look. "There were things in the woods … in

MacInnes woods … that didn't belong there last night, Rowan. I've never heard of them going anywhere near Pack territory before, but there was no mistaking it."

His words hit her along with a sick certainty. She hoped she was wrong. But she was fairly sure she wasn't. "Do you mean … vampires? You think there were vampires in your woods last night?"

Gabriel nodded. "Not many. Two, maybe three. But even that's unheard of, that sort of intrusion. There's never been all-out war or anything, but our kinds don't mix. They never have."

"I did gather that," Rowan murmured, remembering the tone in which Gabriel had called her a "bloodsucker" on the night they met. Not, from what she had seen of actual vampires, that she particularly blamed him.

"It's not really the blood drinking," he rushed out. "I mean, I wouldn't want you to think that. You're not one of them, and none of the Pack would ever treat you like one." He looked concerned, and Rowan felt a bit of pleasure that he would seek to reassure her that he didn't hold her kind in the same contempt. When she gave a small nod, he continued. "It's the way they take it. The way they live. Twisted bastards. Ah, again, no reflection on other types of blood-drinking people. Creatures. Whatever." Gabriel stammered the last part out, then heaved a frustrated sigh and glared at the narrow road ahead. He seemed to think he'd mucked up his qualification. And he had, Rowan thought with a small smile. But it was kind of cute.

"No," she replied. "They're cruel. I saw plenty of it firsthand. I'd be lying if I said I didn't feel some kinship with them, though." At Gabriel's obvious surprise, she nodded. "I do think there is some Dyadd blood in them, though weak in most. But there's so much more in them that's tainted. I wondered quite often while I lived in the nest whether they might not also be part *daemon*." She shuddered. "It's a nasty thought, but it makes sense. Especially considering your own kind managed to cross the barrier between our realms. Why not them?"

Gabriel glowered at the road ahead of him. "And a *daemon* would be what? Yet another kind of Drakkyn?"

He sounded so displeased by the notion that she had to laugh. "There are many different kinds, I'm afraid."

Gabriel grimaced. "Then God help us all."

"Oh, you just managed to meet some of the worst to begin with, that's all. And I'll remind you that you, too, fall into the general category."

Gabriel conceded the point by shifting in his seat, slouching down and muttering something unintelligible that sounded as though it contained more than one curse word. Since that was all she got, Rowan went on.

"In any case, *daemon* are allied closely with the dragons, though they occasionally spill one another's blood. They're foul things, talented with dark magic but fairly weak otherwise, and unable to walk in even the weakest sunlight. They burn up if they do. And with them it's less about drinking blood and more about inflicting pain."

"Sounds like you might be right, then. Not that it makes me feel any better about them wandering the Hunting Grounds." He shook his head, a lock of his hair falling across his eye. It took all of Rowan's willpower not to brush it back, and after a moment he did it himself.

"Is that what you call your woods?" she asked, trying to distract herself from the thought of running her fingers through his thick, soft hair. She had done it only last night. It already felt like forever ago. And in light of their current conversation, it seemed like touching Gabriel again might not be the best idea. Though she was disturbingly unsure whether she was truly going to be able to help herself.

Gabriel, at least, seemed blissfully unaware of her inner conflict. "Mmmhmm. Before there was ever a castle, there were the Hunting Grounds. It's where we contained ourselves, with a little help from the human branch of the MacInnes clan. To, ah, make sure we behaved. Bit of a rough start, but we do all right." His voice suddenly sharpened. "Oh, for the love of … get out of the way, damn you!"

It took her a minute to figure out what he was shouting at, but when she did, Rowan burst into laughter. A large cow had wandered directly in front of the car and now stood stock still, gazing placidly at them and looking as if it had no intention of moving anytime soon. Gabriel laid on the horn, and the cow's expression clearly said, "You've got to be kidding me."

Gabriel threw up his hands and glared at the impassive bovine.

"Um. Does this happen often?" she asked, trying not to choke on the words.

"Often enough," he grumbled, still giving the cow a death look. "At least the sheep have the sense to move. Damned Highland cattle, though. I wonder if pushing it would work?" He turned his head, mouth curving a little at her expression. "What?" he asked, just daring her to tease him. "You think I can't move it?"

Rowan shrugged lightly, unable to help the smirk. "It's an interesting picture either way, but no, not exactly. I was remembering. My favorite stories about your kind were the ones where you were behaving the least." She chuckled. "Wrestling with an innocent cow might fall into that category."

Gabriel grinned then, and the way his sudden amusement lit up his face made her heart stutter in her chest, just a little. "There are stories about us?"

She kept her tone light, but it took effort. Gabriel was far too close to what she'd pictured for so many years. He was also, she thought irritably, far too beautiful for his own good. Or hers. "Yes. Most of them involving your kind tearing the clothing from your manly bodies and rushing off to dismember whoever had impugned a Dyim's honor. They were very romantic. And extremely bloody. I loved them as a child." The cow, possibly having heard Gabriel's threat to remove it bodily, meandered slowly from the road and back out to graze.

Rowan grinned at him. "Maybe the cow's heard the stories as well. It's obviously quaking in fear."

"You heard these stories as a *child*?" Gabriel asked, eyebrows raised incredulously. He sounded as though he thought that was more than slightly inappropriate. Rowan rolled her eyes. Humanity in general, she had noticed, could be decidedly prudish. She hoped it didn't rub off on her.

"Yes. So why do you think there were vampires on your Hunting Grounds?" she asked, turning the subject back to something important as the car began to move forward again. She didn't really want to sit here thinking of Gabriel in the context of those old stories, a wild and untamed hero. And still, it was hard for her to believe he hadn't been mistaken about the vampires. Why would they come here? True, they had played host to her and Bastian. But they had seemed to her to be a cold sort, not any more interested in her and her brother than they were in anything. That they would pay a visit all the way out here struck her as bizarre. Kin they might be, but only in a very mild sense anymore. A Dyim and a *daemon,* she thought, disgusted. Some of her sisters had had poor taste in men, but that was really pushing it.

"I *know* there were vampires in the woods, Rowan," Gabriel said, sounding slightly annoyed. "They smell fouler than anything I can think of, which, considering my nose, is saying something. And it didn't feel right out there. Whispers. Shadows that kept disappearing when I got too close."

The levity of only a moment ago evaporated in an instant, and Rowan's mood sank like a stone. It was only one more reminder of the impossibility of their circumstances, and the insanity of pursuing the simmering emotions Gabriel produced in her. For the millionth time that morning, she wished everything were different. But nothing was, nor would it be. She needed to remember that.

"Did you tell the others?" she asked, her anger at having slept so deeply last night resurfacing. She should have known. She could have helped. These were creatures she knew, and understood in some ways, even though she didn't care for them.

"I did," Gabriel sighed, raising a hand to rub the back of his neck. "But by the time I got everyone up and out there, they'd vanished. And no amount of provocation called them back." He smiled, the slow, sexy lift of his lips that never ceased to turn her thoughts to mush no matter how angry he was making her. "Believe me, we tried. But the scent was there. And we've all agreed that getting you out, and bringing more Pack in, is best for now."

Rowan bit her tongue, trying not to take offense at the "we've all agreed" and failing miserably. She never seemed to be involved in the "we" anymore, and it was increasingly tiresome. Still, she didn't like the sound of any of this. And she was glad that the MacInneses were bumping up their security, even though she was still skeptical that any vampires would be lurking around a remote estate in Scotland just on her account.

"I still don't see why we had to leave entirely just on the basis of some shadows and a *smell*," Rowan muttered. "I would rather be close to the Stone, in case Bastian returns soon."

"And I would rather you weren't, for reasons I think we both understand," Gabriel returned. He looked infuriatingly smug. She could only glare at him. It was that or punch him, and since she couldn't drive and didn't really fancy walking, dirty looks seemed like the only decent option. For now, anyway.

"Look, Rowan," Gabriel pressed. "I can see you think this is crap. But Lucien sounded pretty confident about getting to you, don't you think? Maybe he's found a way to use the vampires. You said yourself, they do have Drakkyn ties. Maybe they kept up on theirs." And then, more to himself than her, he murmured, "We've never actually fought them. It could get interesting."

"I was with them for quite a while, remember?" she said, looking at her hands so she wouldn't have to look at Gabriel and see the certainty she didn't want to feel about this. "I just think that's very unlikely." Her stomach knotted up, though, at the very idea. Was it possible? She supposed it wasn't any more impossible than her brother's apparent ability to jump from world to world with little more than a thought. But she didn't want it to be true. Because that would mean that the danger they were facing was far more real, far more imminent, than she had feared. And while she wasn't certain how the vampires would fight either, since they'd never seemed to find it necessary, she was certain it would be more about cunning and less about brute strength. And it would be as dirty as possible, she thought with a sinking feeling.

Oh, by the Goddess. I hope not.

"You're as unlikely as it gets, and you're still here," Gabriel pointed out. "The *Lia Fáil* didn't do anything but sing at the full moon for centuries, and now it's brought us homicidal shape-shifters and blood-drinking sorceresses in just a matter of months. Maybe we could stop it if we could figure how it even works. But the damned thing never came with an instruction manual."

"Is there that much guesswork involved with something your people have guarded for a thousand years?" Rowan asked, only half joking and more than a little perturbed. She had simply assumed that the werewolves had an implicit understanding of how to use and protect the *Lia Fáil*. That had given her some comfort, since she herself possessed no such knowledge. Now, however, it seemed they were all at a very steep disadvantage.

"I'm afraid so," Gabriel replied, looking morose. "Apparently my ancestors were just fine with forgetting their roots. Blind faith in the saint who civilized us, and in his instructions, sufficed for this long. Saint Columba felt guided by God to try to assimilate us into humanity, into the Clan MacInnes. They gave us their name, and their history, and it was a wondrous gift. But," he sighed, rubbing at the back of his head, "we're paying now for forgetting. We had a place in that other world too. Along with enemies we don't even remember having."

"But they remember you." Rowan watched him, sensing his frustration with the limited information he had. She couldn't imagine how he and his people must feel, discovering that there was so much more to their identity as a group, much of which they might never know. It would be like losing a piece of herself, she thought, if it had happened to her. Then her eyes narrowed as a thought struck her.

"*He* remembered you. Lucien. How? What happened, that you even came to meet the Andrakkar?" she asked, the questions coming out in a rush of words. She tried to tell herself it was natural concern for the safety of Gabriel's Pack.

Yeah, right.

He just looked again at her, puzzled. "Don't you know?"

"Should I?"

He frowned and looked away, tapping his fingers on the steering wheel. "It's just, after last night I seem to know a little more about you. Tiny bits and pieces. Your childhood. The way you lived." His lips quirked slightly. "Quite a party. I'd only ever toyed with the idea of being worshipped as a god who walked upon the Earth, but I have to say, it looks to be a hell of a lot more fun than even I'd imagined. And that's saying something."

Rowan arched one slim brow. "Music, dance, joy. All things that serve the Goddess. Morgaine is the mother of creativity, and as her descendants the Dyadd seek to inspire that in others. I don't think 'party' is really the right term."

He shrugged. "Whatever. It didn't look half bad, anyway." He paused, then said, "So. Didn't you get a look inside my head as well?"

Rowan tilted her head to consider him, but he pointedly avoided her gaze. She supposed he was worried that she'd seen … well, exactly what she had seen. And it was true—the careless conquests were less than admirable. But there had been plenty of good to outweigh that.

"I did," she said, "but only bits and pieces, like you. Pictures. And nothing to do with Mordred or Lucien except for a sort of image of the two of them crossing the threshold over the Stone. And of Mordred transforming into his prettier form." He laughed, and it pleased her. "But I never got a good sense of what it was all about."

"It's a long story."

"I think we have a little time."

So he talked in that wonderful husky burr of his as the green rolled away outside, and the ocean swirled around jutting rocks as ancient as time before disappearing once more beneath a gray and threatening sky. She simply listened. First with interest, then with concern, then with outrage as Gabriel related how Gideon had been betrayed by their cousin, nearly killed by Wolves working under his orders, and how all of it had been orchestrated by none other than Mordred Andrakkar. It seemed that one of his exiles had inadvertently found the lost *arukhin,* once protectors of the vast *Carith Noor,* then powerful and coveted slaves of the dragons. The slight of the shifters' escape into this realm had never been forgotten, and knowing how Mordred operated by now, Rowan knew he would see them as a challenge. He always wanted what he'd been told he could not have. All dragons were that way, pillaging lands and then leaving them, stealing women only to mistreat them, and seeking to claim all power they could find as their own.

This world, this Pack, would all be irresistibly appealing conquests for the dragon king.

Mordred was, as misfortune would have it, both power hungry and in danger of losing his house's centuries-long grip on power. A lethal combination. And one, when combined with the fact that his son's erstwhile intended was now among the descendants of his people's escaped slaves, that could conceivably get not only Gabriel but his entire Pack slaughtered.

Rowan's headache intensified as Gabriel fell silent once again. Could the fates really be so cruel as to condemn her to be the downfall of not one but two whole families? It was mind-boggling, and utterly disheartening. She was going to have to get back, and as fast as she could. No matter Lucien's reaction should he discover she had twined her fate with

Gabriel's, she would at least be a distraction until the others could be warned to get away. It hurt both her head and her empty stomach to think about it. As if to illustrate this point, the latter picked that moment to growl, loudly.

"Sorry," she muttered, though she wasn't. If she hadn't been dragged out of the house this morning without so much as a slice of bread, then her stomach would be behaving itself.

"Don't be. You can have lunch at my place once we get there. That is, if you, um …"

She rolled her eyes. "Yes, I eat real food. Normally, anyway, though that's been in short supply for some reason since I got to Scotland."

"Reasons like you've been hiding from everyone and refusing to join us for meals?"

Rowan paused, looking blandly at Gabriel's amused expression, then sniffed, "I'm never very hungry after such a long trip."

He laughed then, a throaty chuckle that had Rowan's lips quirking despite her best intentions. "You're about as good at lying as you are at sitting in trees."

"As though you had nothing to do with that."

"Nope," he grinned, relaxing once again behind the wheel. "It's all gravity."

They drove on in silence for a while after that, but it didn't seem as fraught. Rowan was thankful for that. Her nerves were on edge enough without the added stress of an uncomfortable car trip with Gabriel. It was as though a weight had been lifted from him upon the telling of what had happened this past December. It was odd,

Rowan thought. As though he'd needed to tell someone who hadn't been there, someone who would see things more as they were. Someone who would tell him if she thought he could have done more.

Rowan sighed, shoving back the sudden desire to relate what had happened the night Lucien and Mordred had come for her. It didn't matter anymore. Not really. Now all she could do was try her best to avenge it, or accept a bleaker fate if that failed and try to go on from there. There was no need to strengthen the bond between them with a sharing of such personal things. Even if she had a strange, unwanted feeling that he might actually understand how she felt.

He'd never been happier to see the scatter of brightly colored buildings rounding Tobermory Bay, painted charms against the gloomy day.

Just as he'd never been more nervous to have a woman over to his apartment. He could only hope he hadn't left anything in the sink that might be growing something. But as housekeeping wasn't really one of his main concerns, he wouldn't know until they got in there and he saw it. Or more likely, he thought with a wince, smelled it.

Gabriel pulled his car into a surprisingly decent parking space just down from the bright blue façade of Wolf at the Door, his beloved pub. Rowan had been craning her neck around curiously ever since they'd arrived, all pretense of cool beauty gone in the presence of the bright pops of blue and pink, yellow and red that was Main Street. She was wearing a simple tank in a different shade than yesterday and the same shorts, as well as a pair of flip-flops that looked as though they needed to be put out of their misery.

Damn. It looked like there was a shopping trip in the offing, whether he liked it or not. And he most definitely did not, he thought, looking down at his own stylish ensemble of a faded Muse T-shirt and a battered pair of cargo shorts. In fact, the idea of shopping with Rowan frightened him. The woman looked like she should be draped in expensive silks and jewels. Had been, actually, from the memories he'd seen. She just looked … decidedly high-maintenance. And while his family had money, he himself lived rather modestly, preferring to live off his own earnings rather than mooch.

He thought about spending a day in and out of stores staring at ridiculously expensive shoes and fought back a shudder. There had to be a better, less painful way.

"It must be really disgusting in there if the look on your face is any indication," Rowan said, distracting him from visions of being asked the question *Do I look fat in this?* several hundred times in rapid succession. The last woman he'd dated for any length of time had been strangely obsessed with the perceived size of her rear end from all angles in any outfit she happened to be covering it with.

It had been, he had to say, a very nice ass. But that opinion had never seemed to be quite satisfactory.

He was never going to understand women.

He turned to look at Rowan, who was regarding him with a sort of amused interest that suggested she found him just as puzzling as he found her. And now she thought he was dallying because his apartment was akin to a landfill. Not a very flattering opinion, even if she might possibly be right.

Hell. He might as well get it over with.

"It's not disgusting. It's just a bit … cluttered."

Her eyebrows, every bit as red as her hair in the patchy sunlight filtering into the car, shot upward. "Mmmhmm," was all she said.

Gabriel heaved an exaggerated sigh and opened the door. There was nothing for it now. "Come on, then."

They crossed the street, dodging the heavier lunchtime traffic, and headed through the side door that led to the upstairs of the small two-story building that housed both his pub and his apartment. He saw Rowan cast a curious glance through the large windows on either side of the front door, but he hurried her past. He was proud of what he'd built, and would be happy to squire her around … when the place was empty. Over the course of the last couple of days, he'd discovered he was a great deal less proud of the lady-killer reputation he'd so eagerly cultivated. He hated to be tethered to a cell phone when he was visiting home, so he'd done as he always had and instructed his partner, Jerry, to call the main house if anything important came up. But a quick glance at the cell, or more specifically the number of messages waiting in his voicemail, had him nervous.

The woman he wanted as his future wife might be at his side, but his past was laying in wait for him as surely as those vampires had been stalking him through the woods last night. And though he was quite sure that Rowan had seen enough during that strange and intimate exchange of memories when they'd made love, having to deal with the living, breathing (and often annoyingly giggly) reality of his romantic proclivities was another thing entirely.

He thought of Rowan hurling indiscriminate fireballs at his ex-girlfriends and wasn't sure whether to laugh or go into hiding.

They made their way up the narrow stairs to the small landing, Gabriel leading the way. He pulled out his keys and began to pick through them, finding the right one all too soon.

"Now just to warn you," he began, turning to Rowan. Her startled eyes shot upward at his movement, and a guilty flush flooded her fair cheeks. A slow, Wolfish grin spread across his face. He felt as though he'd cornered a particularly delectable rabbit.

"Enjoying the view?"

It pleased him that he wasn't the only one who was having a hard time keeping his mind off of last night. Especially when he wasn't exactly dressed to seduce, and she still had that hungry glint in her eyes. They turned even more vibrantly green when she was possessed by some strong feeling, Gabriel thought. For once it didn't bother him at all to be the cause of it.

Rowan took a breath, then thought better of it, stopped, and had a look at the ceiling. She started again, got no further than "I," and then found something very interesting on the worn carpet to study while he waited. Finally she just threw up her hands.

"I give up," Rowan said. "Anything I say to that is just going to sound stupid. Just open the door, okay?"

"With pleasure." Hopefully, anyway. He had a bed and a couch, and last night had given him cause to hope that one of them was going to remain unoccupied while they were here. He turned the key in the lock and pushed the door open, bracing himself for commentary on the semi-imploded state of his living area.

Instead, he found the hackles on the back of his neck rising as a familiar, pungent odor rolled out to greet the both of them. Rich, overpowering, an overripeness on the verge of decay. He'd smelled it twice in as many days, and that was twice too many as far as he was concerned.

Vampires.

Gabriel growled, his gut churning, and stepped inside. If there were any of the damned bloodsuckers here, he was going to rip them limb from limb. In all of his life he had never had his path intentionally crossed by a vampire, and he had certainly never heard of one of his Pack having their home desecrated by one's presence. Still, it was obvious to him, from the strength of the god-awful stench, that there had been more than one vampire in his territory.

Any lingering doubt evaporated. Lucien Andrakkar had found himself a new set of minions. And he and Rowan were going to have to be very, very careful. He gritted his teeth, felt them sharpen into fangs. The Wolf within him snapped and snarled at the end of the thin tether that kept him in check. The beast wanted to take revenge for this insult, to tear and bite.

Gabriel was inclined to agree.

"They haven't touched anything, at least," Rowan said softly as she stepped past him, her voice huskier than usual. She moved slowly, like a woman in a dream, touching a lamp, a table, a stack of papers with a light brush of her fingertips. He knew she was blaming herself, wishing she had escaped into the waiting arms of her enemy as she'd tried to do so that no one else would be targeted. The very thought had fur sprouting from his knuckles, had his claws lengthening as though the Andrakkar were standing right there. Taunting him. Threatening him. But he would show her, somehow, that her worry was misplaced. That he was strong enough to protect them both.

He'd been given one task: to keep Rowan safe. He would use everything in his power to do just that.

"Wrong," Gabriel replied, trying to keep his fury in check. "I'm quite sure they touched everything. And if they've made off with anything," he began, thinking of the few small things he had from home that had a great deal of sentimental value, "I'm going to stake every last damn one of them."

Rowan didn't reply. She simply went to the large picture window that looked out onto the street and pulled back the curtains, flooding the small living area with light. As she stared out, Gabriel quickly canvassed the apartment. At first glance nothing was changed, not a thing out of place. A haphazard stack of magazines sat on the coffee table just where he'd left them. The ever-thickening layer of dust on top of the television appeared to be intact. There was, as he'd feared, a stack of semi-cleaned plates in the sink. Everything was just as it had been.

And nothing was.

He *knew* they'd laid hands on his things, cold, lifeless fingers trailing all across his personal property. Doing it simply because they *knew* he would know. Warning him.

Gabriel went over the living area, the debris stacked on the small table, and in the kitchen. But nothing was obviously amiss until he opened the door to his bedroom. The stench was so bad it had his gorge rising. He had to back away and take several cleansing breaths of comparatively cleaner air. They had lingered there, in the place where he slept.

Once he'd gathered himself enough to go inside, he immediately saw why.

His bed linens were drenched in blood, so much that it might have been from some ritual sacrifice. He wasn't entirely sure he wanted to know. What he did know was that what had once been a simple beige comforter had now been drenched with viscous liquid that had undoubtedly ruined his beloved pillow-top mattress. Gabriel walked slowly to the bedside, noting that the crimson stain was still tacky in places. Not that it made it any more salvageable, unfortunately.

Another flash of red at the corner of his eye, and he turned his head to find the words *You're next* smeared across the mirror hanging above his dresser. The letters had been formed painstakingly, and in a sort of flowing script that seemed out of place, considering the medium. Of course, gothic showmanship was everything.

Christ, how he hated vampires.

He heard her come in behind him as he stood surveying the damage, heard her sharp intake of breath when she saw what had been done. Still, Gabriel wasn't quite ready to look at her. The part of him that was all killer was far too close to the surface. A normal reaction, he supposed, considering his bedroom now looked like the gateway to one of the outer rings of hell.

"Any more doubts," he growled after several more minutes of silence, "now that a certain type of creature I won't mention right now has taken a sudden interest in sacrificing goats on my bed?" The simmering cauldron of emotion that seemed to be constantly on a low boil these days rose up, threatening to spill over. He hoped she wouldn't.

But he knew she would.

She hesitated, and then muttered something unintelligible. Well, mostly unintelligible. He heard just enough to get the ball rolling.

"What was that?" he snapped. Her sharp tongue was one thing when all that was at stake was his pride. It was quite another when it was their well-being on the line.

"I said," she replied peevishly, though at a satisfactory volume, "it's *cow* blood."

Gabriel turned slowly to look at her, nastily pleased when Rowan took a step back once she caught sight of the look on his face. "Oh, I don't think that was all you said, was it? The last word sounded a lot like *moron,* in fact."

Rowan glowered and crossed her arms over her chest. "I suppose it … might have been something like that. And aren't you supposed to have an acute sense of smell like mine?"

"Certain scents never held enough interest for me to learn about. I don't tend to snack on livestock. Which is beside the point." He advanced on her, slowly, deliberately, enjoying the way her eyes narrowed to slits of glowing green at his approach as she dug in for battle. She wasn't the only creature with strength to be reckoned with, and it was time she understood that.

"You didn't answer my question. Do you still think I was hallucinating last night?"

She shrugged, a casual lift of the shoulders that incensed him more than any words could.

"All right, then. Why would they pick that particular love note to leave on my mirror?" he continued, his voice deepening until it was little more than a guttural growl. "Why threaten me now, when it's been years since I've even laid eyes on one?"

"Maybe you did something to make them angry," she offered lamely, prompting him to cut her off immediately.

"For your information, I've had exactly one dealing with our small Scottish nest of neck-biters, who, by the way, live all the way in *Edinburgh,* and the outcome of that little encounter has had them leaving me in peace ever since. A bit odd, don't you think, that they decide to redecorate for me shortly before I bring my esteemed guest back here?"

"Not really."

He'd reached her now, and he had to give the woman credit. Not only was she standing her ground, there were actual sparks beginning to flare around her head, flashing through her hair in bright bursts as though each strand carried its own electric current. Hell, maybe they did. But all the stress of the past two days, traceable to the exact moment Rowan had been shoved into his arms, had finally reached its breaking point. Truth be told, he was spoiling for a fight with someone. He would be thankful

Rowan seemed so willing to accommodate him if he didn't currently want to destroy her.

She didn't even flinch when he leaned in, inches from her face, and snarled, "Just admit I was right. Damn it, after the constant stream of insults, you can at least admit I knew what the hell I was talking about here."

He seriously considered throttling her when she looked directly back at him.

And tried to change the subject.

"Whatever they were doing, it obviously isn't safe here. We'd be better off back at *Iargail*," she said, chin tilting up defiantly.

"The hell it isn't," Gabriel snapped. "Or the cowards would have waited until I got back. Now that I am, they'll stay away or find a skewer through their hearts. We stay here."

Rowan tossed her head in the way Gabriel was noticing either turned him on to the point of insanity or made him start thinking about ways to annihilate her. Unfortunately, this time it was the less pleasant of the two reactions.

"A skewer? You think you're going to keep me safe with *kitchen utensils*?" she hissed. "Yes, I'm sure that'll work. You'll just have to excuse me if I lock myself in this room while you save the day with ironclad cookware. I seem to recall, in fact, that vampires are *terrified* of chafing dishes. Happen to have one of those?"

Her fangs had lengthened in her fit of temper, her eyes turned to burning embers. Gabriel bared his own teeth, allowing a fair portion of the Wolf within to show. Two could play at this game.

"Actually, what I do have is a stubborn, mouthy Drakkyn who seems to think that pushing away those trying to help her is somehow going to fix everything. I know you think that you can fight better on your own, Rowan *an* Morgaine, for some stupid reason or other. But this damned refusal to accept help could very well get us all killed!"

He could feel the temperature in the room rising as he told her what he thought. It was high time the two of them started working together, instead of this ridiculous push-pull that was getting them nowhere. It might not be the situation he'd envisioned, but because he wanted her, he wanted to help her. She was his, just as he was hers. And she was going to accept it no matter how much fur she singed off of him in the meantime.

"Like I got my own family killed, you mean?" she snarled, her eyes flashing dangerously. And this, he could see, was truly the heart of the matter for her. "That *is* what you mean, isn't it? That unless I let you and your hulking band of shifters do everything for me, I'll probably just do something stupid and cause another bloodbath?"

"I think the only stupid thing is that you keep blaming yourself for that! I've dealt with the bastards, remember? Who the hell could blame you for saying no to marrying one? And I *don't* want to do everything for you!"

She waved a hand in front of her face, a sharp and dismissive gesture that told him she didn't want to hear anything he was saying. He growled and clenched his fists, utterly frustrated. She growled right back.

"Oh, really? You could have fooled me, Mr. Let's-Run-Off-To-Tobermory-Because-I-Said-So. Mr. Bite-Me-I-Insist. Mr. Save-The-Day-At-All-Costs ..."

"You were starving to death! Your brother wanted me to keep you safe! He …"

"What about what I want?" she cried, digging her fingers into her hair, caught in helpless fury. "Do you have a single idea what I want? Have you asked? Damn it, Gabriel, I'm not some weak-willed female who needs looking after! I had a home once, a tribe that I was born to lead! The blood of a Goddess runs in my veins, and yet no one, not even my own brother, has bothered in all these months to really consider what I want. Did I *want* to take my clothes off for hordes of pathetic human men? Did I *want* to depend on the mercy of some foul creatures that were abominable mirror images of my own? Did I *want* to be desired my a madman, forced from my home, then abandoned and again left at the mercy of creatures as foreign to me as I am to you? What do you *think,* Gabriel?"

Gabriel stared at her, utterly nonplussed. Her rant had left him momentarily speechless, his reactions to her words too muddled to piece through right this second. So he clung to the one thing he had clear sight of, which was his anger. Though he had a nagging and unpleasant feeling that he was going to regret it later.

"I think you need to tell me what the hell is really going on in that head of yours. Why you have so little faith in me, in my people, that you're determined to throw yourself at Lucien Andrakkar. And by the way, I *thought* that one of the things you did want was me. Or was I just another worshipper to you? Another one of those sniveling, starstruck idiots who came crawling to you to offer you their blood, their lust, anything you saw fit to take?"

"Don't," she said, her voice going deadly, dangerously soft. "Don't you dare malign what you don't understand. Especially when I've seen some of your own past, full of empty-headed females and your own lovely habit of running away as soon as you've gotten what you were after. At least I'm honest about what I am, Gabriel. So don't pretend that having me meant something to you, and be honest with yourself for once. You only want me because you can't have me."

She was right. And so completely, horrendously wrong. She had seen what he had been, yes, but she refused to acknowledge that he could be more to her. That he was more than his failings, though she expected that courtesy from him. And still, he burned for her in that way he knew he never would for anyone else, the longing to have her acceptance … her love … making him nearly sick. He had shared that sacred bite with her, had given her all of himself. There should be no further barriers between them, and yet it seemed that as soon as one was knocked down, another one arose.

In desperation, he heard himself saying the words he had promised himself he would save for a better time, a perfect moment. The day she confessed she wanted him as her own. Her only.

A day he wasn't truly certain would ever come.

"You want honest? Then hear me now, Rowan," he said, his voice ragged. "I will never leave you alone. I will deal with your lack of trust, and your mouth, and your myriad of irritating habits. Because when my kind find our mates, we know. And we never have another."

She shook her head, slowly at first, then more firmly. The look in her eyes had shifted almost entirely to denial, and fear. "No," was all she said. But he had begun, and he wouldn't be stopped now.

"Yes," he said, taking her shoulders in his hands, hating the way they went rigid. Heat, so intense that she might have been nothing more than a live flame, burned his fingers where they dug into her flesh, but still he hung on. She needed to know, and if this was the way it was to be between them, it might as well be now. "You are my mate, Rowan. Just as the women of your tribe have mated with the men of mine since the beginning. I can't change it, and neither can you."

"That's not possible," Rowan insisted, taking a step back. "I would have known. You should have told me this could happen. Why didn't you tell me this could happen?" The pitch of her voice steadily rose with her distress.

Gabriel glared at her, if at all possible even more affronted than he had been a few minutes ago. Would she have avoided him had she known they would bond permanently, irrevocably? It certainly sounded like it. And he didn't care to know that at all.

"What did you think, woman?" he snapped, his gestures becoming more exaggerated the more agitated he became. "That I always telepathically share memories when I make love? That biting in the heat of passion is commonplace for werewolves? That's the kind of thing that kills people, Rowan! It killed my own mother." He saw the shock like a slap her across the face and ignored it as best he could. He had said it to make a point, not to earn her pity.

"Yes, Rowan, believe it or not, I've lost people I loved too. Yet somehow I manage to stay true to my family, and to who and what I am, no matter what you think. And no, I didn't *want* to bond with you, just for your information. I didn't really want a mate at all. Especially not one who's so prickly and uncooperative. But I'm stuck with you, just like you're stuck with me. I don't give a damn how high-handed you think it is. I'm keeping you, and that's all there is to it."

There, Gabriel thought. He'd said it. They could go on from here, wherever that was. Rowan was back to looking like she wanted to incinerate him, and that was actually somewhat comforting. At least it was a footing with her that he understood.

"I don't care what blood runs in your veins, Gabriel. You can't *keep* me, as you've so charmingly put it. I've sworn to marry no man. I'm afraid you qualify. And I have things to do that you have nothing to do with."

Gabriel crossed his arms over his chest and looked down his nose at her. "I do now."

She looked up at him, aghast. "I have to go home, Gabriel. I'm leaving. That was never negotiable."

He didn't budge. "Then I'll come with you. Our mating is also non-negotiable."

Her mouth dropped open, and Gabriel had to suppress his satisfied smirk. He was not a MacInnes male for nothing.

"Just because we were together *once* …"

"A mind-altering once, as you said earlier."

"And I happened to bite you …"

"Right after asking *me* to bite *you,* which sealed it right there."

Rowan stopped talking for a moment, eyes wide. She looked, if he wasn't mistaken, like she was about to shoot right over the edge of angry and land smack in the middle of apoplectic.

"You barely know me!" she cried, gesticulating wildly. "I barely know you! We argue constantly! You seem to think that my presence may get you killed, and yet you refuse to think with any useful part of your body! I don't have *time* for this, Gabriel!"

"You know what? You're right. Neither do I," Gabriel replied in a flat voice, suddenly desperate for a little air, a little space between him and Rowan so he could clear his head. "I'm going down to the pub for a bit. You stay here, and don't think of taking off. The vamps and God-knows-what-else are obviously laying for us, and I'd rather not have them ruin anything else around here."

"I can take care of myself," Rowan retorted.

"Certainly. Right here in my bloody apartment. Until your would-be boyfriend makes his move, this is the best that can be done. If anyone unpleasant shows up, just light them up or whatever you like and then yell for me. My sense of hearing, you'll be pleased to know, is a little better than my sense of smell."

"I *can't* be your mate, Gabriel!" she screeched. "You're just … just blinded by lust. It happens all the time. With some time and distance you won't remember me at all. And anyway, I have no desire to be tied to some big, boorish, overbearing, controlling, potentially violent Wolf for the rest of my life. So I won't. I make my own decisions."

Gabriel swept past her, heading for the door. "Not this time, you don't," he managed in a half growl. "You're officially overruled by nature. And maybe while I'm out you can decide to start telling me all of the truth, instead of just what you think I should hear."

"I don't want this!" she finally yelled in despair. "And I don't want *you*!"

"Yeah you do. Deal with it," he snarled, and slammed the door.

Chapter 11

ROWAN SAT AS SHE HAD FOR THE PAST WEEK, SLUMPED IN Gabriel's ratty old armchair, flipping idly through yet another of his seemingly endless pile of *Maxims* and half watching something called *Monty Python* on his humongous television. Gabriel was at the pub. Again. She might have thought he slept there, in fact, but for the rumpled blanket and pillow on the couch every morning.

Truth be told, she was tired of not speaking to him, mainly because she was bored out of her skull. She would sooner die than tell him that, though. He might have ripped away most of her pretense, but she still had her pride. Which was a good thing, since if she watched too much more about Vikings who sang about something called Spam and people who seemed inclined to randomly explode, there wasn't going to be much of her mind left. The human sense of humor was always going to be a mystery to her.

Though, the Goddess preserve her, she'd found she'd actually begun to laugh at some of it.

Rowan uncurled herself from the chair, which she'd begun to think she was somehow melding with, and got to her feet. She stretched, yawned, and then looked around her tiny prison with a heavy sigh.

Something was going to have to give. Dying was something she knew she would do one day, possibly soon, but dying from boredom was completely unacceptable.

She'd heeded Gabriel about staying put, though she hardly knew why. Some days she told herself it was because he was right about the danger, even if there had been no further sign of the vampires since the day they'd arrived, though that alone made her very uneasy. Some days she told herself it was because she didn't know where the hell she was anyway, and leaving and getting lost was a lousy idea. Particularly because she needed to get back to *Iargail,* where she would undoubtedly be held up by even *more* annoying werewolves.

Other days Rowan simply tried not to think about it and just skulked around in the oversized sweats and T-shirt she'd swiped from Gabriel's closet (taking great pleasure in his obvious irritation about it, which he stubbornly refused to express) and found things to do. Unfortunately, ever since the tense, painfully silent cleanup operation she and Gabriel had undertaken for his bedroom the day they'd arrived, there hadn't been much to do in what basically amounted to three rooms, four if she were being generous and counted the kitchen separately. The entire place had been spotless since Tuesday. It was now Saturday, and even her inner voice of denial was beginning to wonder whether she was hanging around because she was prolonging the inevitable, pretending that there would be some way to avoid presenting herself to Lucien like a beribboned gift. Pretending she could stay with the company she probably liked a little too much.

Or would have, if the man would say more than two or three monosyllabic words to her at a time.

She had to give him some grudging credit. Gabriel was as stubborn as she was, and among her family she had been the gold standard for intractability. But any pleasure she'd gotten out of the tension in their current situation had worn off days ago. She was tired of lying around in borrowed and extremely ill-fitting clothes, wiping at the occasional dirty dish and waiting for Gabriel to show up so she could eat and watch him scowl for a few minutes. She was tired of worrying and wondering what Bastian was getting up to back at home, feeling as though the other shoe dropping was always just around the corner. If she'd had money, she might have tried to distract herself for a bit and redecorated the place in silks and pillows like her tent back in the *Carith Noor* since she was stuck in it all the time. The look on Gabriel's face alone would have been worth the expense.

Instead, her only option for artfully posed lounging was on the bed she'd burned a massive hole in when she'd attempted to cleanse it of blood.

Gabriel had graciously offered her the bedroom for herself after that, which would have been slightly more of a triumph if it would stop smelling like a fire sale in there.

"Damn you, Wolf," she muttered, wandering into the bedroom to glare at herself in the mirror. She looked like the Drak's own wrath, that was the truth. Rowan wound her fingers in her hair and tugged irritably, growling at her wan reflection. Never had she taken so little care of herself, slouching around in the same shapeless clothing day after day, only occasionally bothering to brush her hair. It was all Gabriel's fault, of course.

But it had even gotten tiresome to sit around blaming him.

If only he hadn't called her his mate. She didn't truly hold him responsible for the fight itself … they'd both been spoiling for one, and in her opinion, a good fight now and then was a balm to the soul. But if only he hadn't given voice to the thing she had felt, the thing she had both known and railed against since she had foolishly shared that magical, singular bite along with her body.

If only it wasn't permanent.

I don't want you, she'd told him.

Yeah you do. Deal with it, he'd replied.

And though she had no intention of telling him, he was right. And she was trying. But oh, it was unpleasant.

The front door slammed, a welcome distraction from a train of thought that had become all too familiar these past few days. *Gabriel this, Gabriel that, what to do, what to do.* She was a sitting duck here, waiting for life to happen to her instead of making her life happen, a situation she had always abhorred, and yet her head was full of her grumpy live-in werewolf. She wished, not for the first time, that the stories of the *arukhin* had been a little more detailed about that tribe's personality traits. It would have been an excellent reference point right about now.

Rowan smoothed her fingers through her long, red waves, cursing herself even as she tried to make the best of what was becoming an increasingly dire beautification situation. It wasn't as though she should care. And it certainly wasn't as though Gabriel seemed to care any longer, she told herself, ignoring the nasty little twist in her gut as she thought it.

Except that might not be entirely true. He might just be waiting for her to grovel a little. But that, Rowan thought, was never going to happen. She had meant what she said. And if Gabriel refused to listen, then their relationship, such as it was, would remain as it was now. She had not been raised to sit by idly and let men make her decisions for her. But perhaps in the end it was better this way. Maybe he was wrong, and leaving things unpleasant between them would tear that piece of him away from her soul, would leave her free to face what remained of her future with one less worry. One less shred of guilt.

Then Gabriel sauntered in, big and unshaven and so deliciously vital, and Rowan felt everything inside of her rise up in yearning for him. She kept her expression outwardly cool, barely acknowledging him with a look, but inwardly everything was turmoil. Her shaking hand, seeking something to do, tucked itself behind her back to toy with the bottom band of the sweatshirt.

Every time he was near her she longed for him so completely that it threatened to consume her whole. And it seemed to be getting worse.

Rowan pushed her hair back over her shoulders, nearly giving in to the urge to play her fingers over the mark his teeth had made on her neck. It hadn't yet healed, even though all Drakkyn were remarkably fast healers. Neither had Gabriel's. Not that she was looking or anything. Not that seeing her mark upon him made her feel the least bit possessive.

Rowan pushed the thoughts away. Instead, she girded herself for yet another tiny skirmish in their seemingly stalemated battle.

Gabriel looked at her with the guarded expression she'd rapidly come to loathe as he hooked his thumbs in his jeans pockets, stance completely casual. The stubble dusted over his cheeks and chin looked rough and dark, giving him a half-wild look that she rather liked despite herself. His deep brown hair grazed his cheekbones, practically begging her to brush it out of his face.

Rowan tucked her other hand behind her back, clasping them, digging her nails into her palms hard enough to hurt. If Gabriel noticed, he gave no hint. And when he spoke, it was with a bland, disinterested politeness that made her want to rip him to shreds. That, or crawl all over the chest that was currently so well showcased in a faded, fitted T-shirt until she got some sort of reaction. The kind she might soon have to admit to wanting after all.

"Brought you some fish and chips," he said, jerking his thumb back in the direction of the kitchen. "It's on the table."

"Thanks," she replied, just as polite, though inwardly she seethed. The fare at Wolf at the Door was delicious, she had to concede, but woefully limited. If she had to eat one more fried thing, she was going on a hunger strike. Fruit, fresh vegetables ... she'd scoured Gabriel's cupboards for any scrap of the sorts of things she preferred, but all she'd come up with was freezer-burned instant meals, several stale bags of potato chips, and a real-life can of Spam. She was afraid to open it and see what processed meat actually looked like. As far as she was concerned, enough innocent animals had been sacrificed in this place. Though it did give her pleasure to remember that Gabriel qualified as an animal, and was not at all innocent, should he really make her angry again.

Gabriel looked at her a moment longer, his head cocked in the way he had when he was thinking deeply about something. Hope rose in her that he might be about to end this ridiculous standoff. But in the end he simply gave a soft sigh, a barely perceptible shake of his head, and turned to go.

"Well. I've got to get back. Getting busy down there, and one of the barmaids never showed, so we're short-handed. Need anything else?"

"Yes," she blurted before she could stop herself. Gabriel turned back, his brows arched in curiosity. This non-conversation, in all its lack of nuance and variation, had become their little routine. She'd just broken the pattern. No one was more curious to see exactly how far she'd run with it than her, though. Because in truth, she didn't have a single clue why she'd said it.

All Rowan knew was, she'd had about enough of seeing the backside of Gabriel MacInnes. No matter how cute it was.

They stood staring at each other for tense seconds as Rowan wracked her brain for something semi-intelligent to need. Gabriel, she noted, had at least lost a little of the studied disinterest in his expression. Though Rowan wished he didn't look suspiciously amused, since it was definitely at her expense.

"Well?" he finally prodded her.

"Clothes," she said. It was the first thing that had come into her mind … well, almost … but once the word was spoken she discovered it was true. She was sick to death of looking wretched, feeling miserable. The Dyadd took meticulous care of themselves, and so had she for most of her life. Beautifying the outside now would at least make her feel more like herself, and would hopefully bring back some of the surety with which she had always steered her own life. Maybe she could find a salon as well, Rowan thought with a welcome spark of excitement. It would be lovely to be pampered again.

If Gabriel was inclined to oblige her. And that, judging by the pained expression on his face, was by no means certain.

"Clothes?" he repeated, as though he didn't actually want the definition of that word to register. Rowan put her hands on her hips, ready to fight for this. Her instincts were true. A shopping trip was just what she needed. And damn it, after spending a week in this dingy apartment wearing men's sweats, she was going to get it.

"I came to *Iargail* with nothing. Over a week later, what I have acquired," she continued, sweeping her hand down her well-worn ensemble with her nose wrinkled, "amounts to possibly less than that. You get to go out. I've been good about it, but I don't. I need some air, Gabriel."

"Clothes?" he asked again, sounding doubtful. Rowan just barely restrained herself from smacking him, but she almost lost it when he examined her outfit as though he couldn't quite understand what was wrong with it. Half of the man's closet was probably ten years old, she reminded herself, and he seemed to think that his collection of bowling shirts amounted to dress wear.

He was hopeless. That didn't mean she had to be.

"You know this place," she said, trying for patience in her tone. "Pick a spot if you don't want to come with me, then give me a time and pick me up."

He shook his head. "Not alone. It's a bad idea."

Rowan gritted her teeth. "I need to get out of this damned apartment. I could just go anyway, but I'm trying to be diplomatic about this so you don't freak out." *And also so I don't have to rob a bank to get some new shoes,* she silently added.

"I never freak out," he grumbled, hunching up his shoulders and scowling like a petulant five-year-old. It was, Rowan supposed, the ugly flipside of his often childlike enthusiasm. Being just plain childish.

"Well, whatever," Rowan said with an impatient wave of her hand. She didn't want to waste any more time arguing. The prospect of a little bit of freedom after all of this claustrophobia had her itching to just run out the door. "Come on, Gabriel. You have your pub. I have a general wearing a tutu." She pointed at the television so he could get the whole visual. The sudden curve of his lips and twinkle in his eyes was a decidedly unwelcome distraction, since her mind jumped quickly from putting new clothes on to just plain taking off the ones she had on.

Since that wasn't going to do either of them any good at this point, Rowan forced herself to look away. She hadn't forgiven him for not understanding her. For expecting her to accept him and his decisions unconditionally, when there was so much standing in the way of that just to begin with.

Of course, she thought uncomfortably, she hadn't exactly been forthcoming about where Bastian was, or the bargain Lucien wanted to strike for his safety. The bargain she was all but certain she was going to take, unless a chance to destroy him presented itself first. But she'd decided right away that telling Gabriel and the rest of his Pack would just complicate everything, endanger everyone instead of just her. Of that she was still certain. Even if she was less so about her feelings on the matter.

Gabriel was watching her quietly, and she could tell he was mulling it over. Finally he sighed, and she knew she'd won. It was all she could do not to launch into a victory dance right there, but somehow she didn't think that would go over very well.

"All right," he said, though it obviously pained him. "I suppose you have been cooped up. But there's enough right on Main Street to keep you occupied, so stay close. And I'm giving you my cell so I can check in every hour, all right?" He must have seen her annoyance at that, because he rushed on with, "I mean, I wouldn't want to lose you. Or anything. Um. You never know who might follow you, and …"

He kept talking, though Rowan quit listening. He was rubbing the back of his neck the way he always did when he was embarrassed or agitated, and it was distractingly sexy. It also told her that Gabriel had ceased to make any intelligible sense whatsoever, so it was safe to tune out. She wanted to tell him that no, it was not really all right to call her every hour, since she was a grown woman who hadn't required the services of a nursemaid for some time. But the flood of relief she'd felt at his answer, not to mention the bit about not wanting to lose her, kept her tongue in check. She still didn't know what to do with it, but she couldn't bring herself to be the least bit snide about it.

"Done," she said, and realized that this was the most they'd spoken since the fight. Gabriel nodded curtly, and she could tell he was thinking the same. He put out his hand for a formal shake, raising his eyebrows with a slight smirk that Rowan found ridiculously adorable.

They were back on some sort of terms, it seemed. Probably not terms that were going to make her unlock the bedroom door at night (whether that was for keeping him out or herself in was something she had refused thus far to think about), but terms nonetheless. After a second, she slid her hand into his, ignoring the sensory jolt of his skin against hers as she shook firmly. Not perfect, she decided. But a truce was better than nothing.

And new shoes were better than absolutely everything. Well, almost.

He'd given her his credit card, God help him.

Gabriel handed a pint to Rich, one of the regulars, and brooded over the woman Gideon had jokingly called the Red Plague. Around him, Wolf at the Door hummed with life. It had been a busy Saturday so far, between the comings and goings of the usual suspects and the wandering tourists. The sort of day that normally would have thrilled him, since it was full of both money and good company. He enjoyed his job, his customers, the ebb and flow of conversation that was all part of the rhythm of the pub. He also normally would have enjoyed the tall, curvy brunette eyeing him from her stool at the end of the bar, surrounded by a laughing, chattering circle of her equally attractive friends.

Not today, though.

Today all he could think about was the woman he'd decided he needed to ignore for his own good, at least until she figured out they were made for eah other. He'd thought it would take a day or two, tops.

Nearly a week later, he would swear that the sexual frustration alone was killing off brain cells at an alarming rate. Why else would he have put his credit rating on the line just to see her smile? He wasn't stupid. He'd been worrying over the depression Rowan had seemed to be sinking into, trying to figure out how to help without putting one or both of them at risk.

So much for that.

And the pub was definitely being watched. But until someone made a move, he would wait. He wasn't afraid of vampires, not by a long shot. And so far, that was all he'd sensed. It was just lucky that humans couldn't smell the bastards, Gabriel thought disgustedly, running a towel over a spill on the bar. This place would be empty. And he would have to head down to that nasty little dive they frequented while in town to extract his lost earnings in ill-gotten blood.

His partner, Jerry, a short tank of a man whom Gabriel respected for his keen business sense and gregarious nature as much as for his skilled fists, eyed him speculatively.

"Not female trouble again, is it?" he finally asked when Gabriel just ignored him.

"Isn't it always?" Gabriel returned, glaring at the soggy rag before tossing it into a bucket beneath the counter.

Jerry simply gave one of his booming laughs and slapped Gabriel on the shoulder. "One of these days, Gabe, you're going to get as good as you've given in that department. And God help you then, because it may well kill you!"

Gabriel gave a wan smile. He enjoyed Jerry, but he was in no mood to tell him that it was too late; it had already happened, and sure enough, his life was in danger. He shot a quick glance at his watch. 6:30. She'd been gone two damned hours, and was nowhere in sight. He'd given her a pretty generous "safe area," not that he was at all sure she'd stay in it. Still, Tobermory wasn't exactly huge, and she wouldn't go in *every single place*. At least he hoped not.

Once more he thought of his poor credit card, and cringed.

Heaving a flustered sigh, he picked up the phone he kept behind the bar and punched in his own cell number for the second time that day. He felt a bit stupid, truth be told. But he also was going to feel infinitely better when he heard her voice, so he was doing just what he'd warned. Every hour, he'd said. And it was just time again.

The phone rang once, twice, three times. Gabriel was just starting to feel uneasy when Rowan picked up, a cacophony of female voices speaking all at once in the background.

"This phone is going into one of your orifices once I get back," her smoky voice offered by way of a hello. It was a testament to his worry for her that the phrase was music to his ears.

"You agreed to this," he reminded her, mood light-ening already. He was a sick, sick man.

"I'm also busy, and I … oh wait a sec, Gabriel." She covered the mouthpiece with her hand while she spoke rapidly to someone else. He could just make out the words "layers" and "fringe," which was enough to strike a cold sliver of fear into his heart.

"Please tell me you're not at the salon," he said, knowing that the one nearest the pub was decidedly high-end and also contained a spa. "Even if you're lying, just tell me you're not."

Her laughter was warm, and decidedly evil. "Okay. I'm not. Happy?"

"Not especially. What else haven't you been up to?"

"Well, let's see. I didn't buy four new outfits, three pairs of shoes, and the appropriate undergarments. Nor did I make appointments to get my hair, nails, and toes done. In fact, I've just been sitting on a bench down the street, humming to myself and drooling."

He chuckled, though he was fairly certain he could hear his wallet crying in his back pocket. "Nothing suspicious to report?"

"Yes, actually. Your nasty old sweats ran off all by them-selves when I tried to throw them away. But if you mean strange men stalking me, you'll be glad to know you're it."

"Ha." Gabriel relaxed against the bar, enjoying spar-ring with her after the silent torment of the past few days. He'd been madder than hell to begin with. But as it had worn on, he'd done some thinking about the things she'd said, the accusations she'd hurled at him. And eventually he'd come to the conclusion that maybe, possibly, she was right. Or at least not entirely wrong. Maybe he *was* being heavy-handed in the name of keeping her safe. Some of it he could blame on his instincts, he supposed. She was his mate. It was natural he'd want to protect her. Some … well, some of it was just him. He'd been so determined to prove himself, not just to her but to everyone, *including* himself. It just hadn't occurred to him before her tirade that he might need to tone it down a bit.

It had been, ultimately, the reason he'd sent her off today. It had been a trying couple of weeks for both of them. Some space was probably needed on both sides. Rowan seemed to be enjoying it, in any case.

He wished he could say the same. But if she came back the way she sounded on the phone, it was well worth it. He'd take the annoying ambiguity of their romantic relationship to tense silence any day.

"Well, Gabriel, much as I'd love to continue this stimulating conversation, I have to go get shampooed now. And quit calling, I'm not going to be able to hear the ringer anyway."

"Oh, I'm sure you will eventually," he grinned. "I'll just keep trying."

"Yes, I know you'll keep *being* trying, anyway. Goodbye, Gabriel."

"Have fun, Rowan. As inexpensively as possible."

There was a wicked chuckle, and Rowan hung up without offering a real answer. Still, Gabriel found he was smiling as he hung up the phone. Finally he'd done something to make the woman happy. Granted, it required some pain on his part, but Rowan had sounded so relaxed and in her element that it was hard to complain. Well, not until the bill came in, anyway.

He was a sorry case, Gabriel decided. But he needed her, to the point where if one more night passed with the locked door between them, he thought he might wind up begging at it like a stray dog. He wanted her smiles, her laughter, her continuous stream of insults. And he wanted to make her burn again, burn only for him.

He'd spoken to Malcolm just this morning. Both the Stone and the woods had been ominously silent since the night Lucien had made contact, but there were about thirty extra Pack prowling the grounds now, with more expected today. Duncan had somehow managed to stuff most of them into the main house and cottages, with the rest camping out in tents in the gardens. It sounded like they were having two gatherings this summer, Gabriel thought, wishing he were there for round two. From the disapproval he'd heard in Mal's voice, he was sure it was shaping up to be just as much fun as the first. He wished he could show Rowan off to his cousins, who were sure to love her, sarcasm being a highly prized trait in prospective family members.

The two of them would head back soon. And if, as Gabriel suspected, Rowan's presence was the draw for the vampires, he wanted his Pack with him when they finally revealed themselves. Then there was the matter of her brother. Bastian, when he returned, *if* he returned, would come to *Iargail*. Except Gabriel was beginning to wonder whether Rowan's brother, strong though he'd seemed, had been waylaid somehow. What state he would return in for his sister, if at all. And how, if he did come back, Gabriel was going to tell him all he needed to.

"Hello, darling! I had no idea you were back!" cried a high, feminine voice, jolting Gabriel from his thoughts and switching his worries smoothly from one track to another. Gabriel cringed before looking up with his usual welcoming smile. He'd left a few loose ends lying about when he'd gone home for the annual gathering, thinking he'd leave them until he came back or until they simply tied themselves back up.

But Mary Ross, who was currently angling to plant a juicy lipsticked kiss on his mouth, probably couldn't tie her own shoes. And as the door opened again, followed by yet another female gasp of excitement, Gabriel realized that he was in trouble. Deep, deep trouble, he thought as three more beauties with sweet smiles and murder in their eyes practically climbed over one another to get to him. He was going to have to find a way to convince everyone that he was finally, officially taken, and fast.

Otherwise, there was a distinct possibility of his going down in flames tonight. Literally.

Chapter 12

THE FIRST TIME SHE DIDN'T THINK MUCH OF IT.

The second and third times were kind of annoying, but she was busy enough to not let it bother her too much.

By the tenth time she answered Gabriel's cell phone to find yet another woman looking for him on the other end, however, Rowan had had enough.

Rowan paused outside of the chocolate shop, pulling the small black phone from one of her shopping bags and glaring at it before flipping it open and answering with a clipped "Yes?"

She'd talked to Gabriel not too long ago, and would have bet all of the truly fabulous chocolates in her bag that this wasn't him.

She was right.

"Umm," murmured a breathy female voice, "is Gabriel there?" There was a soft giggle after the question, and Rowan felt her grip tighten as she tried to restrain herself from hurling the phone beneath the tires of the nearest passing car.

"No," Rowan replied, keeping her voice artificially sweet. "He's in the shower right now, actually. I'll be joining him in a minute, so I guess I could give him a message if you really want."

"Oh." The giggler's voice had gone from breathy to brittle in the blink of an eye. Rowan smiled with true pleasure. She'd unwittingly given Gabriel's whereabouts to enough of these creatures today. It had gotten to be a lot more enjoyable once she got creative with her replies. In the last twenty minutes, Gabriel had been cooking her breakfast in bed, giving her a foot massage, out buying her jewelry, and now, awaiting her in the shower. The reactions had varied from poutiness to fury, and she'd savored every last one of them.

"I, um, guess not. Who is this?" There was no coy laughter left in the woman's voice, which was a relief.

She didn't know what made her do it, but the words were out before she considered. "His fiancée, of course. Listen, is this about the wedding invitations? We do seem to have missed a few people accidentally, but if you want to leave me your address, I can always send one along. It's been such a whirlwind engagement," she confided, hoping she sounded just the right amount of giddily-in-love.

There was a soft choking noise on the other end of the line, then a muffled sob right before the unmistakable *click* of the connection being broken. Rowan gave the silent phone a smug smile, closed it, and then rewarded herself with a chocolate caramel before continuing down the street toward the pub. Nothing like the satisfaction of staking your claim on a man and driving away the competitors, she decided. Though the pleasure she felt was clouded by the undeniable fact that she would have been even more pleased with herself if all of the things she'd said were true.

Well, *most*. Whether or not that included the "fiancée" thing was something she was just not going to think about right now, lest it spoil the soothing effects of the chocolate, which were just beginning to kick in.

She frowned and picked up her pace, troubled. Her day out, not to mention the barrage of calls from Gabriel's ex-conquests, had really helped to clarify some things for her. It had also helped to get her out of those grubby old sweats, for which she was eternally grateful. But doing what she could to return herself to her usual pampered state, from the flattering movement of the long choppy layers of her new haircut, to the floaty fabric of her new sundress, even down to the delicate low-heeled sandals that laced up her ankles, had only served to show her that the only person she wanted to admire her beauty was Gabriel. That she wanted, in fact, to knock him on his ass with awe and then drag him upstairs to have her way with him. Many, many times.

That there was no particular reason why she couldn't do just that only served to complicate her feelings on the subject. Because after all that had happened, after a week of locking him out of the bedroom, if she just hauled off and ravished Gabriel, he was going to know that she couldn't help herself where he was concerned after all. That she might actually care.

That she might actually …

Oh no. Uh-uh, not going there. Rowan huffed out a breath, blowing the newly cut fringe out of her face, and popped another chocolate-covered caramel. Life had been so much easier when she hadn't been this *involved.* When the excitement of taking a lover for the evening had been only that, holding no deeper meaning. Nothing but the taking of blood had ever felt particularly important back then, though the occasional squabble over a particularly handsome male had amused her. Especially, Rowan thought with a smile at the memory, since she always won. Gabriel, though … he was different, on so many levels. She wasn't concerned about the bevy of fluttering women who were probably, right this moment, tossing themselves at him (though the fact that she'd given up his location to a few of them rankled a little, she had to admit). She was more concerned about how quickly the two of them had returned to the sort of sarcastic, intimate banter that had evaporated after they'd fought. And how natural it felt to speak of him, to think of him, as hers.

She shoved the nagging feeling that she was on the verge of making some decision of monumental importance (whether she liked it or not) aside and tried to focus on the fact that she was rapidly approaching Wolf at the Door, which no amount of chocolate, no matter how delicious, was going to prevent. Her heartbeat picked up despite herself as she saw the bright façade, heard the faint strains of music tumble from the door as patrons wandered in and out.

Rowan paused in front of a small travel agency, giving herself a final once-over in the glass of the windows. Not at all bad, she decided, running fingernails that had been painted a deep rust color through her hair and turning this way and that, smiling over how well the gauzy material of the thin-strapped dress skimmed down her waist, only to drop in asymmetrical layers to mid-calf. It wasn't quite the glittering raiment of her past, but the jade green matched her eyes exactly, and she couldn't help but think of how well the fabric would move if she decided to dance in it. Alone, perhaps. For an appreciative audience of one.

Rowan's eyes glazed as she let her mind wander, so she barely registered the sight of a burly Scotsman who was so busy staring at her that he stumbled into the bumper of a parked car. Up ahead a ways, a trio of over-done blondes flounced into the pub. Her sensitive ears picked up the distinct sound of one of them fairly sighing the word "Gabriel."

It was a voice she recognized from one of her many abbreviated phone conversations from earlier. And as she'd expected, it looked as though her erstwhile protector was being ambushed. Rowan's brows drew together, eyes narrowing as she stopped, considering. Her plans for the rest of the day had originally encompassed nothing more than heading back to the apartment, dropping her bags off, and stopping into the pub to show off a little. Oh, who was she kidding. She'd planned to drive Gabriel crazy with lust and then lure him away from work in what she'd almost managed to convince herself was a perfectly normal way of thanking him for the afternoon of shopping. Kind of stupid, but it had been working well enough for her.

Now, though, it appeared that she had more of a rescue mission on her hands. That didn't preclude the "showing off" part of the program. And actually, making a spectacle of herself again after all this time was an incredibly appealing thought, with the added side benefit of laying waste to some of Gabriel's bimbo groupies. But that still brought her back to the issue of Gabriel finding out exactly how much he had begun to mean to her. Not to mention having to take a good, hard look at what all of these intense and often irritating feelings of hers really meant.

Rowan hissed out a breath, tapping a finger on her hip.

"All I wanted to do was go shopping, damn it," she muttered. She wished she knew what she was walking into so that she could figure out how best to approach the situation. Or, she thought with a flash of temper, how best to annihilate a bunch of trespassing, bubble-headed females. Barely realizing she was doing it, she reached out to Gabriel with her mind, and was rewarded almost immediately with a shocking little sizzle of connection. It was much like the one they'd formed the first time they'd made love, though instead of memory, she felt Gabriel in the present. Part of her thrilled at her newfound ability. Part of her recoiled at what it must mean.

All of her agreed that she should have known better. Instantly, her nostrils were filled with the earthy, woodsy scent of him, provoking a wave of longing that she was completely helpless to protect herself against. It made her want to be instantly close to him, against him. Rowan's eyes fluttered shut as she tried to concentrate and glean something useful from this strange new connection she'd forged. Slowly, she began to make out the other, underlying smell of smoke, the chatter of many voices, the pulsing beat of music. Then a woman's voice spoke, and Gabriel's discomfort rippled through her so strongly that the tiny hairs on the back of her neck stood up.

"You can't be serious, Gabriel. Everyone knows you're not the marrying kind. Though you are *my* kind … which I don't think you could have forgotten."

"Lori, I'm taken. I've found my match. What about that is so hard to understand?" He sounded slightly desperate, which told Rowan he'd been making this argument to one person or another for some time now. At Lori's reply, she could understand why he sounded as he did.

"Oh, stop teasing, Gabriel. Whoever this new fascination is, she's not here, so she doesn't count. I know how it works with you. And I want to dance before that little bitch Moira Douglas gets over here … look, here she comes. And is that Marisa Maclaren? What's *she* doing looking over here?"

Gabriel's rising panic was a sick twist in Rowan's gut. "Good Christ, woman, just … fine. *Fine.* Come on. I don't want to be in the middle of a catfight, but I'm warning you, Lori, dancing is *all* we're doing."

"Sure, sexy." The voice now held a gloating note that had Rowan's claws lengthening. "Whatever you say. I'm all yours."

Rowan's eyes snapped open, and the connection to Gabriel was instantly broken. Her rising fury probably hadn't helped that any, she supposed. But she'd heard and felt all she'd needed to. She knew, well and truly, that Gabriel wasn't interested in what any of these circling sharks had to offer him. It sounded, in fact, like he'd been telling as many tall tales about her as she had about him today. It would have been funny if he hadn't been under such blatant attack.

Instead she found herself possessed of a steely resolve, stronger than it had ever been in the days when vying for the attention of a handsome man had been sport and competition. Gabriel MacInnes was *hers*, damn it. No Orinn woman would ever have dared trespass on the chosen of a Dyim, recognizing the danger to life and limb if she should even try. Apparently these human women were going to have to be taught the same lesson.

Rowan tossed her head, threw back her shoulders, and reached within to the brightly glowing flame at her center. Instantly her ire calmed, and she felt the fire suffuse her with the old assurance, knew it lit her form so that she glowed more brightly than any human woman could ever dream. She felt primal, her beauty and desire both amplified and impossible to ignore. She breathed deeply, then started forward again, less a walk than a prowl. Inside her bag, Gabriel's cell phone jangled into life once again, slicing into her thoughts like a buzz saw. This time she didn't even break her stride, just grabbed it and threw it, with deadly accuracy, into the road. Moments later it fell silent with a satisfying *crunch*. Rowan's lips curved with pleasure. She felt her incisors lengthening in anticipation.

A bookish-looking middle-aged man was walking in the opposite direction, but at the sight of Rowan seemed to lose all sense of where he was going and plowed into a garbage can. Another tripped over his own feet as she passed and went sprawling onto the pavement. She barely noticed, focusing only on the task at hand. It felt amazing to cruise on the old power again, to feel sure about something. And despite all her worries, all the potential pitfalls and problems, there was no denying it: she wanted Gabriel MacInnes all to herself.

And she was going to take a great deal of pleasure in making that abundantly clear. No one dared touch the desired of the Dyadd Morgaine.

Rowan grinned as the door flew open before her without so much as a touch. She'd always been good at making a spectacle of herself, just as she'd been a master at kicking ass when ass-kickings were due. Tonight, with Morgaine's blessings, she'd get to do a little of both.

She stepped into the pub and surveyed her domain.

The goddess, Rowan decided, was back.

Gabriel was completely trapped, hemmed in on all sides by a bunch of sweetly smiling beauties. They fawned over him. They discreetly shoved one another out of the way in the constant battle to be his next dance partner. He'd thought it might be better on the small dance floor, easier to take on his determined adversaries one at a time. But if he heard one more time how *adorable* he was, how they'd *missed* him so on his too-long vacation, the Change would happen here and now, and he'd have to make a run for it, breaking through the glass if necessary.

He finally told his current partner outright that he was getting married. Lot of good that had done.

"Oh, Gabe, you're *sooooo* funny! You're never taken for long." A pair of big hazel eyes blinked up at him. "Can I be the woman of your dreams next?"

He bit back a grimace as Marisa Maclaren leaned into him for the umpteenth time, giggling, and wanted to die. Had he ever actually enjoyed this? He didn't remember ever feeling that his female fan club was quite this vapid and inane, but then again, he had spent less time listening and more time deliberating over who was going to be his latest flavor of the month. And, of course, how long it was going to take him to get her upstairs.

Gabriel glanced at the door for the millionth time that night. The light outside was fading fast, and there was still no sign of Rowan. It had been almost an hour since he'd managed to peel himself away for long enough to call her, and then she'd indicated she was nearly done.

Maybe she'd been tired and gone up to bed, he thought.

Or maybe she'd poked her head in, seen this debacle, and was currently burning everything in his closet. That some of the closet's contents probably ought to be burned was beside the point. They'd finally had a thaw in their little cold war, and here he was blowing it all to hell because he had too many manners to flatten women just to get away from them, which was looking more and more like the only way to extract himself … and to escape from the undulating Marisa, who had already tried to crawl up his leg a few dozen times.

He closed his eyes. So this is what it felt like to be mated. You got to realize exactly what an ass you used to be, then figure out how to fix it so that your mate wouldn't kill you at some point in the future. He thought of Carly and her running war with Gideon over the hamper, and smiled wistfully. If only laundry were his biggest issue. He didn't know why or how God had seen fit to curse him with so many of his ex-girlfriends all at once, but instead of enjoying the promise of a warming in his relations with Rowan, he felt as though he was spending a night in hell. That the beer was incredibly good was, for once, doing nothing to change that perception.

Lori, he saw, was eyeing him again and staring daggers at Marisa, a petite brunette with considerable assets, none of which were located in her head. She was already edging closer, circling with the others like a bunch of sharks as the song ended and another began. And as his rotten luck would have it, this one was a heavy, mid-tempo rock number with a driving beat that lent itself well to lots of grinding.

He was going to have to make a run for it.

He had just begun to back away from the group of women that were as ferocious and intimidating as his own Pack in this element when the door to the pub flew open so quickly, and with such force, that it nearly blew off its hinges. Gabriel stopped dead, along with every other soul in the pub, as a vision unlike anything he'd ever seen came striding in as though she owned the place.

It was Rowan. That much registered in his fuzzy brain, if only dimly. But this was a Rowan he had never encountered. It was as though all the vestiges of being an Earth woman had been stripped away, leaving only the ruling Dyim of another realm in all her otherworldly glory.

And oh, but she was glorious. She had gone from wearing his sweats to some flowing green dress that coiled and uncoiled around her legs as she moved, suggesting length and shape and form, even exposed and creamy skin, while revealing little. Her shoulders were wonderfully bare, and whatever she'd done to her hair showed off her exquisite face even more effectively than before. That outrageous hair was fire in the dim light, as though it had retained a few of the rays of the sun.

This, Gabriel realized as all of his functioning circuits went up at once, was what Rowan was, what she might be again. A goddess who walked among men.

And she was headed straight for him.

Gabriel automatically opened his senses to her, all of him craving her as he watched her approach. *Rowan,* he thought dazedly. *My mate.*

It was painful at first. His senses were really too acute to do anything but hurt him in the pub, which was why he normally made an effort to dampen them. Turning the acuity on and off was something most Wolves learned young, and he was no exception. But it was always a shock to the system when you turned them on in a place like this, full of movement and noise and scent.

Then, all at once, his senses cleared. Where there had been smoke and noise and the cloying, nauseating sweetness of too many intermingled perfumes, there was only Rowan. His nostrils filled with her intoxicating autumn scent—leaves and smoke, candles and spice. Warmth flooded him, as well as a fierce need to be with her. Now.

Abruptly, Rowan stopped. Placing one hand on her hip, she lifted her chin and surveyed the area around him, eyes touching briefly and disdainfully on each of the women who'd been vying for his attention this evening. Gabriel felt a smile tugging at his lips, humor breaking through his awe. He didn't know how she knew who his exes were, but she sure as hell did. And the way she was dismissing them without a word, looking for all the world like some glorious warrior queen, warmed his heart. She was saving his ass, and he didn't mind a bit. All he wanted to do was shout to the rafters that she was his.

Rowan, it appeared, had her own ideas about displaying her affection. After giving Marisa a look that by rights should have caused her to drop dead on the spot, she turned her green gaze to him. It turned from subzero to scalding in less than a second, and Gabriel felt his blood rising in response. *Come to me, then,* he thought. *Come and get me.* He couldn't think of anything he wanted more. But Rowan, obstinate creature that she was, arched an eyebrow as though she'd heard him, and then crooked a finger at him.

She couldn't have been any clearer if she'd spoken. *No,* you *come to* me. Gabriel frowned. Rowan smiled, a slow, sexy curve of her lips that immediately had a half dozen indecent and possibly illegal fantasies about her running through his mind. Which was, he knew, exactly what she'd intended. But though he tried to muster a little indignation over being pushed into the position of the claimed instead of being the claimer, as he had always done, it was completely impossible. Because she wanted him. And he needed her so badly that in that moment he knew he would have crawled to her if she'd commanded it. Now he knew how it must have felt to be a villager singled out to worship a daughter of the Goddess.

But this was infinitely better. Because he knew that for Rowan to stake her claim upon him, she had to have decided she didn't want to let him go. And after this there was no way in hell he was going to let her.

Beside him, Marisa's voice sliced sharply into his thoughts, making him wince.

"Well who the hell does she think *she* is? Queen of the fucking universe?"

He looked down at her, at the ugly expression on a face he had once thought attractive, and gave her a pitying smile.

"Exactly. It's just one of the many reasons I love her."

It felt good to finally say the words out loud, he thought. Good to finally give voice to the intense feeling he'd been carrying around with him since Rowan had landed in his arms. Marisa's mouth dropped open so far he wondered whether it would hit the floor. Then he refocused on Rowan, and Marisa simply ceased to exist for him.

The band, a popular outfit out of Leeds who favored the sort of piano-driven electro-rock that Gabriel himself did, chose that moment to dig into their next song with a vengeance. It was dark, sensual music, especially with the added dimension of his heightened senses as he listened. And as the song wove its dark spell, he went to her, feeling as though there was no one in the crowded room but the two of them. It wouldn't have surprised him if his feet had only scraped across the ground as he was drawn inexorably toward Rowan, so strongly was he pulled. All around him, couples moved with one another, melting into each other to the beat of the song. Rowan waited for him, swaying gently, her eyes locked with his.

Then his arms were around her, his hands linked with hers as she melted into him, and Gabriel knew that whatever heaven might end up being, it would never hold a candle to this.

"I must say," he breathed against her ear, enjoying the way she shivered, "you know how to make an entrance."

"I got what I wanted, didn't I?" she asked, her voice huskier than usual. She wound her arms around his neck, pressing even more closely against him. Gabriel's thoughts scattered at the slow, subtle movements of her hips to the beat. It was a full minute before he could collect them enough to form a coherent sentence to answer her with.

"And what do you want, Rowan?" he finally asked, part of him dreading what she might say, but needing the answer nonetheless. His heart lifted instantly, however, when she drew back just enough to look up at him with an expression that clearly said "duh."

"I don't waste my best entrances on just anyone, you know. Now come on, genius. Everyone's watching us anyway." Her grin was wicked. "Dance with me."

Before he could insist that dancing wasn't really his thing beyond the usual bob and sway, she was off. Gabriel stood stock still, watching in speechless fascination as Rowan spun effortlessly across the floor, her body moving with a long-limbed and effortless grace that seemed to belong only to true dancers. She looked absolutely amazing, Gabriel thought foggily as his eyes tracked her.

Rowan's hair rippled and shifted in the lights like a live flame, flowing behind her as she dipped and spun, arched and turned. It was like watching music-made flesh, Gabriel thought. Tonight it was easy to picture her under some alien sky, being worshipped beneath the moon and stars to wild and ancient music. He might have worried that he looked like a complete idiot next to such perfection, but somehow she managed to draw him into her dance seamlessly, guiding him with her hands and body, making him her partner without taxing his limited dancing ability. As the crowd cleared a space for them, cheering the two of them on, Gabriel knew that for once he was utterly secondary, serving only to showcase his exquisite partner.

It was fine with him. All he wanted to do was watch her too.

As the final chord of the song reverberated throughout the pub, Rowan spun into him one last time. Gabriel caught her against him, his mouth a breath away from hers. He could feel her heart pound against him as he held her, and was glad he wasn't the only one so affected by the contact. As the hoots and hollers began, egging him on, he slowly grinned.

"Well?" she asked, so softly that only he could hear. "I did all the hard work. How about a decent finale?"

"With pleasure," he chuckled. This, at least, was something he'd been able to do since he'd been trying to impress (and get his hands all over) girls at his high school dances. He put his hand at the small of Rowan's back and dipped her low, his breath catching at the sight of the long, pale column of her throat as she arched back, her eyes shut in pure bliss.

His next act was born out of complete, possessive instinct. Gabriel pulled her up quickly and drew her against him, sliding his fingers up into the silken mass of her hair. He caught just a glimpse of Rowan's bemused expression before he claimed her mouth in a long, hot kiss that felt as though it burned right through him. Rowan's throaty purr told him she was more than pleased by his very public display as he took his time tasting her, reveling in the sweetness of her, enjoying the bold strokes of her tongue against his. When he finally drew back, only because he knew it was that or have her right there on the floor, Rowan's eyes were glazed with desire.

The crowd erupted at the spectacle, roaring their approval.

"Well," he said softly. "Now that you've caught me, your highness, what are you going to do with me? Because I think you've ruined my chances at getting another date for the evening."

Rowan laughed, a long, lusty roll of amusement, and looked over to where a disconsolate Lori was grabbing her purse before slamming out of the pub. "Hmm. How sad. I suppose I'll have to take you upstairs and have my way with you, then. It's only fair. Unless," she grinned, "you have to stay and work."

"Let me put it this way," he growled, a split second before bending to catch her behind her knees and hoisting her off the floor. Rowan yelped, then gave him a long-suffering look as he settled her in his arms and made a beeline for the door.

"This isn't quite the exit I had in mind."

"You can't set my ex-girlfriends on fire. It's frowned upon around here."

She wrinkled her nose at him even as she linked her fingers behind his neck. "At least then I would have maintained a little dignity."

Gabriel just snorted. "You're heavier than you look," he commented as people scrambled to get out of his way. Rowan smacked him smartly on the arm.

"My hero," she sighed, fluttering her eyelashes at him. "How do I ever keep my hands off of you, with your romance and flowery words?"

"I thought the sex was enough," he replied with a quick grin, nearly knocking over a group of drunken college students in his rush to get her the hell away from the crowd and upstairs alone with him.

He saw Jerry give him the thumbs-up and heard his raucous laughter just before he headed out the door. He was absolutely going to hear about this for ... well, probably forever. But he'd deal with that later. Right now he swung around the corner of the building and headed up the stairs to his apartment. Having no time for keys, Gabriel simply kicked the door open and marched on in.

"You've lost it," she informed him, sounding deeply amused. "Completely, absolutely, one hundred percent lost it. You may need professional help."

"Werewolves don't do therapy," he said, kicking the door as shut as it would consent to go behind him and depositing Rowan as gently as possible on the couch.

She shook her head slowly back and forth. "Werewolves don't ... you know, I can hear the *Sexual Healing* joke coming a mile away."

Gabriel grinned as he pounced on her. He loved this, the way Rowan gave him hell even when the scent of her arousal was driving him to a near frenzy. "Damn. That was all I had. So before I remove every stitch of your clothing with my teeth, I must know ..."

"Oh no you don't," she warned him, eyes narrowing. "This is brand-new, and I happen to like it."

"I like it too."

"Then don't eat it."

He pretended to consider, toying with the ends of her hair as she lay back, almost completely beneath him. "We'll see how quickly you can get it off. So anyway, how did you know what you were walking into?" He smiled at the memory. "I honestly thought there might be blood. And it wouldn't have been you trying to draw it."

She gave an elegant little shrug. "I might have received a few phone calls inquiring about your whereabouts. From people who didn't seem to care for the fact that an unidentified female was answering your phone."

Gabriel cringed. He hadn't even considered the possibility of that, which had been utterly moronic on his part. His only excuse was that giving her the phone at all had been a split-second decision, and after that he'd been too preoccupied with her general safety to worry about irritating phone calls. Still, he hated that it had happened.

She cocked her head at him, looking genuinely perplexed. "What's wrong?"

"I'm just surprised that you danced with me instead of tossing one of your fireballs at my head."

Rowan raised her eyebrows. "No more surprised than I was that some of those women showed up even after I told them I was about to get in the shower with you."

He laughed despite himself. "Count me surprised as well. Did you really say that?"

"Among other things. And since it was obvious that they were all suffering greatly from prolonged lack of contact with you, I didn't figure a fireball to your head was warranted. I did think you might need a little help. So I decided to, you know … check."

Gabriel shook his head in wonder. "That may be the understatement of the year. You were bloody amazing, as you well know." Just the memory had him reconsidering not tearing apart her new dress. Something she'd said had caught him, though, and it was only intense curiosity that gave him pause. "So what else did you say to put them off? On the phone, I mean?"

"I. Well, I …" She trailed off, frowning, which surprised him. After she'd gone to the trouble of winning him in front of the masses, he figured she'd want to gloat just a little. He hoped she wasn't having second thoughts about it, about taking the extra step and letting him know without a doubt that she wanted him to herself. Worry began to creep back into his thoughts, chipping away at his pleasure over how Rowan had come after him. He wanted, badly, for her to stop resisting what was between them, to set his mind at ease and accept their bond. But he knew from sorry experience that if he pushed too hard, she'd run the other way.

It was definitely some sort of cosmic punishment that he'd fallen for a woman as obstinate as himself.

Gabriel nuzzled her nose, trying to get her to look at him. "Rowan," he coaxed. For her part, Rowan kept her eyes averted, though her faint blush was telltale.

He leaned in, very, very close. So close that he could feel her warm breath fanning his face. And he whispered, ever so softly.

"Don't decide to be upset now. I'll let you blow up my cell phone, if you like."

"Hmm," was her only answer as she continued to be greatly perturbed by something on the other side of the room. Gabriel was a little surprised. He'd expected a snappy comeback, possibly even a slap upside the head, but not this pensive avoidance. Was she that embarrassed about what she'd said? Rowan didn't really seem the type to be embarrassed by anything. Intrigued, he pressed her further.

"Is there …" He angled his head down, trying to catch her eye with a soft smile. "Is there something wrong, love?" He couldn't imagine. But this time at least he got a response.

"Exactly," she muttered, huffing her new bangs out of her face with an irritated little puff of breath, looking for all the world like a forlorn child. Gabriel found himself unexpectedly charmed, if confused.

"Exactly?" he repeated. That earned him the expected eye-roll, at least. She shoved at him until he sat up, then curled her knees into her chest, frowning.

"Yes, exactly, Gabriel. *Love* is the something wrong."

He shook his head, not sure what exactly he was hearing. "Are you saying … are you still upset that …"

Then Rowan did look at him, and what he saw in those exotic, otherworldly eyes stunned him into shocked silence.

"I think I love you, damn it. And I don't have a clue what to do about it."

Chapter 13

PLEASE TELL ME THAT DID NOT JUST COME OUT OF MY *mouth. Please ...*

Rowan stared at Gabriel in horror.

She hadn't meant to say it out loud. She hadn't even meant to think it, but the realization had just sort of landed on her all at once. All she'd wanted to do was enjoy her triumph, not to mention the tall, dark, and handsome spoils of that triumph, without ruining it by getting all introspective again. And really, the whole thing had gone off even more beautifully than she'd imagined. The look on Gabriel's face, not to mention on the faces of those annoying creatures ogling him, had been priceless. Their dance ... she'd never danced with any man quite like that before. It had been perfect. It hadn't even bothered her that he'd hauled her out in his arms when she'd planned on dragging *him* out. She had won. Gabriel was hers. Life was good. And then he'd had to ask what she'd said, and she couldn't bring herself to say the words. All she could think of was talking about weddings, and rings, and of what he might see in her eyes when she told him. And suddenly, she knew.

She loved him. There it was, just like that. As though it was the simplest thing in the world, instead of the absolute worst thing that could happen. Being mated was one thing, and bad enough in its way. Love, though ...

Rowan winced, as much at her own muddled thoughts as at the expression on Gabriel's face. He looked absolutely floored. It was a look she might have enjoyed putting there had it not been for the subject involved. But it was out now, and there would be no taking it back.

Strangely, she wasn't entirely sure she wanted to. That might depend on Gabriel, she guessed. This was all new to her. To Gabriel as well. That much was painfully obvious.

"I don't think I can discuss this with you unless you stop looking at me like I've grown a third eye," she said.

"You love me?" he asked, sounding as though he'd recently sustained some sort of head injury.

"Yes. I … yes, I love you." She nodded, hoping it would get easier to say as time went on. Right now, it was a little like chewing on shards of glass. It hardly seemed possible; her kind did not take mates, did not love the men they took. But they had once, she reminded herself. They had loved men, Wolf shifters like Gabriel. And now the two were united once again. She would try to focus on that right now, and deal with the numerous impossibilities later.

Gabriel's eyes were glazed. "Really?"

Rowan arched a brow. "Yes, Gabriel. Really."

"You actually love me, you're serious?"

She looked at the ceiling and prayed for patience. "You're being an ass, Gabriel." She was just beginning to wonder whether she had made an even bigger mistake than she'd thought when a beautiful grin lit Gabriel's face like the sun after a storm. His eyes, those forest-colored eyes, glowed with a fierce joy that took her breath away. And despite everything, her past, her misgivings, the terrifying uncertainty surrounding her future, her doubts about Gabriel vanished like so much smoke. This was right. No matter what was to come, this was right.

He grasped her hands, then touched her face, smoothing her hair from her eyes, his hands roaming restlessly as though he was afraid she would suddenly disappear.

"You love me," he said softly. "Thank God, then. Thank God for that."

She smiled. "I prefer to thank the Goddess."

"Whatever," he growled on a laugh, gathering her against his chest, touching his forehead to hers. "We can save the theological arguments for later. I'd like to bask for now, thanks."

But as she snuggled into his embrace, and Gabriel began to trail soft kisses down her jaw, Rowan's pleasure clouded. She had given him her heart. Was she not entitled to his? He must have felt her stiffen, because he immediately pulled back to look at her, concerned. He rubbed a thumb across her cheek, frowning.

"What's this, now? Don't be sorry already. I can be much more irritating than this, I swear."

"No, no," she said. "It's just … I thought …" She trailed off, searching for the right words. And she found them, to her surprise, in her past, on the night she had refused a man who had said he was incapable of giving her the one thing she would demand from a marriage.

"Will you love me?" she asked, her voice soft, afraid to hear the answer. Would a man who was still, in his heart, a warrior give her such a precious gift? Or would he say, as Lucien had, that he could give her anything but? That his kind were incapable of such a weakening emotion?

Gabriel's eyes cleared at once. "Rowan," he said, his voice rough. "I'm sorry. I just assumed you knew."

She shook her head, heart thudding painfully in her chest. What should she have known? That only Drakkyn women were capable of love? That Gabriel would never be able to give her his heart?

"I've loved you almost from the moment I saw you." He grinned as he remembered. "I mistook it for annoyance at first, but it wasn't long before I figured it out."

"And were still annoyed," Rowan guessed, sliding her arms around his neck with a relief so great she was dizzy from it. He loved her. She loved him. Such a simple thing that meant everything.

"Only sometimes," Gabriel replied, nuzzling her hair. "Like when you're burning up my bed and then locking me out of my own room. Or when you decide to climb trees to get away from me. Or when …"

"Stop," Rowan laughed, nipping his ear. "That's a great deal more than *sometimes*."

"And yet I still love you," Gabriel sighed, pressing a kiss to her temple. "I may be insane, but I'm happy. Or I will be once we've taken care of our dragon friend and you and I are properly wed."

Wed. The word sent chills of both fear and anticipation through her. She would be breaking with tradition to do it, but then it was a tradition that had started when the *arukhin* had been lost to them. And that was the least of the problems that now faced them. Gabriel made it all sound so easy … she wished it were truly so. Rowan drew back, placing a hand on either side of his hand-some, beloved face, so open and excited. She knew that there could be no more secrets between them if she were even to try and accept him as her one mate. For them to have a chance at a future, there was a fight ahead of them. One he was going to have to let her lead.

"I'll take you as my mate, Gabriel. As my husband. But there are things that may change your mind, things I can't compromise on."

He cocked his head to one side, listening. "Such as?"

Rowan took a deep breath and then blew it out. "Such as the fact that I am still *Dyana* of the Dyadd Morgaine, whoever might be left. I have a responsi-bility to them. I can't stay on Earth. And I can't demand that you leave here when your family is here. So where does that leave us?"

His look was unreadable as he considered her. "I've been thinking a lot about that, actually—what we would do if you decided to open your eyes and embrace the wonder that is me." He smirked, and she couldn't help but return it, despite her apprehension. "And I want to be wherever you are. I've never really been sure where I belong, you know. And I've been looking for something, something I didn't even understand, for years. But I've found it." He traced a rough thumb down her cheek, eyes warm and full of what he felt for her. "I'm not about to let that go."

She shook her head, hardly daring to believe it. "You'll be giving up everything."

"Nope. I'm gaining everything. And it's not as though I have to give up my family, Rowan. Not as long as they have the Stone of Destiny. Anyway, I love them, but vacations with them are quite enough."

She didn't know what to say. She had doubted him, and fought him, and here he was ready and willing to leave behind his entire life just to be with her. There weren't words enough to encompass the tumultuous swirl of gratefulness, guilt, and, above all, love so over-whelming that it threatened to rob her of her wits entirely. So instead she drew him to her, putting every ounce of that feeling into a single, soul-searing kiss. His lips were warm and soft beneath hers, and it was so tempting to simply succumb and let only passion come through. But she was gentle, rubbing her mouth against his, catching his breath in dozens of tiny sips until she could stand it no longer, and had to have more.

He wound his fingers in her hair, his soft groan as she let him taste her with his tongue sending lazy ripples of pleasure coursing through her entire body. Her hands were restless, as though they might be able to imprint the memory of each part of him in her mind forever simply by moving over them. She rubbed his broad shoulders, his strong back, stroked down his arms over muscles that jumped at her light touch. And all the while, she let herself drown in his kiss, sliding her tongue against his in a slow, seductive rhythm.

Two halves of the same whole. Gabriel had been right.

Rowan finally drew back, but only reluctantly. She knew she could lose herself now, could take the pleasure and leave the rest until later. But she wanted to be honest where she hadn't been, wanted to tell Gabriel what she needed to. Even if it angered him.

He isn't Lucien, she told herself firmly, and knew it was true. No matter what she ever did to him, this man would never hurt her or hers. She had to believe that he would also understand that there were some things she needed to do on her own.

"Well, you can't stop *now,*" Gabriel said, his voice a low, sexy growl. He tried to pull her back to him, but stilled when Rowan put a hand to his chest.

"There's something else," she said.

"More than that we'll be making an interdimensional move?" He wrinkled his nose. "You're sure it can't wait until morning?"

"No." Best to get it all out at once, she decided, and told him everything on a rush of breath. "Bastian is back in our own realm, and Lucien knows. He's got the dragons hunting for him, and Lucien has promised he'll kill him if I don't marry him."

Gabriel went silent and still. Regret flooded her as his eyes darkened with anger, all the pleasure evaporating in an instant. So easy, she thought, to say the words. Why hadn't she just told him? But she couldn't go back in time, so she would have to deal with what came. She didn't think he would leave her, no. Trusting her, however, was another issue entirely.

"Your brother is being hunted, and you were going to …" Understanding dawned, and it wasn't pretty. His jaw hardened as he finally understood what had been going on in the chamber of the Stone that night. "So that was why you were going to let him take you, wasn't it? You would have *married* him, bound yourself to him forever, rather than just asking me or my family for help. Just sacrificed yourself to that bastard when you didn't have to."

He was angry, all right, Rowan thought with a sinking feeling. "I didn't want to involve you. There was no reason."

His eyes flashed along with his temper. And though it was on a longer fuse, she knew it was just as dangerous as her own. "No reason. Except that your brother left you with us because he knew what we were, and that we could help you. You knew by then, too. So that doesn't leave much of a reason but your own pride, from where I'm standing."

"There was plenty of reason," she snapped, feeling her own anger beginning to burn. "I had already been responsible for the deaths of my own family. I didn't really feel like repeating the experience with yours."

Gabriel sat back and glared at her. "You didn't kill your family, Rowan! The dragons did!"

"I could have saved them if I had just submitted and gone with Lucien."

"Let me ask you something, Rowan," Gabriel said flatly. "Was there a single member of your family, your *tribe* or whatever, who thought your marrying Lucien Andrakkar was a good idea?"

"It doesn't matter. I should have known what would happen …," she began, but Gabriel rolled right over her.

"Why, because you're psychic on top of being able to throw fireballs? That's news." He moved closer again, taking her by the shoulders. Rowan had the distinct feeling that he wanted to shake her, but fortunately for them both, he refrained. "Rowan, I know what went on that night, okay?"

Rowan blinked, startled. "But … from my memories?"

"No, that was more like snapshots. Nothing that coherent, you know?" When she nodded, because it had been like that for her, too, more like watching a moving photo album than anything, he continued. "It sounds crazy … hell, no, I suppose it doesn't at this point … but I had a dream the night you tried to take off. Except it didn't feel quite like a dream. And I saw …"

"Everything," she murmured, recalling it with perfect clarity. Remembering how Gabriel, instead of Bastian, had been there to save her in the end. The intimacy of sharing such a private thing as dreams shocked her. And yet it confirmed the depth of their connection. Something about it was comforting, that the Gabriel in such a terrible dream had truly been him. And it was a relief that she would never have to retell the story to him. Because in a way, he'd been there.

His eyes were dark and serious. "I didn't want to say anything, because you haven't been in much of a mood to talk to me, and I know that's a touchy subject. But there was no way your mother wanted you to go with them. Not her, not anyone else. Your family loved you to pieces," he said, his voice softening a little as he felt her tremble. "You had no reason to expect what happened. And sacrificing yourself would probably just have prolonged the inevitable. I mean, you come from a tribe of outrageously gorgeous women. They'd only just rediscovered you. What would happen the next time a dragon decided he needed one of your Dyadd for a wife?"

She shook her head, eyes welling with hot tears she refused to shed. She had stopped crying for them, thinking she had no tears left. She should have known there would always be more. "It might not have been that way," she said weakly, even knowing he was probably right. The dragons had few females of their own. Once Mordred had turned his eye back to the forests, no matter what, it was only going to be a matter of time. They had been doomed. And none of them, not she, not even Elara, were ever going to be able to stop it. Not every time, once the dragons lay siege.

A few tears escaped, leaving their warm tracks on her cheeks. But that was all she would allow. "I just wish so badly that it had been different," she whispered hoarsely, baring her emotions in a way that she had been unable to do, even with Bastian. "I miss them so much … I wish I could go back, that I could change it so that I would at least know they were all still there. And now I'm going to lose Bastian. I'm going to lose you."

Gabriel sighed, moving to sit beside her on the sprung old couch and gathering her back into his arms. "For once I can't stay mad at you. I wish you'd told me, but I can't change that. I know now, so we'll go from here. You're not going to lose me, Rowan. Or Bastian. You don't have to worry about that, okay?"

She looked up at him, trying to take some of the heat that always seemed to radiate from his body into herself. Her worst fears given voice, she simply felt hollow, and cold.

"I need to do this on my own, Gabriel," she said, seeing the reluctance on his face as soon as the words were out of her mouth. "No. They killed my mother, and I'm sure they killed others. I need to find whoever is left, and then we're going to have the revenge we deserve. You would demand no less for yourself."

"I'll fight for you, Rowan. My Pack will fight for you if you let us," he sighed, though his tone indicated he knew that her answer would stay the same.

"I know," she said, taking his hand to stroke it. "And I cherish it. But this is my battle. The Dyadd's battle. We have no need to hide behind anyone, no matter how strong or well intentioned. But we would be honored if any *arukhin* would face the dragons at our side."

"I won't let you get hurt, Rowan," he replied, his expression guarded. "I'd give my life to protect yours."

"I want your word that you'll step back," Rowan said. "I'm not just a woman, Gabriel. I'm descended from the Goddess Morgaine herself, mother of the Drakkyn, consort of the great Drak. I can do a lot more than throw fireballs at you when you make me angry."

Gabriel's response was to press her back onto the cushions and settle himself between her legs, gently pinning her arms above her head when she tried to hold him off. Rowan swallowed hard as she began to throb and ache at the very center of herself. She wanted to deal with this, to hear that he had faith in her. To know that his love, though so much sweeter than Lucien's, would not just be another kind of cage. But Gabriel seemed to have given all that he could for now. And she needed him. Oh, how she needed him.

"Tomorrow," Gabriel murmured, sliding a hand up to cup one of her breasts. She arched into his hand, unable to temper her body's need for him with any kind of reason. "We'll talk about it tomorrow. For tonight, just let me love you, Rowan. Let me show you how I love you."

The words fell sweetly upon her ears, resonating deep within her forever and forever and forever. She slid her hands into his hair, the dense silk of it, and pulled him down to her in temporary surrender.

Tomorrow, then. For tonight she would content herself with the fact that they belonged solely to each other. But there were still things she wanted of him … things she knew he could give her right now.

Rowan slid against him, flicking her tongue against his ear and feeling him shiver as the heat between them built. Her voice rough with desire, she whispered, "Give me your Wolf, Gabriel. When we make love, I want all of you. Call your Wolf."

He claimed her lips in a series of quick, hot kisses, edging up her dress. "I don't think … I'm not sure that's a good idea." His voice was rough with desire, but Rowan didn't miss the apprehension beneath it. It was as she had supposed; Gabriel had never shared that part of himself, the elemental force of the *arukhin*, with any woman. Even the night they had bonded, he had held back some of that wildness to let her have the control she'd needed. It had been a gift to her, and she would never forget it. But tonight she wanted the beast as well as the man.

She wanted it all.

So she reached within herself, to the flame that always burned within, and called what was Morgaine's. She called the divine, so that she might give it freely. It was more instinct than actual knowledge, but it seemed there was a part of her that had always understood, had always needed to do this to complete herself.

Power flared, shimmering just beneath the surface of her skin as she gave over to the magic that was hers, and hers alone. She let Gabriel slide the dress down to her waist, enjoying the way he hissed in his breath at the sight of her bare skin, her breasts. He skimmed his hands down her torso, a look of wonder on his face. His hair hung in his eyes, giving him a boyish, disheveled look that tugged sweetly at her heart.

"You're so beautiful," he said, his voice ragged. She loved the way he looked at her, as though he had just seen the Goddess herself.

Rowan smiled as her beautiful new shoes were carelessly discarded on the floor, as her dress soon followed in a crumpled pile, leaving her in nothing but an intriguing scrap of fabric she had chosen while imagining the look on Gabriel's face should he ever see it.

The reality was even better.

"Red," he growled with a wicked grin, his eyes flaring with intense green light.

"Of course," she replied as Gabriel finally tugged his own shirt over his head and threw it, exposing a rippling expanse of dusky skin that radiated with a heat as intense as her own. He didn't look like an Earth man as he knelt before her, she thought, purring with pleasure as she ran her hands greedily over his chest. He looked like a warrior.

"Mmm, mine," she said, lowering her head to trace a path up his collarbone with her tongue.

"Absolutely," Gabriel agreed, then gave a grunt of surprise when Rowan raked her fangs across the same skin she had just canvassed so tenderly. Blood welled in the thin cuts, and Rowan latched on eagerly, suckling at the crimson liquid that contained the essence of him. In it, she could feel the quick pounding of his heart, a beat echoed with increasing intensity between her legs. She raised her knees on either side of him, cuddling his hardness against her, digging nails that had lengthened into claws into his hips to hold him there.

Gabriel braced himself on his elbows as he gave more of his weight to her, recovering from his initial shock to urge her on, holding her head to him as his lifeblood flowed into her. She knew it was bringing him pleasure. It was the way of it, exchanging blood for a pleasure that would only intensify the longer she drank. But she had no desire to drain him at all, only to draw out the side of him she sought tonight. Wild called to wild.

And she was going to make certain that the Wolf couldn't hide.

He knew what she was after. And though he was determined to keep that part of him tightly leashed, once Rowan began biting him he knew he was going to lose the battle.

Beneath him, Rowan stopped sucking in favor of flicking the tip of her tongue over the shallow wounds. He never would have believed that such a small movement could make him so hard, but the sensation was so intense that he knew he wouldn't be able to let her continue much longer. He felt the dagger points of her claws at his hips, felt the escalating beat of her heart as surely as he felt his own.

As surely as he felt the beast within racing to the surface, breaking free of the cage he tried to keep it in while he walked as a man. Her scent, so rich, like a crisp October night lit by a harvest moon, filled his senses. The comfortably shabby trappings of his apartment seemed to vanish around him, leaving nothing but this feeling of rushing ever faster down a river of liquid sensation. Rowan's claws dug in harder, the soft gasps of her breath a fascinating counterpoint to the aggressive way she urged him on.

She rose up to nip at his ear. Again, a quick bite, then that delicious suckling that seemed to pull at his very center. His Wolf pushed forward, snarling, wanting out. He felt his own claws come out, felt his every perception sharpen hundreds of times over. Teeth lengthened, sharpened. Anything remotely human faded away. And instinct ruled all.

He wanted to taste her. The desire came quickly and refused to depart, until Gabriel was consumed by it. He rose above her, letting her see what she had asked for. Letting her see the need she had inspired. The beast that lurked beneath his skin rippled over it now, not quite shifting, but blending with the man. And Rowan, her eyes green fire as they burned into his, traced the tips of her claws down his chest with a feral growl of approval.

"My *arukhin*. My Wolf. I want you inside me." Gabriel's breath caught in his throat as one of her hands slipped into the waistband of his jeans, then wrapped around the hard length of him to give a testing stroke. His hips moved in time with her strokes as she picked up the rhythm, pleasure and tension coiling in his lower belly until he had to make her stop. He wanted to savor her tonight, not just give in to the hot rush of lust he felt every time he got near her. The last time they'd been together it had been all about urgency, need. Those things were still very much there, but this time there was so much more. They had exchanged the words.

Now he would show her exactly how deeply he felt them.

Gabriel claimed her mouth for one more bruising kiss before slowing the pace, then he began to gently kiss and lick down the length of her. Rowan put up a gentle struggle at first, groaning her frustration.

"*Gabriel*," she complained, trying to drag him back upward. "I want you *now*."

He raised his head only to grin at her. Considering the state he was in, it was a look that might have sent many women running for the door. With Rowan, however, this was what she understood. What she knew.

What she wanted.

"Just relax, love. We're both going to enjoy this."

She heaved a heavy sigh and gave him a frown he found ridiculously sexy, then tossed herself back on the couch. She did not, however, relax. He could sense her tension without even touching her, running right beneath the surface of her skin. Gabriel chuckled. This really was going to be his pleasure.

Slowly, deliberately, he worked his way back down, dipping his tongue into the hollow of her neck, where her pulse beat fast and strong. He licked along her collarbone, then kissed a path down the center of her chest to nuzzle right between her full, perfect breasts.

"Are you feeling relaxed yet?" he asked placidly, then smiled when she muttered an obscenity in response as her pulse continued to flutter. "Hmm," he continued. "That didn't sound like it. Let's see if you like it better over here."

He scraped his teeth up the mound of one breast, pausing to sneak a look at his mate before he began to tend to it in earnest. She'd shut her eyes, fully focused on his mouth and what he was doing with it. Still watching, he flicked the tip of his tongue over the taut bud of her nipple once, twice, relishing her breathless little gasps. Then he fastened on it with a long, hard pull. Rowan's hips jerked beneath him, and those gasps quickly became moans.

Gabriel turned his attention to the other breast, licking and teasing until Rowan's entire body was a thrumming live wire beneath him.

"Really, sweetheart, you're awfully tense. I suppose I'll have to try something else," he growled. She gasped and arched into him, making the insistent throbbing between his legs intensify. He needed to be in her, and soon. But first he wanted to give her this.

He licked a hot path down her stomach, swirling his tongue around her navel, then traveling lower still until he reached the delectable scrap of fabric she'd chosen to tease him with. It was a lacy scrap of nothing, leaving just enough to the imagination. If, that was, he had any interest in imagining anymore.

The thin straps on either side of it snapped easily, and Gabriel tossed it to the floor without looking to see where it landed. He was far more interested in the thicket of dark red curls that nestled at the apex of Rowan's thighs, already slick with moisture. Again he watched her as he slipped a finger inside her tight sheath, sliding it slowly in and out. Desire had made her skin incandescent, her entire being shimmering with her own, singular magic. Her cry was music as she writhed against him, begging him without words for more. He closed his eyes, savoring the sweet scent of her. He knew she would taste like honey, like succulent nectar. More, he would gladly give her.

Gabriel parted her curls, lowered his head, and began to feast.

The first touch of his tongue was nearly enough to make her come.

The second sent her over the edge.

Rowan gave a hoarse cry, gripping the cushion beneath her and pressing her hips against Gabriel's wicked mouth as her orgasm burst through her, as wild and unexpected as a summer storm.

"So sweet," he breathed against her, making her shake as he plied her with both his tongue and his finger. Perhaps it was the sight of his dark head between her thighs, or the rough scrape of his night beard against her sensitive skin, but the shaking soon subsided. Impossibly, almost immediately, Rowan began to tighten again. She knew she would be quick to reach the peak again, and this time she wanted to bring Gabriel with her.

She threaded her fingers through his hair and gave it a rough tug. When he finally looked at her, she only said one word: "Now."

Gabriel slid up the length of her, half-man, half-wolf, muscles corded tightly with desire. Somehow he'd gotten his jeans off in record time, and it seemed that every fiber of her being cried out in thanks as skin connected with skin. She lifted her hips, urging him into her heat. On a shuddering breath, he slid into her, and Rowan arched against the exquisite intrusion. He filled her completely, the thick length of him stretching her so tightly that the slightest movement provoked a tidal wave of sensation. His scent, like the forest after a rainstorm, enveloped her. All thought vanished, to be replaced by simple want and need.

Rowan drew her legs up higher, until she had taken all of him into herself. Gabriel's eyes were glazed with pleasure, she saw, and it satisfied her on a purely primal level. Then he began to move, buried his head against her neck with a groan, and satisfaction tumbled into the bottomless well of desire that was only for him. She would have echoed that groan if she'd been able to breathe at all. But his long, controlled thrusts had robbed her of speech as well as thought.

Their harsh breaths synchronized as they moved together, slow at first, then faster as the intensity of the sensations rocketing between them increased. Rowan heard her own soft, panting cries at the peak of each rough thrust, helpless to do anything but clutch the fabric of the cushion beneath her and silently will him to ride her as hard as he could. She heard the ripping sound as her claws tore right through the ancient couch, but couldn't bring herself to feel the least bit guilty. She was racing toward that blinding flash of light at the end of a long, hot tunnel, and she clung to Gabriel for life itself.

Without warning, Gabriel withdrew on a guttural snarl. Rowan didn't even have time to voice her displeasure, though, before he had flipped her to her stomach, risen to his knees, and resumed making love to her with a ferocity that she had never experienced. This was the animal in him, claiming her fully for his own. And as he gripped her hips, holding her still while he slammed into her again and again, Rowan gladly gave over all control in favor of what he gave in return, feelings so intense they threatened to drive her mad. All of her focus narrowed to a single point in space, each powerful thrust making her flex ever tighter, and everything inside of her was coiling, coiling.

Sensing she was nearly there, Gabriel slipped his hand between her legs, seeking out the swollen bud of her sex, and pressed against it, *hard*.

Rowan came apart, bucking back against him with a broken cry. The release was blinding, tearing through her like a tornado, obliterating all of her but for the part that was simply *feeling*. Gabriel was caught in it, roaring when he emptied himself into her. His tight grip loosened as his tremors subsided, and Rowan heard him gasping for breath. She could still feel his pounding heartbeat in the most intimate part of herself. For her part, she simply collapsed beneath him. No part of her body seemed capable of holding her own weight any longer, so she gave in to the delicious lethargy stealing over her, knowing Gabriel would take care of her.

And so he did, flopping down beside her with a force that shook the abused and ancient piece of furniture. He dragged the blanket he'd used the night before down over the two of them, snuggling up behind her so that she fit perfectly into the curve of his body, and sighed contentedly into her hair. With what small amount of energy she had left, Rowan curved her lips upward into a lazy smile. There was only one word in her mind, and she decided to share it.

"Wow," she murmured, and heard Gabriel's soft chuckle in return.

"Wow," he agreed, nuzzling into her hair and inhaling deeply, as though he would breathe her instead of air if he could. It took her a moment, on the edge of sleep, to recognize the feeling that was trying to take hold inside, like the seed of some fragile flower trying to take root. But it was something she had once had, what felt like long ago. That, and better. It was peace. It was contentment.

"I love you, Rowan." Gabriel's voice, fading into sated sleep.

"I love you, Gabriel," she replied.

And for tonight, whatever else came, it was enough.

Chapter 14

"IT IS TIME."

Lucien jerked in surprise, then whirled, furious, as the *daemon* approached him. He hated to be startled, hated to be reminded that his back was not always protected. Especially now, when he was so close to truly having everything he wanted. Jagrin, pale and emaciated in a leather tunic of storm gray, seemed to know all of this, and gave him a smile that was very close to a sneer.

These are my allies, Lucien reminded himself. He meant to bolster himself. Instead, the thought left him slightly ill. May the Drak protect him if these creatures ever decided his rule was not in their best interest.

He stood in near-darkness, the only light the eerie silver of the sky above the borderlands between the Black Mountains and the Blighted Kingdom. He had flown here alone, against all better judgment, and at the risk of his father discovering his plans and flying into a rage that could conceivably end both his quest and his life. Mordred's mind might be consumed by the *arukhin,* but his temper was very much intact. Hearing that his only son had promised himself to the *daemon* in order to cross into a world that he himself was increasingly desperate to enter would hardly be well received.

Yet Lucien could do nothing else. Jagrin had at last summoned him to this place, where crumbling ruins dotted a flat and barely lit landscape that stretched, dusty and lifeless, to a blank horizon. What sun there was had sunk below it, leaving barely enough light by which to see the *daemon* king's trusted adviser. Soon, Lucien knew, there would be nothing but blackness and the creatures that prowled it, hunting for the unwary. It made his skin crawl, thinking of bloodless figures creeping through the darkness. The Black Mountains existed in a state of eternal twilight, it was true. But to him, that dusky half-light filled with lightning was beautiful, a fitting setting for the powerful creatures that inhabited it. The Blighted Kingdom, however, even in what light reached it, was a horror.

He did not want to be here. Not alone. But though he had taken to haunting the Cavern of the Tunnels, hoping that somehow they would again bend to his wishes, there had been nothing of the sort. Not even a whisper of Rowan. And Mordred had begun insinuating that old Ragnath's daughter, the only female dragon of child-bearing age, would do for a mate. Lucien clenched his jaw at the thought of touching Auriel, a shuffling and unkempt creature who was more than a little mad. He knew he must produce an heir, must further the dying Andrakkar line. But the price, in that case, would be far too high.

He needed his witch, and now.

Jagrin beckoned him to a small, free-standing arch that had once been part of a magnificent gateway, back when the Blighted Kingdom had been a land of plenty and the gods had walked the world. Now it stood alone, weathered black stone inscribed with golden letters that had long since lost their meaning. Remaining, despite wars and curses that had robbed the kingdom of almost everything, a testament to a lost and glorious history that would never be recaptured.

Lucien strode quickly to meet the *daemon,* painfully conscious of how the last light was fading. His cassock swirled around his long legs in a sudden gust of wind that seemed like a warning. But it was too late. He had come, and there was no turning back.

"Your Dyim wench and her lover are surrounded, my lord Andrakkar," Jagrin said when Lucien reached him. "The moment to seize what we both want is upon you. Are you prepared?"

The words took a moment to fully register. But when they did, the rage had scales emerging briefly to shimmer across his skin, and the points of his wings threatening to burst from his clothes. *Her lover.* There must be some mistake, he told himself.

"Rowan *an* Morgaine has no lover," he growled, his tongue forking, smoke hissing from his mouth. The thought of her with her perfect body entwined with another's, her fiery hair spilling across another's chest as she rested in someone else's arms, was almost too much to bear. Jealousy, white hot and unfamiliar, surged through him. That, and the more familiar and even more distasteful fear that he was alone in this world, in all worlds. That the connection he felt to Rowan was nothing but a cruel figment of his solitary and twisted soul. *Lover.* He would kill the man if this were so. Rend him limb from limb as Rowan watched, to teach her that there could be none for her but Lucien Andrakkar.

Jagrin's look was entirely unsympathetic. "The Dyadd have many lovers, my lord. You know as well as I it is their way. Just be pleased she has chosen an *arukhin* to dally with this time. It makes your promise that much easier to fulfill. You get what you want. I get what I want. If, that is, you can set aside this ridiculous anger to do the job correctly. You won't have much time." He smirked knowingly. "And you really don't want to be here once the light has gone entirely, dragon or no."

Lucien had to fight to get his anger under control, but managed to push it back just beneath the surface. Still, the knowledge that Rowan had spurned him, only to take the wretched MacInnes as her lover, cut him deeply. More deeply than he had ever thought possible. The pain it caused threatened to spill over as a rage unlike any he'd ever known. He wanted nothing more in that moment than to taste the blood of the *arukhin* who had taken what was not his to take. But the *daemon* had a point, he told himself, breathing deeply, drawing into himself, focusing. Several, actually. So he would focus on the task at hand. And perhaps if the *daemon* were willing, he could watch some of Gabriel's "training." He would venture into the bowels of the Blighted Kingdom for that, Lucien thought. The *daemon* would be incredibly cruel masters. The shifter who had crossed his path one too many times would have his mind and body broken long before he was allowed the repose of death.

The idea gave him some small amount of peace. He had felt the shifter's teeth, after all. It was time to return the favor … but later. Once he had made Rowan his, again and again, until she had no doubts as to who she truly belonged to. She would heal him. She would love him. All would be well.

Lucien inhaled once more, deeply, and this time his exhalation was more air than smoke. Jagrin nodded approvingly.

"You are ready. Good. Because when the time comes, there will only be minutes to do what must be done. And your anger will not open the door."

Lucien tracked the tiny, glittering vial of his own blood that hung around Jagrin's neck, a reminder of the consequences should he fail to live up to his end of their bargain. Now that he was so close, the worry grew. His promise had been rash, he saw that now. There was no way he would ever consent to being enslaved by Jagrin and his kind. But he also had no doubt that the vial was enchanted with dark magic. So he would have to be clever, and careful, and be sure he himself could never be claimed.

So close. And as though it knew he was ready, the letters set into the archway began to glow with golden fire, increasing in intensity until they were hard to look at. White lightning erupted from the gray dust beneath it and snaked around the stones, charging the air with power that was so solid Lucien felt he could almost reach out and grab it.

"It senses your need," Jagrin murmured, as pale as the dust as the sky darkened. "It wakes." He looked as though this were a sight he had never before witnessed. Lucien wondered whether it might not actually be.

"If anger will not open it, then what will?" he asked, unable to tear his eyes from the wonder of the thing that would save him.

"Passion. Lust. Love. Even," Jagrin said with a pointed look, "the most desperate sort of impotent longing. Emotions, feelings that are lost and useless to my kind, but some of which you, my lord, seem to have retained. And how fortunate for you, for this is the ancient gateway of the *Balan Nalath,* goddesses of pleasure, rulers of the City of *Urum.* With this gate they summoned their lovers from all the corners of the universe, and through this gate came their destruction when men's devotion turned to obsession and madness." Jagrin's red eyes were cold as he spoke, and Lucien had a sudden but intense impression that the *daemon* thought history would, in a way, be repeating itself tonight.

"I would open this door, Jagrin," Lucien snarled, feeling the pull of that empty archway as though the Upper Kingdom itself were just on the other side of it. He didn't care what the *daemon* thought. He cared for nothing but getting what the gods and goddesses had so long denied him.

Jagrin's smirk was knowing. "Lay hands on it then, and focus on nothing but your desire for the witch. When the door opens, step through. There will be others there who have been instructed to help if need be. But be quick, dragon. Only the *Balan* themselves could hold the way open for long, and they were lust incarnate. If the door shuts, there will be no opening it. Your Dyim will escape. And you will be held until I can personally come for you." His grin was full of teeth that were made for nothing but pain. "A deal is, after all, a deal."

"How … ?" Lucien wanted to know how there could possibly be these vampires waiting at the ready, how such instructions had been given. He wondered, too, what specific instructions had been given regarding himself. Again he felt exactly how unwise it had been to have come alone. If he simply vanished into some unimagined torment, would anyone ever suspect the ones who were responsible?

Jagrin's eyes narrowed, as though sensing the direction of Lucien's thoughts. His thin lips curled into a sneer. "We are promise-bound, dragon. *Daemon,* at least, respect that power. And as to the ways of my people ... there are some things still sacred, still secret among my kind. They will remain so."

Lucien gave a curt nod. That he could understand. And beyond the arcing lightning that raced ever faster over the ancient stones, his future awaited.

He reached out one hand, then the other, his entire body reacting as the energy sizzled though him. Lucien thought of Rowan, of that missing piece of himself that she carried. Of completion, and to finally be loved. His mind filled with the sinister, seductive whispers of goddesses long vanished from this world. There was a rush of hot, incense-laden wind.

A doorway opened.

And Lucien stepped through.

Rowan dreamed of violence.

In her sleep she ran endlessly through a blackness so thick she couldn't see what was before or behind her, nothing to break the oppressive darkness but the heavy sound of approaching wings. It was the worst nightmare she'd had in months, full of a terror so intense, so immediate, there was no doubt in her mind it had to be real. Sleeping, she felt doomed.

Waking was worse.

She had fallen asleep cradled in Gabriel's arms, drawing from his warmth and surrounded by a protection she finally accepted, even cherished. It was the abrupt removal of that feeling of security, more than the foreign hands that replaced Gabriel's upon her, that jolted Rowan awake. And all around her, there were whispers.

"He's coming ... hold her, Lars ..."

"Ah, there it is, can you feel it? No, he warned us not to mark the Wolf. Careful with the needle, that stuff's potent ..."

"Watch her hands, remember what Jagrin said about her hands ... damn it, here it comes, hold her now ..."

Rowan forced her eyes open when she felt the air itself begin to quiver, though she desperately willed all of this to be just part of her dream. What she saw, however, left no doubt that this was a waking nightmare. The room was full of pale figures with vibrantly red lips and burning eyes, all moving quickly as they readied for an arrival Rowan barely had to guess at. Cold hands gripped her by the arms as someone behind her made quick work of chaining her hands together before she quite registered what was happening. All she knew was that she had been safe, and happy. And now she was neither.

Oh, Ama Dyana, *where is Gabriel?*

The thought slid like a knife into her heart—cold, sharp, immediate pain. She jerked her head to and fro, scanning the darkened room for him even as the intruders finally noticed she was awake. She had just caught sight of Gabriel's large, powerful frame crumpled in a heap off to one side of the couch when an unpleasantly familiar face inserted itself directly in her line of vision.

"Well, look who's awake," he grinned, looking for all the world like the reanimated corpse he aspired to be. "You've really been slumming it since you ran out on us, beautiful." He jerked his head toward the area where Gabriel lay. "A werewolf, when you could have had me? I should be insulted."

"Get your hands off of me, Mace," Rowan growled, terror for Gabriel warring with impotent fury. "I don't know what brought you all the way here, but I can assure you it isn't worth your while. And you had better pray to whatever god you worship that you haven't harmed the werewolf."

Mace Ravenwood, the head of the nest she and Bastian had lived in back in Reno, winked unrepentantly. He had been the one to take them in, to find her a job, such as it was. The one who had seemed so generally unconcerned with the presence of two strange blood-drinkers in the sprawling compound at the foot of the mountains.

Apparently he had seen more than she thought.

"Don't worry, baby. We only drugged the big guy. Though where he's going, he'd probably rather be dead." Mace chuckled a little at Gabriel's expense, fangs flashing. "You, we're just holding for your fiancée." He swept his eyes dispassionately over her exposed skin, then glanced at Gabriel's still form, which was similarly unclothed. "Somehow I doubt he's going to be happy about the picture. Hey, Lars. Go find me a shirt or something for Rowan." He looked back at her. "Not nice to tempt the mercenaries, you know."

Rowan growled, exposing her own fangs. She was terrified. She was also completely furious. Lucien, not satisfied with making her life miserable on his own, had enlisted help. And Gabriel, as she had feared, was paying the price. She didn't want to keep looking at him, didn't want to let these vile creatures know the extent to which she cared, but it was nearly impossible. At least from the steady rise and fall of his shoulders, she could tell he was still breathing.

"Now, now," Mace clucked as he caught what Lars threw at him and shook it out to reveal one of the loud Hawaiian shirts that Gabriel was so fond of. The sight of it, so cheerful in such an awful situation, made Rowan want to weep. Mace simply looked it over, shrugged, then tugged it around Rowan's shoulders and began to button it up despite the fact that her hands were chained together behind her back. She didn't miss the fact that his hand brushed against her breasts repeatedly as he went about the task. Nor, she saw from the black amusement in his eyes, did he mean her to.

Her jaw clenched with determination. The chain was going to hinder her a little. But Rowan had no intention of going quietly.

The air rippled again, and she knew she had no time to lose. The vampires, eight in all, turned their heads in unison to look at the open apartment door. But instead of the dingy landing, the doorway was suddenly filled with blinding blue light.

Rowan concentrated, digging deep to stoke the flame she carried within her. She could only hurl it from her hands, it was true. But she could drink it in, take it into every part of herself until lovely warmth had suffused her skin. Warmth to her, however, was not going to feel quite the same to any who lay hands on her. Rowan closed her eyes, willing her inner heat outward, until she knew she was flushed from it.

She embraced her gift, and burned.

Mace, his attention completely diverted by the light at the door, didn't even look as he reached for her arms to pull her to her feet.

There was a spark, then a hiss like water thrown on a hot griddle. Mace cast her one horrified look before his dark eyes rolled back in pain. In a split second he was engulfed in flames. Rowan kept up the heat as Mace staggered from her, a terrible, inhuman shrieking emanating from the fireball he'd become. He moved blindly as Rowan watched, the other vampires shrinking from him, from the light and heat. Then, all at once, Mace stopped still as though struck. His voice disappeared in mid-shriek, and just like that, he crumbled into dust in the center of the room.

Silence, but for the strange electric hum rising from the light in the door. Then one of the bigger vampires stepped toward her, eyes going red with anger.

"You … you killed Mace, you bitch! I don't give a damn who wants you, you're going to pay …"

She hissed in reply, ready to fight. She'd burn them all in a heartbeat if she could. But then a familiar voice, low and silken, reached her ears. And all of the fire she'd been ready to use turned cold.

"I know she can be trying, but I wouldn't suggest it."

Lucien. And this time there would be no escape.

Rowan was filled with a sick certainty. He would never stop chasing her. She would never be safe. But even if it were true for her, it didn't have to be for Gabriel. With all the strength she had, she would make sure of that.

She turned her head to watch Lucien as he strode across the room, heading directly for her. She had wondered, on occasion, whether Lucien would hesitate when the moment came. He was a puzzle to her, a violent maelstrom of a man who kept his own counsel beneath the shadow of his father. But she had no illusions. Lucien was all dragon. There would be no mercy from him this night.

He stopped in front of her, violet eyes ablaze. She tensed, waiting for him to simply scoop her up and try to carry her off, but instead, after a moment of thought, he extended his hand. And behind her back the chains fell away. He was taking a big chance in setting her free, Rowan thought. And she needed to exploit that as best she could. But she would have to be careful. He would be expecting something. Frantically, she tried to think of a way to get him to spare Gabriel.

"Do you now concede defeat and accept me, my Rowan?"

She cringed a little at the sound of it, at the possession inherent in his tone. Had she truly thought Gabriel was overly possessive? She'd been a fool then, Rowan thought bitterly. A fool about many things, most of all love, until it was too late.

Holding on to what she had of him, and the knowledge that he was safe, would have to be enough. And the last she swore she would see to, no matter the cost. Taking a breath, she slid her arms through the sleeves of the oversized shirt and placed one hand into Lucien's, long and elegant and graceful … and capable of such evil.

His skin was surprisingly warm to the touch, she noted. That, and much softer than she'd assumed. But then he had been raised to rule, not toil. He looked at their entwined hands for a moment, his brow slowly furrowing as though something he'd expected had not occurred. She couldn't imagine what he had thought would happen. She herself felt nothing, only the touch of a man who could have been anyone. Not like Gabriel, the slightest brush of whose hand sent countless delicious currents running wild just beneath her own skin. Whose rough and calloused palms scraped like softest velvet over her body.

Gabriel. He still lay quietly, deep in a drugged sleep mere feet away and surrounded by vampires who looked like they would love to drain him of his blood and throw his carcass out into the street.

Rowan rose to her feet, allowing Lucien to draw her up and stand before him. He was taller than she'd remembered, she thought as she faced him. Taller, and decidedly more dangerous looking. Coiled strength radiated from him, at odds with the gentleness of his touch. Still, that gentleness did nothing to put her at ease. The hungry desperation that she'd seen in Lucien the night she had first refused him had only intensified, making dark hollows beneath his eyes and causing his mouth to look tight and drawn. He kept looking at their hands, eyes reflecting puzzlement ... and, it seemed to her, worry.

Rowan felt an unexpected flash of pity.

He's searching for something, but it isn't me. I can't fix this, she thought bleakly. Being raised by Mordred Andrakkar, deprived of any kind of love with his mother who-knows-where, would take a toll on anyone. It had twisted this creature into something she didn't understand and had no idea how to reason with. She had thought to force some sweetness to try to bargain for Gabriel's safety. But Lucien's eyes slid to her beloved before she could begin to try to bring Lucien around, and the jealousy and rage she saw there frightened her to the core.

There would be no gentle bargaining.

His gaze returned to her quickly, softening somewhat, though not enough to make her comfortable. "Come. Come home and be with me." He looked toward Gabriel, at the vampires who surrounded his still form, and said, "Bring him to the portal." Then more softly, just to Rowan, he added, "He's nothing to either of us anymore."

The words felt like a knife in her heart. Did Lucien really think she would simply take his hand and leave Gabriel to whatever dark fate he had planned? That a loveless marriage and years trapped in the stone prison of the dragon castle would ever feel to her like home? What a mockery. She had always been a fighter. She swore she would use all the strength she had left to fight for the man who meant everything to her. And when she reached for them—the power, the anger, the ability she needed— they were all blessedly there.

"I'm not going anywhere with you," she replied in a near-whisper, letting her rage fuel her heat, letting it flood her anew. Fire flashed white-hot between their joined hands, and Lucien pulled away with a pained hiss. His palms were smoking and blackened, she noted with vicious pleasure. He studied them for a moment in seeming disbelief, and when he raised his eyes to hers once again, they were full of wounded anger.

"I won't let you take him," she said. "I was prepared to go with you if it would end this insanity. But you go too far. Gabriel has nothing to do with this. I swear on the blood of the Goddess herself that I will fight you with every breath left in my body, there will never be a time you have me that I don't leave you scarred, unless you *let him be*. A small price for my submission, Lucien."

Lucien seemed to collect himself, but for the first time he seemed unable to shut his feelings down completely. His striking face, normally cool and impassive, contorted with pain. And Rowan knew she would, indeed, have to fight. "Why?" he gritted out. "Why, when I offer you everything, do you insist on tormenting me this way? And with one so unworthy?"

Rowan remained silent, knowing any answer she might make would do nothing to sway Lucien. It surprised her, the depth of his hurt, palpable in the air between the two of them. But she had done nothing to inspire such feeling. It seemed the height of unfairness that she should have to pay the price for it nonetheless.

Lucien raised his palms to study them. "I ask so little of you. All I wanted … all I needed …" Then his gaze darted back to Gabriel, and Rowan saw that on some level, Lucien knew that the *arukhin* had touched her in a way he himself would never be able to. The knowledge in his eyes, she saw with horror, looked like death. "Doesn't matter," he growled roughly, more to himself than anyone. "You will come with me. And I know someone who'll be happy to train *him* for other things. Things," he continued, lips curling into a smile that looked more like a grimace, "he might actually be good at. Like serving those superior to him."

"I won't let you do this," Rowan said, and she hated the note of desperation she heard in her own voice. She darted a look at the vampires, gauging the distance she would have to cover to clear the area. "He's done nothing but keep a promise to my brother." Then, before she could stop herself, she again asked the question that she felt she would never be able to understand the answer to.

"I don't want you! I will never want you! Why, for the love of the Goddess, can't you just leave us *alone*?"

Lucien's hand shot out to fasten on her wrist, but this time her blazing heat didn't faze him at all. With a terrible sinking feeling, she realized that his hands were now covered in glistening black scales. Lucien smiled, and it was a terrible thing, bloodthirsty and cruel. The smile of the most dangerous type of man: one who had nothing left to lose.

One who was lost himself.

"You should have learned the lesson your mother could not," Lucien said softly. "There's no denying a dragon." He began to drag her toward the door, the light of which was now perceptibly faded. Rowan dug in her heels, thrashing violently, skin nearly aflame with terrified magic. It only slowed him a little. Even in this form he was possessed of fantastic strength.

"I've made promises too, you see," he snarled as they reached the threshold. "And this particular *arukhin* deserves no less than his fate. I don't give a damn about how honorable you think he is. He touched you. It is my dearest wish that he will suffer greatly before he dies. And for once in my life, I will have *something* I want!"

"No!" Rowan tried desperately to pull free. Her body whipped from side to side as they struggled, half wild in her terror and grief. She couldn't lose Gabriel. Not when he was all she had left to hang on to. Not when she loved him so much that his death would kill the best parts of her.

"We're leaving. *Now,*" Lucien hissed at her. "You're *mine.*"

"You're insane!" she screamed. "You think you can win me by destroying my protector?"

His smile was bitter. "No. Just destroying him is enough. Be happy it's only a lover, Rowan, and not your brother. Bastian does not even bother to hide from us in the forests of the *Carith Noor.* He lives because I knew you would see reason."

She bared her teeth, straining to get away from him. "Because you wanted one more thing to taunt me with."

Her struggles barely fazed him. He knew he had won. "Whatever the reason, he will live. The *arukhin* is no longer my concern. Or yours."

Her vision clouded with pure hatred. She wanted to burn him, to cut him to the quick as he had her. So without thought to the consequences, she hurled the deadliest arrow she had.

"He will always be my concern," she hissed, her face inches from his, her wrists bruising beneath the pressure from his grip. "You may lock me away forever, Lucien Andrakkar, but for one thing you come too late. Gabriel MacInnes is my mate, bonded full and true. He has my heart. And whatever you do, that you will *never* have!"

Lucien stared at her, his pupils dilating until his eyes were almost all black, only a thin ring of glowing violet remaining. She had gone too far, Rowan saw as smoke began to curl from his mouth and nostrils. His lips pulled back from teeth that had grown long and deadly, rows of needle-sharp spikes. She had provoked the dragon, and now she would pay the price.

"No! You lie!" His voice had deepened to a roar that shook the walls. But she didn't lie, and he knew it. She had never seen such raw pain, such fury. His hands shook, black claws lengthening to encircle her wrists.

"What did you think, Lucien? That I would bond with you simply because you willed it? Haven't you figured out that there is nothing meant to be between us? You may want me, Lucien, but that's all it will ever be! By all the gods and goddesses above, *I am not for you!*"

Scales shimmered over all of his skin, black as night, as his inner dragon fought to the surface. With a deafening shriek, he pushed forward, hurling her through the doorway. She didn't even have time to gasp before she was flying through the air, passing through light that was shimmering and warm before landing hard on the ground in a cloud of grayish sand. Her breath rushed painfully from her lungs as she skidded to a stop on her side, body already aching from the surprise assault. Her wrists burned, and Rowan could see the deep purple welts in the shape of fingers already rising on her pale skin. Those, she knew, would stay for some time. Drakkyn healed incredibly fast, but for the wounds they inflicted on one another. It was why they had been intended only to look after the various parts of Coracin in the gods' stead, not to fight one another.

A lofty idea, and utterly unworkable. Perhaps that was why the Goddess had turned a deaf ear to Rowan's own petitions for so long. She was no longer listening.

Seconds later there was another dusty *thump* as a body landed near her. Rowan rose, wincing, to a sitting position. She didn't know where she was, or what was going to happen. But she knew with only a glance that the body in the sand was Gabriel.

She crawled to him, her heart in her throat. He lay so silent and still, limbs in disarray, naked and vulnerable as a newborn babe. She could see no marks, but that didn't mean that Lucien had let him be. Rowan swallowed hard, leaning over him to touch a tentative hand to his forehead. Gabriel's skin, which normally looked tawny and gold-dusted, was waxen and pale. His face was impassive, long sooty lashes entwined to conceal the luminous eyes she had grown so accustomed to in such a short time.

Rowan bit back the sob welling in her throat, smoothing his hair back from his face and trying to ignore how cool he was to the touch. He couldn't be gone. He was too strong, too full of life, too *hers* to be gone. She tipped her head back to look at the deep gray of the sky, thinking to beseech her Goddess. But her heart was empty and hollow. In this forsaken place she knew there was no hope. She had no prayers left to offer.

Once again she had failed.

A faint flutter tickled her fingers, splayed now across Gabriel's broad chest. She looked down, startled, and the flutter came again, followed by a shuddering, shallow breath. It was all she could do to keep from crying out. He was alive. Maybe not by much, but he was not lost yet.

She stroked his hair again, and then noticed two small puncture wounds up high on his neck that she hadn't seen before. *Bastards!* Her hand shook as she gently touched the tiny holes, heart aching when she heard Gabriel's faint moan. They had drugged him, and hadn't been able to resist having a taste. As a result, he was dangerously weakened and unconscious. And she could do nothing.

She heard footsteps in the sand nearby, heard low voices conferring. Lucien's fierce growl was unmistakable. So was the fact that he was arguing, rather viciously, with whomever he'd met. But she didn't turn, didn't bother to look. She no longer cared. She seemed to cause the destruction of all that was beautiful in her life, without knowing quite how or why. Her birth had been accursed, it seemed. That day had not marked the arrival of the future *Dyana an Morgaine*, but of their doom, and the doom of all who dared to love her.

She was afraid, and hated herself for it. Rowan looked at Gabriel's face, which frowned slightly as though he was having an unpleasant dream, and wished desperately that at least she could right this wrong. But she had nothing to give, no healing powers to call upon. She had only herself.

Rowan stopped still, wondering. She didn't know whether it was madness to hope, whether such a thing could bolster him at all. But he was still her mate, and it was better to try than to just sit here and wait for him to be taken away or to stop breathing altogether. Now she did sneak a glance at the two figures engaged in heated discussion a small distance away. Lucien, smoke still streaming from his mouth, gesticulated angrily at a lonely looking stone arch while his companion folded his arms across his chest and glared back. Neither acknowledged her presence. *Good.*

Still, she knew there would not be much time. Extending a nail, which she lengthened immediately into a claw, Rowan slashed across one abused wrist so that blood began to flow freely from her body. With the other hand, she gripped Gabriel's head and propped it on her lap, pressing the wound to his mouth. The thick crimson liquid spilled into his mouth, down the side of his chin, and he showed no sign of response. Rowan gritted her teeth, willing the blood and all it contained into Gabriel. Her magic. Her strength. Above all, her love.

"Come on, Gabriel," she whispered. "If I can eat fish and chips for a week and get some energy from it, you can certainly do something with this. Drink, baby. Drink."

She didn't know if he heard her or was just reacting to the flow of liquid, but Gabriel swallowed once, then again. It was weak at first, but his sucking grew steadily stronger as he drank. Rowan cradled his head in her lap, eyes closed, concentrating on her connection to this man. To her Wolf, her warrior shifter. It felt so natural, sending her energy into him, even as she got to feel his body reawakening in return.

Lucien roared. She tensed, holding Gabriel tighter because she knew they had finally noticed what she was doing. When she opened her eyes and looked down, Gabriel's looked back, bright and alert and full of concern. Rowan, robbed of the right words, shook her head gently, removed her wrist, and gave him a soft kiss on lips she herself had warmed. Then massive claws seized her from behind, ripping her from Gabriel's returning heat and lifting her into a sky full of emerging stars she had almost forgotten. Above her there was nothing but the steady beat of wings, the sound she hadn't managed to escape after all. Still, as she watched Gabriel grow smaller and smaller, saw his mouth move while he shouted words she couldn't hear, she could not feel total despair.

He would live, for now. In these last moments before he vanished from her life, she would focus on that. She had at least given him a chance, slim though it was.

Such a shame that hers were all gone.

Chapter 15

"SHE'S GONE, SHIFTER."

Gabriel knelt in the sand, staring at the far-off black shape in the sky that was Rowan and Lucien. She'd saved him. After all his reluctance to let her face the enemy on her own, she had proven herself brave as any warrior, and she had saved him. He knew it as surely as he knew anything, could still feel her blood racing through his veins and setting his weakened body to rights.

Just as he'd known her kiss had meant good-bye.

He'd tried to stand, to run after her and the monster that was carrying her off. But his legs didn't seem to want to hold him, and he'd managed to stagger only a short way before falling to his knees here and shouting her name until he was hoarse. But there was nothing he could do. The Andrakkar had won her after all.

She was gone.

And slowly, awareness returned.

Gabriel swallowed, wincing at what he'd done to his throat with the shouting. His head pounded dully, and his tongue felt as dry as the desert he now found himself in. It was still evening here, he saw, though the light was going fast. He saw nothing but a dead and barren landscape full of crumbling structures and slinking shadows that left him uneasy.

Though he hadn't yet acknowledged it, he was also aware of the voice that had spoken. He knew he wasn't alone. He'd also recovered enough of his wits to understand that this was bound not to be a good thing.

"I see that damned dragon was right; you aren't quite dead after all. Perhaps you'll still be of some use to me." The voice was soft, but there was a quality to it that set all of Gabriel's nerves on edge. It grated, scraping painfully against his ears. He turned his head slowly to the figure who was waiting just to the left of him, and if he'd been in Wolf form, his ears would have immediately flattened to his head.

He had never seen anyone quite like the creature who regarded him with a sort of clinical interest through painfully red eyes. The man was tall, slim, and willowy and garbed in a simple gray tunic and leggings. He had no hair to speak of, just a smooth pate of skin so white it looked powdered. The rest of his features were normal enough, though there was an unshakable sense of *wrongness* about him, malevolence surrounding him like an aura. And those eyes … Gabriel was reminded of every gorefest of a horror movie he'd ever seen, and decided that none of them contained anything as remotely horrifying as the eyes now looking at him. It was like gazing into an abyss— cold, inescapable. Endless. But not empty. In the abyss of those eyes lived things that would always be hungry.

Gabriel shuddered, unable to help it. The creature, who had folded his hands patiently behind his back while Gabriel studied him, smiled.

Good Christ, his teeth …

He wanted to scream, but managed to tamp it down. Teeth like that were made for one thing, and one thing only—tearing flesh.

He was going to have to be very careful it wasn't his.

"Finished looking?" the thing said. "Good. I am Jagrin, *arukhin*. Your new master. Technically you'll belong to the king, but I'll be overseeing your ... training."

Gabriel said nothing, cringing a little over the relish with which Jagrin had said the word "training." A soft noise distracted him then, a sly skittering that had him whipping his head around behind him. He caught sight of a shadow melting away behind one of the massive bricks that were scattered about this place like the forgotten blocks of a baby giant.

"Pay no mind to that, shifter. They won't hurt you." Jagrin grinned, and it was hideous. "Unless I let them, of course."

"What the hell are you?" The words were out before he could stop them, but Jagrin didn't appear to mind.

"Why, I am *daemon,* shifter. Blood kin of the vampires of your world, ally to the dragon. And now master of you, a very special pet indeed. I must apologize for your condition ... I will be having words with whoever drank from you." An ugly expression flitted across his face. "More than words, possibly. Unfortunately, the *sarasin* mirrors we use to communicate do not always show me everything I would wish to see, but they are what we have. Still, the Dyim Lucien is so fixed on did me a great favor by restoring you. I would have thanked her if he hadn't been in such a hurry to have the bitch." He grimaced. "Lust is so entirely useless. *Daemon* are rarely afflicted with it, thank the gods."

Gabriel must have made a sound, some disgusted, furious sound in the back of his throat, because Jagrin suddenly looked at him more sharply, his interest more keen. Gabriel hardly cared, so overwhelmed was he by the need to get to his mate, to prevent her from being violated by that scum of whatever-the-hell-dimension this was. She was *his*, damn it! And the thought of her with Lucien, of him hurting her, taking her by force …

Gabriel was suddenly overcome by a wave of nausea. How was he supposed to get *out* of here? Another shadow slithered through the stones, and he could feel it looking at him, heard it slide a tongue over dry and hungry lips before moving reluctantly on. There was a faint smell like curdled milk, like rotting garbage.

He began to sweat, though the air was cool.

"Well. Interesting. The red-haired witch must be quite something to have ensnared the both of you so entirely." He stepped closer, squatting down to study Gabriel as one would a particularly fascinating insect. Then Jagrin closed his eyes, inhaling deeply, savoring the air around him like a fine wine. Gabriel could only watch, using all of his willpower not to shrink away.

"Mmm," sighed the *daemon*. "I can taste your fear. Your pain. Delicious. I can only imagine what your flesh would be like." He opened his eyes again, and there was a new and terrible hunger in them. "Just a small nip wouldn't hurt, I suppose. A reward, I think, for my own cleverness in having gotten you in the first place. After all, you're going to be a very useful boy, aren't you? *Arukhin* blood is said to have been quite potent for the darker spells … and perhaps we can finally work out how to shift ourselves so we don't have to depend on those disgusting dragons."

"You … you depend on the dragons?" It was the only thing he could think to say, but he had to keep the conversation going no matter how disturbing it got. There had to be a way out. Or maybe he could lure Jagrin close enough to rip into before the snacking began, though he had a bad feeling the *daemon* was smarter than to set himself up for that. Jagrin tipped his head to one side, smirking. He knew Gabriel was stalling. But there was nothing for it.

"Mmm. Mordred Andrakkar thinks he's so *special*, a descendant of the Drak himself. Just ask him. But we are all children of the gods, are we not? Narr, god of night, son of the Drak, fathered my kind. Why should *we* not have the ability, somewhere within, to change these weak and useless forms? But we need the dragons for protection, so taking one to study is out of the question. *Your* kind, however, is long gone from Coracin. Who is to know if we keep just one?"

So *this* was going to be his future? Experimented on and tortured so that these creatures could better fight the dragon who'd made it all possible? *Lucien Andrakkar, you are a flaming stupid ass, and I hope I get to tell you that someday, right before I rip your bloody throat out,* he thought.

"I don't suppose you've discussed this with Lucien," he commented. Jagrin shrugged.

"He cares for nothing but the witch. And he didn't ask. He'll make a much better ally than his father, who is often inclined to watch us more closely than we'd like." He looked faintly amused. "Though of late, I must say, he's been somewhat consumed with hunting down a rogue group of *arukhin* who had the audacity to continue existing in another realm. The attempts he's made …"

Jagrin shook his head slowly, though there was no sympathy in his eyes. "The Andrakkar are fools. The bloodline seems to have been tainted with madness somewhere along the way. And yet they're the best the dragons have to offer at present. No wonder they're in such decline."

"You sound so disappointed about it," Gabriel returned, earning him a grating laugh from his captor.

"It will be centuries before the damned things die out completely. And we do need them, at least until the Orinn stop sending their little bands of crusaders to kill us off while we sleep. But if we could discover the secret … *your* secret … come up with just the right way to harness your essence … we would have everything we required. We could leave the Blighted Kingdom and walk in daylight."

"Rule the world," Gabriel added, only half joking. But he'd apparently said the wrong thing, as Jagrin's smirk faded and his hunger returned.

"You should not speak of things about which you know nothing," Jagrin said flatly. "Coracin cannot be ruled. But it has many treasures for the Drakkyn, should they be bold enough to grasp them. And ah, you're afraid again, aren't you? That's much better. You're diverting, shifter, I give you that, but I have better things to do than waste my time *talking* to you."

Gabriel clenched his jaw, cursing this *thing* that could sniff out his emotions so easily. He was glad for the information Jagrin had provided, yes, but in his current situation it did him no good whatsoever. Not liking the look on the *daemon*'s face, he grasped at straws.

"Wait. Isn't there going to be some, ah, god or goddess angry about your making me a pet?"

Jagrin's patience for the conversation was apparently at an end. "They've been gone a long time, shifter. One measly *arukhin* isn't going to bother anyone, least of all Ronan ... not when there are so many nymphs and the wine flows so freely in the Higher Kingdom." His eyes moved over Gabriel's biceps, the meat of his calves. "No, a small bite won't hurt you at all, I think. Not compared to what's coming. And I'm so ... *hungry.*"

Gabriel swallowed hard, and all he tasted was the metallic tang of rising panic. There was only one choice, and he knew it. It was just going to take most of his strength to do it. Still, he knew he had to Change if he was going to have any chance of escaping this abomination's teeth. There was a burning sensation as his limbs stretched to legs and paws, as fur burst through skin to cover and protect and his muzzle lengthened. His mind cleared, always a pleasant side effect of embracing his animal side. And as a Wolf there were only two things he was focused on:

Escape.

Find Rowan.

Jagrin sneered as he looked at him, but the hunger in his expression had been joined by what might have been jealousy. Gabriel growled, a low warning sound that echoed across the desolation around him. He lowered his massive head, crouched low to the ground, ready to attack at the slightest provocation.

"Foolish beast. Even if you could escape me ... which you *can't* ... night has fallen on the Blighted Kingdom.

You'll be eaten alive, consumed while you can still watch. I can protect you. I have powers you know nothing of. Or I can drag your half-eaten yet still-breathing carcass back to the castle after I've joined in the feast. Your choice."

Gabriel took a step back, then another, still growling. Jagrin narrowed his eyes to red slits.

"Last chance, *arukhin.* Let me show you how unwise this choice would be. *Ness'eth!*"

Jagrin raised his arms, and Gabriel felt himself being lifted as well, paws working helplessly in the air that was suddenly beneath him. He rose high above the *daemon,* dangling between earth and sky. Jagrin watched him for a moment, then gave a guttural cry and threw his arms forward. Gabriel, too, shot through the air, slamming into the ground with crushing force as sand hissed up into a cloud around the divot he had made.

He felt his rear leg snap, and the pain made the world go as gray as the sand for a few seconds. It would heal … hopefully quickly, since the *daemon* hadn't done it with his own hands … but it wouldn't heal in time to save him from this. He struggled back to his three good feet, ready to fight to the end. He thought of his family, of Gideon and Duncan, Carly and Malcolm, in bright bursts of images that brought him some small comfort. But mostly he thought of Rowan. The hair as bold as her mouth, the way she moved, as though she were always dancing. The way she had looked at him when she had finally said "I love you." He loved her too, with all the strength he had. But it had not been enough. And for that he had oceans of regret.

As the darkness deepened, Gabriel saw more of those creeping shadows slink into the open. The smell that accompanied them, foul and rotting, increased until Gabriel's eyes were watering. The noise they made, a throaty moan that turned delighted as one by one they spotted him, made him want to put his paws over his ears and bury himself deeply in the sand. It was awful, and at last fear unfurled its black petals deep in his chest. Jagrin approached him slowly, red eyes brimming with terrible glee. Still, Gabriel stood his ground.

"Desert dwellers," he purred. "Scavengers. Do you hear them? Feel them? They are without mercy, shifter. Without conscience. They are *daemon* in the most ancient and raw form, and they will eat you while you beg for death. You cannot fight me, for the darkness is my power, and the light is gone. What will you choose? Be quick. I won't hold them back forever."

The moaning grew louder, and Gabriel's eyes darted to and fro in the near-blackness. There was sandy shuffling all around him, and his sharp eyes could make out over a dozen figures approaching quickly. God, maybe he could have run were it not for his stupid leg. But there was a sharp twist of pain each time he jostled it, and he could barely even put it down.

So this was it. He would not be taken. Ideally, it would all be over with quickly, but he had no intention of going down without a fight. Despite the fact that his vision began to gray once again, he lowered his back leg to the ground, throwing out his chest, ears forward and alert.

A MacInnes Wolf, even at the end.

He tipped his head back to give his battle cry, one final act of defiance and pride. His howl rose into the dark and star-studded sky and echoed across this waste-land, rising to a high and mournful crescendo before falling, falling back to the desert floor. The sound was beautiful and wild, giving pause even to the things that stalked him as the last of it faded away. But all too quickly the shuffling resumed, and Jagrin's voice sliced through the night like a blood-encrusted blade.

"So be it. I'll let them have your limbs, *arukhin,* before I return you to the king. I'm not going to let you die just yet. There are things you're going to assist us with before you go … and you can't escape without legs, now, can you?" He laughed, the most evil sound Gabriel had ever heard. And he began to worry that he might not die after all. He was going to have to try.

But I want to live so badly …

There was a sudden flash of blinding light and terrible screaming as the white and malformed creatures who had come for him threw up their arms to shield them-selves from the burning poison of it. Jagrin himself cowered, throwing himself to the ground and curling into a ball. But Gabriel only caught a quick glimpse before he had to shut his eyes against the glare himself, which was why he didn't know how to respond to the arms that wrapped around his midsection and pulled him backward with a force no human could possibly have.

"It's Bastian," rasped a familiar voice behind him. "We're leaving."

Gabriel growled in agreement, the only sound he could muster. He hoped it sounded grateful.

"No!" Jagrin was shrieking as Gabriel was pulled into the light. "Damn you, damn all of you, *someone stop them before they …*"

But his words faded into the tortured wails of the wretched *daemon* still cowering, some beginning to smoke and catch fire from the heated glow. Gabriel had only time for a brief instant of vicious satisfaction at the scene.

Then he was in the light, and they were gone.

"I warn you, Rowan. Do not mention to my father where I found you. His obsession with crossing into Earth knows no bounds, and he would torture you into revealing how you came to be there. With me, that secret and your brother are safe. With him, what is left of the Dyadd Morgaine is wiped from Coracin forever. And the rest of your precious arukhin will burn."

She had been smuggled into the depths of the mountain the dragons called home, had been commanded to wash Gabriel's scent from her skin and abandon the comforting armor of Gabriel's shirt for a maiden's gown of soft emerald green. She did it all with tears in her eyes, since it felt like washing away all traces of her bond to him. Still, she did it, heeding Lucien's warning. For whatever reason, the son only wanted her. The father would want everything else she held dear, and more.

Though it was difficult right now, she tried to be grateful for the small blessings that had been given. Even if she would have to count Lucien's unwanted devotion among them.

Now Rowan stood before the dragon king, locking her secrets tightly away inside and trying to conceal her shock at what he had become.

Once tall and proud, Mordred Andrakkar sat slumped on a massive throne carved into the stone of the mountain wall itself. His handsome features were sunken, his fair skin marred by shadows. Around his neck was wound a dark strip of fabric, beneath which Rowan could see black fluid oozing continuously. Only his eyes were the same as she remembered—glowing violet coals devoid of anything but a cold and ruthless self-interest.

This was still, despite everything, a dangerous man.

Other dragons milled around the great hall, with its soaring ceiling and ornate stonework. It looked, she thought with bleak amusement, like a human church in a way. Though she doubted any Earth priest would find much to celebrate here. The pile of bones in the corner, for instance. Probably not left there for any sort of religious reason. And the dragons, some rangy, some muscular, most male, and all looking ready for a fight, would have scared off the most intrepid human explorer—explorers who probably would have been roasted or eaten before they ever got out the doors. Doors that had just slammed shut behind her.

"Father," Lucien said, anchoring an arm around Rowan's waist and hauling her up against his side, "I have returned with my bride."

Rowan shot him a look as Mordred leaned forward to peer at her, but his arm didn't budge. Already she had grown to loathe his touch. She wasn't sure how she would tolerate what was bound to come after this. The part where he took her back to his chamber and … and …

She inhaled deeply, trying to fight off the dizziness that threatened to take her down. She'd made it this far.

She wasn't going to show weakness now. Rowan had already decided that she would just try to survive it, taking her mind far away from her body while Lucien did as he would. At this point there would be no fighting him, no deterring it. Too much was at stake. But he would take as little pleasure as possible from their joining. That, at least, she could make sure of. It was infuriating, that being a terrible mate was the only punishment she could inflict on the one who had left Gabriel to die among the *daemon*.

The very thought of it had Rowan fighting to keep her lips from trembling. She had no doubt Gabriel was dead. He would never have allowed himself to be taken, and she had heard his beautiful, terrible, final cry. High in the air, clutched in a dragon's claws, she had wept. But she would not cry here, in front of the Andrakkar. In front of the dragons who had taken from her all she'd ever had, and might have had.

Mordred arched one slim silver brow, thin tendrils of smoke coiling from his nostrils. His thin, brittle smile was the only indication Rowan had of his pleasure. That, and the way he rubbed his hands together as he regarded her, the dry hiss the motion produced scraping her nerves raw.

"So you've finally caught the Dyadd witch, have you?"

"I have," Lucien replied. "She has agreed to the marriage." He gave her a sidelong glance full of silent warning. "She won't escape again."

"Indeed," Mordred murmured. His gaze shifted to pin her where she stood, making her feel naked despite the layers of fabric. "You've caused a great deal of trouble, my girl. You should thank the Drak himself that we have such need of you here in my mountains. If there were another as well suited, you would burn where you stand."

Rowan kept her spine straight, her gaze steady as Mordred gloated over the fact that she was, or would have been, the *Dyana an* Morgaine. It seemed that Lucien had inherited his habit of saying the most awful things in a calm, reasonable tone of voice from his father. If one hadn't been paying attention, one would have thought he was complimenting her on something. Instead he spoke of wishing her dead. There was a soft, irritated growl from her side, and she knew Lucien didn't appreciate his father's sentiment.

It was a sad day when she would be the least bit thankful to have Lucien Andrakkar at her side, but when faced with the father, she would take Lucien's question-able defense.

"I'll have you know it was on your account I had to banish one of my best soldiers," Mordred continued, his tone smooth and pleasant. "On your account I have been punished by the Goddess Morgaine." He bared his teeth at Rowan in a grotesque parody of a smile, and they were sharp. "My wounds no longer heal, you wretched little Dyim. Does that please you?"

She looked again at Lucien, trying to gauge how truthful she could be with Mordred without some sort of retaliation on his part. But Lucien was utterly fixed on his father, looking as though he wanted to rip the elder Andrakkar's throat right out. And through her misery and fear, cold calculation slowly filtered in.

There was a rift here she could use, playing one against the other. And if she made her moves wisely, the Andrakkars' destruction might come without a wave of her own hand, or a drop of her own blood, though that she would gladly give.

These two were primed to kill each other. She must be strong enough, and wise enough, to push the right way. Rowan knew she could. It was the least she could do for her brother, her people. And for Gabriel.

"It does please me," Rowan finally said, drawing a surprised snarl from Mordred, even as she covered Lucien's hand with her own. From the corner of her eye, she saw his surprise, as well as a flash of pleasure. *Good,* she thought, and forced herself to begin thinking not just of survival, but of gaining justice. Her fate was, in large part, in Lucien's hands. If she fed his anger at his father, if he would allow it, he would be that much easier to use as a weapon.

She would learn the boundaries, Rowan decided. She would see just how far Lucien would let her go to have the pleasure of seeing Mordred cut by her words. She would let him think that she stood with him. And then, when the time was right, she would destroy him.

It was against her nature to be so cold. And yet with these Drakkyn it felt good. It felt right. She was not Elara's daughter for nothing … her wrath, once unleashed, would carry the power of a thousand tempests. Emboldened by Lucien's silence, she continued.

"You broke faith with the wishes of the Drak himself, that the Drakkyn children coexist in peace."

Mordred's lip curled. "Foolish girl. There has never been true peace."

"And never has there been a slaughter of an entire tribe by fellow Drakkyn," she snapped. She was not going to stand here and be lectured by the one who bore the responsibility for the carnage. "You deserve to bleed as you do. To wither away into dust."

She had reached that first boundary. Rowan could feel Lucien's claws biting into her side now, but she didn't care, keeping the warm pressure of her hand on his. To vent even a little of her fury at Mordred was a gift she would treasure.

Mordred looked angrily at his son. "You will need to learn to control your woman, Lucien. If her tongue remains this sharp, I would suggest cutting it out." Then he chuckled nastily, a thick sound that caused a thin rivulet of black to leak from beneath the binding on his neck. "After all, it isn't her tongue you'll be needing."

She could feel Lucien's temper rising as they stood there, pouring from him in venomous waves. His eyes glittered like twin amethysts as he watched his father stagger to his feet, throwing off the hands of the attendants who sought to help him rise. Still, he said nothing, moved not a muscle. *So much for defending my honor,* she thought, thoroughly disgusted. She knew she was only here to be used for breeding. She would rather not have had the fact wielded to humiliate her publicly. Nor would she forget the insult of Lucien's silence.

Rowan wished the two of them would just kill each other now and be done with it, saving her a great deal of trouble, but she doubted it. She was bone weary, emotionally exhausted, and in no mood to continue this distasteful exchange, much less plot death when she'd had enough of it to last several lifetimes. Unfortunately, Mordred descended the steps slowly but without incident, though he nearly lost his footing several times. Finally he came to stand in front of them, and in his bearing was a shadow of the great and terrible king he had once been.

"So this is where you've been," Mordred purred, reaching out his hand and extending one long, black claw to run down her cheek. Rowan held still, knowing that to flinch would just be encouraging more of the same. "Shirking your duties, vanishing at all hours." His eyes, slightly darker than Lucien's and infinitely colder, shifted to his son. "Meeting with *daemon* behind my back." An uneasy murmur ran through the crowd. Rowan found it interesting. It seemed that even the *daemon*'s allies didn't trust them. From all she had ever heard of them, that didn't come as a surprise. Still, the dragon kingdom seemed to be on less sure footing than anyone had known.

Rowan felt Lucien stiffen a little, and guessed he'd thought his machinations had escaped Mordred's notice. Mordred smiled, pleased to have caught his son off guard.

"Yes, Jagrin has told me of your efforts to scour the *Carith Noor* to find our wayward new *Dyana*." He nodded approvingly, missing, Rowan was sure, the relief that flickered briefly over Lucien's face. "Very industrious of you. I had hoped you would take the initiative to drag this creature back here. I've had quite enough to do, keeping watch over the scouts I've sent through." His eyes went far away for an instant, and in them Rowan saw the beginnings of madness. "Such riches. Such potential. I have seen wonders through the crystal beyond imagining."

"If you're speaking of the valuable warriors who were lucky enough to make it to Earth after you had them tossed into the abyss of the Tunnels, I don't suppose you've figured out how to bring them back yet?" Lucien sneered. "Or have our young and able-bodied become so expendable to you in your rush to open the borders of Earth?"

It gave her a start, hearing that. She had only heard whispered tales of the Cavern of the Tunnels, always assuming that such a place couldn't be real. Endless openings, endless worlds, all in a maelstrom of uncontrollable magic that could tear a person apart, or cast them into the farthest reaches of the universe. If Mordred was insane enough to try to use power so violently unpredictable to return to Earth, what would he do if he ever learned of her brother's ability? Rowan's stomach began to hurt. Lucien had been right. She could not afford to be anything but perfectly acquiescent. She also began to understand that Mordred's days had been numbered before she ever arrived.

She vowed to make them shorter still. The MacInnes Pack had no idea that even now dragons walked the Earth. With luck, they would pose no threat once Mordred was deposed, but dragons were notoriously greedy. There were no guarantees, no matter what happened.

Rowan thought of *Iargail*, of the men who cared enough to guard the gateway stone, and wished there were a way to warn them to be on their guard. Obviously, there were other, albeit less reliable, ways in. And they'd been used.

"We rushed in too quickly the last time," Mordred said with a dismissive wave of his hand. "The three who lived have been taking their time, collecting information. We will understand how to conceal ourselves, how to live among these *humans* and best exploit them before we take the *arukhin*'s Stone."

"The promise of wealth and women will not hold our people forever, Father," Lucien rasped in a voice so soft only Rowan and Mordred could hear. "Better to rebuild the glory that was Coracin, land of our gods, than to die in a world we do not understand and cannot control."

Mordred looked at Rowan when he spoke, though his words were intended for his son. "You must forgive Lucien his weakness. His mother was a weakling drag-oness who broke within a year. Full of fear, and she gave it to my son. I did not always choose wisely when I bred." He considered her, calculating. "A *Dyana* with the gift of fire, though. He has made a fit choice, I will give him that. You're soft yet, but cruelty can be learned." He leaned forward to whisper in her ear. "Perhaps you will kill him and rule in his stead one day. I can teach you to love the kill. It is in your blood, after all."

He drew back with a cryptic little smile as Rowan felt her skin go cold. What was she to say to something like that? *In her blood* … The Dyadd were no killers, and the old dragon knew it. He only wanted to make her uneasy, Rowan thought, angry at herself for letting him succeed. There was nothing more to it than that. He hadn't even known her name until his ill-fated excursion to the forests. How could he profess to know her character?

And to even insinuate that he would allow a mere woman to succeed him, much less one not of his own blood, or even tribe …

Still, something in his whisper, in the way he looked at her with his hard and glittering eyes, refused to leave her mind. Rowan frowned into the distance, ignoring her fuming future husband as his scales began to show.

"Your refusal to listen to reason will be your downfall, no matter what you may think of me, *Father*."

Mordred raised his eyebrows as their curious onlookers hissed in anticipation, obviously relishing the prospect of a bloody fight. "Was that actually a threat, Lucien? Well done, then." His laugh was soft, mocking. "Late, but well done."

Mordred turned and made his way slowly back up the steps to the obvious disappointment of his subjects, who returned to their small groupings and resumed whatever they had been doing before. Rowan noticed, however, that a few bright gazes lingered on her and Lucien. Some were hostile, some hopeful. All served only to reinforce the impression that change was heavy in the air in the Black Mountains.

Violent, sudden change, she had no doubt. And in her heart she wanted no part of it. All she really wanted right now was the one she would never be able to have again.

Her vision suddenly grayed at the edges, making her sway a little on her feet. Rowan struggled to stay alert, realizing that the endless night was finally taking its toll on her body. She was hungry, exhausted, and, above all, severely drained from the grief she was forced to internalize. Lucien, to his small credit, seemed to realize it as he tightened his hold to steady her.

"My woman is tired," Lucien informed his father's back. "I'm taking her back to my chambers."

His chambers. Rowan had to force herself to be still, to not run screaming. She dared a glance at her captor, and it was as she'd feared. There was concern there, or some reasonable facsimile, she supposed. But there was also a smug satisfaction, and, though she didn't want to see it, hungry anticipation. Rowan knew she must accept him if her plans to manipulate him were to have any chance at success; still she wished futilely for anything to postpone the inevitable. She was in no shape to deal with Lucien anymore this night.

Though it shouldn't have shocked her, considering recent events, her salvation came in the oddest of forms.

"Nonsense," Mordred said, panting a little as he reached the top step, then settling himself back upon his throne. "Take a close look at your intended, Lucien. Do you really think she's in any shape to survive you right now? It's hard enough for one woman to sate a dragon's appetite under normal circumstances." His gaze swept over her, his disgust at her current condition obvious. "If you truly want to kill her, be my guest. It would be an interesting departure for you. But after going to all the trouble, destroying such a promising breeder seems a waste."

Lucien turned to look at her, and Rowan could feel his indecision, desire to claim her warring with uncertainty. She supposed he hated to listen to Mordred, but in this case the elder Andrakkar had brought up a point she hadn't even considered. The sexual appetites of dragons were legendary, yet another reason why so few women survived any sort of association with them. Would it kill her? She hardly knew. But beneath Lucien was one of the last places she'd want to die. Battle would be better.

If only ...

"You may be right," Lucien reluctantly conceded. Rowan let out a shaky breath she hadn't known she'd been holding. She knew he'd noticed when his tone sharpened.

"I'll give you until tomorrow evening, Rowan. Then the ceremony will be held. And at sunset ... you're mine."

Rowan inclined her head to acknowledge this truth. It was all she could do. She was afraid she'd be sick if she opened her mouth.

"Excellent," Mordred said. "I'll have her shown to her room."

Lucien opened his mouth to protest, but Mordred cut him off sharply. "No need for such temptation. And you and I, my wayward son, have things to discuss." His lip curled slightly. "Unless you don't wish to even maintain the pretense of an interest in ruling one day."

Lucien glared at him until Rowan's hope sparked anew that there was going to be a fight after all. At last, though, Lucien gave a small bow.

"As you wish."

He strode away from her, gliding smoothly up the steps his father had so struggled with, as Mordred snapped his fingers several times. Rowan's side ached so from Lucien's clutching her that it took her a full minute before she noticed the familiar beast who had slunk from the shadows to cower at his master's feet.

When she did, her mouth fell open in shock.

"I can see your surprise," Mordred preened, laying a long-fingered hand on the miserable creature's head.

"There has not been an *arukhin* warrior in our world for a thousand years. But I assure you, this is one. Though he can hardly be called 'warrior.'" He laughed, amused, even as the Wolf cringed at his touch.

Rowan wondered how this pitiful thing had come to be here. She had seen only Gabriel in his animal form, a huge, black, glossy-coated Wolf that looked as though he could defeat anything that dared challenge him. This one, though, was pitifully thin, bones visible beneath a gray coat that looked scorched in places and was burned away altogether in others. The look in its huge gray eyes was utterly defeated.

"Why does he not walk as a man?" Rowan asked, finding it hard to believe there was anything in that skin but wounded, abused animal. Except for the eyes ... there was something utterly haunted about them.

"I do not allow it," Mordred replied, "and Malachi serves me well. He failed me as a man ... so he keeps the form best suited to use around here. Though he does tend to get underfoot at inopportune times. The fur generally grows back." He grabbed the animal by the scruff of the neck and shoved it forward while Rowan watched in horror. So this was Gabriel's traitorous cousin, the one everyone assumed was dead. Even though she knew what he had done, how close he had come to destroying the Pack, it was impossible to feel good about what had happened to him. She had never seen a beast so wretched and broken.

"Take her to the chamber beneath the north face," he instructed the Wolf, who padded silently and slowly to Rowan and then waited at her side. She noticed a small chunk of purple rock swinging on a thin chain around his neck and recoiled. It had been a long time, but she knew a slave stone when she saw one. They could not be removed unless the one who had put it there did it. That, or died. But until then your thoughts, your actions were never entirely your own.

No wonder he couldn't shift from his Wolf form anymore.

Rowan gave a shallow curtsy, all the respect she could manage to feign, and turned to go. The great hall, despite its grandeur and soaring ceilings, was devoid of windows. There were only torches and smoke and shadows, and it was making her claustrophobic. Though she doubted her room would be better. Dragons were cave dwellers by nature. Fresh air would be in short supply here, as would sunlight. But then the skies over the Black Mountains almost always looked bruised, and the lightning storms were fierce. It was a place uninhabitable by all but the most dangerous creatures.

"If you wish for something, send the *arukhin*. I'll station him near your door. He has yet to fully appreciate the honor it is for the low Drakkyn to serve the high, I think."

Rowan stiffened at the reference. There had always been those who considered certain Drakkyn tribes to be above the others, and the dragons especially, since the Drak himself had been one. Though she herself was descended from his consort Morgaine, greatest among the goddesses, the entire notion was offensive to her. It had always sounded like nothing but a hollow excuse for oppression and war.

"The gods made no such distinction. All Drakkyn are the same in their eyes."

The laughter she heard in response was not kind, and she cursed herself for having risen to the bait as she felt Lucien's attention return to her. When Mordred motioned to the silent and waiting Wolf, she felt dizzy with relief. She had much to plot. But first she must rest.

"Ah," Mordred replied as the Wolf who had once lived as a MacInnes took her hand gently in his mouth and led her away. "But not in mine."

Chapter 16

HE AWOKE ON THE OTHER SIDE OF THE WORLD.

At least that's how it felt at first.

Every muscle in Gabriel's body protested as he began to stir, stiff and miserably uncomfortable. He made a soft, irritated noise in the back of his throat, wanting nothing more than to return to the oblivion of sleep. He did have some vague memory of the nightmares that had robbed him of much of his rest, though. Darkness, and screaming, and fire. All the more reason to try to catch a few more winks. He just wished the blanket hadn't fallen off again, and he didn't remember his couch ever having been so uncomfortable.

When reality returned, it was both brutal and instantaneous. Gabriel's eyes snapped open, his own tortured voice echoing in his ears as he called out, again and again, for the one who had been stolen from him.

"*Rowan,*" he whispered, and as he took in his unfamiliar surroundings, he knew that his nightmare had been reality after all. Gabriel sat up quickly, a mistake since his head began to pound immediately. He hadn't a clue where he was. The last thing he remembered with any clarity was facing down those *things* in the desert as a Wolf. He'd known he was going to die. But then there had been a flash of light … things had begun to burn …

Gabriel groaned softly, sliding his hands into his hair and propping his elbows on his knees. He had been rescued by Bastian *an* Morgaine, by some strange stroke of luck or fate. At least whoever had saved his hide had mentioned something about being Bastian before he'd blacked out. And he certainly wasn't in the desert anymore.

These were mountains.

He looked around him, absorbing his surroundings and trying to make some sense of them. He'd been resting beneath an overhang of smooth, black rock, so enclosed as to be like a small cave. There was a crumpled blanket of rough material on the ground beside him, which told him he had been covered at some point. A blast of wind blew past him, smelling faintly of smoke, and Gabriel shivered. Making a quick decision, he wrapped himself in the blanket, crouched so as not to hit his head, and made his way out under the open sky.

Wherever he'd ended up, he needed to know.

If only he'd had some kind of frame of reference for what he was seeing.

Gabriel's eyes widened as he took in a landscape unlike any he'd ever seen, one of stark yet breathtaking beauty. He stood on a large, flat outcropping of rock on the side of a mountain that was black as night, looking out on the tall and jagged spires of more of the same as far as the eye could see. The ground, far below him, was invisible beneath a layer of silvery mist that roiled and shifted like some alien ocean. And above it all stretched a sky of deep bluish purple, the color of twilight on Earth, and yet somehow more. There was a faint hint of shimmering movement in the depths of that endless canopy, a constant blending of color as it balanced between fading light and deepest darkness. Occasionally there was a quick and jagged flash of lightning.

It was both beautiful and terrifying, Gabriel thought as he stared into the distance. But unlike the barren desert he'd been rescued from, this air crackled with an energy and vitality all its own. He drank it in eagerly, feeling immediately more alert, feeling his faded strength return.

Good, he thought. He would need all of it he could spare, because he was more certain by the minute about where he had arrived. Unless he was mistaken, these were the mountains of the dragons. And he had no illusions about why, of all places, this was where he'd been brought. His enemies were here. Mordred and Lucien Andrakkar were here.

And somewhere in these fields of stone, so was Rowan.

"Good. You're up."

The soft, raspy voice startled him. At first glance he'd been utterly alone. Now, however, he saw that there was a tall, blond-haired figure perched at the far edge of the outcropping, his back to Gabriel. Clad in a rich blue tunic and tall black boots, the figure never moved a muscle, never turned to make eye contact. Still, though Gabriel had only ever met him once before, he had no question about who his company was.

There was no mistaking Bastian *an* Morgaine.

Gabriel made his way to the edge, steeling himself against the wave of dizziness that wanted to throw him off balance when he saw exactly how high up they were. Slowly, deliberately, he lowered himself to sit beside

Bastian, determined not to show any fear. He felt he succeeded admirably, though it was a full minute before he could speak.

He was a werewolf, not a bird. And oh, how he hated heights.

"I'm up," he said simply, and it was then that Bastian turned the full force of his crystalline blue gaze on him. The difference in his appearance between this meeting and last shocked him. Weariness and worry were etched deeply onto Rowan's brother's face, revealing lines that Gabriel didn't remember being there before. His first impression of the lone male Dyim had been one of quick mind and a sort of dangerous vitality. Now it was like looking at a different man.

Then again, Gabriel thought as another strong gust of wind tore through him, chilling him to the bone, he supposed Bastian could well be thinking the same about him.

"Do you know where we are?" Bastian asked, his expression unreadable.

Gabriel nodded. "Dragon country, right?"

Bastian smiled thinly. "The Black Mountains, lair of the dragons. And of the Andrakkar. I'm sorry for having brought you here so quickly, without much rest, but there was no time. If the Goddess is kind, you'll be able to heal properly at the camp after this."

"I would have kicked your ass if you'd brought me anywhere else," Gabriel replied, and Bastian's amusement was a little less strained this time.

"You can try that … and fail, of course … later. Right now all that matters is getting Rowan out of this mountain while she's still able to leave."

Gabriel looked around him, at the unforgiving landscape. Then he looked back at Bastian. "I hope I'm missing something. Because flying, for my kind at least, is out of the question."

Bastian was unruffled. "You can't see it from our position here, but behind us is the Lunin Desert," he explained patiently. "The dragon fortress of *Drak'ra Tesh*, upon which we now sit, touches it."

Gabriel's eyes shot immediately to the sky, scanning it for any sign of enormous serpents with large teeth. "We're sitting *on* their fortress? I just thought it was a bloody mountain! Don't you think we should be more ... hidden?"

Bastian waved his hand imperiously in a gesture Gabriel had seen from Rowan more than once. Just that small memory of her calmed him somewhat, and refocused his agitation. Still, he wasn't sure that hanging around atop a dragon castle in plain sight was the best idea. His companion, however, disagreed.

"It's early in the day yet. The dragons don't stir themselves if they can help it before afternoon at least. That should work to our advantage, since the palace within the mountain is vast. It may take you the day, and the hidden way in is long. Among other things." He frowned and looked away for a moment, and a chill rose the hackles on the back of Gabriel's neck. Still, whatever had to be done to get Rowan back, that he was willing to do. And as far as he was concerned, the sooner, the better.

No matter what "other things" were involved.

"Just point me in the right direction, then, and I'll go," Gabriel said, impatience welling up and threatening to spill over. "If that bastard has touched her already … and she doesn't know I'm alive, what if she doesn't fight? What if she's already given up?"

"No," Bastian said sharply. "She's fine right now. Frightened, but fine. And more than a little furious, which in her case is a good sign." At Gabriel's puzzled stare, Bastian simply shrugged. "Sometimes I can sense things. Emotions, intentions. Especially when I'm close to the person in question. It's nothing much, really. But I can't say it wasn't useful last night. Just as I'm glad for it right now. I'd rather know she's all right."

"Last night?"

Bastian arched one slim brow at him. "How do you think I knew where you were? I heard … felt … Rowan. Screaming for you."

Gabriel felt ill. "Screaming? She was screaming?" He hadn't caused her anguish on purpose, but knowing he'd done it at all didn't settle well.

"No, not the way you're thinking," Bastian said, shaking his head as though he were teaching someone a wee bit slow. "In her mind. She was crying out for someone, anyone, to save you from the *daemon*. Her love came through like nothing I've ever felt before. Not," he continued with a bitter twist of his lips, "that I've ever been in love before. But even I couldn't mistake it."

"She saved me," Gabriel said softly, blowing out a breath. It was humbling to think that the woman he'd been so determined to save had flipped the tables on him so neatly. She had protected him when he had been rendered incapable of protecting himself. And she'd done it selflessly. Now it was his turn.

"I think I deserve maybe a *little* credit," Bastian said with a faint shadow of a smile. "Nonetheless, yes, she did. You seem to have captured my sister's affections completely, something I never thought I'd see happen. Especially not under these circumstances. But then she always did like to do everything the hard way."

Gabriel looked into the distance, trying to wrap his brain around it. Not only had Rowan given him her blood to survive, she'd managed to call her brother to him to get him the hell away from those foul, flesh-eating *daemon*. He'd started off thinking she was a hot-tempered, blood-drinking menace. Actually, he thought wistfully, he still thought those things. But in the best sense possible. Turned out she was one hell of a warrior besides. Christ, how he missed her. It had only been hours since he'd seen her.

It might have been years.

"She doesn't really need anyone to protect her, does she?" Gabriel wondered aloud. In truth, it was something that had nagged at him since she'd hurled him against a wall the night they'd met. "Why did you leave her with me? She can obviously take care of herself, so why?"

Bastian shrugged. "Rowan takes everything onto herself. And she's brave to the point of insanity some-times. I know she thinks I live to try to run her life … and I do occasionally try, I'll admit, though that's the surest path to self-inflicted pain I know of. But in truth, I just didn't want to leave her alone. Your possession of a *Na'an Taleth* was wonderful luck. Best to leave her among equals, with a sparring partner she couldn't readily defeat and extra eyes that were trustworthy.

Drakkyn are stronger united, and I'm glad that the bond between our people hasn't died. I can see I was right about your stubbornness."

"There may also be some insanity involved," Gabriel returned. He thought for a moment, then said softly, "She's my mate."

Bastian seemed to mull that over, then gave a short nod. He gazed into the distance. "The circle rejoins. That's as it should be. And when this is over, our tribes will need to meet. Perhaps some of the *arukhin* will want to return to the *Noor*. It's high time, I think. Ultimately, it isn't my decision, of course. But I have no doubt our sisters will have plenty to say about the possible return of the forest warriors. Particularly in light of the attack. They're ready for a change."

Gabriel studied him, almost afraid to ask, but needing to know. "You've been here. How many of your people, your sisters, are left?"

The answer was an unimagined surprise.

"All nine sisters of the Dyadd live by some miracle, though all will carry scars of one sort or another. Many more of the tribe survived as well, though there were nearly as many who did not." He shook his head. "The heart of the Dyadd survives. But it will take time to heal the wounds that the dragons inflicted upon us."

"Still, they're alive and here. All with your help, no doubt," Gabriel added, certain that Bastian had been instrumental. The man exuded quiet, slightly unnerving competence. But Bastian's voice, when he replied, was rife with frustration.

"There's no need to be impressed with me, Gabriel. I'm only just beginning to figure out my abilities. Being the only male Dyim made me novel and got me coddled, but encouraging the development of any power I might have was pretty far down on the list for my mother, may the Goddess keep her."

"She's gone, then? You're sure?" he asked. He'd hoped, when he'd heard that her sisters had survived, that Rowan had somehow been mistaken about her mother. It was obviously not to be.

"I'm sure." Gabriel turned his head to look at him, and saw that his jaw was set in a grim line. "The survivors lit the pyres the next night. I'll always be sorry I wasn't there. But the dragons couldn't be allowed to take two *Dyana* in one night."

"And now we have to get Rowan back," Gabriel said, turning back to the subject that weighed so heavily on him. Mere minutes had passed, but still he felt like he'd wasted hours of precious time. God only knew what she'd been put through already. It made his own heart ache to know that she must be mourning him.

"Tell me what to do," Gabriel said, keeping his voice low. He began to be nervous again about sitting out in the open here, despite Bastian's assurances. Maybe it was because he knew he was about to invade the lair of creatures that were more than capable of killing him in any number of interesting ways. Certainly the fact that each breath he took carried a hint of fire was doing nothing for his confidence.

"I already want to crawl out of my skin, knowing what could be happening to her at any moment," he said. "Wondering. I'm going to get her out of there, and anyone who tries to stop me is going to end up with pieces missing."

Bastian looked at him a moment. "I'm glad you feel that way, Gabriel. You're going to need that anger if you're caught. But I'll do all I can to ensure you get in. After that it'll be up to you to find her. And bring her home." Bastian stood, unfolding his long, broad frame to rise and walk back toward the overhang under which Gabriel had slept.

"Come," he said. "We need to talk, brother Wolf, and quickly. And then I'll show you the way in."

Panic began to flutter in Gabriel's chest like a caged bird as he followed. He had never worried about winning a fight—ever. Not only was he big and strong by human standards, he was a damned *werewolf*. Who was going to beat him? Well, except Gideon, and then it was usually a draw. But dragons … bloody *dragons* …

He was no hero. He was only Gabriel MacInnes, the second son of the Pack Alpha, who had never had to work for anything, who had never really known what he wanted to work for in the first place. Now that he'd finally figured it out, it happened to be the hardest thing he'd ever had to do, not to mention something most men would never even have the option of doing. He had to rescue his damsel in distress from a den of dragons. Or rather, he thought wistfully, he would be helping Rowan to rescue herself, as she would no doubt claim.

Of course, this was if he ever even got started, much less managed to get anywhere near her.

Gabriel took a deep breath, trying to keep the old fears at bay. He was one man. He'd always had his family to back him up. He didn't feel that he'd ever really proven himself, and in the depths of his soul there was an insistent little voice that said it was because he wasn't truly up to the challenge.

"The *arukhin* were both feared and coveted by the dragons for their intellect and bravery, stealth and speed. You must use all of these, or you'll be taken down by the first dragon you encounter," Bastian was saying as he ducked beneath the rock.

It's all on me, he thought dully. *Every last bit of it.* And for an instant he knew what it was like to be Gideon, the brother he'd always envied for having that set purpose, the duty that he alone was fit to carry out. He'd wanted such things for as long as he could remember, thinking that Gideon's life held all the answers that he would never find on his own. That being chosen, whether by nature or circumstance, brought comfort and security.

Turned out it was just loneliness. And if it had been him first in line to be Pack Alpha, he probably would have run straight past America, which was where his brother had fled to, and ended up in an ice cave in Antarctica or something. Gideon, though, had found a few things worth fighting for, love chief among them.

Now so did he. Along with a heinous gauntlet to run.

If he managed to pull this off, he swore he was going to buy his brother a beer or ten and have a real conversation for once, minus the egregious name-calling and wrestling. Well, mostly. No sense robbing himself of one of his favorite pastimes.

"I can't shift," Bastian was saying, "so you'll have to go down alone. As my abilities stand now, I'm completely conspicuous. But we know more about their mountain than they think, knowledge passed down from the time when dragon and Dyadd often came together. Showing you how to get in where they won't expect it is the best use I can be to you. They might expect one of the Dyadd to make some stupid last-ditch effort on Rowan's behalf. But they won't expect an *arukhin*. Much less one who's supposed to be dead. There's been no movement either in or out of the castle since we arrived, so I don't think word of your escape has traveled here yet."

When he could go no farther forward, Bastian stopped, leaned down, and studied the rock for a moment. Gabriel had just begun to think that what he was looking for wasn't there when Bastian reached out and slid his finger down an invisible groove. Immediately, a large square of the rock slid inward and to the side, revealing an entrance into the silent darkness of the mountain.

Bastian turned back to look at him. "These upper Tunnels are ancient, and treacherous. They were built by the *daemon* long ago, when the dragons first claimed this mountain as their own, and were made to destroy those who didn't truly know the way. The way out will be easier, an old Dyadd path, and the circle of stones you must use is only a short distance from there. But there are things you'll need to remember, or you'll never get that far."

Gabriel nodded stiffly. He would remember whatever he needed to and then he would go, because just standing here while the woman he loved was somewhere below him was becoming physically painful. Something still nagged at him, though, refusing to let him imagine everything would be tied up neatly should he succeed.

"They're not just going to let her go," Gabriel said softly. "Not after all this." He would never understand

Lucien's psychotic determination to have a woman who he knew despised him, but he knew it would only get worse if she disappeared from his grasp again. That meant risking a repeat of the massacre that had brought Rowan to Earth in the first place, and he had no idea how they planned on preventing that.

Bastian seemed to understand. "Yes. If you get her out, Mordred and Lucien are going to give chase." His jaw was set, determined. "But the dragons need to understand that they're not welcome in the forests, nor welcome to our women. That the Dyadd are a force as formidable as their own. For now, you just worry about using your strengths to get Rowan out." His eyes hardened.

"Then we'll play to ours."

Gabriel descended into darkness.

And in the darkness, time ceased to exist.

In a narrow passage devoid of both light and sound, he felt deprived even of his senses, which were of no use to him here. Bastian had explained that this was part of the enchantment that worked on this place, that it would lift once he reached the warren of caves and chambers that comprised the castle proper. Still, he felt both blind and deaf as he padded forward, a black Wolf as one with a shadow.

He moved slowly, carefully. Occasionally he would feel that disconcerting sense of openness that meant he was passing an offshoot of the tunnel. Sometimes he took a required turn, sometimes he pressed forward. Once, he saw a flash of fire far off in the distance, writhing like a tortured soul before vanishing with a ragged breath. Another time, he swore he felt the brush of dead and clammy fingers vying for purchase in his fur as he passed one of the open places.

All the while, Gabriel became more and more certain that there were horrors he couldn't begin to imagine encompassed within these labyrinthine passages. He walked endlessly, possessed more and more strongly by the creeping dread that whispered he would never get out, and he would never find Rowan. That he would eventually lie down, weary and weak, and succumb to the blackness that weighed more and more heavily on him the farther he went.

Gabriel pushed the despair aside, concentrating on his steps. *Three more passages, left. Two, then right. Don't look down. Don't look back.*

And whatever you do, don't run.

A soft crunch, as of a foot crushing the tiny stones that littered the floor, sounded not far behind him, down the passage he'd just passed. Gabriel swallowed hard and forced himself to control his speed. Hopefully it was just the continuing darkness beginning to play tricks on his mind. That crunch could have just been his imagination.

Just like the scrape of that same imagined foot dragging as whatever owned it started to follow him. And the footfall after that. And the soft, moaning gasp that accompanied it.

Don't run. Don't run.

Gabriel pressed on, his gait steady, even as whatever nightmare had caught his scent continued to shuffle along behind him, just a little ways back. He had to focus. Stopping, indecision, were no longer options of any kind. He couldn't be caught.

Especially not by whatever that *thing* was.

This was how he'd always imagined hell: dark, dank, enclosed spaces where everyone was lost, with only taunting illusions of a way out, and unseen horrors dogging your every step, watching, waiting just out of sight, anticipating the moment you would finally fall. The only thing that kept him moving through it was the vision of Rowan's face, glowing vibrantly in his memory. He had to pretend he could smell her warmth and spice rather than the decay that permeated this godforsaken place. That he could hear faint echoes of her husky laughter, urging him onward, instead of the inexorable forward movement of the thing that stalked him.

Gabriel's heart thudded rapidly in his chest as he continued on through the abyss of the dragon Tunnels. Had the Dyadd lovers of the dragons really once used these passages to meet their amours? It was astounding to him that this had been done by anyone with any frequency. But then love created compulsions that were very close to madness.

Shuffle, scrape. Shuffle, scrape. Breath.

Fear closed in on him. His sense of time, he knew, had been horribly distorted. How long had he been walking? Ten minutes? Three years? It could have been anything. All of his instincts rebelled against what he was doing, demanding that he run like hell. All, that was, but the strongest of all, the one that dovetailed perfectly with one of the most important rules Saint Columba had given his Pack, their Sacred Dictates.

Protect thy mate.

So he pressed on. And after what might have been an eternity, the air began to freshen, the impenetrable darkness to lessen degree by minuscule degree. Until he walked in grayness, the black cut by a nimbus of light just ahead.

The exit. Rowan. Thank God.

Whatever he might face with the dragons, nothing would compare to this horrifying journey into their lair. He would rather fight what he could see, no matter how terrible. He picked up his pace as he drew closer to the light, seeing now that it was the outline of something covering the exit, hopefully nothing difficult to move. Behind him the pace of that steady shuffle picked up as well. And to the left of him he heard something else stir into life down another passage, nothing more than a black hole in the barely existent light.

Don't run. Do NOT run, he told himself. Until the shuffling, faintly moaning somethings were joined by a third, and a fourth. And just ahead, in the very last dark opening before freedom, a white form so misshapen and revolting his joints began to leaden at the barest hints of what it might truly look like dragged itself hungrily toward him, trying to head him off.

To hell with not running.

He was too close to lose now, damn it. Gabriel put his head down, took a deep breath, and barreled forward, hoping that whatever was blocking the exit had at least a little give to it. Because it was either hit it or deal with his pursuers, and at this point an ice pick under the claws sounded better than the second option.

His speed kicked in immediately, like nothing he'd felt before. Even at his initial Change he'd noticed that his Wolf form seemed enhanced in this realm. More powerful, bigger, faster. As though the air on Coracin had been tailored specifically for his benefit. He wondered briefly what else he might be capable of in this place, and just as quickly decided he would find out later. It was time to get out of here.

The creature ahead of him snarled and made a swipe as he rocketed past, numbing the area where its long and malformed fingers brushed. Behind him the moans had turned to howls of anger, muffled and wordless torment that was painful to hear. Gabriel bunched his muscles as the rest closed in behind him, feeling how their speed increased to match his own, feeling the hands swiping at the air just out of reach.

He leaped as the cries behind him reached a deafening pitch. Then he found himself passing directly through the dark square in the center of the light, coming to land hard on the other side as the miserable voices fell silent all at once. He had crossed some sort of invisible barrier, Gabriel thought as he straightened, looking around cautiously. Beneath him was a smooth stone floor, black as the mountain itself. On either side of him a high arched corridor stretched and curved away, lit by flickering torches that produced no smoke. And just in front of him, where he would have expected to see some hint of the opening he had just passed through, hung a faded and dusty tapestry depicting what could only be *daemon* feasting on … on …

Gabriel curled his lip and turned away. It seemed his people and the *daemon* had never gotten along very well. And he had better things to do than look at the evidence.

All that mattered was that this corridor was blessedly deserted, that even now he could begin to catch hints of the one he sought beneath the overpowering scents of smoke and incense. And that he would not have to bring her back the way he'd had to come in.

It was time for the Andrakkar to understand a little something about *arukhin* tenacity. They might have been gone a long time, but they hadn't lost the traits that had made them worthy adversaries of the dragons. He was an Earth man, yes. But he was also a Drakkyn who had discovered that some things were truly worth fighting, even dying, for.

And he had come for his mate.

Chapter 17

ROWAN SAT ON THE EDGE OF THE BED, STILL ENOUGH THAT she might have been a statue, waiting for the inevitable knock at the door. Though there was no natural light in the room, which was lit only by small torches on the walls that had been enchanted to burn endlessly without smoke, she knew it must be getting on toward evening. And apart from the ghostlike Wolf hovering outside the door, she had been left completely alone.

It couldn't last. And perhaps that was best, she decided, running a hand absently over the heavy and sumptuous fabric of the bed coverings. Best to get it over with, so at least she would be rid of this terrible sense of impending doom. Rowan wasn't quite sure what to expect, but she supposed the Andrakkar had enlisted some of those wretched *daemon* for whatever ceremony they would perform. What evil might yet be done to her she couldn't begin to guess. But no matter what, she would be playing the willing victim, pretending to soften toward Lucien. Beginning to set him up for what would be, if the Goddess were just, a terrible fall. Yet it would never be as painful as what he deserved.

She still couldn't believe Gabriel was dead.

Rowan rose, moving restlessly about the small chamber looking for something more to occupy her thoughts. Anything but that final image of Gabriel reaching into the sky and shouting her name while his captor waited and watched, smiling. But there was nothing she hadn't already looked at a thousand times. The bed, a small table, a chair. Heavy fabrics and dark colors, jewels glittering dimly around an empty fireplace. Nothing to help her. No way out.

So she thought of Gabriel, and that cut through her numbness and sliced the wound open anew. Rowan tipped her head back, digging her fingers into her hair and tugging, closing her eyes. Maybe she truly was cursed. She almost hoped she was, if she was to belong to Lucien. If she must make some pale imitation of a life here, among the dragons.

How she hated them. And yet found she hated not Lucien, but Mordred most of all. He had led the dragons to new depths of destruction, had twisted his son into a creature that couldn't comprehend real love. He hunted the *arukhin* because they still existed, because he was afraid of beauty and courage and beings who fought with their hearts along with their teeth and claws.

He had turned what the Drak had made in his own image into a violent, amoral waste. But the Drak had turned a blind eye long ago. And she was no dragon to make it right.

If it weren't for Bastian and whoever was left of the Dyadd, she would have gladly fought them all to the death. It would have been worth it if she could have taken one of the Andrakkar with her. As it was, she was cornered. Heat gathered at her fingertips, and she raised her hands before her to watch as they glowed, pulsing gently in the dim light. So much power. So utterly useless.

A bitter smile twisted her lips. If ever there were a time when she would have consented to Gabriel rescuing her, this was it.

The soft scratch at the door made her jump, her heart swelling with hope even as she cursed herself. But when she opened the heavy wooden door, it was only Malachi, cowering a little as though he thought she might decide to strike him at any minute.

"What is it?" she sighed, but the Wolf couldn't answer, just pinned his ears back and whined softly. Rowan frowned, and the animal shrunk away from her, though he didn't leave.

"No, no, I'm not going to hurt you," she said softly, giving in to her instincts to soothe him though she hadn't been able to soothe herself. She held out her hand, feeling slightly foolish about it once she realized what she was doing. This wasn't really a Wolf, after all, but a man. He probably didn't want to sniff her hand or be petted. And sure enough, Malachi surprised her into smiling when he ducked his head away and gave her a look that was plainly disgruntled.

Whatever had been done to him, there was still man in the Wolf, she decided. He looked nervously over his shoulder, into the shadows of the hall that had been carved from the mountain itself, then back at her and whined again.

"Is it," she asked haltingly, "is it time to go?" She could think of no other reason for the intrusion. The only way she'd known Malachi was even there before this was because she'd poked her head into the hallway twice earlier on, and he'd been sitting sentry by the door both times. But instead of taking her hand in his mouth and leading her off as he had earlier, he backed away slowly, still whimpering and darting quick looks into the shadows.

She looked in both directions to make sure that no one would catch her out of the room, then took a step toward Malachi.

"Look, whatever it is, maybe I can help. You don't need to be afraid of me …"

But she saw then that it wasn't her the Wolf was afraid of at all. Rowan went completely still as she looked into one of the pools of darkness that was untouched by the flickering torchlight. And as she watched, a great pair of glowing golden green eyes opened to regard her, seeming to float in blackness.

Her hand fluttered to her throat to catch the sound that threatened to erupt from her mouth and bring all the dragons running. She knew those eyes.

Gabriel padded smoothly into the light, his inky fur making him look like a shadow come to life. Rowan swallowed hard, frozen in place. Something in her feared that if she moved, he would just fade away. But the black Wolf seemed to have no such worry. His gaze never wavered from her face as he approached, finally coming to a stop inches from her. His great head, which came up to her waist, lifted slightly as he continued to look at her.

It was the yearning in his eyes that was finally her undoing.

With a strangled cry, Rowan dropped to her knees before him, threw her arms around his neck, and buried her face in thick, soft fur that smelled of forests and wild, far-off hills. Her will to remain here shattered at that first blessed touch. She couldn't stay here with Lucien knowing Gabriel was still alive, not for another second, though she knew it would mean the fight of both their lives. She had no idea what would become of them, but one thing was certain, for now and evermore. From this day forward, Gabriel MacInnes could rescue her all he wanted to.

As long as he accepted the fact that she was occasionally going to rescue him as well. The man was utterly hopeless. But he was alive. And he was hers.

She felt him Change, felt the fur become warm flesh and a pair of strong arms wrap around her. Rowan wanted to tell him not to, that it was too dangerous, but the ability to speak seemed to have gone entirely by the wayside. Anger had become easier for her than joy over the past year, but there was nothing to work up even the slightest bit of ire where he was concerned. All that mattered was that Gabriel was alive, and that he had come for her.

"We have to go," he said, the rumble of his deep brogue like chocolate for her ears.

"That would mean letting go of you," Rowan said breathlessly, covering his face, his mouth, in thousands of tiny kisses. "Not interested."

He drew back to look at her, cupping her face in his hands. He looked tired, she saw, and unshaven, and generally distressed. He also looked like he wanted to hold her as tightly as he could for as long as he could. She wanted, with every fiber of her being, to allow just that.

But not now. There were voices down the corridor, drifting from far off but getting closer. And one of them was Lucien's.

"I'm going to Change back now, love. We're not far from one of the passages your ancestors used to get in when they were carrying on with the dragons. Stay close."

Rowan nodded, suddenly so anxious to be gone from this place that she felt a little ill. She almost forgot about the Wolf huddled against the wall, watching the two of them intently.

"Wait!" she breathed, making Gabriel turn back to look at her, concerned.

"What is it? What's wrong, love?"

"What about your cousin?" she asked, gesturing to Malachi. When Gabriel's brows drew together, she continued, "I know he's done horrible things. But he'll die here. He's nothing more than a slave. Look at his fur, Gabriel … they've been burning him."

She could see that she had a great deal more sympathy for Malachi than Gabriel did, and probably for good reason. But Gabriel appeared to at least be thinking about it.

Finally he grumbled, "I'm not forgiving you, Malachi. I don't know that I ever will. You knew what you were doing. But as little as I like it, you're still family, though my father will have the final say on that. You deserve bad, but not this. Come on. Come with us and let's get out of here."

Malachi made a sound, some strange and unhappy sound, and lifted one paw to swipe at the stone that glimmered at his throat. Then he backed slowly away, looking unspeakably miserable. Rowan sighed, finally understanding.

"He can't come. Not while Mordred is alive. That stone around Malachi's neck is as good as chains, binding him to his master's will. It'll show Mordred where we are if he should decide to ask. He has to stay here until Mordred is no more." She shook her head sadly. "There's no other way. Malachi can no longer Change to a man, and he can't remove the collar. His best bet is to wait. Then he can come to us."

"Brilliant," Gabriel said flatly. "Sorry, cousin. Looks like it's a little more fun with the fire breathers until we get this sorted out."

Malachi's glare was unmistakable when he looked at Gabriel, but his expression when he turned to Rowan was decidedly softer, more questioning. Pleading. She nodded.

"We'll come back for you," she said. And with that, Malachi shrank back into the shadows and disappeared. Gabriel sighed.

"We've just made a lot of people very unhappy. He would have killed my father, Rowan. It's not as though he doesn't deserve what he's gotten."

She just shook her head. "It's not right, Gabriel. Mordred Andrakkar has caused enough pain."

Rowan gave a soft gasp as Gabriel grabbed her and planted a hard kiss on her mouth. "Damned right," he said gruffly. "Now let's get the hell out of here."

In seconds, man had become beast once more, taking off down the empty corridor with a swiftness that had Rowan racing to keep up. Lucien's voice still echoed from somewhere behind them, and she waited with dread for the moment her absence was discovered. All she could hear as they ran was her own thundering heartbeat and labored breathing, while she expected to hear the angry shouts and the pounding of feet in pursuit at any second. But there was nothing but the sounds of their own escape. Not that she would feel better until they were out, and gone.

Sheer luck, she decided, that she had been installed in a part of the mountain castle that looked to be little used, probably in case she decided to be difficult. The ornate rugs covering the stone floors of these hallways were threadbare and dusty, and no tapestries covered the craggy walls. Rowan knew without a doubt that Gabriel would have found a way no matter what, but as he slipped behind a stone jutting from the wall at a strange angle to duck into a narrow, cobwebby passage, she thought that Morgaine might be looking after her daughter after all.

Rowan had to crouch a little as she moved along the dark, downward-slanting passage, but other than that movement was easy. It was odd to think that once her people had traveled this way full of an entirely different kind of anticipation. Maybe the dragons had been different then. Or maybe it had been the Dyadd. Either way, those days were long gone.

Down they raced, ever downward, until Rowan began to wonder if they had made some mistake and were now headed for the center of the world. There was no light, only the insistent padding of Gabriel's feet in front of her. And still there was only silence from the mountain. After what felt like hours had passed, Rowan started to believe they might just make it out unnoticed.

Their luck held until just before they emerged through a slice of pale light into the young evening. Rowan had just caught sight of the large, red moon hanging low in the sky, had just taken her first breath of pure mountain air, when a furious roar barreled up through the bowels of the mountain to shake the ground beneath their feet.

"Shit," she hissed as dust rained from the ceiling, and prayed for speed. They were going to need it.

The two of them burst through a small arched opening at the base of the mountain and made a beeline for the distant haze of blue that Rowan knew must be the portal to carry them home. She picked up her skirts, wishing desperately for her jeans and a pair of sneakers instead of a heavy gown, and ran. Gabriel loped alongside her now, urging her on with his continuous glances behind them and upward, at the flat, massive shelf of rock and enormous doors near the top that marked the formal entrance to the castle. They were still shut, but not, she feared, for long. Soon the air would be full of great leathery wings. And in the night their eyes would look like violet fire.

She remembered. And as she did, the past began to blend with the present, opening around her like some dark and malignant bloom.

Ama Dyana, *help me … they're coming for us all …*

They reached the true base of the mountain and sprinted across the valley floor, kicking up clouds of gray sand in their haste. She could hear the rapid in and out of Gabriel's breath beside her, matching her own. Rowan clung to that, and to the rapidly approaching light.

So close ... almost there ...

There was a terrible metallic squeal, then a long and drawn-out groan as the doors of the mountain began to swing outward behind them. The sound underlying that, however, was so much worse. It was the sound of dragons, hissing, snarling, thirsty for blood and ready to take flight. And she and Gabriel had no cover. Not making it was not an option.

She'd be damned if they would catch her now.

Rowan focused intently on that point in the distance, the ire of the dragons fading into background noise. Bursts of coolness spread over her skin, and she felt herself lengthening, stretching forward. Her feet were lighter, catching more and more air beneath them as she ran. And suddenly, strangely, she felt something within her begin to change. She didn't have time to breathe and consider what it was, but it felt as though the varied loose and hanging threads of her past chose just that moment to wind together and tie themselves up.

The air above them was suddenly filled with noise and movement, the heavy *whoosh whoosh* of massive wings pressing in on them from all around. And though she was terrified, something deep within her responded to that rhythm with wild joy. She began to pick up speed, something electric rippling through her as though there were thousands of tiny wires beneath her skin newly awakened to life. The circle of stones was just ahead, and through the bright blaze of blue she could see the place she had thought she might never see again—*home*.

An ear-splitting shriek sliced through the evening like a dagger, so close it was painful. Rowan didn't have to turn to know she would find a dragon as black as midnight in hot pursuit, almost close enough to touch.

Almost there … If only I could fly, I might just make it …

The truth slammed into her all at once. The threads pulled tight. Everything she had ever questioned suddenly made sense. The ramifications were staggering, but there was no time to think it through right now. Only one thing mattered right now: if she didn't just go with it, she wasn't going to make it. Lucien was almost on top of her. She had no choice.

Goddess, give me strength.

With an ease that shocked her, Rowan gave herself over completely to her body's instincts, concentrating only on the steady beat of dragon wings, and on her destination. Something she had never known reared its head inside, demanding to be set free. There was a searing flash of pain down her back as she leaped alongside her mate into the light, her wings bursting from her back and unfurling to catch the air. Fear gave way to an unexpected, brilliant burst of exhilaration, and for the first time in her life, Rowan knew what it was to soar.

Then the light was gone, and the dragons' roars abruptly gave way to the gentle whispers of the trees overhead. Familiar arms reached out for her, and cries of delight fell from lips she thought had fallen silent forever.

She was home.

Gabriel stared as Rowan was enveloped in a laughing, squealing, crying crowd of women, none of whom seemed to be the least bit perturbed by the iridescent green wings that were already retracting, seeming to melt back into her gown without the slightest disturbance to the fabric.

Maybe he'd missed something. Maybe she grew wings under duress and had forgotten to mention it. He had to be glad she had them, since they were probably the only thing that had kept her out of the claws of Lucien Andrakkar. But obviously the Dyadd Morgaine had a different idea of "unusual" than he did.

Small wonder, considering the place they lived.

Then he began to see what else surrounded him, and Gabriel momentarily forgot everything else as his senses tried to absorb their first encounter with the *Carith Noor*.

It was a forest. That much he could see. But that was as far as the familiar extended, because it was like no other forest he had ever seen, or even imagined. He stood amid a scatter of brightly colored tents in a small clearing, their bold hues and high peaks more sophisticated than circus-like. Pennants, each with a single and unfamiliar symbol, fluttered in a warm breeze. He couldn't quite tell how many tents there were or how large the encampment actually was, but it was a question that vanished almost immediately as he caught sight of the wonder that was the trees.

Not far from where he stood, just past a large wooden cart and a small gathering of zebra-like animals that grazed peacefully on the emerald green grass, silvery trunks at least ten times the circumference of a man erupted from the ground and shot into a sky that shimmered faintly in hues of deepest purple and royal blue. Somewhere out of sight, lost to his vision above the canopy of trees, the moon continued to cast its red glow. And the bit of sky directly above him was framed all around by leaves of palest green. There were some scattered on the ground around him as big as his foot, and the ones still on the trees rustled comfortingly, rippling in waves of exquisite color off into the distant shadows of the forest, which looked, from where he stood, to stretch on forever.

It was the sudden musical cry of some exotic bird that finally shocked Gabriel into drawing a breath. He had never seen a place of such exquisite beauty. There was a wildness here that seemed to be in the very air, already seeping into his blood, running through his veins until he didn't think he would ever be able to separate from it.

He had never been to this place, and yet something in him called it *home*.

Forcing himself into movement, Gabriel finally collected his wits enough to step from the ring of white stones in which he stood. He grabbed the clothes offered him by one of a veritable sea of breathtakingly beautiful women, grousing inwardly a little at the fact that Rowan didn't seem to have the clothes-ripping-during-a-Change issue that his own kind did. Then, forgotten, he slunk a short distance away so that he wouldn't be crushed in the stampede. He pulled the garments on quickly, a simple brown tunic over fitted leggings. Then he watched Bastian, with a bigger smile than he thought Rowan's serious brother was capable of producing, pick up his sister and give her a bear hug so tight that she had to punch him, laughing, to get him to let go.

It was amazing, he thought. Rather than dissolving into tears at her ordeal, Rowan's eyes were alight, glowing like two jewels in the near-darkness. Her entire being seemed lit from within, exuding a vitality that surprised him after all that had happened. *Wings,* he told himself, trying the idea on for size. He found that he was surprised, but not totally shocked. *She's got wings.* Well, he guessed, why not? He'd come to terms with the fact that she was a blood-drinking sorceress pretty early on. The addition of wings was relatively minor. Not so different from him sprouting fur. Mostly.

And God, he thought as he watched her lift her arms to the sky and execute a joyful dancer's turn, but she was beautiful.

Whatever else came, he was glad he'd been able to give her this.

"I don't know how to thank you," Bastian said, appearing as suddenly as he usually did to stand beside Gabriel and watch the continuing display. His voice was thick with emotion. "There's nothing I could give that would come close to being enough. The Dyadd is whole again."

"Your blessing for Rowan and me is enough," Gabriel replied, accepting Bastian's brotherly cuff on the shoulder.

"You have that, and gladly," Bastian said. "Though you may change your mind after a few days surrounded by all of my sisters." He shook his head ruefully. "It can get interesting. And I warn you, I won't always be here to protect you from their wrath."

Gabriel raised his eyebrows at Bastian's smirk. The reality of living with a tribe of women hadn't really occurred to him, but he wasn't afraid. Yet. "You planning on going somewhere?"

Bastian just shook his head. "Later. Right now we need to concentrate on strategy, because we have maybe an hour, not much more, before the dragons arrive. They'll be on their way as we speak, no doubt."

"You mean you haven't got a bloody plan?" Gabriel growled, dumbfounded. He and Rowan had just risked -their necks getting out of the mountains, making it by the skin of their teeth. He'd assumed they weren't just fleeing back into certain annihilation. Though he supposed throttling a spell out of Bastian was always an option. Bastian, however, was watching his sister with a speculative expression that for whatever reason made Gabriel uneasy.

"I think," Bastian said, "all things considered, that the plan has just changed."

Gabriel looked back at Rowan, who was caught in the embrace of three of her sisters. "You mean the wings?" he asked, feeling more than a little stupid. Was this not something Rowan had been known to do before?

Bastian raised his eyebrows incredulously. "I mean considering your mate is half dragon. Don't you think that changes things somewhat?"

Dragon.

Dragon?

Gabriel opened his mouth to say something intelligent and perceptive about this. It was no great surprise to him when nothing came out. He frowned, gritted his teeth, and tried to collect his thoughts, which were suddenly awhirl with visions of making love to a sharp-toothed serpent. It wasn't pretty, and it was beyond distracting.

Rowan ... a dragon ... wait a minute ... what?

By the time he remembered he had an audience, Bastian looked ready to punch him. "Don't tell me that after all of this you're considering having a problem with that."

"No. I ... no. It's just ... I mean, how did you not *know* that?" Gabriel stammered, trying desperately to get his bearings. It wasn't that it changed his love for her, he thought. But it was a hell of a thing to have suddenly sprung on you. He really shouldn't be expected to be at all coherent about it right now. He would get over it. He was just going to need some time to wrap his brain around it.

"Look," Bastian snapped, beginning to look dangerous. "I assume that Rowan mentioned this, but the *Dyana* hasn't taken a mate in over a thousand years. *All of Elara's children* have different fathers. Some of us know who they are. Some don't. And no one particularly cares." He flung out a hand, pointing at a delicate, sloe-eyed beauty with curly brown hair that fell to her waist. "Reya's father is a faun. The man is half goat, for the Goddess's sake, and runs around naked as the day he was born. Are you going to start gawping like a fish every time she gets near you now, too?"

Gabriel hated feeling like an ass. It was something he tried to avoid, though often unsuccessfully, at all costs. But for a man who could change into a beast at will, it occurred to him that he was being awfully stupid about bloodlines. He exhaled loudly and scrubbed his palm across the back of his neck.

"No. Of course not. Sorry. It's just, ah … different. That's all." He shot a look at Bastian's fists, which he was pleased to see loosened slightly. "I don't care." When Bastian looked at him skeptically, he repeated, more irritably, "I don't. But I'm allowed to be surprised, aren't I?"

Bastian gave a noncommittal grunt. "Hmm."

Gabriel considered Rowan, who glanced over to give him a look that was both questioning and full of love. The wings were gone, but the glow remained, as though she'd just discovered something wonderful.

So, Gabriel decided, had he. That was really all there was to it in the end.

He responded to the question in her expression with a wink, earning him a brilliant smile in return before her attention was captured again by the sisters competing for it. She would always be his Rowan. He was just going to have to make certain he always had adequate cover before he pissed her off from now on. The thought made him grin, and when he addressed Bastian again, it was with a different tone entirely.

"Have some sympathy, man. I've got myself a mate who's higher on the food chain than I am. Give me a minute to mourn, all right?"

His sense of humor had always been his way of apologizing. Making Gideon laugh when he might otherwise have killed him had been his way of life for many years now. And, he was relieved to see, Bastian was just as receptive. His mouth gave a reluctant twitch.

"You're an ass, MacInnes."

"Agreed."

"Well, as long as you recognize it, I'll let you live." He gave him a wry smile, but his gaze was serious. "She'll need to know you're comfortable with it. Especially considering who her father probably is. I didn't put two and two together then, but it all makes sense. It's why Rowan's gift is fire. And why my mother was so determined that Lucien shouldn't have Rowan. An 'abomination,' she called it. Brother and sister …" He trailed off, making a face. "She was right. I only wish she'd mentioned the connection, but it wasn't her way."

Gabriel blew out a breath. He'd made the connection right after Bastian had said the word "dragon." Well, once his brain had started forming words again.

"Yeah. I know."

They stood in silence for a moment, each lost in thought. Until finally, Gabriel, who'd never been able to tolerate long periods without conversation, elbowed Bastian to get his attention.

"Do you think Mordred knows?"

Bastian shrugged, wrinkling his nose in disgust. "I don't know. Maybe. Sick bastard. But I'm willing to bet Lucien doesn't. That isn't going to sit well." He smiled, a cruel little twist of his mouth that made Gabriel pity anyone who ever got on his bad side. He didn't even want to speculate on what sort of combination produced a blood-drinking, world-hopping wizard. And he sure as hell wasn't going to ask. So instead he pictured the coming fight, and Rowan in whatever her full glory turned out to be.

He had no doubt she would be amazing.

"She's going to kick ass," he said, imagining it with a slow, savoring smile.

Bastian appeared to consider this, then returned the smile.

"Yeah. I know."

Chapter 18

Rowan waited alone in the clearing.

It was how she had wanted it, at least in the beginning. Though she knew there were others, more than the dragons might imagine, just out of sight in the trees, it had been incredibly important to her that she be able to stand for the Dyadd this way. For the first time, she had been granted the respect accorded the *Dyana*. It was humbling. And as she waited, Rowan thought of her mother. She wished Elara could see her, because she stood for her now too.

Nothing would ever be the same. But she was going to do all in her power to make things right. It couldn't hurt that she appeared to be the natural daughter of the enemy, and a dragon besides. If that wasn't leverage, she didn't know what was.

At the moment her wings had burst from her back, she had known. There was no horror, only a sense of completion that she finally knew, and understood, both halves of herself. The dragons were the children of the Drak himself, for all their faults and shortcomings. She had the half that was Dyadd to temper those things and embrace their strengths. Handy, as the protector of her people, to have a dragon's claws and teeth at her disposal.

It didn't bother her that Mordred was, in all likelihood, her father, nor that Lucien was her brother. Elara had not always chosen the kindest or the most magnificent for her conquests. They were all Daughters of the Goddess Morgaine, and that was what mattered. Still, she had been worried about Gabriel. His way was different. The Andrakkar were his people's enemies. And for all her faith in him, she had felt his eyes upon her wings and worried that he would turn away from her completely.

As usual where he was concerned, she ended up feeling like an irrational idiot. He hadn't skipped a beat. Or at least, she thought with a warm flush, the kisses she'd gotten when he cornered her against a tree had felt a lot like acceptance to her. As had his willingness, though somewhat reluctant, to allow her to be out here on her own.

Now their enemies had only to arrive. Since she was wanted alive, Rowan didn't think they would attack immediately. She planned to try reason first. Then she'd just see how her dragon skin felt when she put it all the way on. And how the dragons felt when they realized just how much the forest had changed.

The moon hung low and red in the sky, which was deep blue and scattered with stars. The forest was strangely silent, as though all the creatures within it knew what was coming. And before long, Rowan's ears picked up that unmistakable sound in the distance, rushing air being pushed by many pairs of great wings, matching with the beat of her heart.

She remembered the same sound on a night that seemed long ago now, the memory tugging at her with old sadness. She knew now that it hadn't been her fault, or her mother's. Mordred had been punished, though it was not yet nearly enough. Making it enough fell to her.

This time she was unafraid.

Shadows soared across the moon, circling high above, then dropping from the sky one by one to land in the clearing. Six dragons in all, hardly an army. But Mordred would have figured that whatever was left of the Dyadd would be easy to bend to his will.

Rowan smiled. He had a very nasty surprise coming. His last, if she had anything to do with it.

He had come himself, she saw, a venomous red dragon with terrible twisting horns. His neck wound leaked openly in this form, black blood mingling with the green poison dripping from his fangs to fall to the ground and scorch the grass.

Lucien landed beside him, folding pitch-black wings tightly against his body and looking at her with eyes that burned like live coals. The four others ringed them from behind, silent, waiting, smoke coiling from their nostrils as their breathing hissed in and out. She folded her hands in front of her, strangely calm. One way or another, she was going to finish this. And then she, Gabriel, and her people could all begin to move forward again without fear.

Mordred's and Lucien's forms seemed to melt and shrink as they shifted form, becoming men as they approached her in the midst of the Dyadd's dark and deserted tents. Mordred managed to walk relatively upright, though there was a stiffness to his gait that indicated he was in pain. Lucien seemed alert, nervous, scenting the air as though he was expecting an attack at any moment.

They stopped when they were only feet from her, and Rowan felt as though she was standing on one side of a battle line she'd drawn without being quite aware of it. They passed a full minute without speaking, and Rowan knew that Lucien had taken note of her appearance.

She had dressed with care, donning the glittering raiment befitting a *Dyana* of the tribe of Morgaine. Gone was the heavy velvet of the dragons. It was a message: *I am not yours.* He seemed to have received it. It was obvious Lucien wasn't pleased.

"I fail to see what the point in causing so much trouble is when you know you have no choice. Now I'm going to kill that worthless brother of yours as well, and I know he must be close by." Lucien's jaw was set. He looked exhausted, Rowan thought, and ill with the dark shadows beneath his eyes. She wondered about the pressure that the father put on the son, the toll that it had taken. About how close his mind was to breaking altogether, and what might happen if it did.

"Him," Mordred growled, his face alight with terrible anticipation, "and the *arukhin* shifter you escaped with. Don't think I didn't recognize him, witch. I'll replace the wretched beast I already have with him. It will be a pleasure to make him pay for the difficulties his family has caused me. And with luck, perhaps he may draw the rest of his kind back as well."

Lucien whirled to glare at his father, curling his lip in disgust. Rowan wondered if he would actually spit at the man, but he only spoke to him in a low hiss.

"For once, Father, I would rather not hear about the damned forest-shifters. This is about my taking a mate, about furthering the Andrakkar line. About what *I* want, for once. It has *nothing to do* with those wretched shifters!"

"Actually, he's right," Rowan said, drawing both sets of eyes to herself almost immediately. They both looked a little surprised, and she thought they might have forgotten there was a third person in attendance to their spat. She felt, though, that it was time to stop the madness of Lucien's pursuit.

"You're … agreeing with me?" Lucien asked, looking puzzled.

Rowan nodded. "Yes. Because all of this has much less to do with the *arukhin* than it does with the fact that I have no desire to marry my own brother."

That produced a reaction, as she'd known it would. But she refused to dance around the truth. Lucien's mouth dropped open in shock, while Mordred's face contorted in rage. He bared teeth at her that had gone long and sharp.

"Nonsense."

"Hardly," she retorted, losing some of her calm. "Though I can understand why you'd lie about it. It's disgusting, to want the two of us together solely for the purpose of producing a purer bloodline." Her temper began to boil. "My mother, my cousins, died for your madness. Thank the Goddess your son hasn't killed any more before finding out the truth."

"The madness is yours," Mordred snapped, smoke rushing from his mouth in his anger. "You're the only one fit to marry my son, because you're a *Dyana,* High Drakkyn of reasonable wits and proper age. Not particularly easy to come by. Your mother died because she was foolish enough to try to stop me." His lips curved cruelly. "I don't know how you escaped, but it won't happen again. No matter who gets in the way."

Rowan just looked at him, feeling nothing. It was sad that she should feel so empty when she looked at the man who had fathered her. But then she supposed she had gotten the best part of him, whatever meager bit that was. It would have to be enough, because there was nothing worthwhile left to have.

"My mother's only mistake was in taking a man like you to her bed," said Rowan. "And I refuse to join with my own blood. Besides … I am already mated."

Mordred snorted, his skepticism apparent. He opened his mouth to reply, but his son, silent all this time, had something to say.

Lucien looked from her, to his father, and back again. The misguided need in his eyes had turned to disgust as reality slowly sank in.

"Is this … is this true?" he asked in a strangled whisper. He was so obviously appalled that Rowan actually felt sorry for him. She had worried a little that Lucien would see things the way his father did on the issue. But it seemed that Mordred had not twisted him enough for that. He had been so sure of what he considered to be love. Now he had the rug pulled out from under him. She remembered he had once told her that she was the only thing that made him feel in his cold and empty existence, and felt a surprising tug of sympathy. He had not been there the night her mother had died. And if nothing else, he was her brother. Maybe he deserved nothing, but it wasn't in her nature to turn away.

She might end up spitting fire, but she wasn't ready to turn away.

She nodded slowly. "I only realized it today. There's no other explanation. I am your sister, Lucien."

"Lies!" shrieked Mordred. "I have no child but Lucien!"

She rounded on him, baring fangs that had gone deadly sharp. "No child that you admit to. But you recognized me that night in the tent, didn't you? Another dragon, and with Andrakkar blood. You encouraged Lucien's selection, and poisoned him with this misguided infatuation as a result. Look at him!"

Mordred lowered his head, his scales beginning to be visible beneath his pasty skin. "There is nothing wrong with my son that a good beating wouldn't cure. He's soft, and lacking in bloodlust, but he's all I have to produce an heir, and he should have the best. A *Dyana*."

"A *Dyana* who carries your blood," Rowan snarled. "I've had enough of your lies, old man. See what I am. See your daughter."

Enraged as she was, the Change came quickly. It was as though the dragon within had only ever waited to be beckoned. She tossed her head back, feeling the dragon blood rocket through her, stretching her, ripping at her as scales shimmered over her skin and her wings tore anew from her back to unfurl. It was freeing, and glorious. And yet her anger, which had seemed great as a woman, had grown along with her and now threatened to become a towering, destructive rage. She wanted to tear flesh, to burn. Flame poured from her throat and lit the sky, along with a roar so full of fury that it seemed as though it could have ripped her in two.

Rowan flexed her wings, almost giving in to the urge to take to the sky, and instead coiled her long neck around to look at Mordred. He looked thunderstruck … and pleased. Incredibly, insanely pleased.

"She can Change," he said, his voice quavering. "She's magnificent. I never dreamed you would gain the ability after so much time had passed, my child. And yet you are all that an Andrakkar should be ... oh, yes," he purred when Rowan hissed at him, "I can see you want to kill me. I would almost allow it, and die happy, but there is so much I can teach you. Such things you will be capable of. And the children you could produce. The restoration of the dragons to their glory." His voice was reverent as he reached out to touch her iridescent green scales. "Let me teach you. I'll give you everything ..."

It was a twisted echo of the promise Lucien had once given her, and infinitely more disturbing. She knew then that Mordred truly had no heart, to cast aside the son he'd raised so easily. That he would do anything to retain his house's grip on power.

And that to end the darkness his reign had brought to Coracin, he would have to die.

"So she tells the truth," Lucien said, his deep voice hoarse and strained. "You would have allowed this union, knowing that we were ... that we were ..." He seemed unable to say it, so repulsive the idea was to him.

"I would have encouraged it!" Mordred screamed, withdrawing his hand when Rowan snapped at it. "I knew when I saw her that the bitch Elara had conceived the one night I convinced her to lay with me. I can see now who is the fitter successor. Perhaps I should just be done with you now and take her back in chains." Smoke poured from his mouth as he spoke, and he and Lucien began to circle each other. "Even as misguided as she is, she has the anger, the lust for the kill. I can feel it!"

Rowan watched intently, barely restraining the urge to tear into both of them. The compulsion to violence was strong, stronger than she would have imagined. And she was so new to this form, controlling it was utterly foreign to her. The dragon came with its own vices as well as virtues. Now was not the time to learn them.

There was a sudden comforting warmth at her side. She looked down to see Gabriel, his Wolf form so big and strong and yet somehow diminutive next to her, come to stand at her side, fur brushing against scale. Her rioting senses calmed almost immediately. His presence reminded her of who she was, why she stood here. And for the first time, he didn't place himself in front of her, but stood where he belonged. Right at her side.

Rowan was filled with a fierce, all-consuming love in that moment. Gabriel, without saying a word, had just given her the most precious gift of all. He had accepted her fully as both an equal and mate. He would not only stand for her, but with her. And in return he would have her heart into eternity.

She felt as though she could defeat an army of dragons.

Lucien and Mordred, however, seemed to have forgotten she was there. They were brewing a battle of their own.

"You would kill me, your only son and heir," Lucien snarled, not looking a thing like the weakling Mordred had described.

"I would do what is best for the House of Andrakkar!" Mordred spat back. "How could that be you, who doesn't believe in conquest, who has no appreciation for the power inherent in being a child of the Drak? You may have my strength, Lucien," he hissed, "but you have no true lust for blood, for treasure. Under you, the dragons will continue to die. If another house takes the throne, the Andrakkar vanish forever. I can't allow either to happen."

"But my own blood. The things I've done, blinded. How you could have deceived me ..." His voice shook slightly with anger and more than a hint of despair, seeking something, anything to assure him that there was more here than met the eye. That his father's selfishness truly did hide some small affection.

But Mordred's eye had been caught by the dark shape beside Rowan, and all else was forgotten. "Enough!" he cried, breathing heavily in his excitement. "The cowardly *arukhin* emerges!" He turned to the dragons at the edge of the clearing. "Take him, and kill any who try to prevent it. And you, my wayward daughter," he growled as he turned to Rowan, already growing, sprouting horns and wings once more, "are coming with me, even if I have to drag you home with my teeth in your neck. I'll teach you what it means to carry my blood. To obey your king."

Rowan knew the time was at hand. The dragons started forward, prompting a loud, deep bark from Gabriel, followed by a low growl. Mordred, now entirely dragon, made a swipe at him with huge and deadly claws. Gabriel leaped to the side, and Rowan shoved herself in front of Mordred when he tried to give chase, breathing a wave of flame that slammed into Mordred's chest. Though he was protected by his scales, he staggered backward from the force. And by the time he recovered, he was immobilized by the sight of the creatures pouring toward him from the cover of the trees.

Rowan threw back her head and gave a battle cry. It was returned by a chorus of voices raised in Wolf song.

The dragons stilled at the sound, hanging hauntingly in the night air.

The *arukhin* had returned to the forest.

They raced into the clearing, some hundred Wolves, golden eyes glowing bright and teeth bared. But whether it was the nature of their enemy that inspired them or just the air of their ancestral home, these warriors were more than they had been in the Earthly realm. Their fur crackled with sparks of power, flickering over their forms until they each seemed outlined in light. Their speed made them a blur, and they seemed able to strike blows that inflicted more damage than their size might indicate. The dragons reared and snapped, their great heavy bodies unused to having to fight creatures smaller and nimbler that were so intent on harming them. The Wolves dodged every angry swipe, leaping to sink teeth into wings, crawling up scaly backs to claw at vulnerable eyes. And the light that filled them looked to Rowan as though it burned.

Rowan watched as a yellow and black dragon, half covered in *arukhin* warriors doing their utmost to disable it, took off in blinded and lopsided flight, only to crash back to the ground moments later with a howl of agony. Bastian was among the attackers, Rowan saw, icy light flying from his fingertips that caused any it hit to bleed. Her sisters hurled their own blasts from the trees, moving constantly, invisible to the besieged dragons but deadly with their aim.

Rowan was deep in the fray, slashing, using her tail as Mordred fought for purchase. She knew that he would do as he'd promised and sink his teeth into her neck to carry her off if he could, whether or not she had much life left in her. He was larger than she, but clumsier. She was thankful for his wound, because with her inexperience at fighting this way, at full power he would undoubtedly have had a huge advantage. As it was, it was taking all of her concentration and strength to hold him off. The rest, thankfully, were occupied by the MacInnes Wolves, though it gradually occurred to her that there was one dragon she had not seen fighting.

A flash of movement beyond the battle caught her eye. She had a brief image of Lucien fleeing into the forest on foot, a Wolf that could only be Gabriel following close at his heels. Mordred had seen them too and turned his head ever so slightly, momentarily distracted.

It was all the opening she needed.

Rowan struck hard, aiming for the already gaping wound in Mordred's neck. Her mouth was instantly filled with a rush of inky blood as her enemy's death cry screamed into the night, Still, she didn't let go, letting all of her rage go in this final act of retribution for all he had done to her, and her people. She shook his neck hard, snapping his vile horned head back and forth with lethal force long after he'd drawn a final, gasping breath.

It was only the howl, distant through the trees, that brought her back to herself.

Gabriel!

She threw Mordred's lifeless body to the ground with a terrible crash and immediately saw that the fight was over for the dragons. Two of the others lay as dead as Mordred, and two more were nothing but rapidly disappearing shadows backlit by the moon. The Wolf shifters were beginning to celebrate, their song raining into the deep blue sky as they gamboled in the clearing. Their wild dance and excited barks were victory itself. The fierce and joyful cries of her tribe reverberated through the trees.

They had won.

But there would be no celebrating for her. Not until this was truly finished.

She felt as though she was contracting into herself as she Changed back, wings, scales, claws compressing until the dragon was tucked neatly away inside. She crouched as her form returned completely to that of a woman, gasping. It had taken more out of her than she'd expected, but there was no time to rest. She picked herself up unsteadily, staggering a little before heading off in the direction she'd seen Gabriel and Lucien go.

Two other Wolves appeared out of the throng to pad at her sides, black like Gabriel but with slightly different features, and one with a hint of silver on his muzzle. She immediately knew them to be Gideon and Duncan, and she was grateful for the backup. Lucien might not want her any longer, but he had to be reeling from the betrayal. Again, she wondered just what he might do if pushed too hard.

They made their way quickly through the trees, her feet as noiseless as their paws on the soft ground of the *Carith Noor*. Dread began to creep through her veins as the silence became oppressive, not a hint of what was happening to Gabriel carried through the night air. She could scent the both of them, Gabriel's warm spice and Lucien's faint incense, intermingled with fear and hatred.

Bastian's voice in her ear made her gasp.

"Wait. We're not alone."

She stopped short, her companions following suit. She looked behind her and saw that Bastian had joined them at some point without her notice. His pale hair shone in the darkness, and his fangs were still lengthened from battle. He jerked his head to indicate that something was ahead of them, then put a finger to his lips. They began to move again, but more slowly, and soon the whispering of the trees became whispers of a far more sinister nature.

Rowan's heart sank.

There were *daemon* in the woods.

Gabriel hunched low to the ground, staring at the familiar creatures who stepped out from behind the trees to stop him and his quarry in their tracks. Their heads were smooth, their faces so nondescript that they were almost interchangeable but for the festering burn on the cheek of the one in the middle. That one he would know anywhere.

Jagrin.

Gabriel fought the urge to recoil, to try to slink backward into the sheltering darkness of the trees. Instead, he stood his ground, stomach roiling as he caught the unmistakable scent of Lucien's fear. It puzzled him that a dragon would be afraid of anything at all. But a quick glance told him that Lucien's pupils were dilated, his breathing catching. And his bright violet eyes were fixed on the tiny vial that dangled from a thin chain around Jagrin's neck, glinting dully in the faint light.

The *daemon* stank of death.

"How fortunate that we meet," Jagrin purred, his red eyes full of hatred as they fixed on each of them in turn. His two companions flanked him, their silence just as unnerving as Jagrin's speech. All looked hungry.

"What do you want, Jagrin? The *daemon* are unwelcome in the *Noor*." Lucien's voice was bereft of its usual resonance, and sounded thin and uncertain in the night air. Jagrin's lips peeled back in a grotesque imitation of a smile.

"As are the dragons, Andrakkar most especially. And yet here you are as well." His eyes flicked down to Gabriel. "Along with that which was promised and not given."

Gabriel growled softly. As obscene as it seemed, he was hoping that Lucien had some better way of defending the two of them than he alone had managed the last time. Of course, that was assuming Lucien wouldn't just hand him over and run.

The chances, he knew, were not good.

"The bargain was fulfilled," Lucien said, his tone warning. "It isn't my fault you couldn't handle him once I left."

"Hmm," said Jagrin, a noncommittal sound. "I have a promise, sworn on the blood of a dragon, that I would have an *arukhin,* or the dragon himself, for my services. Yet I have nothing but the promise. That remains, and so we are still bound."

He slid his fingers beneath the chain to dangle the vial before them, swinging it back and forth, back and forth. It was the pendulum. And he and Lucien lay in the pit, watching it slice ever lower.

"We are bound by nothing, *daemon,*" Lucien snarled. He began to Change, only to have Jagrin give an amused little chuckle and hold out one hand.

Immediately the process stopped, and Lucien let out a choked noise, shuddering as his scales disappeared and his claws retracted.

"Not so fast, my lord Andrakkar. You should know better than that. I can't be so easily killed, nor the promise so easily broken. And your father is dead. Be mindful that I have little incentive to take any care with you anymore."

Lucien seemed to take the news without surprise, though the scent of his fear increased exponentially. "If he is truly dead, then I am now the dragon king," he said. "Remember how much easier my rule will be on your kind, and leave this place."

"Your *rule*," Jagrin sneered. "Even now the dragons move to choose another to lead. They assume and hope you to be dead. Your people grow weary of the name of Andrakkar, Lucien. And my kind demand the payment that was promised."

Though Gabriel had expected Lucien to turn on him immediately at that, as he had gathered that *he* was supposed to have been the payment, the dragon lord hesitated. "Surely," he said at length, "there must be another way. I can't allow you to take me. Or," he murmured, casting a quick and inscrutable glance at Gabriel, "I'm afraid, the *arukhin*."

Gabriel could only stare, incredulous. *What was this?*

Jagrin snorted, looking as disbelieving as Gabriel felt. "Have we forged a friendship with our enemy in the heat of battle, Lord Andrakkar? How sweet. And how pathetic."

Lucien's expression, shrouded in shadows, revealed nothing. His voice stayed steady. "Be that as it may, the situation has changed. There must be *something* else you desire ... besides a battle with the two of us."

Gabriel had heard enough. He shifted in the blink of an eye and stood to glare at the man who had recently put a lot of effort into becoming the bane of his existence, certain that Lucien was trying to play him for a fool one last, deadly time.

"You bloody lunatic," he snapped, poking a finger into Lucien's chest to push him backward. "I don't know what you're up to, but I sure as hell don't need your protection."

Lucien's eyes flared. "*Protection?* You're as much a fool as I thought. I don't give a damn what happens to you," he spat back. "You can burn in the fiery pits of Azgaroth for all I care. But because you matter to her ..." He trailed off, the words seeming to catch in his throat. And intermingled with the fury in his eyes, Gabriel saw something he had never expected, nor thought this dragon capable of—regret. "Because you matter to my ... my sister ... you won't be sent there by my hand. I have caused her enough pain, more than she will ever forgive, or should. I wish I had recognized ... but then," he said with a sharp, bitter bark of a laugh, "it's far too late for foolish wishes. There is just you, and me ... and a few bloodthirsty *daemon.*" Lucien shook his head, and Gabriel saw, with a sinking feeling, that there were indeed things that the dragons feared. "Why didn't you just let me run?"

Jagrin watched the two of them, intrigued. "Really? The object of your desire is your own flesh and blood? Well, well, well. *Very* unfortunate." His voice took on a note of malicious amusement as he focused his attention solely on Lucien. "I don't suppose you have anything left to live for then, do you, Master Lucien? No woman. No kingdom. Bastard of a father newly deceased. Why, I'm surprised you don't just want to die."

Very slightly, Gabriel saw Lucien flinch. A nerve had clearly been hit. "There's been enough death here tonight," he said softly.

"Oh, I think not," Jagrin replied, letting the vial around his neck drop back against his chest. "Not if you choose to fight what you've agreed to. Look at it this way. I'm doing your people one last favor, ridding them of the madness of your house. Besides, while the forest shifter still has his appeal, I can think of a great many more uses for a dragon." His grin was hideous. "A *great* many." He turned his head slightly to one of his companions.

"Take him." He considered Gabriel for a moment, then shrugged. "And the other. Though I think we'll just tie him to a stake and let the scavengers have at him. It's no less than he deserves."

It was all he needed to hear to set him to action. Gabriel sprang at Jagrin with a snarl, Changing in mid-air to barrel into the *daemon* as a Wolf. Jagrin screeched as they flew backward, rolling when they hit the ground in a tangle of teeth and claws. Gabriel howled as Jagrin's needle-like teeth sank into his shoulder, but managed to get in his own blow soon after, raking his claws across Jagrin's face. Vile green liquid welled in the deep slashes and ran freely into the *daemon*'s eyes and mouth. Still he struggled, gagging on the dark words he meant to use on Gabriel.

A sudden shout, a flash of light, and suddenly it seemed there were a great many more fighting on his side. A voice he recognized as Bastian's cut through the bloody haze. The howls of the other *daemon* rose into the night as his friends joined the battle.

"Get him! Rowan, watch yourself, he's going to move …"

Another flash of light, a tortured scream, and a whiff of brimstone immediately followed Bastian's command. Gabriel wanted to look, but he finally had the lead *daemon* pinned beneath him. All that was left was to end it. But as Jagrin's red eyes stared up at him, something was badly amiss. He didn't look like a creature about to die.

"Not … this time," he gasped, spitting out blood. "*Kethamra … natar …*" Without warning, Gabriel was thrown backward, landing hard on the ground as a dark figure leaped onto Jagrin, grappling fiercely. It happened so fast that he barely had a moment to register what was happening before it was over. There was a blur of movement, a snarl of triumph, and a tortured, unearthly scream.

A blinding burst of light, a whiff of smoke, and finally, silence. Gabriel struggled to his feet to find a dazed-looking Bastian staring at a spot on the ground a few feet away, Gideon at his side. The ground before them was pouring white smoke.

The world went gray when he tried to gain his feet, and he remembered the blood streaming from the wound in his shoulder. Then, mercifully, there was the scent of autumn, and Rowan's arms were around him, giving him heat, lending him support where he felt like he might not be capable of it himself. Gabriel wrapped himself around her, gladly submitting to the touching, stroking, caressing fingers that roved over his face, through his hair.

Her voice was shaky as she admonished him. "Very nice job, but please stop fighting with things that have bigger teeth than you, okay?"

He laughed softly, nuzzling into her hair and realizing that he was going to need to go to sleep for roughly a week to recover from this adventure. Which meant Rowan was sleeping for just as long. Because his current plans involved never letting go of her again. "Nice try. I'm still going to fight with you, no matter what you say."

"You shouldn't. I'm meaner than the *daemon*."

"Don't I know it." Gabriel sighed contentedly, aware that they were not alone and not particularly caring. He'd seen Gideon and Carly all over each other often enough. It was his turn to be disturbingly mushy.

"When I saw him bite you … this is twice in as many days that I've thought I lost you." Rowan's voice wavered, and he knew that her humor was just cover for worry. It was a mechanism he understood well.

He opened one eye to look at her through a curtain of red hair.

"Well, I think we can safely say that dragons and *daemon* are no match for me. So unless you've got anything else for me to fight, I'll take a couch and some palm-waving servants from now on. Maybe a cold beer, once I smuggle it in. Naked lap dances once in a while from my goddess of a wife. I'm an easy man to please."

Rowan stroked Gabriel's hair absently as she knelt beside him. "I think the servants are out. And I don't do lap dances. Though I may consider making an exception for my very furry husband." She kissed him softly on his cheek, which was rough with stubble.

"We may as well go back to the camp," Gideon said from beside them. "It's over."

Gabriel turned his head slightly to look at his brother, crouched by the still-steaming ground, and sighed. "I hope so, Gid."

Gideon shook his head. "No, they're gone, the both of them. Strange, the Andrakkar jumping on that *thing* right after he threw you off. I don't guess we'll ever know why, since they melted right into the ground before we could do anything. Though it looked like the other one had the advantage." He shook his shaggy hair, the slash across his eye very stark in the moonlight. "I wouldn't want to be Lucien right now. But it's no less than he deserves."

"Maybe," Gabriel said, though in his heart he was no longer sure that was entirely true. But no matter what, it appeared to be a moot point. And right now all he wanted was his mate's arms, and some long-awaited peace.

Rowan looked at him, the fatigue on her exquisite face filling his heart with thoughts he would never have the words for. He wasn't a poetic man, nor particularly romantic either. But he would always give her what he had. And he had a feeling Rowan would think it was more than enough.

"I love you," he said softly, breathing the words against soft, porcelain skin.

"And I love you," she returned, his woman, his lover, his fire-breathing dragon. His mate.

"Then come on. Let's go home."

Epilogue

Rowan MacInnes an Morgaine reclined on a bed of silken pillows and cushions, enjoying the shade of the gently billowing canopy above her. She breathed in the sweetly scented Highland air, basking in the dappled sunlight filtered through the branches of an ancient oak tree as she relaxed upon her little oasis at the edge of *Iargail*'s terrace. One hand curved protectively around the magnificent swell of her belly, which she had managed (with perhaps a little bit of help, she conceded) to swath in shimmering green fabric along with the rest of her for the day. The other hand was busy with what had lately become a favorite activity: directing.

The directee, however, was being less than accommodating.

"I really don't think you should put your thumb there," she commented, waggling a finger at him. That earned her not one, but three matching scowls, along with some colorful muttering she pretended not to have heard.

"He's still putting his thumb there." Carly MacInnes looked skeptically at Bastian, Gabriel, and Gideon as they labored over a small, simple wooden thing that looked like it might one day aspire to be a piece of furniture. "Are you *sure* the father has to make the cradle? Even if he's …" She trailed off, wincing as Gabriel exploded in a torrent of curse words, shaking his wounded thumb as Gideon shoved his brother aside to have a go with his own manly expertise. Bastian regarded the misshapen structure with thoughtful intensity, then offered some tidbit of wisdom that earned him a rude comment from each of the brothers. "Kind of inept?" she finally finished. She then shot Rowan a sidelong glance that had them both dissolving into laughter.

"It was traditional once," Rowan replied, wiping at her eyes when she could finally speak again. "I think it's a lovely way to begin again, now that so many Pack have returned to the *Noor*."

"Yeah, no wonder you've escaped back to the Highlands for a little while," Carly smirked, her blue eyes twinkling as she propped herself on her elbow. "And this cradle-making thing is also a lovely way to keep entertained when your husband is always nipping at your heels otherwise, if I do say so myself." Her eyes narrowed playfully. "This wouldn't be revenge, would it?"

"No." Rowan paused, thinking about it, then qualified, "Mostly."

Rowan relaxed into the softness of the pillows behind her neck and back. She was lucky, she thought as she watched Gabriel continue to hammer away at the almost-cradle. So very lucky in so many ways. And she'd never dreamed that now, nine months to the day since they had driven the dragons out of the *Carith Noor*, life would have become so beautifully normal.

The Dyadd Morgaine was once again a tribe bursting with color and music, enhancing the forests with their magic as they traveled. Throughout the *Noor* there was merry laughter and conversation, the wild and beautiful trills of their songs carried on the warm air. There, on the other side of the Stone, the silverwood trees had burst into lush and glittering bloom, and the gentle breeze brought the petals down around them in a gentle, fragrant rain of white. All as it should be, as she had always imagined it.

And more. Because she was not alone.

"I give up," growled the deep, delicious brogue into her ear, giving her a start. As she seemed to do more and more often as her time approached, she'd dozed off without realizing it. Rowan opened her eyes with a sleepy smile, gladly accepting the comfort as Gabriel sank in beside her and readjusted her position so that she now rested against his chest. Beside them, Gideon arranged himself at Carly's side and grabbed a tiny fruit from the loaded platter the women had been sharing, popping it in his mouth and dropping a playful wink at her.

Rowan grinned and winked back as her brother settled himself at her feet, closing his eyes with a relaxed sigh.

They had promised to come to the *Carith Noor* for the birth, Carly and Gideon, Duncan, and even Malcolm (who had insisted he only wanted to see Gabriel finally get his just desserts but got suspiciously teary every time he was anywhere near something remotely baby-related). It touched her deeply, the love and loyalty of the MacInnes Pack, and their willingness to make her and hers a part of all that. Since she and Gabriel had married, on the grounds of *Iargail* and then again beneath the majestic trees of her homeland, his family had become her own. And Carly, though she saw her only sporadi-cally, had become as one of her own sisters.

Marriage to a MacInnes male, Rowan had decided, was a solid foundation for friendship all on its own. Sometimes, like when Gabriel had asked her for the hundredth time in an hour whether she thought she ought to just sit down, it was nice to know that elsewhere in the universe she had a one-woman support group who was bound to sympathize.

Though right at this moment the big, handsome man with the swollen thumb was making her feel like the luckiest woman alive, just by holding her in his arms. He did have a way about him.

What came out of his mouth, as always, was another matter entirely.

"I think, unless you want the baby to sleep on a board, that you might want to consider hiring someone else to build the cradle, love." He nuzzled her hair, sighing contentedly, and the familiar warmth he provoked in her suffused her. "I'm a big enough man to admit it. I've been defeated by carpentry. You may as well put me out of my misery."

Rowan felt him slip a hand against her belly. The baby's answering kick was hard enough to take her breath away, but after a minute Rowan threaded her fingers through Gabriel's with a contented smile. It had been a surprise, finding out that the lovemaking that had bonded them had also resulted in a rather life-altering side effect. Still, it was a welcome one. This child would know and be loved by her father, the first Dyim in a thousand years to be able to make that claim. Rowan hoped that she had her father's eyes, though personally she was rooting for another redhead.

Gabriel, apparently delusional, still thought he would somehow get a boy.

He had a better chance of her letting him off the hook about the cradle. And *that* wasn't happening either.

"You can't quit," she murmured. "The baby needs a bed. You could always ask Malachi …"

"I'd rather hammer my finger a few hundred more times," Gabriel replied mildly, "but thanks for the suggestion. I'll get the hang of it. I'm not going to have our son sleeping in a basket."

"Daughter, you mean." Rowan opened one eye to fix Gabriel with a baleful stare before snuggling back up. His answering grin was typically unrepentant. Still, she wished he would take her advice about his cousin. It would do both of them some good to begin that healing.

Just a few days after Mordred's death, the battered gray Wolf that had once been Malachi MacInnes had dragged itself into camp and collapsed at her feet. He'd been freed, as she'd thought, at the moment of Mordred's passing. But it had taken weeks to nurse him back to a point where he could become a man again. Longer still to get him to say more than two words at a time, yet the dark, silent MacInnes kept more to himself than anything. There were deep wounds there that Rowan wasn't sure would ever heal. But he was clever with his hands, and had asked her privately to keep him busy … solitary, if possible, but busy … around the camp with whatever required attention.

Whatever he had been, whatever he had yet to become, Rowan knew this was his way of thanking her.

And because of it, she wasn't afraid. Duncan had met privately with Malachi not long after he'd come, and whatever had passed between them, the Alpha had seemed satisfied. Gabriel and Gideon, she realized, were probably never going to accept him. There was too much bad blood there for her to ask her husband to forget. But Gabriel had never asked her to throw him out. He'd never questioned the wisdom of allowing Malachi to stay.

Just more of the thousand or so reasons she loved him so fiercely. He trusted her judgment. So today she would let the matter drop.

Still, she hoped that someday things might begin to improve between them. A fantasy, probably, but one never knew. The Goddess had set her on a strange path, and that had turned out wonderfully in the end.

Mostly wonderfully, she amended. Because Gabriel was going to ask her something silly, probably about whether she might like to go lie down. Again. She could feel him being overvigilant again, and made a point of keeping her eyes shut so he couldn't see her rolling them.

He'd been wonderful about standing aside while she kicked ass as a dragon, but her carrying their child in her womb seemed to have done strange things to his brain. He was suddenly suspicious of any activity that might somehow break either her or the baby, up to and including lifting, walking, laughing too hard, screaming, and/or not chewing her food well enough. Gabriel, Rowan had decided, would have been perfectly happy if she had taken a nine-month-long nap. Well, with frequent awakenings so that she could be ravished.

Somehow that had escaped his "do not" list. It was a good thing, or she would have been screaming a lot more, she thought with a curve of her lips. And the Goddess knew she did enough of it anyway, since the hormones had done some interesting things to her temper. Which in turn never failed to prick her husband's.

She'd come to find it perversely amusing.

"What? You might as well just say it."

"Well …"

"Though I would like to point out, I am sitting down," she added. Gideon snorted.

"You look tired," he grumbled, slightly defensive. "I just wondered whether you might, ah …"

"She's not lying down right now, Gabe," Gideon said, rising to pull his wife to her feet. "And neither am I, for that matter. The day is too beautiful, and I'm on vacation. Come on, love. Let's go for a walk."

Carly, fairly glowing in a deep-blue sundress that perfectly matched the color of her eyes, looked wistfully at the cushions and the platter of treats as Gideon began to tug her away.

"Some vacation. The MacInneses don't sit still very well, have you noticed?"

"Enjoy the activity while you can. It gets deadly dull here in pillow land, believe me." Rowan gave her a pointed look. "You're in for it now, you know. You have my sympathy."

Carly just laughed as she was led off. Rowan smiled as she watched Carly put on the brakes and tell her tall, long-legged husband to slow down already. Then she pulled him down to her much lower level to plant a kiss on his lips.

Once they were out of earshot, Gabriel regarded her quizzically.

"What's Carly in for?" he asked, tucking a lock of hair gently behind her ear.

"Oh," Rowan murmured, "you'll see." She wasn't about to steal Carly's thunder on that one. But it would be nice for the baby to have a cousin so close in age.

It would also be nice to watch someone else be asked to get off of her feet every time she moved. Though she was sure that Gabriel would have moved on to other things by then, like crawling-related paranoia. She must be crazy, Rowan decided, sighing contentedly as he began to nibble at her neck. Because she couldn't wait.

"Behave, you," she instructed him. "I'm as big as a house."

"You're beautiful," Gabriel replied as he continued to tease her. "And now you can't run away from me."

"I can still waddle pretty quickly," she replied, swatting at him and then shifting around to try to get comfortable again.

"For the love of the Goddess, Rowan. I can't rest in the middle of an earthquake." Bastian, a wicked grin on his handsome face, got to his feet from where he'd been quietly resting and stretched. "For the record, I still think you must have at least two in there. Maybe even three." He laughed as Rowan pelted him with fruit, her only defense.

"Damn it, Bastian. I'm going to teach her to bite your ankles as soon as she can crawl. We'll see how you like *that*." Inwardly, though, she rejoiced. He hadn't been sleeping well for some time now, Rowan knew, and she didn't care at all for the dark smudges beneath his eyes, or his increasingly frequent desire for solitude. Her

brother had always been serious, but his reclusive tenden-
cies had become even more pronounced since the victory
over the dragons. Today, for the first time in months,
Bastian seemed better. Maybe whatever cloud he'd been
under had lifted. She hoped very much that it had.

"He says he'd like to stay here for a while, see what
he can do to help Dad and Malcolm run things," Gabriel
said, indicating Bastian with a tip of his head as her
brother jogged away.

Rowan sighed, unsurprised, trying not to be hurt that
Bastian didn't want to stay with the Dyadd, his family.
"Yes, he mentioned it to me. In a way it's a relief. I'd
worried that he might just take off into the wilds, especially with whatever's eating at him. Maybe this place
will do him some good." She stroked the back of
Gabriel's hand. "It always does me."

"He'll be fine," Gabriel soothed. "He just needs to
find his place, like I did."

"Hmm," Rowan returned, noncommittal. She willed
her husband to be right, but it didn't ring entirely true
with her. There was more. But Bastian, contrary as ever,
didn't want her to know, and refused to share the burden.
"He's as bossy as I am. He and your father are going to
drive each other nuts."

"Speaking from experience, that's really not such a
bad calling," Gabriel offered, finally drawing a smile
from her. "And I don't know about him not finding some
way to make himself useful around here. Dad's been in
a bit of a mood the last couple of days. Something about
unwanted company headed this way, and he's been
muttering a lot about integrity and family honor and

'damned hippies,' of all things." He paused, considering. "Could be the old man's losing it all by himself. He might not need any help on his way there."

"Sounds fascinating. And stressful. I think it's a perfect distraction for Bastian," she sighed warmly, turning her head to catch Gabriel's soft kiss. For now, she tried to put her worries about Bastian from her mind and concentrate on all the good that she'd been blessed with, and the infinitely more to come.

Soon. She felt it in each breath she took, in every turn of the baby within her. It wouldn't be long. And by some miracle she had all of her sisters to share the joy, along with a host of Gabriel's Pack who had so fallen in love with the land of their ancestors (and in more than a few cases, with the women of her tribe) that they had decided to remain. Some stayed on Earth, of course. The *Lia Fáil* remained guarded and safe, as it had for centuries, and there was talk of searching for the dragons that had been stranded on Earth by Mordred, though nothing had yet been decided. Still, in the realm beyond the Stone, the *arukhin* had returned at last. And among the women of the Dyadd there was a contentment not felt in generations.

As *Dyana,* Rowan found she enjoyed helping the Orinn of the many villages in the *Noor.* There was always need for their abilities, and despite the fact that she was often tired lately, she was always happy to do what she could. She'd found, though, that the celebrations had grown to be a bit much for her at present. She would simply choose one of her sisters to preside over the festivities, and then Gabriel would fuss over her in the peace of their tent. The man gave a fantastic foot rub, she had to admit. And as chosen leader of the Pack contingent now living in the *Noor,* he had risen to the challenge of playing both strong Alpha and loving husband with a confidence and ease that filled her heart nearly to overflowing.

She only wished her mother could be with her. But when it weighed on her, Rowan reminded herself that Elara was no doubt sharing a goblet of ruby wine with Morgaine herself in the Higher Kingdom, watching and smiling on them all. In fact, since her return to Coracin, she had begun to have dreams about just such things, and always awoke with a sense of warm comfort. Her mother, she was now sure, watched over her and hers well.

Elara had been avenged. For now, at least, the Drakkyn were at peace. And thanks to the circle of stones in her forest, the doorway between her and Gabriel's worlds was used often, and without fear.

Bastian was teaching her about using the stones herself. Though she worried over his reasoning, she treasured the gift he was trying to give her. She had come close to opening the portal several times now. Soon she would succeed, and Rowan held back for that reason. Because once she did, she knew Bastian would go. Even if it was only to *Iargail,* she hated to lose his steady and constant presence. And she couldn't help but be concerned about why he was removing himself.

Still, they were all here now, enjoying a final bit of calm before she gave birth to the first of the next generation of the Dyadd. And as much as Rowan loved her home, she found herself ever more enchanted by this little corner of the Scottish Highlands, a place full of hidden magic that had come to feel like her second home. She would focus on that and try to be content.

"I didn't think it was possible, but this is even more peaceful than the *Noor*," she sighed contentedly, her eyelids beginning to droop.

"If you want to call a bunch of rowdy werewolves living side by side with your trigger-happy sorceresses 'peaceful,' be my guest," Gabriel chuckled. "But I think pregnancy must have addled you a bit if you really believe it."

"They're not trigger-happy," Rowan protested, and the face he pulled had her laughing again. "Okay, so Samuel's horns might have been a little rash on Reya's part."

"Along with the hooves," Gabriel added.

"Well. That's what you get when you don't keep your paws to yourself," she sniffed.

There had been an adjustment period with some of the Pack learning the rules of the tribe. Actually, she was beginning to wonder whether that was just going to be the natural state of things, but she was trying not to dwell on it. The werewolves had plenty of redeeming qualities that stopped the Dyadd from outright bloodshed. And her people, she was pleased to note, appeared to have an endlessly entertaining gift for clever retaliation.

Besides, Reya had removed the horns and hooves.

Eventually.

Gabriel gathered her close, tucking her head beneath his chin. They were quiet for a long time, and Rowan snuggled into him, feeling centered, feeling his love as though it were a tangible thing. As she drifted, she thought about her family and his, and about the new one they were about to create. She thought of the future, and the past. She wondered about the brother who had let himself be taken by the *daemon,* trying to atone at last for the pain he had caused, and whether he was still alive. Though she couldn't truly be sorry he was gone, Rowan did wish him a release from his pain, for his own chance at redemption and peace.

But most of all, she cherished this moment—that she was here in her mate's arms, their child stirring in her womb, surrounded by love and family beneath the ancient and sheltering trees.

Not even in the wildest of the tales she had loved as a child had the Wolf ever ended up with the dragon. But that, Rowan decided as she sank into contented sleep, was somehow better.

That story, ever and always, would be their own.

Acknowledgments

Many, many thanks to my fabulous critique partner, Katey Coffing, without whom this story would never have made it off the ground (or my laptop, for that matter). The next round of green bean fries is on me. Big thanks also go to my family, who helped me keep it together and keep writing despite moving, deployment, and the usual insanity. I couldn't do it without you.

About the Author

Kendra Leigh Castle started out stealing her mother's romance novels and finally progressed to writing her own. She brings her love of all things both spooky and steamy to her writing, and firmly believes that creatures of the night deserve happily-ever-afters too. When not curled up with her laptop and yet another cup of coffee, Kendra keeps busy in California with her husband, three children, and menagerie of high-maintenance pets. For news of upcoming novels, or just to drop her a note (she loves to hear from readers!), visit her online at www.kendraleighcastle.com.